USA Toda... been writi... Mills & Bo... Depp, cupcakes and colour coordination, she spends a lot of her time shopping for cute shoes, scrapbooking and hanging out on Facebook.

Readers can check out Tawny's books at her website, www.TawnyWeber.com. There, they can also join her Red Hot Readers Club for goodies like free reads, chapter excerpts, recipes, contests and much more.

Annie O ...eil spent most of her childhood with her leg draped over the family rocking chair and a book in her hand. Novels, baking and writing too much teenage angst poetry ate up most of her youth. Now Annie splits her time between corralling her husband into helping her with their cows, baking, reading, barrel racing (not really!) and spending some very happy hours at her computer, writing.

Olivia Miles lives in Chicago with her husband, young daugh... and two ridiculously pampered pups. As a city ... with a fondness for small-town charm, she enjo... ...orporating both ways of life into her stories. ... da... goes by that Olivia doesn't feel gratefu... ...able to pursue her passion, and sometin... ...oes have to pinch herself when she reme... ...found her own Happily Ever After. Olivi... ...s hear... ...readers. Visit her website, www... ...amile...

The Night Before Christmas

TAWNY WEBER

ANNIE O'NEIL

OLIVIA MILES

MILLS & BOON

First Published in Great Britain 2018
By Mills & Boon, an imprint of HarperCollins *Publishers*
1 London Bridge Street, London, SE1 9GF

THE NIGHT BEFORE CHRISTMAS © 2018 Harlequin Books S.A.

Naughty Christmas Nights © Tawny Webber 2013
The Nightshift Before Christmas © Annie O'Neil 2016
'Twas the Week Before Christmas © Megan Leavell 2013

ISBN: 978-0-263-27532-2

9-1118

MIX
Paper from
responsible sources
FSC® C007454

This book is produced from independently certified FSC™ paper to ensure responsible forest management.

For more information visit: www.harpercollins.co.uk/green

Printed and bound in Spain
by CPI, Barcelona

NAUGHTY
CHRISTMAS NIGHTS

TAWNY WEBBER

To my awesome brothers, Ron and Kevin!
I love you guys.

Prologue

HOLIDAYS SUCKED.

Gage Milano had no issue with the *idea* of a holiday. Celebrations were great. Kinda like parties, which he rocked. Or remembering and commemorating events, which showed respect. Gage was all for respect.

But holidays?

Holidays meant family.

Obligation.

That freaking heritage crap.

Gage looked up from his plate. Crystal glinted, china gleamed. Ornate flower arrangements in fall tones lined the center of the rosewood table big enough to seat two dozen people. Which was twenty-one more than were sitting here now.

Stupid.

There was a perfectly sized, comfortable table in the breakfast room. But no. Couldn't eat Thanksgiving dinner in the breakfast room. Not because it wasn't fancy enough. Nope. Gage figured it was because his father was still trying to drive home the fact that in the Milano dynasty, he still had the biggest…table.

Marcus Milano was all about who was biggest. Best. Holding the most control. Something he loved, probably more than his sons. He'd taught Gage and Devon to be fierce competitors. From playing T-ball to pitching deals, he'd set the bar high and dared both his sons to accept nothing but a win. Unfortunately, with two of them, that meant one of them was always losing. Something Marcus always found a way to capitalize on.

As if hearing Gage's thoughts and ready to prove them right, Marcus looked up from his perfectly sliced turkey and portion-controlled serving of carbs to bellow down the table.

"Gage. New venture for you to take on."

Ahh, dinnertime demands. The Milano version of conversation.

"No room." Gage scooped up a forkful of chestnut dressing and shot his father a cool smile. "I'm in meetings with my own clients next week, then I'm on vacation."

"Make room," Marcus barked. "I want this account."

Ahh, the joys of being under the cozy family umbrella. Gage might be thirty years old, have a rep as a marketing genius, be the VP of a Fortune 500 company and own his own marketing start-up, which was quickly racking up enough success that he'd be forced to make some decisions soon.

But in his father's mind he was still at the old man's beck and call. There to do the guy's bidding.

It wasn't that Gage didn't appreciate the opportunities Milano had afforded him. But dammit, the company's success was as much because of him as anyone else. When he and Devon had come on board six years previous, it'd been sinking under the economic collapse. Between Devon's restructuring and Gage's marketing, they'd turned it around.

The old guy didn't see it that way, though. To him, he was Milano and his sons simply adjuncts.

Gage glared down the table. Pointless, since his father was nearsighted and too far away to notice. Not that he'd care if he could. Marcus Milano had built his rep on not giving a damn. So Gage shifted his anger across the table at his brother.

Devon, his black hair and blue eyes the spitting image of their father, only grinned.

"You're the king of the sales pitch, little brother. You know how we depend on you for these special projects."

Devon was also the king of bullshit.

"I don't have time," Gage repeated, his words delivered through the teeth of his own smile. "I've been going full speed ahead for six quarters with no break. When I signed that multimillion-dollar deal last month for the electronics division, we all agreed I was off the books until the end of the year."

Five weeks away from Milano. Time to chill, to relax. Hightail it to the Caribbean, where he could lie on the beach, chug the booze and check out the babes. And think.

Think about his future.

Think about leaving Milano.

Weigh the risks of going out on his own.

The old man had built a multipronged business with its fingers in various consumer pies. Milano made everything from tech to textiles. Devon was R & D, Research & Development. He came up with the ideas, put together whatever new product he thought would reel in more coin for the very full Milano coffers.

Gage was marketing. He could sell anything. Water to a drowning man. Silicone to a centerfold. Reality to the paranoid.

He knew people. What made them tick, what turned them on.

A trait that served him well, in business and in pleasure.

A trait that told him that getting away from this dinnertime trap was going to be one helluva feat.

"Off the books except in an emergency," Marcus said

around his mouthful of oyster stuffing. "This is an emergency."

"An emergency is pictures of Devon doing a donkey being displayed on the cover of *People* magazine. An emergency is the accounting department being caught using our computer system to embezzle from a foreign government or your last wife showing up pregnant, claiming the baby is yours. Whatever new product you want to peddle isn't a marketing emergency."

"I say it is."

Gage ground his teeth. Before he could snap, his brother caught his eye.

"Look, it's an easy deal," Devon said quietly, forking up a slice of turkey and swirling it through his buttery puddle of potatoes. "We're launching that lingerie line. The merchandise is ready. We just need a platform. Marketing came up with a great idea."

"Then why do you need me?"

"You know Rudolph department stores?"

"Dirty old man with the Midas touch and a handful of elite stores in California and New York?"

"That's the one. His spring fashion launch is an exclusive deal guaranteed to put any line he includes on the map. He's never missed. Whether it's because he has a keen eye or because the fashion industry is a bunch of lemmings, waiting for him to call the next trend, I don't know. But if we get that lingerie contract, Milano is gold in the fashion field."

Gage shook his head. He was a marketing consultant. He specialized in consumer branding, digital management and online strategic development. Nothing in that description said anything about talking to eccentric billionaires about women's underwear.

"Seriously, it's not going to take up more than a few days of your time. Rudolph is announcing his choices next weekend, and the contract will be signed and delivered before Christmas. You go in, make the deal and leave." Before Gage could point out that anyone could go in and pitch this, Devon dropped his voice even lower and added, "You can even add the time you lose on this to the New Year. You'll still get your five weeks off."

"This isn't about the time off." Even though that was a part of it. "It's about respecting our agreement."

"Look, I've had to set aside my projects to take on this new online store the old man wants to launch. It's not going to kill you to hit the beach a few days—or even a week— later than you'd planned."

So that was it. Lifting his pilsner glass, Gage gave his brother a dark look. Someday, one of them was going to be at the helm of Milano. The question was, which one? Marcus had made it clear that to run the company, his sons had to do three things: Be absolutely loyal. Prove they were more worthy than the other. And not piss him off.

Gage and Devon had realized a few years back that it was going to take building their own business success separate from Milano to prove their worth. The trick, of course, was doing that while not jeopardizing rules one and three. And more important, doing it faster and better than the other brother.

Or in Devon's case, while sabotaging the other brother's chances of doing it first.

"You're playing dirty," Gage said decidedly.

"I'm playing to win."

"What're you two muttering about down there?"

"We're talking about our tradition of breaking the wish-bone," Gage shot back, not taking his eyes off Devon. "I'm thinking we should sweeten the pot. In addition to the 10K for the winner, I think the loser can take on this new project of yours."

Devon's grin slipped. He couldn't talk his way around a

wishbone bet. There were no cards to slip out of his cuffs. It was a straight-on deal with lady luck. And of the two of them, Gage always had better luck with the ladies.

"Fine. You win, I take the deal. But if I win, I get to pick your costume for the Christmas party this deal requires you to attend."

Gage grimaced.

A Christmas costume party? What the hell kind of joke was this?

Appetite gone, he shoved his plate away.

Yeah. He hated the holidays.

1

HAILEY NORTH LOVED the holidays.

All the glitter and fun. Smiling faces glowing with joy, the secrets and excitement. And the gifts. Gifts and surprises always rocked. Especially hard-earned ones, presented at a fancy dress-up ball. Or, in this case, a ballroom packed with the rich and influential of the Northern California fashion scene all dressed up like holiday cartoons.

She should be ecstatic. Over-the-moon excited.

Tonight she'd finally be sure that her lingerie company wouldn't be joining Father Time in waving goodbye at the end of the year.

Instead, she was afraid the past couple of months of financial worries and stress over keeping her company had sent her over the edge into Crazyville.

Here she was surrounded by male models and wealthy designers, many of the most gorgeous specimens of the opposite sex to be found in the Bay Area. And it was the six-and-a-half feet of green fur, snowshoes and a bowling-pin shaped body across the room that was making her hot.

Hailey squinted just to be sure.

Nope. There was absolutely nothing enticing about the costumed guy at the bar. But sex appeal radiated off him like a tractor beam, pulling her in. Turning her on.

Green fur, for crying out loud.

Wow. Month after month of no sex really did a number on a healthy woman's libido.

Or maybe it was a year dedicated to the objective of making romance sexy. Of studying romantic fantasies, and finding ways to tastefully re-create them in lingerie form and show women that as long as they felt sexy, they were sexy.

Or, possibly, it might have something to do with the glass of champagne she'd knocked back for a little social courage when she'd walked into a ballroom filled with high-powered movers and shakers, most of whom had more money in their wallets than she had in her bank account. And all of them here to impress Rudy Rudolph, a department-store tycoon with a wicked sense of fun and prized openings in his new spring fashion lineup.

She glanced at her empty champagne flute, then at the bar. She should trade this in for something nonalcoholic. Something that didn't make her go tingly over green, grouchy holiday figures.

Then the Grinch pushed back his fur to check the time. When the hairs on his fingers caught on his leather watchband, he yanked off the gloves in an impatient move, tossing them on the bar.

Thirst forgotten, Hailey stared at his hand as he reached for his own drink. Long and lean, with tapered fingers. Even from across the room, his palm looked broad. Her mind played through every hand-to-penis-size euphemism she'd ever heard and came up with the only conclusion possible.

The Grinch was hung.

The only question was, did he go for cute elves? Or was he strictly a man-and-his-dog kind of guy? Maybe she should have dressed up like a Who?

She'd taken two steps toward him, her body desperate to find out, before she caught herself.

No. She was here for business.

She peered at the baggy, saggy, furry back and grimaced. Not for fun. No matter how big the fun's hands were.

"Hailey, darling."

Relieved, both at the distraction from lusting after the Grinch and at there actually being someone here who knew her name, Hailey turned.

Her social smile shifted to genuine delight at the sight of the man who'd made this night possible for her. Jared Jones, assistant to the wealthiest—and most eccentric— tycoon in the department-store business.

Jared had taken her under his wing last summer when they'd met in an elevator. Hailey had been on her way to pitch her lingerie designs to the sales team and Jared had been bemoaning a rip in his shirt. Before they'd reached the sixth floor, she'd pulled out some fabric tape for a temporary mend, earning his gratitude and his endless devotion.

Apparently, a fashion faux pas was, to some, the end of the world.

"Jared," she greeted, leaning in for a hug but careful not to let him bump her head. It'd taken her twenty minutes to get the bell-festooned elf hat pinned to her curls in a way that didn't make her hair look like fluffy poodle ears.

"I love your gingerbread-man costume. Is that your favorite holiday character?" she asked, flicking her finger on one of his cheerful, oversize buttons. Her eyes widened before she laughed aloud as she noted the words *Eat Me* etched on the red plastic.

"Edible goodness, that's me," he said with a wink. Then he shifted his head to the left and gave a little wag of his chin. "And if all goes well, that drummer boy over there will be having a taste before the night is out."

Used to Jared's aggressive sexuality by now, Hailey

gave the drummer an obligatory once-over before sharing an impressed look with her horny gingerbread friend.

"But look at you," he gushed, his loud enthusiasm aimed as much at getting the drummer's attention as it was appreciation for Hailey's costume. "You know, I've seen at least a dozen elves tonight, but you're the best by far. You look fabulous. Is everything you're wearing straight from your lingerie line?"

"Everything but the skirt," Hailey confirmed, arms wide as she gave a slow turn to show off the goods. Her candy-cane-striped bustier with its red satin trim and white laces paired nicely with her red stockings and their white seams up the back that ended in clever bows just below the hem of her green tulle ballerina skirt. She was proof positive that the right lingerie could make any woman feel sexy.

Nothing like a year in the gym, a carb-elimination diet and a great tan to make a girl look damned hot in lingerie.

Too bad she'd only hit the gym maybe four times in the past twelve months, loved carbs like she loved her momma and was closer to winter-white than sun-kissed tan.

But that was the beauty of Merry Widow lingerie. A girl didn't have to have a supermodel body to look—and feel—fabulous in it.

"Oh, darling," Jared breathed in admiration as he completed his inspection.

Hailey didn't have to follow his gaze to know where he was staring. After all, the guy might not be interested in what her lingerie was covering, but he was all about fashion.

And her boots were pure fashion candy.

The white Manolo booties were an early Christmas present from her father. Well, not really *from* him, since he never knew what to get her. But she'd bought them last month with the holiday check he'd sent, so that made them his gift to her.

"Hailey, you have the best taste in footwear," he sighed. "Those boots are perfect. And such a great touch to bring the outfit from cute to couture."

"Thanks. Will Mr. Rudolph be arriving soon?" she asked, shifting from one foot to the other. She wiggled her toes in her most excellent boots as a reminder that a girl could handle anything if she was wearing fabulous footwear. "Since he's announcing his choices for the spring exclusives, shouldn't he do it before all the designers are drunk?"

While she was still tipsy enough to use getting one of those prized exclusives as an excuse to seduce the Grinch.

"Drunk designers only add to Rudy's sense of fun," Jared told her with a sly grin. He didn't say a word about the contracts, though. She knew he knew who'd been chosen. And he knew she knew. But they both knew she wouldn't ask.

"Quit obsessing," Jared said, giving her a nudge with his shoulder and leaving a streak of glitter on her arm.

"Maybe you should see if the drummer boy's sticks are worth checking out." She tilted her head toward the guy he'd been scoping. "I can't clear my head enough to be fun company."

"Darling, I'm here to enjoy the party with my favorite designer. If there was anything I could do to set your mind at ease so you could give the party the appreciation it deserves, I would. But you know me—I don't kiss and tell."

Giving in to her nerves, and reminding herself that she'd taken a cab here, Hailey traded her empty champagne glass for a full one, then arched one brow at Jared.

"Okay. So I don't spill company secrets." He hesitated, then wrinkled his nose and leaned closer. "At least not the ones that could get me fired."

Then he looked past her again. This time when his face

shifted, it wasn't into lustfully suggestive lines. Instead, he came to attention.

"I don't think the news will be secret for long, though," he told her, twirling his finger to indicate she turn herself around.

"Welcome, welcome."

Hailey, along with the rest of the ballroom, turned around and came to the same subtle attention that Jared had as a skinny Santa took the stage with two helpers dressed in swaths of white fur and a whole lot of skin.

She leaned forward, peering at the trio. The nerves in her stomach stopped jumping for a few seconds as she stared in shock. "Wow. Mr. Rudolph sure looks different without his tie."

Or maybe it was the fact that the pervy old guy was shirtless under his plush red jacket. Wasn't he in his seventies? Now, that wasn't a pretty sight. Afraid to look at it too long, in case it rendered her blind, Hailey glanced at the rest of the crowd. Nobody else seemed surprised.

"Thank you, everyone," he said, "for joining the Rudolph-department-store annual holiday costume party. As you can see, my favorite character is Santa Claus. Appropriate since I'm the man giving out the gifts tonight."

Fingernails digging into the soft flesh of her palms, Hailey puffed out a breath, trying to diffuse the nerves that'd suddenly clamped onto her intestines.

This was it. The big announcement.

She felt like throwing up.

"This year, instead of simply awarding spring women's-line contracts, I've decided to make things fun. I've chosen two favorite designers in each department. Women's wear, shoes and lingerie. Those designers will compete through the holiday season for the top spot."

Hailey's stomach fell. Competing? That didn't sound good. She wasn't the only one who thought so, either, if the muttering and hisses circling the room were anything to go by.

She gave Jared a puzzled look, trying to shrug off the sudden despair that gripped her. The contracts weren't being awarded tonight? But she needed to know. Without that contract, she was going to lose her business.

Jared ignored her stare, tilting his head pointedly to get her to pay attention.

She dragged her gaze to the stage with a frown. Instead of looking abashed, the old man seemed delighted by the angry buzz. His grin shifted from wicked to a visual cackle as he held up one hand for silence.

It took all of three seconds for him to be obeyed.

"So without further ado, here are the finalists in women's wear," he announced. A model featuring an outfit from each line crossed the stage behind him as he named the designer.

Hailey swallowed hard, trying to get past the tight worry in her throat. It wasn't as if she'd irresponsibly put all of her hopes on this deal. It was more a matter of everything else falling apart until this deal was all that was left to hope for.

She shifted from one foot to the other, trying to appreciate the gorgeous shoes as Rudolph announced the designer finalists for footwear. But not even the studded black leather stilettos could distract her worry.

Then he got to lingerie.

She didn't even listen to the names.

She just watched the models, her eyes locked with desperate hope on the curtain they entered from.

One strutted out in a wickedly sexual invitation in leather. It was the complete opposite of the Merry Widow's style, a look that screamed sex. Hot, kinky sex.

Hailey frowned. It wasn't her style, of course. But it was appealing. *If you like hot, kinky sex.*

Did she like hot, kinky sex? She'd never had the opportunity to find out. For a second, she wondered if the Grinch was into leather. Before she could imagine that, worry crowded the sexy thoughts right back out of her brain. She held her breath.

"And last but not least, Merry Widow Lingerie." Echoing the announcement was a model in a white satin chemise trimmed in tiny pink rosebuds, a design Hailey had labeled Sweet Seduction.

Fireworks exploded in her head, all bright lights, loud booms and overwhelming excitement.

"Ohmygod, ohmygod, ohmygod," she chanted, hopping up and down in her gorgeous booties. She spun around to grab Jared in a tight hug, then did another little dance. "That's me. That's me. I made it."

She made it. She had a chance.

An hour later, she was still giddy. It wasn't a contract, but it wasn't a rejection, either. And she'd learned young to take what she could get.

"This is so cool." Ever since Santa Rudolph's announcement, people kept coming up to congratulate her. That part was great. What was even better, though, were the compliments about her designs, which were displayed all around the room.

She felt like a rock star.

"I'm excited for you, darling. I am sorry it's not a definitive answer, though," Jared said quietly, his face taking on a rare seriousness. "I know how bad you need this deal, and I've been pitching hard for you. But Rudy got this wild notion that a contest would bring in more publicity and make it more fun. He'll decide before the New Year, though. He has to for marketing purposes."

"What kind of publicity?" Big publicity? Good publicity? Could it net her some new clients, maybe a few features in the fashion rags? Hailey's stomach danced again.

"Well…" Jared drew out, wrinkling his glittery nose. "I

honestly don't think he has a lot of publicity lined up. We were all under the impression that he was simply choosing a single designer for each line. But Friday he talked to some marketing guru who convinced him that it'd bring in great promotion if he made it a competition of some sort instead of a straight-up announcement."

"Who makes the final decision?" she wondered.

Jared pulled another face and shrugged. Clearly he didn't like not being in the know any more than she didn't like not having a clue.

But before Hailey could ask more questions, they were joined by a dapper-looking guy dressed like a festive reindeer with his green-and-red-plaid bow tie.

"Congratulations, Ms. North. I'm Trent Lane, the photographer for Rudolph department stores. I was happy to see your designs in the running. I've taken test shots of each submission and yours is my favorite."

"Really?"

"Really. It seems to epitomize romance. But sexy romance. The boudoir-photo kind, not the *Hustler*-spread kind."

Hailey giggled, wondering if the leather getups were *Hustler* material.

"It's my favorite, too," Jared agreed. "I told you when I first saw the line. It's perfect. Next season is all about nostalgia with overtones of passion. Bridal fresh but womanly confident."

Hailey wrinkled her nose, wondering if he realized he'd just described her gorgeous designs in the same terms used for feminine-hygiene products.

"Baby's breath and air ferns lining the runway. Satin backdrops. Maybe one of those long couch things, like Cleopatra would lounge on," Trent mused, falling into what she immediately saw was a creative brainstorming habit between him and Jared.

"A chaise. Perfect," Jared agreed. Tapping his chin, he added, "Maybe carried down the runway by four muscle-bound sex slaves?"

"That's not romantic," Trent dismissed. "You know Rudy really wants to lead the trend this season. If you suggest sex slaves, he might seriously consider Cassia Carver's mesh love sleeves for a part of the women's-wear line."

Hailey barely kept from shuddering. Avant-garde minis and maxis made up most of Cassia's line, and while they were edgy and fun, they would hardly compliment Merry Widow's lingerie. They would, she realized with a frown, go great with Milano's leather.

Suddenly the simple contract she'd thought she'd have was now even more complicated. All of the choices were going to have to flow together into a single, cohesive spring debut.

"Even if Rudy wants mesh and love slaves, there's no way marketing will go for it," Jared dismissed. "They'd bury him in the horrible sales data from the last time mesh hit the runway."

Oh, yay. A point in her favor. She just had to make sure she racked enough to win this baby. Hailey held her breath, willing herself to look invisible. Maybe if the two men forgot she was there, they'd spill some insider info that she could mop up and use.

"Well, Rudy wants Cherry Bella to model the entire spring line, and Merry Widow will look perfect on her."

Hailey couldn't contain her little *eep* of excitement.

Her designs? Perfect? Cherry Bella?

Oh, man. That shooting star was getting close enough that she could almost feel the heat.

"She'd look great in Merry Widow or Milano's," Trent agreed. "It's really going to come down to whichever line Cherry wants to wear. She'll be the final judge of all the lines, I'm guessing."

"Rudy has to get her signed first. And so far, she's not interested."

Trent looked to the left. Jared and Hailey looked, too. Then he looked to the right. They obediently followed his gaze. Forgetting that she was supposed to be invisible, Hailey leaned in just as close as Jared did to listen.

"I hear Rudy's pulling out all the stops. He's crazy to get Cherry signed. He's tried everything. Promised her the moon. So far, no go. He's shifted all his promises to her agent now." Trent gave them both a wide-eyed look, then nodded sagely, his reindeer ears bobbing in emphasis. "Whoever gets him Cherry Bella? They're golden."

Excitement ran so fast through Hailey's body, she shivered with it. Her lingerie was perfect for Cherry. The statuesque redhead had started as a soulful torch singer, but lately had branched into modeling and a few minor acting gigs, as well. Merry Widow's flowing, feminine designs would suit her as though they'd been custom made.

All Hailey had to do was cinch the deal.

She'd find Cherry's agent, charm him or her into listening to a personal pitch on how perfect Merry Widow designs would look on the retro singer.

"Do the other designers know?" she wondered aloud. Seeing the guys' arch expressions, she scrunched her nose and gave a shrug. What? They all knew she wasn't really invisible. "Just wondering."

"It's pretty hush-hush since a lot of competitors are always big to get a jump on Rudolph's spring debuts. So unless the other designers are chatting up Rudy's staff, I doubt they have a clue."

Jared's snort of laughter was more sarcastic than amused.

"Which means no," he explained at Hailey's questioning look, a little of the sugary glitter flaking off his face as he sneered. "Your competitors are all well established, with top-of-the-line reps, darling. They, unlike you, have huge egos. None of them see the need to fraternize with the help. They talk to Rudy, or they don't talk at all."

She peered through the costumed crowd, looking for any of the lingerie-clad models circling the room. She sighed as one lithe blonde floated by in a Merry Widow nightie. Cotton flowed. Lace rippled. The pearl buttons down the front caught the light, even as the delicate fabric molded to the woman's perfect body.

So romantic.

And so perfect for the Rudolph account, especially if he got Cherry as his spokesmodel.

She didn't want to jinx it but the little voice in her head was already planning the victory-dance moves.

"I'm surprised Cherry's agent isn't all over this deal," Hailey mused, wondering what they were holding out for. "A contract with Rudolph department stores would rocket her from national to international exposure, wouldn't it?"

"Oh, yeah," Jared agreed, looking like a dejected gingerbread boy with his furrowed brow. "We can't figure out what the problem is. Rudy'd be tearing his hair out if he wasn't already bald."

"Best we can figure, it's because the agency is one of those co-op places. The agents all work together on every client. Make decisions by consensus. We don't even know which agent is at the party. Guy, gal, nobody's got a clue," Trent complained, looking like a very grumpy reindeer whose gossip rations were being withheld. "Like I said, whoever reels her in is going to be golden."

Then a passing model dressed in a fishnet candy cane and spangles shaped like question marks caught his eye. He straightened his bow tie, gave Jared and Hailey an absent smile, then tilted his head. "Well, I think I'll go talk up the models and see if any of them are repped by the same agency as Cherry."

With that, and a leering sort of grin, he was gone.

"So what do you think? Do I have a shot?" Hailey asked as soon as he left. Her gaze flew around the room as if the infamous agent might have hung a neon sign around his or her neck, just for fun. If she could find the agent, she could pitch her own designs for Cherry. If she could get the agent enthused, she'd have an inside track. Maybe even a guaranteed deal.

Excitement bubbling, Hailey gave the room another searching look. Her gaze landed on Trent, who'd apparently given up on seducing the woman in mesh and was now talking to the sexy Grinch.

Her excitement took on a totally different edge at the sight of that Grinchy butt. The hood of the costume now pushed back, she could see his hair, so black it reflected the blue and white Christmas lights of the tree next to him, wave into the green fur of his collar.

Her nipples tingled against the tight satin layers of her bustier. Her thighs turned to mush, only the sheer red silk of her stockings holding them together.

Oh, yeah. He was definitely the hot, kinky, sexy type of guy.

All she had to do was look at him and she was more excited than she'd been with any of the lovers she'd ever had. Or even all of them, combined.

And all she was gazing at was the back of his head. That was better than being turned on by his furry back, wasn't it?

Her breath a little on the shallow side, she sighed and wondered how great it'd be to strip that ugly fur off and see what kind of body was beneath the costume. Could it be as sexy as she was imagining? Long and lean, with strong thighs and washboard abs? Shoulders she could cling to as she rode him like a wild stallion?

She'd just flown a few miles closer to catching her

shooting star. Didn't she deserve a treat? Could she do it? Go talk to him? Ask his opinions on hot, kinky sex. Leather or lace. Roses or studs.

Her face, throat and chest all on fire now, either with lust or embarrassment, Hailey quickly drank the rest of her champagne and exchanged the glass with a passing waiter, hoping the bubbles would cool the fire blazing in her belly.

"Hailey, darling? Where'd you go? I've been filling you in on all of the Rudolph stores' holiday plans and you haven't said a word. What's got you so distracted?"

Unwilling to admit the horrifying truth, that she was all hot and horny for a guy whom she'd only seen from the side and back, both of which were covered in puke-green fur, Hailey tore her gaze away and gave Jared an apologetic look.

"Nothing. Just, you know, wondering if that guy Trent's talking to might be Cherry's agent," she improvised.

Almost on tiptoes to see around the crowd, Jared peered in the direction of the bar. Then he gave a shrug.

"No clue." He looked again, this time giving a little hum of appreciation. His eyes were as wide as the buttons on the front of his gingerbread suit as he fanned one hand in front of his face. "I'll be happy to go find out, though."

She looked over again herself, wondering what had got his attention.

And almost fell to the floor, thanks to her weak knees.

Oh, baby.

The Grinch was gorgeous.

Her lust cells stood up and did a victory dance, vindicated in their attraction.

Her brain couldn't argue.

Because the man was definitely lust-worthy.

Raven-black hair swept back from his forehead in soft waves, framing a face that would make Michelangelo weep. Sharp planes, strong lines and intense brows were balanced by full lips and wide eyes. Even though she couldn't tell the color, she was sure those were the most gorgeous eyes she'd ever seen.

For the first time in forever, Hailey didn't know what she wanted more.

Success? Or the man across the room.

2

"THIS IS THE most ridiculous idiocy I've ever seen," Gage said decidedly, his glare spread equally across the ballroom at his cousin and at those butt-ugly green fur gloves he'd been forced to wear to this stupid party. "And what's with the babysitting duty, Trent? You lose a bet yourself?"

"More like blackmail," Trent muttered, watching yet another leggy blonde slink by with a regretful sigh. "Believe me, if I had a choice, I'd be long gone by now."

"Yeah? Well, so would I."

Once, a party like this would have appealed to Gage.

A bachelor's playground, complete with booze, babes and enough variety in the guest list to stave off boredom.

The requirement to dress like your favorite holiday character, though? That was where it all tipped right on over to idiocy.

Yet, here he was. Smothered in freaking fur. Didn't matter that it was almost December. San Francisco didn't get cold enough to make this costume anything but miserable.

"How'd they con you into this?" Trent asked, craning his head to one side to watch a woman's leather-clad ass as she worked the crowd. Gage vaguely recognized it. The leather, not the ass. It was one of the new Milano designs. Sexy Biker Babe, Devon had called it. Stupid, really. It looked hot, and definitely sent a strong sexual message. But who wore leather lingerie?

He gave an absent scan of the room, measuring the crowd, the reactions. There were enough people eyeing the leather with an appreciative look, as opposed to the ones peering in confusion at the mesh dresses some models were suffering in.

The most admiration seemed to be for the lacy getups floating through the room, though. The kind of lace you'd see on a forties pinup model, rather than the kind you'd see on a favorite internet porn site. Classy, he supposed it'd be called.

Noticing his attention, a tall brunette in a tasteful teddy and floor-length robe in white satin with fluffy trim gave him an inviting look before she stopped to exchange comments with a guest. The model moved on.

But Gage's gaze was locked on the woman she'd spoken with.

Helloo.

Interest stirred for the first time since he'd heard of this party, Gage straightened.

She was blonde and cute, with an air of sweetness surrounding her like a holiday promise. The women he usually went for were dark, sultry and cynical. So what was it about her that made him want to sit up and beg?

Sure, she was sexy. But even though her costume was obviously lingerie inspired, she was still stepping pretty close to the sedate line. His type usually danced on the edge of the slutty line.

Yet he wanted nothing more than to cross the room, toss her over his shoulder and haul her off to someplace where he could lick her wild. Obviously this work overload and insane costume were taking a toll on his sanity.

"Gage?"

"Huh?" With one last look to assure himself that she

wasn't his type, he yanked his attention back to his cousin. "What?"

"I said, how'd you get stuck with this gig? I thought you were on vacation."

"The old man played the emergency card, deeming getting the Rudolph contract to launch this new project top priority." He wasn't about to admit that he'd pulled the short end of a wishbone. A guy could only take so much humiliation at a time.

Used to his uncle's games, Trent didn't seem surprised.

"You do well enough on your own. And you hate working for your father. Why don't you just resign?"

Good question.

"It's not that easy. Nor is it something I want to talk about at a party full of people in their underwear and me in green fur."

Or anywhere else, for that matter.

Not because he was so private.

But because he really didn't know himself.

Money was a major factor. He'd seen plenty of successful people sink under the weight of running their own show.

Loyalty was another. He might hate the dictatorial way Marcus Milano ran things, but it was still a family company founded by his grandfather. As far back as he could remember, his father had claimed that Milano was run by Milanos. And Milanos were expected to make it a success. So much so that if one left, he was out. Out of the company, off the board and in the case of Gage's uncle when he'd quit, disinherited and ostracized by the family.

And there was always the competition between him and Devon. Gage glared at the furry gloves again, damned if he'd lose to his brother in an even bigger way. When he went out on his own his start-up would be bigger, stronger, more successful than any and all of Devon's put together.

None of which were thoughts he was particularly proud of.

The perfect distraction, the pretty blonde elf caught his eye again. Her eyes were huge, so big they dominated her face. A cross between adorable and arousing, with full lips and round cheekbones both a glossy red to match her stockings. Gage's gaze dropped again to those legs. They were very excellent legs, long and lean. The sheer red hose and sexy little boots reminded him of a candy cane. An image echoed by the striped bustier hugging breasts so sweet they almost overflowed the tight fabric.

Gage rocked back on his heels, humming in appreciation.

She didn't belong here.

Her costume might.

Her party partner might.

And the holiday theme might.

But she looked too sweet to be interested in something as lame as this event.

So sweet he wanted to invite her to a private party. One where he could taste her, just there where the satin met that soft flesh, and see if she was as tasty as she looked. Like a delicious Christmas treat.

"So, hey, I've got instructions from Devon I've gotta follow." Trent's uncomfortably muttered words pulled Gage's attention away from the sexy blonde.

"You babysat, you probably took pictures to share on Facebook, and you verified that I stayed until the announcement." Gage was still irritated that the best he'd been able to get out of this deal was to be in the competition for the contract. Despite his best pitch, Rudolph hadn't been willing to set aside his initial favorites. "I've done my part. I'm done. Showing up in this stupid costume was the end of my assignment."

"Yeah, sure. But, well, my instructions were to wait until after the announcement, and if Milano was in the running for the contract, to issue a new bet." Trent looked a little ill at this point.

Gage laughed so loud, half the room glanced their way.

"Is that reindeer headgear pressing too tight into your brain? You really think I'm going to take another one of Devon's bets?"

"C'mon. You know he'll make my life hell if I don't follow through," Trent beseeched, looking so pitiful even his antlers drooped. "It's not a big deal. I just have to mention that there's a bet on the table, and give you this."

This, Gage found out when Trent pulled it from the inner pocket of his Fruit-Stripe-gum-colored jacket, was an envelope. "That's it?" Gage asked, gesturing with his gloves to the paper. The envelope was thick and black, and he figured his brother had been trying for ominous. The guy was a little too dramatic.

"This is it," Trent agreed, holding the envelope closer. When Gage didn't take it, he set it on the bar with a shrug. "My instructions were simply to make sure you knew there was a bet and to make it available if you were interested."

"You did, and I'm not."

"No skin off my nose," Trent dismissed. Now that he was free, he was more focused on catching the eye of one of the mostly naked women than trying to change Gage's mind. "I'll let Devon know you met the terms of the bet. Oh, and can you tell him I did offer you the insider info? He promised to burn the pictures of… Well, it won't matter what they are after tonight."

If Trent's grin was anything to go by, the evidence Devon had used to blackmail him was probably wearing a wedding ring. And just for handing over an envelope, that evidence was getting burned?

Gage frowned at the heavy black paper. His brother wasn't the type to let go of blackmail material that easily.

Always resourceful, Devon figured good dirt was worth using at least twice.

So whatever plan Devon was playing, it was big.

"Hold on," he said through his teeth, snatching up the envelope and ripping the heavy paper aside. He read the thick, purple papers quickly, shock seeping through his irritation. Then he read through them once more to be sure the itchy green fur hadn't impaired his comprehension.

No way in hell…

"He's willing to let me go?"

Trent leaned closer to read the letter, then gave a shrug. "Is that what it says? He told me to assure you that he's not bullshitting." Seeing Gage's doubtful look, Trent plastered on his most earnest expression. It went pretty well with the antlers and bow tie, actually. "He didn't give me details, just told me what to say if you opened the letter."

"What are you? His windup toy?"

"Funny you should mention toys. That's actually what those pictures…" Grimacing, Trent shook his head. "So, you gonna take the bet?"

Gage considered his options.

Being the trusting soul he was, Marcus Milano hadn't just used the threat that he'd cut them off if they ever left, he'd contractually tied his sons to Milano's.

But if Gage got this contract, his brother would arrange for an entire year of freedom. With full pay. Gage could do whatever he wanted, without losing his safety net or walking out on family obligations. In exchange, he just had to seal this lingerie deal.

"You gonna fill me in on what it'll take to win this Rudolph contract?"

"Why? You don't have any pictures of me, three blondes and a battery-operated rabbit."

All Gage did was shift. Just an inch. His shoulders back. His spine straighter. His chin lifted.

Then he arched one brow.

Trent's grin wilted.

"Look, I don't know anything. And what I do know is mostly rumor. But it's company rumor, so I can't tell. Your games with Devon aren't worth my job."

Unfazed, Gage nodded.

"I win this bet, I'll be gone for a year," he mused, taking a second to revel in that vision. A whole year, free of Milano. To travel without a tightly controlled, money-making itinerary. No board meetings, no R & D meetings, no personnel meetings. Just him and his own business.

He eyed his cousin. Yeah. He wanted that dream. Enough to take the bet and to bump the stakes.

"I'm gone a year," he repeated, "I got two choices. Garage my 'Vette. Or let someone play car-sitter."

"Your 'Vette?" Trent's eyes glazed over as if he was having a personal moment. Then he shook his head. "No way."

"Way."

It didn't take two seconds before his cousin grabbed his hand to seal the deal.

Everyone had a price.

Gage listened as Trent babbled on about a torch singer, a weird old man's trend obsession and secret agents.

"So whoever gets this singer to wear their line is gonna get the deal?" he confirmed.

Trent nodded. "If you get Cherry Bella to wear your lingerie line, you nail the contract."

And win the bet.

"And you're saying her agent is here, at the party, scoping it out to decide if any of the designs are worthy?"

"That's what I hear."

Gage's gaze shifted across the room again to the blonde.

There was only one person here who didn't belong.

One very sexy, very tasty-looking person who seemed

out of place among the eccentric designers and the narcissistic models.

If he had to guess who the agent was, and apparently he did, he'd pick her.

And now that he'd picked her, he just had to charm her into choosing Milano for her client.

"Not a problem," he decided.

This was going to be quite the treat.

Beat his brother.

Win a year's freedom.

And make some time with a very sexy blonde.

Looked as if this party wasn't quite as idiotic as he'd thought.

HAILEY GULPED.

He was coming her way.

She'd lost count of how many glasses of champagne she'd had. Enough to make her head spin. But the tingling swirls going on right now had nothing to do with alcohol and everything to do with the Grinch.

The oh-so-deliciously-sexy Grinch.

"Trent looks like someone just gave him the keys to a houseful of horny women. I'm going to talk to him," Jared decided, clearly oblivious to Hailey's tingles, swirls or even her overheated cheeks. "I'll bet he figured out who the agent is."

"Go, go," Hailey encouraged with a little wave of her hand. She wasn't really shooing him away, so much as making room for the Grinch.

"Oh, baby," she sighed as he stopped next to her. He was even yummier up close and personal. A faint shadow darkened his chin, making her wonder if he was one of those guys blessed with a luxurious pelt of chest hair. She'd always wanted to get close enough to a guy like that so she could bury her face in the silky warmth and snuggle.

Her fingers itched to tug the zipper of his costume down and see for herself.

"Hello." The greeting was accompanied by a smile that, for all its charm, edged just this side of wicked.

His eyes were dark, so dark they seemed black in the party lights, with thick lashes and slashing brows. And they were staring at her with an intensity that made her want to check herself to make sure nothing had fallen out.

"Hi," she said, giving him a bright smile. At a delicate five-one, which was why the elf costume had been so inspired, she had to tilt her head back a little to see his face. Bells jingled. At first she wondered if that was a sign from Cupid. Then she remembered that it was Christmas, not Valentine's. And that she was wearing bells on her hat.

"I'm Gage," he murmured, taking her hand.

"Hailey," she said on a sigh as her fingers were engulfed by his. He was warm. Strong and gentle at the same time, and his skin felt so good she didn't want to pull away.

Her usual nerves at meeting a gorgeous, sexy man were nowhere to be found. Probably doing the backstroke through a river of champagne. But she wasn't drunk enough to do anything stupid, like unzip his costume with her lips right here in the middle of the ballroom.

After all, she didn't want hair between her teeth.

"What do you think of the party?" he asked, not taking those intense eyes off her as he tilted his head to indicate the room. It was as if he were looking past her cheerful smile and holiday bells into her soul, where he could peek at all of the secrets she hid there. Like her dreams. Her darkest, sexiest fantasies. And every single one of her fears.

That was both sexy as hell and the scariest thing she'd ever imagined.

"The party's great," she said, nerves starting to poke through the champagne bubbles. "I thought it was a fun theme, coming as your favorite holiday character. At least I did until I saw the guy dressed as a pair of Christmas balls waving his candy cane around."

The words echoed in Hailey's head as she realized what she'd said. Eyes wide with horror, she slapped her hand over her mouth. Not that she could take the words back, but maybe it'd help slow down the next stupid thing she tried to blurt out.

Gorgeous Gage the Grinch just laughed, though. A deep, full-bodied sound that eased her fear and made her grin right back. His gaze changed, softened, with his amusement. He was still sexy as all get-out, but now he seemed real. Not quite so much like a sexual fantasy sent to rip away all her inhibitions. More like an intriguingly attractive man who made her want to toss them away on her own.

"I guess I don't have to ask if you've been entertained by the various displays here this evening."

A movement across the room caught her eye. Hailey shifted her gaze, noting Jared, flanked by Trent and Mr. Rudolph, heading toward the door. He looked frantic, doing a subtle wave of his hand behind his boss's back and jerking his head around. Either he was trying to give her a message, or he was being hauled off against his will.

She tilted her head, trying to figure out what he was saying. Then she realized he was pointing at Gage and mouthing something. She gave a helpless shrug, totally clueless. His disgusted sigh came across loud and clear, though, then he held his hand to his ear, thumb and pinkie outstretched.

Call him.

Then, just as he was swept out the door by a jolly old man, he jabbed his fingers toward Trent.

"Looking for that pair of Christmas balls?" Gage teased.

"Oh, sorry," she said with an abashed grimace. "It's just

so distracting here. Like a circus, but instead of performing animals, it's a bizarre fashion statement, all wrapped in holiday tinsel."

"And you're not into bizarre?"

Hailey arched her brow. Why did that sound as if he'd just passed judgment and she'd somehow failed?

"Should I be?"

"Hardly. *Bizarre* generally means weird and confusing. I'm not a fan of confusion."

"And the holidays?" she asked, gesturing to his costume. "Are they high on your list, or is your heart three sizes too small?"

He opened his mouth, then shook his head and shut it with a grin. "I'll skip over any size comparisons, if you don't mind."

Delighted at his sense of humor, Hailey laughed.

"How about we leave size issues to my imagination and skip right to the holiday question," she said with an impish smile.

"Just as long as you have a good imagination."

"It's amazing."

"A lot of dreams?"

"Big ones," she assured him. "Huge, even."

He gave an appreciative grin, then at her arch look, it faded to a deep, considering stare before he shifted his gaze to the decorated trees and holiday props around the room.

"I don't have a problem with the holidays, per se," he admitted. The way he said it, slow and careful, as if he were measuring each word, told her that he was a man who valued honesty. He might dance around the truth. He might refuse to answer. But whatever he did say, he expected to be held to it.

That kind of integrity was even sexier than his gorgeous

smile. Maybe not sexier than his body, but she couldn't say for sure since it was still covered in lumpy green fur.

"But there are parts you're not crazy about," she guessed, trying to stay on topic and quit undressing him with her mind. Especially now that her imagination was using the word *huge* in all its naked images.

"Sure. But you have to take the bad to get the good, right?"

No. She wanted to shake her head. The bad might show up from time to time, but the whole point was to avoid it if possible. To think positive and flow with the good.

But she wasn't sure her Pollyanna-esque argument was going to get very far with a guy who favored the Grinch.

"So which good parts are your favorite?"

"The food," he mused, gesturing to the Mrs. Claus walking by with a tray of sugar cookies. "Gotta love the desserts this time of year."

A man after her own heart.

"But as good as those cookies look, I'll bet you're sweeter. Like the candy cane your outfit reminds me of. But instead of peppermint, you'd be cherry flavored."

His words were low and flirtatious, his eyes dancing and hot as his gaze swept over her body as if he wanted to taste her and see.

Hailey swallowed hard. She knew she was totally out of her league. But she didn't care.

It was as if she were drowning in desire, passion burning low in her belly with a heat she didn't think anything could douse. She sure was ready to let him try, though.

Then his words washed over her like a lifeline, tugging at her attention.

What had he said?

Cherry?

A bright light went off in Hailey's head, clearing away the foggy fingers of passion. Ooh, she smiled as excitement pushed back—but didn't in any way extinguish—the hot desire in her belly.

Jared must have been trying to tell her that Gage was the agent. The man to persuade that her designs were perfect for his client.

Seriously?

Hailey almost laughed out loud.

First her designs were chosen as semifinalists.

Then the sexiest man she'd ever seen hit on her.

And now she had to do everything and anything in her power to make him crazy about her lingerie?

It was all Hailey could do to keep from clapping her hands together in delight.

This night rocked.

3

"So you don't seem like a designer or model," Hailey said, sliding a sideways glance at Gage. Not that all designers were, well, feminine. But the gorgeous man next to her was way too masculine, deliciously and temptingly masculine, for her to imagine him playing with ribbon and lace. Or even mesh and leather, unless they were exclusively in the bedroom.

His laugh echoed her assessment.

"Oh, no," he assured her. "I'm not a model. And I'm definitely not a designer."

And he didn't work for Rudolph's, or Jared would have told her. Which left, *dum da dum,* him being the agent.

Sweet. So sweet, she almost did her happy dance again.

"So you're clearly a fan of the holidays," he guessed, gesturing to her outfit. "And you look as if you're enjoying the party. Anything in particular impress you tonight?"

He had.

But she didn't think he was fishing for compliments.

Hailey tried to clear the champagne buzz from her head and pull together a strategy. She needed to pitch her heart out here. To make wow and impress him, not only with the designs themselves, but with her knowledge of the industry, of his client. And, because he was just so freaking yummy, maybe with herself.

It wasn't as if she was offering up her body in exchange for a good word to his client. More like she was willing to worship his body while never directly mentioning the client.

That wasn't stepping over any lines, was it?

"Hmm, there's so much to choose from," she mused as if her mind had retained anything other than impressions of him and the words *Get Cherry*. "I was really impressed with Rudolph's clever contest. The designs were all so diverse, weren't they?"

His eyes sharpened, as if she'd just triggered a switch. To what, she wasn't sure. But since he stepped closer, she hoped she could figure it out so she could trigger it at will.

"And your favorite?" he asked, so close she could feel his breath on her forehead. So close she could feel the warmth of his body wrapping around her.

She wanted to lean in and breathe deep. To snuggle in and nuzzle her nose in the curve of his shoulder. The tiny part of Hailey's brain that was still functioning at normal levels was trying to figure out what the hell was wrong with the rest of her. All she did was look at this guy and all of her senses were sucked into the lust cycle.

"Hailey?"

"Hmm?" She frowned, trying to remember what he'd asked.

"Do you have a favorite?"

"A favorite…?" Position? Flavor of body oil? Term for the male genitalia? "Oh, favorite designs?"

"Yeah. Are you drawn to any particular designer?"

There was that intense look again.

Hailey started to pitch her own line, then bit her lip. Maybe it was better to charm him first, before he realized she was one of the designers. That way, then she could gently lead him into the idea of Cherry and Merry Widow being the perfect match. She'd noticed one thing in this past year of trying to sell her wares—the minute someone thought you were pitching something, they went on the defensive.

Her gaze roamed over the masculine beauty of his face, making her sigh. Nope. She'd much rather he be receptive to anything she had to pitch.

So she shrugged instead and said, "There are a lot of great looks here tonight. I think it'd be fun to try to match each one to their perfect person." Hailey wanted to bounce in her Manolos, she was so proud of that subtle hint. Kinda like subliminal sales. She'd just lay a few bread crumbs here and there, and he could nibble his way to her line of thinking. "That's the key to a great design, isn't it? That it enhance the features, the personality, of the person wearing it."

"Do you really think there's someone that suits all of these, um, outfits?" he asked over the band, who'd turned their amps up louder now that people were hitting the dance floor. He gave a pair of sequined hot pants and a satin, cropped tee a doubtful look before arching a skeptical brow. Maybe because the outfit was the same nauseating green as his fur.

"I think everyone, and everything, has a perfect match," she said. Then she grimaced, worried her enthusiasm might be taken the wrong way—as if she were about to chase him down like a lovesick crazy woman who was looking for happy-ever-after forever promises. Instead of the right way, which was that they should get naked and see what happened when their bodies got sweaty together.

What'd happened to her? Hailey was almost as shocked at her body's reaction—instant horniness—as she was at her wild thoughts.

She rubbed one finger against her temple, as if she could reset her normal inhibition levels. She needed to stick with cheap champagne from now on. Clearly she couldn't handle the expensive stuff.

"What type of lingerie would match you perfectly?" he wondered aloud. His tone was teasing, but the look on his face made her stomach tumble as the lust spun fast, tangling with nerves.

To hell with resetting her inhibitions.

This was way more fun.

Her perfect match was a man who was there for her. Who wanted her for the long-term, not just for a convenient window of time. Perfect was fabulous sex, unquestioning support, faith in her abilities and enough love to want to actually dig in deep and be a part of her world, instead of flitting around the convenient edges.

But that was all someday thinking.

Tonight? Tonight perfect was dressed in green fur.

As if he heard her thoughts, the flirtatious heat faded from Gage's demeanor and his smile shifted from seductive to charmingly distant.

Hailey frowned as his look intensified, as if he were inspecting the far corners of her soul. The parts she kept hidden, even from herself.

Was he reading her mind when his eyes got all deep and penetrating like that? Did he know she was wondering if he was her match? Or was he the kind of guy who'd run, screaming with his furry tail between his legs, if he had a clue she was interested in more than business?

Before she could wonder too much about it, though, the floor show kicked off. All of the models hit the dance floor, "Gangnam Style." And Gage's attention shifted, so the heat in Hailey's belly had a chance to cool a little.

"Now, that's entertainment," he said with a laugh, wincing as more than one model had to grab her chest to keep it from flying out while dancing.

"It's getting wild," Hailey agreed, both amused and impressed at the same time. Wild or not, her designs looked great out there. Feminine and sexy. And it was nice to know her lingerie could dance horsey style.

"What do you say?" Gage asked, leaning in close so his words teased her ear. Hailey shivered, her nipples leaping to attention and her mind fogging again. "Want to get out of here?"

Despite her nipples' rapid agreement, Hailey hesitated.

She was willing to do a lot for her company. She was willing to do almost anything to get this contract. But while she was insanely attracted to Gage, she wasn't sure leaving with him was something she'd be proud of once the champagne cleared her system.

Correctly reading her hesitation, Gage gestured to the glass doors.

"How about a walk through the conservatory? It'll be quieter. We can talk, get away from the, um, dancing."

As if echoing his words, the music shifted to a raunchier beat. Hailey winced as the dancers shifted right along with it.

A walk. That was safe. They would still be in a fairly public arena and she'd be close enough to the party to remind herself that this was business. That should keep her from trying to rip that fur off Gage's body to see what was underneath.

"Sure," she agreed, accepting his invitation to tuck her arm into his. She tried to ignore the dance floor, where the hired help was doing a dance version of the upright doggy style. But she couldn't help blushing. Not because the moves were tacky. But because she wished she could do them, too. She couldn't, of course. Mostly because she was a lousy dancer.

She could—and should—get out of here before the dancers, and the champagne, gave her any more naughty ideas, though.

"A walk would be lovely."

GAGE WELCOMED THE cool night air like an alcoholic welcomed that first hit of gin. With greedy need and a silent groan of gratitude.

He'd been sweating like crazy in there.

Was it because of this god-awful hideous costume?

Or because of his body's reaction to the sweet, little elf next to him?

It had to be the costume.

Because he never sweated over women.

The lust wasn't a new thing. He'd spent most of his life surrounded by gorgeous women, so lust was as very familiar to him as breathing.

And it wasn't as if he had problems mixing business and pleasure. Gage worked with too many beautiful women to hamper himself with silly rules or false moral restrictions.

And while he wasn't a cocky ass, he'd had enough success with the ladies to feel both comfortable and confident that he could handle anything a woman had to offer.

Nope. He'd never had women problems.

So clearly, it must be the costume.

"Mr. Rudolph puts on quite a party," Hailey said as she wandered between marble columns wrapped in twinkling white lights. "Do you attend often?"

"This is my first," he admitted. "How about you?"

Gage didn't wander. Instead, he scoped the room, found a semisheltered wall and leaned against it. That way, she could come to him. She didn't, though. Instead, after an inscrutable look through those thick lashes, she shrugged and continued her slow meander through the conservatory.

"This is my first, too. I've talked to plenty of people who are involved behind the scenes, though. If the rumors are true, things are going to get pretty wild and naked in there soon."

Behind the scenes?

She must have a few models in there showing off the

wares. Theirs, and the designers. He debated how long to wait and steer the conversation toward some of her other clients. A minute or two, maybe. First he needed to figure her out. Usually by this point, fifteen minutes into their first meet, he'd completely pegged a person.

But Hailey the elf was a mystery.

"You don't sound disgusted by the idea of wild and naked," he observed.

Was she wilder than her sweet face and cute demeanor portrayed? His body stirred, very interested in finding out.

"Everyone has the right to enjoy the holidays in their own special way," she said, her laugh as light as the bells jingling on her hat. "And I like the idea that the lingerie samples might be so sexy, they inspire that kind of thinking."

"On the right woman, an elf hat and ballerina skirt inspires that kind of thinking," he murmured quietly.

Not so quietly that she didn't hear, if the pale pink washing over her cheeks was any indication. She didn't say anything, though. Just kept on wandering.

"So what did you find most interesting this evening?" she asked, trailing her fingers along the edge of a larger-than-life, white wicker sleigh filled with a tree, gifts and more lights. "Were you here for the shoes? There were some gorgeous new lines being shown. Or are you more a women's-wear kind of guy?"

Her arch smile was teasing and filled with as much light as the twinkling display around them. Gage had to wonder if she was always this cheerful or if she'd been hit with a little too much holiday cheer.

"I was only interested in the lingerie," he said, figuring it was time to start winding the conversation toward her coveted client. "At least I was until I saw you. Everything else sort of faded at that point."

"Uh-huh," she laughed. "Me versus a dozen perfect

women in lingerie. I can see how you were torn between the two views."

"Do you doubt me?"

At his mock offense, she stopped wandering and gave him a wide-eyed once-over. Then, finally, she joined him next to the nice, semiprivate wall.

"Doubt the Grinch? A figure known for his good cheer, holiday honesty and love of everything sweet and cuddly?"

Gage grinned. Damn, she was cute.

"Is that what he's for?" He looked down at the green fur monstrosity he was wearing and rolled his eyes. How appropriate. He had to hand it to his brother; the guy was clever with the inside jokes.

"You don't know? You're supposed to be portraying your favorite holiday character."

"I lost a bet."

"So you're not really all Grinchy about the holidays?" She tilted her head to one side as she asked the question, her bells tinkling as if to dare him to deny the joy of the season.

Gage hesitated. He never tried to hide his disdain for the holidays, nor was he worried about offending a potential business associate over differing views. But he couldn't quite bring himself to dim the sparkle in Hailey's eyes. Sharing his opinion of Christmas would be akin to telling a four-year-old that Santa was a sleighload of crap. Which was exactly what his stepmother-du-jour had done to him.

Instead, he did what he was best at. Sidestepped the question with a charming smile. "I promise you, I've never been called Grinchy in my life."

The speculation in her big eyes told him he might need to toss out a little more charming distraction. Otherwise, she seemed like the stubborn type. The kind who sweetly nagged at a person until they'd spilled their every secret, then thanked her for dragging them through the ugly memories.

"How about you?" he asked. "Why is an elf your favorite holiday character?"

"Elves are clever. They bring joy and create beauty, but they stay behind the scenes. They're the cute and cuddly part of the background." To emphasize her point, she offered a bright smile, tilted her chin toward her shoulder and twirled around so her skirt offered a tempting view of her stockings. Which, Gage's mouth watered to realize, were thigh-high and held up with garters.

"But elves don't have their own movie," he pointed out. "As grumpy as he is, even the Grinch gets top billing."

"*Elf* is a movie. And top billing usually comes with top headaches," she pointed out. "Expectations and demands of excellence. Appearances, groupies, haters. Is all of that really worth the spotlight?"

Gage frowned.

Hell, yeah, it was worth it. The other option sounded kind of…forgettable. Who aspired to that?

Maybe that was why she was an agent instead of striving to be the star, he guessed.

Still…

"Being on top is better than being on the bottom," he pointed out.

"Not always." Her words were low, teasing and lilting with innuendo. The look in her eyes was hot, sexy. And way more appreciative of the view than he figured his costume warranted. But who was he to dissuade a gorgeous woman from appreciating him?

His momma didn't raise no fools. Of course, she didn't raise her sons, either, but that was beside the point.

Right now, the point was seeing how hot this spark could flame between him and the deliciously naughty elf.

He stepped closer.

Amusement and desire both clear on her face, Hailey stepped back. With a quick glance over his shoulder, as if gauging their privacy, she wet her lips.

Gage almost groaned.

He probably could have walked away before.

Probably.

But now? Seeing that full mouth damp and inviting?

He wasn't leaving without a taste.

"Being on top has a few definite benefits," he decided quietly, now having completely switched places so her back was against the wall and his toward the ballroom.

"Does it? Like what?" Her eyes were huge, so big they were lost in the curls tumbling out from the white fur brim of her hat.

Need, stronger than any he'd felt over a simple flirtation, surged through Gage's body. He angled his body so Hailey was trapped between him and the wall.

For a second, one delicious second, he just stared.

Enjoyed the anticipation in her eyes.

The rapid pulse fluttering in her throat.

The tempting display of luscious flesh, mounded above the tight satin binding her breasts.

The need intensified. Took on a sharp, hungry edge.

"Like this," he said, giving in to its demand.

He took her mouth.

He'd intended to be gentle. Sweet, even.

But the kiss was carnal and raw and dancing on the edges of desperate. Tongues tangled. Lips slid, hot and wet.

She tasted as sweet as she looked.

But the sounds she made were sexual nirvana. Low, husky moans of approval as his hands skimmed over her waist to that tempting place just below her breasts. He didn't touch. He just tortured the both of them with the idea that he could.

Public, he forcibly reminded himself. They were practically in public, and if he did what he wanted, they'd be putting on a display for a ballroom full of people.

Knowing if he didn't stop now, that display was a very real possibility, Gage slowly, reluctantly, pulled his mouth from hers.

It was harder than he'd thought it'd be. And not just between his legs.

Unwilling to let go completely, his hands flat against the wall on either side of her head, Gage leaned closer. His body trapped hers as he pressed tiny kisses along her throat. Hailey's head fell back, her breath coming fast, filling the air with tiny bursts of white fog.

The move arched her back, so the long, delicious length of her throat was bare and those glorious breasts pressed higher against his chest. His hands burned with the need to cup her bounty. To weigh the soft flesh. To slide that candy-cane-striped fabric down and see if she was as tasty as he thought.

Public, Gage reminded himself again. *Keep it in control.*

Because while he wasn't averse to a little public display of passion himself, he had the feeling that Hailey would be. Especially if some of those models in there were hers.

Then her hands shifted, moving off his shoulders to press their way down his chest. Gage could feel their heat even through the thick fur of his costume.

He shuddered with need, taking in the flush of rosy color washing over Hailey's cheeks and pouring down her throat and chest to meet that tight satin.

One taste couldn't hurt, he decided.

Even as his mind listed all the ways it actually could, he moved closer, so his body was tight against hers. As Hailey's hum of pleasure filled the air, he pressed his mouth against the side of her throat, just under her ear, and gave in to the need to taste.

She was delicious.

Seriously worried for his sanity if she kept teasing him with those delicate fingers, Gage folded his hand over hers and pressed her palm flat against his chest. Then he grabbed the zipper tab and yanked.

It didn't move.

The grabby need clawing at Gage's libido slowed, even as the foggy desire tried to pull him back.

He yanked again.

Nothing.

"Hell," he muttered, pulling his mouth from Hailey's.

Unwilling to separate their bodies, he angled his head to peer at his chest. He got a better grip on the tab and pulled again.

The zipper was stuck.

"I can't get it down."

"Well, I guess I'd rather hear that than you can't get it up," she said, her eyes dancing with laughter. Clearly a smart woman, Hailey pressed those lush lips together to keep it contained, though.

Gage growled.

And yanked.

Nothing.

This was not happening.

His body straining against the thick fur of the costume from hell, he considered ripping it right off.

"I guess the moment's lost," he said with a reluctant smile when she couldn't hold back her laughter any longer. He figured that was better than acting like a spoiled, tantrum-throwing asshole.

Although he was reserving the right to throw the tantrum later in private.

"Maybe not lost," she said, her smile gentle now, her eyes bright with promise. "Maybe just delayed."

Gage considered the option of a delay over cancellation.

It had a lot more appeal. And while he wasn't so uptight that he had stupid rules about sex, clients and associates, he was also smart enough to know that women got funny about stuff. If Hailey thought he'd slept with her to get to her client, and to snag the deal, she'd go one of two ways. Give it to him because he was so damned good. Or withhold it out of spite.

He didn't see her as the spiteful type, but she didn't come across as the kind of woman who'd take kindly to ulterior motives, either.

Time for some careful maneuvering.

"Why don't I call you?" he offered. After a quick mental review of his calendar, he added, "I'm out of town for the next couple of days. Are you available for dinner on Wednesday? I'll pick you up at six."

Her eyes were huge as she gave him a long look.

It was the kind of look that'd usually make him nervous.

A look filled with hope. With trust. With all those sweet, innocent emotions he'd never experienced in his life.

It was scary as hell.

His feet itched to run, even as his dick ached to stay.

"I have a meeting on Wednesday," she finally said. She reached up to trace her index finger over his lower lip, making Gage want to growl and nip at her soft flesh. Then, without warning, she ducked under his arm and shifted away.

Scowling at how lost his arms felt all of a sudden, he turned to watch her stop a couple of feet away. What? Did she think looking at her instead of touching was going to simmer down the need boiling through his system?

Impossible.

She was pure eye candy.

Still clinging with one hairpin, her hat was askew, dangling to one side. Blond curls, so soft when he'd tangled them in his fingers, were a bright halo around her face. And that face.

Gage wanted to groan.

He'd never gone for sweet. Sweet was dangerous. Sweet came with expectation, with demands. Sweet set off the run-don't-walk sirens in his head.

But he couldn't resist Hailey. He wanted all of the sweetness she had to offer.

But she was also the key to his winning this bet. And that, even more than the sirens, warned him to back off. At least until they'd settled their business.

"Well, if you have plans…" he started to say. Before he could excuse his way out of dinner and suggest a more businesslike meeting, she interrupted.

"Do you know Carinos?" she asked.

He gave a hesitant nod. Upscale and trendy, Carinos was the latest see-and-be-seen hot spot.

"How about I meet you there on Wednesday? We'll need to make it seven instead of six, though. I'm not sure how late my meeting will go."

This was it. His chance to back out.

But he couldn't make himself suggest alternate plans.

Gage tried to sort through his confused thoughts. Not an easy thing to do when he could barely stand, thanks to the throbbing hard-on he was sporting.

Before he could decide if he should accept or counter, she smiled.

That sweet, sexy smile that shut down his brain.

Looking like a naughty elf, Hailey wet her lips. He wanted to groan at the sight of her small, pink tongue.

And then, moving so fast she was a blur of blond, she kissed him. Hot, intense. A sweep of her tongue, a slide of her lips. Just enough hint of teeth to make him growl to keep from begging.

Then, before he could take control, or hell, even react

with more than a groan of appreciation for the hot spike of desire shooting through him, she moved back.

"See ya Wednesday," she said.

With that, a little finger wave and a smile that showed just a hint of nerves around the edges, she was gone.

Gage wanted to run after her. To grab her and insist she do something about the crazy desire she'd set to flames in his body.

Except for two things.

One, his dick was so hard, he couldn't walk for fear of something breaking.

And two, his mind was still reeling.

He'd tried to blame the costume. Because he didn't get stupid over women.

Ever.

But that cute little elf, with her candy-cane-sweet taste, had sent him so far into Stupidville, he might as well set up camp.

Until he'd figured it out, he needed to stay away from her.

Far, far away.

Because horny was all good and well.

And, he had to admit, stupid-horny was a pretty freaking awesome feeling.

But stupid-horny and business?

Not a good combination.

At least, not when his freedom was on the line.

4

"YOU'RE GRINNING LIKE a kid who just found a dancing pony under her Christmas tree. What's wrong with you?"

Wrong?

This was afterglow. Sexual anticipation. And a big ole dollop of nervous energy. It'd been three days since her kiss with Gage, and she was still floating.

Hailey inspected her image in the ornate standing mirror in the corner of her workroom-slash-office. Behind her were swaths of billowing silk, yards of lace and spilling bins of roses and romantic trim.

Only Doris would look at that and say it was wrong.

Hailey peered past her reflection to the woman behind her.

Doris Danson, or D.D. to her friends—which meant Hailey called her Doris—looked as if she were stuck in a time warp.

Rounded and a little droopy, her white hair was bundled in a messy bun reminiscent of a fifties showgirl. Bright blue eye shadow and false lashes added to the image. Doris's workday uniform consisted of polyester slacks, a T-shirt with a crude saying by a popular yellow bird and an appliqué holiday sweater complete with beribboned dogs, candy canes and sequin-covered trees.

The sweater and tee didn't bother Hailey. But as a designer, she was morally offended at the elastic-waisted polyester. Doris knew that. Hailey had a suspicion that the older woman haunted thrift stores and rummage sales to stock up on the ugly things.

"Nothing's wrong," Hailey said.

Not really. But she couldn't meet her secretary-slash-seamstress-slash-bookkeeper's gaze.

Despite her afterglow, she was kind of freaked out. She'd made out with a potential business associate. Now, granted, *associate* was a pretty loose term. But she was still walking a moral line here. Should Gage be off-limits? Maybe she shouldn't be obsessing over that kiss. Hailey bit her lip, chewing off the lip gloss she'd just slicked on five minutes ago.

"Might want to eat something besides your lipstick. Not like they feed you at these fancy meetings. Why you think it's a good idea to go talk to this guy after he burned you is a mystery, though."

"Mr. Rudolph didn't burn me. He'd never offered an actual contract. I'm sure I'll still get the exclusive. It's just going to be a little more interesting now." Jared and Trent wouldn't have praised her designs like they had if they didn't think she had the contract in the bag. And Hailey had a secret weapon now. A very sexy, very delicious one she was meeting for dinner.

"Interesting. Right. Instead of getting a solid deal you expected, you get to play some rich man's game." The wheels of her chair creaked as Doris shifted. The woman was barely visible behind the stacks of paper, catalogs and the tiny ceramic Christmas tree on her desk. Too bad she wasn't barely audible, too. "And where are you going to be when that other guy walks off with the contract? On the street, that's where."

Turning to give Doris a chiding look, Hailey insisted, "It's going to be fine. I'm going to get this deal."

Doris tut-tutted. "I'm telling you, Hailey, you are wasting your time. Better to accept reality than to keep dragging this out."

Hailey hated reality.

Especially when Doris dished it up with such bitter relish. It was as if she reveled in negativity. Hailey shifted her gaze from her own image to the woman behind her.

What a contrast.

Preparing for the meeting, Hailey was dressed in business chic. A black leather mini paired with leopard-print tights, a black silk turtleneck and a brushed cotton blazer with satin lapels. Along with her favorite boots and black knee-high schoolgirl socks, the look was savvy, sassy and modern. Just right for wowing a department-store tycoon and a fashion powerhouse.

And behind her was the elf of Christmas gloom.

An elf that knew the business inside and out, could finagle suppliers' fees down to pennies, worked magic with the books and, next to Hailey, was the best fill-in seamstress Merry Widow had ever seen. Which made her indispensable.

Indispensable gloom.

Not for the first time, she wished she were the kind of person who could tell Doris that her bad attitude wouldn't be tolerated and suggest the woman get her act together or clear out her desk.

But every time Hailey thought about doing it, she thought of everything the woman brought to the company. Then she remembered how lousy Doris's home life was, how Merry Widow was all she really had.

And whenever the older woman pissed her off so much that she forgot all that, the minute she got ready to get in her face, Hailey's tongue swelled up, her head buzzed with panic and she freaked out.

It wasn't that she was a wimp. She was a fierce negotiator in business, a savvy designer who insisted her company be run her way. She was smart. She was clever. She was strong.

She just sucked at confrontation.

Partially because her father had once told her that arguments always left scars. That even after making up, the memory of the conflict would forever change the relationship. Given that his advice had come on the heels of a hideous family drama that'd cost Hailey a whole year away from her new half brother, she'd taken the lesson to heart.

But mostly because she hated making people mad at her. Her mom had got mad and left her dad. Her dad got mad and refused to talk to Hailey. She'd seen plenty of mad in her life. Which was why she tried to avoid it like the plague.

"You want one of these cookies?" Doris asked, a frosted reindeer in hand. Doris shot Hailey a sour smile, bit the head off, then said around her mouthful, "Might as well eat up now, since things are gonna get tight after we go out of business."

"We're not going out of business," Hailey insisted, lifting a cream lace scarf to her shoulder to compare, then switching to one of vivid red cashmere.

"Right. Bet you still believe in Santa Claus, too."

"We're not going out of business," she said again. "Our sales are up ten percent over last year. Our projected first quarter should double that, easily."

"The Phillips kids are calling their daddy's note the first of the year," Doris reminded her like a persistently cheerful rain cloud.

Rotten kids. Or, really, greedy adults.

When Hailey had bought Merry Widow Lingerie from Eric Phillips three years ago, they'd agreed that he'd take a percentage of the profits for five years, with a final payment of the agreed-upon balance at the end of that time.

When he'd died in the fall, though, his kids had found a loophole in the contract, insisting that they could call the entire debt. They'd given Hailey until the end of the year, which was mighty big of them, in their opinion.

Without a significant contract the size of, oh, say Rudolph department stores, the bank wouldn't consider a loan in the sum the Phillipses were demanding.

Just thinking about it made Hailey's stomach churn, an inky panic coating the back of her throat.

No. She put the mental brakes to the freak-out. She wasn't going there. She'd found her answer; she just had to believe in it. She was going to snag this Rudolph-department-store contract.

Negative thinking, even the kind that had her second-guessing her date tonight, would only drag her down.

Giving her reflection a hard-eyed stare, Hailey vowed that she was going to rock this meeting and wow her date. As long as she didn't strip him naked and nibble on his body, she wasn't crossing any ethical work-relationship boundaries. Right?

Right.

Now she just had to get Doris off her back.

"When I pull in this department-store deal, we're golden. I can pay off the note, Merry Widow will be mine free and clear, and we'll be set," she assured the other woman.

"Do you bake special cookies to set out for Santa, or are you comfy settling for store bought? And those stars that fall from the sky, how many of those wishes actually come true for you?" Doris gave a pitying shake of her head. "You listen to me, miss. You keep going through life with your head in the clouds like you do, you're gonna fall in a big ole ditch one of these days."

What was it with the people in her life? Her mother was always warning that she'd get taken advantage of. Her friends worried that she was wearing rose-colored glasses. Even her father… Hailey bit her lip. Well, her father barely noticed what she was doing. But every once in a while, he did throw out a caution warning of his own. It wasn't as if she were Pollyanna with no clue. Hailey was a smart, perceptive woman. She'd made it to twenty-six without a major heartbreak, owned her own business and paid her bills on time. And unlike anyone else in her family, she hadn't had to resort to therapy and/or addictive substances along the way.

"I'm just saying, you might want to look at your alternatives. Me, I can retire anytime. But the rest of the team, don't they deserve a little heads-up so they can start looking for new jobs? It's all well and good to keep your hopes up," Doris said, her tone indicating the exact opposite. "But you can't let your Mary Sunshine attitude hurt other people, now, can you?"

"Everything is going to be fine. Why don't you focus on doing your job and let me do mine," Hailey snapped, her words so loud and insistent that the other woman dropped her cookie and stared.

She closed her eyes against Doris's shocked look. Hailey never snapped. In a life surrounded by simmering emotional volcanoes, she worked hard to be calm water. Mellow. Soothing, even. She'd grown up watching the devastation negativity and emotional turmoil caused, had spent her childhood trying to repair the damage.

And, of course, on the oh-so-rare occasions that she did respond to stress with a negative reaction, she always got that same horrified, might-as-well-have-kicked-a-puppy-and-cussed-out-a-nun look from people.

"I'm sorry," Hailey said with a grimace. "I'm just nervous about the meeting this afternoon. I want to make a good impression, to show Mr. Rudolph and his team that I'm the designer they want."

"You think the perfect scarf is going to make that dirty old man pick you as his lingerie designer?"

"I think the right look will show him my sense of style and savvy use of color and patterns," Hailey defended, lifting one scarf and then the other against her neckline again. "How a woman feels about her outfit affects her confidence, after all. If *I* think I look good, I'll project a strong image. And that might be all I need to get the deal."

"You might be a little overoptimistic about business stuff, but you've always had a firm handle on how well you put together fashion," Doris said with a frown. "Silly to start worrying about it now."

"I really want this contract." *Desperately needed it* was closer to the truth. But why put that fine a dot on the subject?

"An exclusive with the Rudolph department stores? It'll be so cool. The rich and famous shop there. They have a store on Rodeo Drive and everything. Can you imagine Gwyneth Paltrow in Sassy Class?" Hailey said in a dreamy tone, thinking of the pristine white satin chemise with delicate crocheted trim.

"Those highfalutin stars are the only ones who can afford to shop at snobby stores like Rudolph's." Doris's sniff made it perfectly clear what she thought of stars, snobs and all of their money.

"Well, unless you really do want to retire early and spend every day at home with your husband, you better cross your fingers that those snobs take to my designs," Hailey said, finally choosing the red scarf. It was sassier, she decided as she draped it elegantly around her neck. Frustrated, she wrinkled her nose. At least she was trying for elegant. It was hard when she'd knotted wrinkles into the scarf, so it looked like a soggy, deflated balloon around her neck.

Doris rolled her eyes, then hefted herself out from behind the desk to come over and adjust the scarf. A tug of fabric here, a tuck there, then she jerked her chin to indicate that Hailey turn back to the mirror.

While Doris fussed with the scarf, Hailey obsessed.

What if the other woman was right about it being impossible to come up with the funds to pay off the Phillips note?

What if Hailey's mother was right about Hailey shooting too high, wanting too much?

What if this was it, her last Christmas as the owner and head designer of Merry Widow Lingerie? What if it was the end of her dream?

"Not gonna happen," she muttered, lifting her chin to emphasize the promise.

"Whazzat?" Doris peered over her bifocals.

"Nothing," Hailey assured her in a cheery tone. With a smile to match, she patted the older woman's shoulder and promised, "Everything's great. Merry Widow is ready to fly, and this account is going to be our launchpad to make it happen."

The older woman harrumphed, but her usual grumpy look softened a little as she tucked one of Hailey's curls back into the faux chignon she'd fashioned at the base of her neck.

"Well, I will say this. If anyone deserves to make those dreams come true, you do." With that, and a stiff smile, Doris clomped back to her tin of cookies.

That was about the nicest thing Doris had ever said to her. It had to be a good omen, right?

Or the kiss of death.

AN HOUR LATER, Hailey stepped into the glass elevator in the center of the Rudolph Building and pushed the button for the top floor. Top floor, baby. Unable to resist, she watched the surrounding buildings of the Financial District as the elevator rose, sighing when the sun broke through the clouds, and off in the distance she could just make out the Golden Gate Bridge. That had to be some kind of sign. Any day that included a meeting with a powerhouse like Rudolph, a pat on the back from Doris and a date with a sexy guy like Gage couldn't go wrong. Hailey practically skipped out of the elevator.

Still, she paused outside the frosted-glass double doors. One hand pressed to her stomach to calm her nerves, she took a deep breath. A quick glance at her feet to peek at her Jeffrey Campbells worked as a reminder that everything went better when a girl wore great boots. Then, resisting the urge to fluff her curls into frizz and nibble at her lipstick, she called up her brightest smile and pulled open the door.

This was it.

Her first foray into fashion fabulousness and the beginning of the best day of her life. A prelude, maybe, to the best *night* of her life.

With that peppy chant playing in her head, she swept into Rudolph Headquarters.

"Hailey, darling." Jared greeted her as soon as she crossed the foyer. He hurried around the high counter where he'd been chatting with the receptionist to offer a hug.

Hailey shifted, suddenly nervous.

"Hi, Jared. What's up?" He looked normal enough. Metro chic in his electric-blue suit and skinny tie, his hair slicked to the side and quirky horn rims perched on the bridge of his nose. But he was all tense, as if someone had just told him shoulder pads and moon boots were about to make a comeback.

"Up? Nothing, nothing. C'mon, let me escort you to the meeting. Rudy isn't in yet, of course. But you can get settled. I'll fetch you a nice latte, shall I?"

Hailey's stomach sank. Now she knew something was

wrong. Jared didn't fetch for anybody. She slowed, all but digging the spikes on the heels of her boots into the plush carpet to make Jared slow, too.

"Seriously. If something's happened…" She swallowed hard, then forced herself to continue. "If I've lost the account, I'd rather know before I go in that meeting."

Quick as a flash, a grimace came and went. Not a small feat considering the amount of Botox injected in that pretty face. "It's nothing, really. Just, well, Rudy finally got hold of Cherry Bella. She's interested, but not committed."

That sounded familiar. Hailey didn't figure reveling in the turned tables would endear her to Rudy, though. She kept her lips still.

"She's in tentative agreement, with the caveat that she gets to be the final judge on the various lines for the spring show. She and Rudy are nailing down those details."

"So how is this any different than it was Saturday night when he announced that it was a competition?" she wondered.

"Well, before we were pretty sure he was going to go with Merry Widow since he had this whole soft spring theme in mind. But Rudy apparently left the party Saturday with Vivo, the shoe designer."

So? Hailey arched both brows. She wasn't competing for the shoe contract.

"Vivo is edgy, modern and quirky. Think eight-inch platforms shaped like dinosaurs."

Eww, tacky. Halfway through her cringe, it hit her why Jared was so upset.

"Rudy's going to want the line to be a cohesive message…." Her words trailed off as it hit her.

Romantic sensuality didn't go with eight-inch platform dinosaurs. But snakeskin and black leather did.

And Rudy had a favor-wielding relationship with a designer who thought dinosaurs belonged on women's feet?

Anger ran, tense and jittery, along Hailey's spine. Fists clenched at her sides, she ground her teeth to keep from shouting that enough was enough. They kept changing the rules, shifting the playing field. Dammit, she deserved more respect than that. She'd worked hard for this deal, and until that stupid party, all indications were that she'd be awarded the contract.

She didn't say a word, though.

Yelling never helped anything. If she jumped all over Jared, it'd just make things uncomfortable, and might lose her whatever slim chance she had left.

Big picture, she reminded herself, taking deep breaths to try to push out the irritation. It was all about saving her company.

"I just found out a few minutes ago, or I'd have called to warn you. Cherry and Rudy are meeting with all of the designers together, listening to their pitches." Jared's words came at such a rush, they were spilling over themselves. Maybe because they'd reached the wide double doors of the meeting room.

"They're making the decision now?" she asked. Her fingers clutched her sassy messenger bag filled with marketing ideas and clever pitches aimed at the media. She'd come prepared to pitch the beauty of romantic lingerie that made women feel sexy. If she'd had more time, could she have found a way to work ugly shoes into her presentation? To show that even with the hideous footwear, a woman could still feel attractive?

His hand on the door, Jared closed his eyes for a second, as if he was fighting some inner battle. Then he leaned close and gave Hailey an intense look.

"Focus on Cherry. She's the key. Rudy will ignore his preferences in favor of whatever she likes, so chat her up. Make friends. She's on edge about something. Don't know if that's her typical personality or if she's having issues.

But she seems to be responding better to soft sells than hard pushes."

Before Hailey could process all of that, before she could do more than give Jared a grateful smile since she knew he was risking his job by showing preferential treatment, he'd pushed the door open and gestured her inside.

She wanted to grab his hand and drag him in with her.

But she didn't.

Instead, she took a deep breath of her own, lifted her chin, pulled back her shoulders and plastered on her best soft-sell smile.

Then, with as much enthusiasm as if there were a bed of hissing vipers on the other side, she swept over the threshold.

And almost tripped over her gorgeous boots.

"Hi," she breathed, the word taking all the air from her lungs.

GAGE SHIFTED HIS glare from the window to the door, ready to get this damned meeting over with.

And, for one of the few times in his life, found himself speechless. He had to blink a couple of times to make sure he wasn't seeing things, then found his voice.

"Hailey?"

Damn, she was pretty.

Her hair, still a froth of blond curls, was tamer than it'd been at the party. Sleeker, as if she'd bribed the curls into behaving by tying them in a knot at the base of her neck. Her big, round eyes were subtly made up, her lips pale and glistening. She was definitely looking more nice than naughty today.

But even without a candy-cane-striped bustier and thigh-grazing ballerina skirt, her sweet curves were mouthwatering. Instead of skimpy holiday wear, today she was decked out in a simple black skirt a few inches short of her knees and another pair of sexy boots. Her scarf and turtleneck screamed class, while her leopard-print tights assured him she was all sass.

He'd never been a foot-fetish kind of guy, but he was starting to seriously wonder what other styles of footwear she had in her closet. And how she'd look riding his body wearing just a pair of boots in thigh-hugging black leather.

"Gage?" Frowning, she chewed on the full pillow of her bottom lip, making him want to offer to take over the task. Then, as if she'd realized something, her eyes cleared and she offered a smile. "I didn't expect to see you."

"I'm surprised you recognized me without the green fur," he said with a teasing smile, walking across the room. He met her wide-eyed look with a wink.

He swept his gaze down her body again, noting the edgy boots and knee socks paired with tights and black leather.

She was a study in contrasts.

"Your suit is a definite step up from that costume," she agreed. "I'm glad to see you finally got the zipper unstuck."

She gave him a once-over just as hot as the one he'd given her. Her gaze slowed when passing over his faulty-zipper zone, making him wonder if he'd be having issues with these slacks. The speed at which she inspired an erection was hell on his clothes.

"I didn't. I had to cut the costume off."

"Oh." Her eyes danced with amusement, but she pressed her lips together in an attempt to keep from laughing aloud.

She was so damned cute.

He wanted to lift her off her feet and pull that curvy body against his, to see if it fit as good as he'd spent the weekend imagining. Not for the first time, he cursed his brother, the bet and that damned Grinch costume. If it weren't for Saturday night's thick layer of green fur— and a faulty zipper—he'd already know what she felt like.

But this was a formal meeting.

In someone else's office.

Getting hot and heavy with a business associate was definitely on the stupid list. Especially since Rudolph was likely to walk in at any moment. If he caught Gage and Hailey making out, he'd probably grab a video recorder and put it up on the company's YouTube channel.

So reluctantly, Gage offered his hand instead. The delicate softness of her palm and her quick intake of breath reminded him that she was about as close to an innocent as he'd been since his teens.

Maybe this was a bad idea.

"I didn't realize you were going to be a part of the meeting," she said breathlessly, her hand still nestled in his.

Gage frowned.

Why wouldn't he be here? This meeting was supposed to be him, Rudy, that singer chick and the competing designer. He'd figured he'd play to Rudy's good-old-boy persona while pitching circles around the designer. Milano's leather designs already appealed to Rudy's misogynistic perverted side. All Gage had to do was play that up, maybe intimidate the other designer a little and snag the contract on his way out the door to meet Hailey for dinner.

A dinner he'd been of two minds about keeping.

Hailey was everything he liked in a woman.

Sexy, fun and sporting a body that'd starred in all his dreams since the party.

And Hailey was everything he avoided in a woman.

Sweet, trusting and sporting an emotional innocence that promised nothing but trouble down the road.

And she was a business associate. Distant, perhaps, but still close enough to this project for it to possibly get messy. If he were smart, he'd offer a clever excuse and get out of their date. He'd keep this business deal simple, and himself out of trouble.

Gage was damned smart.

And here he had a chance to pitch to the singer's agent, just him alone. Might as well use it. Maybe it'd help keep his mind off stripping Hailey bare of everything but those boots.

"Since Rudolph is late, why don't we get comfortable? You can fill me in on what you think Cherry Bella likes best. And, of course, tell me what you're wearing under that skirt."

So much for keeping his mind off her naked.

Eyes wide, Hailey's mouth rounded to a surprised O before she let out a gurgle of laughter. As he escorted her to one of the half dozen club chairs by the window, she slanted him a teasing look.

"Under this? What better under leather than lace? Merry Widow lace, of course."

Releasing her elbow, Gage frowned.

What the hell?

She wore the competition?

"I'm a little confused," she said before he could point out the blatant conflict of interest. "Wouldn't you know better than I what Cherry likes?"

Why would he?

Gage gave Hailey a hard look.

Before he could ask exactly what her connection to Cherry, and to Rudolph, was, the department-store mogul swanned in with all but bugles blaring a fanfare. The small, bald man apparently made up for his lack of stature by surrounding himself with as big an entourage as possible. Mostly made up of busty women in short skirts, Gage noted. Two carrying briefcases, one with coffee and another with a tray of tiny pastries.

The women paraded in, each setting her item on a wide, glass-topped table, then without a word, doing a snappy about-face and parading right back out.

Leaving Hailey to stare, wide-eyed, Gage frowning and Rudolph posing in the doorway. And Cherry Bella nowhere to be found.

Was that why Hailey was here? To rep her client?

"Darlings, I'm late. So let's not dawdle. Sit, sit." Rudolph waved his fingers at Gage, who, after a second's debate, sat. But opposite Hailey instead of next to her. He had a feeling he was going to get more out of watching her face than whatever the old coot spouted.

"It'll just be the three of us, I'm afraid." As if to emphasize his statement, he came over to sit with them, rat-a-tat-tatting his fingers on his knee and frowning. "I know you're both anxious to hear the decision of who'll be awarded the contract. I'd intended to give it today, with Cherry's help. But as she's ill, we'll have to reconvene tomorrow."

"Tomorrow?" Tension spiked Gage's system. And not the happy, sexual kind he'd been enjoying thanks to Hailey. This meeting was supposed to finish up his commitments to Milano for the year. He had his own clients to see, several projects in the works. He didn't have time to play babysitter to a leather lingerie line and a kooky, old guy.

"Unfortunately, Cherry felt ill after lunch," the old guy said, sounding more irritated than sorry. "She apologizes for missing the meeting, but insists on talking with the designers herself and having a say in the decision if she's to take the role of spokesmodel. I hate to inconvenience you, but we'll have to meet again tomorrow. Cherry feels the lingerie is the linchpin of her agreement to signing on as the face of Rudolph for next year."

Gage barely heard a thing after the words *talking with the designers*. His eyes shifted to Hailey. Her eyes were round, those full lips parted in a silent gasp. Not a gasp of pleasure, either.

Nope. She looked about as horrified as he felt.

"Inconvenient for the two of you, but as much as I'm sure you both want this contract, I'm sure you'll make adjustments." With that pronouncement of misperception, Rudy bounced up and scurried over to the tray-topped table. "So are you in the mood for cocoa? And a sweet, of course. What's Christmas without cookies? Then we'll take a quick look at the test shots my photographer took of Cherry in each of your designs. Consider it an early gift, since it gives you a chance to refine the pitch you'll need tomorrow."

Hailey closed her eyes, taking a deep breath, then shaking her head as if trying to shift the new facts into the old picture. If the pinched expression on her face was any indication, she wasn't liking the way it looked now.

Gage could relate.

Son of a bitch.

There went his Christmas treat.

5

WELL, THIS DAY had totally sucked.

Sinking deeper into the worn booth, Hailey looked around the retro diner and took a deep breath to keep from crying. Then wrinkled her nose as the acrid scent of burning burger filled the air. On opposite sides of the room, two babies screamed their dissatisfaction with dinner, their cries echoing off the curved glass window in stereo.

Carinos this wasn't.

Of course, there was nothing to celebrate, either. So a cheap diner was much more fitting than a four-star restaurant.

She wanted that account. She'd worked her ass off for it. She was damned good, her designs were high quality and on trend, yet unique and memorable. Her costs were reasonable, her profit margin solid. She'd put together a fabulous proposal.

She was perfect for Rudolph's spring line.

Her designs were perfect for Cherry Bella.

Now she was afraid perfect might not be enough. That this time, just like so many others, she'd get within touching distance to getting what she wanted, only to have it swept away.

She glared at the glass on the table in front of her.

Other than being made of melted sand, it in no way resembled the sexy, seductive wineglass she'd thought she'd be sipping from right now while flirting her way through a very promising date.

Nope, this glass was thick, with hot fudge sliding down one side and a puddle of melting, sprinkle-embedded whipped cream pooling on the stem.

She licked a smudge of chocolate off her knuckle, taking comfort from the bittersweet richness.

She was wearing her favorite lingerie under this chic outfit. A sweet, dove-gray demi bra with picot lace and tiny pink satin rosebuds. She'd imagined describing the matching thong and garter belt to Gage over candlelight and appetizers, letting that image set the tone for the rest of their evening.

Her garter belt pressed tight against her overfull tummy, a reminder of just how mistaken she'd been. No pleasant alcohol buzz and sexual zing happening here for her.

Instead, she had an ice-cream gut ache and felt as if she'd been beaten around by a bag full of gloom. Heck, she could give Doris a run for her money for the biggest downer award in this mood.

And it was all Gage Milano's fault.

As if her thoughts, or an ice-cream-inspired fantasy, had called him up, Gage suddenly appeared right there at her booth.

Sexy as hell, his black hair windswept from the chilly San Francisco weather and tumbling over his forehead in a way that made her fingers itch to tidy it. His eyes were intense, wicked and amused as he arched one brow. And his body. Yes, he was wearing a leather bomber jacket, so she didn't have full view of those delicious shoulders. But hey, she'd correctly pegged how gorgeous they were when he was draped in green fur. She could imagine them just fine covered in leather.

Leather.

Something he specialized in.

Hailey blinked a few times, sure he was just a sugar mirage. But he didn't disappear. Instead, he smiled.

Damn him. And he didn't even have the courtesy to look out of place. Instead, he was perfectly at ease. It was so irritating.

"What are you doing here?" she asked.

"I followed you."

She shook her head. No, he hadn't. She'd been here, stuffing her face and getting sick on ice cream, for almost three-quarters of an hour. Her body would have sent up horny signals if he was anywhere near her.

"I'd have been in sooner, but once I saw you were settling here for a bit, I had to make some phone calls."

Perfectly at ease and acting as if he had no doubt she'd be thrilled to see him, Gage shrugged out of his jacket and slipped into the seat opposite her. She was distracted from feasting her eyes on his shoulders when, with a grimace, he shifted to lift one hip, then slid back toward the seat's edge. Hailey smirked at the contrast of his sleek looks cozied up in an ice cream and burger booth. She hoped his hundred-dollar slacks had just got stuck in a chocolate smear.

Was that mean of her?

Sure.

But dammit, she'd really been looking forward to their date—and the sex she'd imagined they'd be having soon afterward.

Talk about disappointed.

It was like every Christmas she could remember.

She'd be promised something wonderful, be it that special gift from Santa or her parents not fighting for one blessed day. She'd spend the entire season winding herself up with excitement, hoping and imagining just how amazing it would be.

And, always, it'd been a huge disappointment.

Santa never brought her what she asked for.

Her family never kept their promises.

And her prettily imagined holiday never came true.

She knew it wasn't really Gage's fault. He hadn't known they were in competition for the contract, either. But she couldn't help but feel that the Grinch had, indeed, stolen her Christmas.

"Why'd you follow me?" For one tiny second she imagined maybe it was to beg her to go out with him still. To tell her how hot he was for her, that a silly thing like business shouldn't stand between what they'd felt for each other.

"I thought we should talk. Maybe work this out between us." His smile was pure charm, his look so potent that—despite her vow that he was now off-limits—she was tempted to start undressing right then and there.

"Really?" Her pulse joined the dance and Hailey shifted in her seat, her waistband a little snug from holding her breath—and all that ice cream.

"Really." He leaned forward and lifted her hand into his. His thumb rubbed along the center of her palm, heating and stirring. "I figure there's no reason we can't both have what we want, right?"

Her mouth was too dry for words, so she settled on a nod. He was so damned sexy. His eyes were hypnotic, as if he was trying to pull her in. She didn't think it'd take much for her to follow just about any suggestion he might offer up.

"I mean, who knows what kind of crazy things Rudolph might want in order to award the contract. Look at how he's dragged this out already. First he was supposed to announce the lineup on Saturday. Then it was today. Now it may be tomorrow. I know you're a busy lady, and I definitely have plenty on my schedule. So why don't we make this easy for him. What do you say?"

"What?"

Her pulse slowed to a thud, matching the feeling of anticipation deflating in her belly.

"How about I make you an offer? Hook you up with some other potential clients, some big names. A half dozen hot leads you could nail down before the weekend. And, probably, before Rudolph would get around to figuring out what he wants." Gage added a charming smile, as if he were plopping a fat, juicy cherry on top of his delicious proposition.

Delicious, that was, for him. She clenched her teeth against the rude words she wanted to spew, leaving a sick taste in her mouth.

When she didn't answer, he craned his head forward to check out her ice cream, then lifted a spoon from the place setting on his side and scooped up a bite.

"Not a bad chocolate," he commented. "I'd have pegged you as a more adventurous ice-cream connoisseur, though. Espresso, some exotic fruit or maybe bourbon flavored."

"But then, you don't know me very well, do you?"

Brows arched, he gave a slow nod and set the spoon down. He had a look of smug satisfaction on his face. As if he'd just been proved right about something.

"I know more about you than I did before," he offered, his smile so full of charm it was dripping in her ice cream. "You're an up-and-coming force to be reckoned with. Your designs are pure romance, created to make any woman and every woman feel sexy."

"How sweet." She reached forward with two fingers and slid her glass of leftover melted ice cream back toward her, out of his reach. "You memorized my promotional materials. Did you also notice that my designs are the perfect look for Cherry Bella?"

"Well, c'mon," he said, his smile teasing and light, even though his eyes were narrowed now, a little more watchful and a little less charming. "Cherry Bella's the kind of woman who can wear anything and make it look great. And she's going to be the total focus of the spring line. The clothes will barely be noticed."

"My designs always get noticed."

"Sure they do. I'm not saying they're not great. They are. But c'mon, we both know leather gets more looks than froth."

He was so sure he was going to win, he'd just given her the pity look. The oh-so-sorry-you're-a-distant-second look. She'd seen that look so often in her life, she'd have thought she was immune.

Except when it was on Gage's face.

Her jaw tight, Hailey had to work to keep her expression polite, when all she wanted to do was stick out her tongue, dump her melted ice cream in his lap and storm out.

She'd be damned if the sexiest man she'd ever met was going to think she wasn't good enough. Even if he was no longer in the running to find out just how good she *really* was.

"Are you trying to say my designs aren't good enough to get this deal when they're up against yours?"

"I didn't say that." His frown was a flash, gone in a blink. But she caught the surprise in it and realized he'd not only thought she wasn't good enough, he'd also thought she was a wimp-girl. As fluffy and frothy and fragile as her designs.

A lifetime of never being quite enough had, if nothing else, taught her to fight like hell for what she wanted. So before he could respond, she leaned forward and offered her sexiest smile. Her eyes locked on his, she trailed her fingers over the back of his hand in a soft, teasing gesture, then arched her brow.

"But that's what you meant." Hiding both her hurt and her frustration, she gave a pitying shake of her head. "A shame, really. Because if you'd played your cards differently, you'd have been able to find out firsthand just how fabulous my lingerie is."

VISIONS OF HAILEY'S curvy little body packaged in shimmering lace and delicate ribbons danced through Gage's brain like tempting sugarplums.

Visions he'd been damned close to seeing in real life.

He'd been so sure when he walked in here that he could charm her into stepping aside. He'd made a few phone calls, called in a couple of favors and lined up a handful of potential clients for her. Nothing as big as Rudolph in terms of prestige. But some solid deals that could keep her in sexy shoes for a while.

She had a good product, but she was still up-and-coming. Not quite in the same league as Milano. He'd figured she'd be so grateful, they'd not only keep their dinner date, but hurry right through so they could get to the dessert he'd been thinking about.

All he had to do was dish up a little charm, weave his marketing magic and ta-da. He'd be licking chocolate off her belly.

Instead, he'd barely warmed up when Hailey flashed those big green eyes at him and he'd totally forgotten his plan. That had never happened before. He'd had women flash their breasts in the middle of a sales pitch and he hadn't missed a beat.

But now, with his freedom on the line, he'd stepped all over his own tongue. Nothing like coming off as an arrogant ass to tip his hand and piss her off. He'd already lost his shot at seeing her naked. Time to table the idea of dinner, and dessert, and just get her to agree to give up the Rudolph deal. That way he could get the contracts nailed down before ole Rudy decided to add another twist or drag it out further. Then Gage could keep his own client appointments and maybe still get in a little holiday vacation.

Noting the chill in her eyes as she pulled out her wallet to pay for the ice cream, he figured he'd better do it before she walked out.

It was going to take some quick talking.

And some clever marketing.

Good thing he was good at both.

"I already know firsthand how great your lingerie is." He waited a beat, enjoying the way her eyes widened and a hint of pink touched her cheeks. Unable to resist, his gaze dropped to her chest. Completely covered to her chin in a black turtleneck, he could still imagine how she'd looked Saturday night. "You have a distinct sense of style, and now that I think about it, your elf outfit featured pieces of your lingerie line, didn't it?"

Like that bustier. The candy-cane-striped one that'd made his tongue ache to lick her.

"It did," she agreed slowly, as if not sure she wanted to trust him. Gage had to hand it to her; she looked like a china doll, but she was damned smart.

"I'm impressed. Most men don't notice what a girl's wearing, let alone remember and recognize pieces of it days later."

"You made quite an impression. Even if I'd known we were competitors, I'm sure I'd still have hit on you, but I might have been a little more aware that this could get awkward."

"Oh, I don't know," she said, her words as sweet as the hot fudge on the edge of the ice-cream glass. She reached out to touch her finger to the thick chocolate, then pressed it to her tongue. His brain shut down. Gage didn't know whether she'd done it because she was nervous or because she just knew it was the perfect way to torture him. Either way, the south side of his body took a quick leap north.

"You don't know?" he repeated, totally forgetting what they'd been discussing. Something about lingerie, probably.

"I don't know that this is awkward, really. More like a disappointment. I mean, we're both trying to win the same contract. That means our dinner date is off." As Gage was trying to find some appreciation for her practical acceptance of that, she gave a deep sigh that pressed her full chest against that lucky black fabric—and made the blood flow to his dick.

It was that rush of blood that inspired his next words.

"I don't think it has to be quite as cut-and-dried as that," he argued. "You can take my offer, reel in some big clients and everyone's happy. Then we can play the rest of the game just fine."

"You see this as a game?"

"The contract?" he asked. "Or our date?"

Her laugh was a soft puff of air, barely there and not enough to reach her eyes.

"Well, I guess that answers that."

"I'm just saying I don't think we need to let this contract business get in the way of any potential pleasure between us," he heard himself propositioning. This was the first time his dick had ever taken direct control of his brain and had him saying things he knew were insane. Gage wasn't sure if he should be impressed or terrified.

"Well, that does sound tempting," Hailey agreed, her look so warm and sexy that he decided terrified was the wisest choice.

"But I've got to ask," she continued, turning the ice-cream glass in slow circles, its tempting fudge and just a smidgen of whipped cream on the side making him crazy with hunger. "Are you comfortable in second place? Because I plan to win that contract."

It took him three whole seconds to rip his gaze off her full lips and realize what she'd said.

She thought she could beat him?

Hell, all she had to do was take a deep breath and he'd be so focused on her body, she just might have a shot at it.

"Babe, you might want to rethink your plan." Despite feeling as if he'd fallen off a very unfamiliar cliff, Gage gave her a cocky smile. "I never lose."

He knew that statement edged him over into total ass territory. But dammit, he was rattled.

Since this was a first, he clearly wasn't handling it well.

"Rethink my plan?" Her thick lashes fluttered over those big, round eyes, but she didn't look intimidated. Nope. If anything, Hailey appeared irritated. "In what way do you think it needs rethunk?"

Was that even a word? From the way she'd lifted her sharp chin, and arched one brow, Hailey looked as though she was challenging him to question it.

Gage shook his head, trying to bring his thoughts back in line. This wasn't about words, silly or otherwise. This was about her potential disappointment.

He might have had to kiss goodbye all of the prurient sexual plans he had for her body, but he wasn't the kind of guy who took his disappointment out on a lady.

He liked to think he was too chivalrous for that.

So he decided to warn her instead. Hopefully keep her from getting her hopes up too high.

"You're clearly the kind of gal who throws herself into things wholeheartedly," he observed. From the tiny furrow between her brows, he figured he'd hit the mark, and she wasn't exactly thrilled to be read that easily. No surprise. Most of his competitors weren't. "But in this case, you'd do better to have a backup plan."

"Because you're so sure you're going to win."

"I'm just saying I don't want to see you disappointed," he told her, his smile as soothing as the hand he gently glided over her arm.

Her green eyes chilled and she shifted her arm to one

side. Only a few inches, but enough to make it clear that touching her had just made the off-limits list.

"Ooh," she said, drawing the word out in a husky tone that made him think of bedtime moans and whispered words in the dark. She tilted her head to one side and nodded. "So you don't want me to be disappointed."

Never taking her eyes from his, she grabbed her jacket and purse from the seat beside her and slid from the booth. Her body moved with a grace that made it impossible for him to look away, even as manners automatically kicked in and sent him to his feet, as well.

Her lips flicked in a satisfied smile, as if she'd expected nothing less.

Then, in a move as deliberate as it was bold, her gaze slowly—oh, baby, so painfully slowly—drifted down his body. When she reached his zipper, and every wonderful thing contained therein, she gave a sad sort of shake of her head, then looked him in the eye.

"Since our date, and any other plans that it might have led to, are clearly canceled, I'm sure the odds of my being disappointed just plummeted."

With that perfect put-down, and a smile more wicked than a woman with a face as sweet as hers should be allowed, Hailey turned on one sexy heel and walked away.

Leaving Gage to stare at her very fine ass while trying to pull his jaw off the floor.

6

THE MAN WAS pond scum. Worse, he was sexy pond scum disguised as temptation. And he was so damned sure he was going to sweep in and snag the contract. Hailey ground her teeth, still pissed. A good night's sleep might have helped, but she'd spent the night having erotic dreams of Gage, covered in sexy pond scum that looked a lot like his Grinch fur.

Damn him.

There was no way she was letting him take this contract from her. No way in hell.

Hailey stepped into Rudy Rudolph's office riding high on a righteous anger, a double caramel latte and the feminine confidence only great lingerie and a new pair of shoes could offer.

The black leather of her double-strap Mary Janes was a perfect contrast to her red tights and purple knit slip dress. She'd offset the aggressive colors by pulling her hair back in a loose braid, letting tendrils curl around her face. As accents, she'd assured herself. Not for something to hide behind.

"Miss North, welcome."

"Call me Hailey," she told the bald little man for the tenth time. Her smile stiffened when she saw that Gage was already there.

Not only there, she noted, narrowing her eyes. But there, cozied up in the seating area by the window. Right next to a buxom redhead who looked as if she ate sexy guys for breakfast and snacked on the more adventurous ones for dessert.

Hailey's fashion eye took in the woman's expensive dress, a Zac Posen cloque in gunmetal, paired with a droolworthy pair of matching Louboutins. You couldn't begrudge the woman's excellent taste. In clothes, shoes or—Hailey noted as the redhead reached over to lay her hand on Gage's wrist—in men.

"Have a seat, Hailey. Can I get you a drink?"

Gage and the redhead still ignoring her, Hailey refused Rudy's offer, her fingers gripping her leather portfolio bag's handle so tight she was surprised the stitches didn't fall out.

"Cherry," Rudy called as he ushered Hailey across the room. "Here she is. The owner and designer of Merry Widow Lingerie, Hailey North. As you can see, she's just as fetching as her designs."

The redhead rose, a slow sinuous move that in the end had her towering over Hailey's petite frame. It was easy to see why Rudolph wanted her as the face of his spring campaign. She was the embodiment of smoldering sexuality.

"It's a pleasure to meet you, Miss Bella," Hailey said, her words stiffer than she'd like. Because Gage was giving her that smug look, she told herself. Not because the woman had just been touching a guy Hailey herself wanted to lick like a melting Popsicle.

"I love your designs," Cherry said, her trademark voice husky and low, more suited for a dim, smoky bar than a business meeting. But her smile was genuine, and her grasp warm and friendly as she took Hailey's hand. Not to shake. Just to hold for a second, as if making a connection while pulling her over and gesturing that Hailey take the seat next to her. "You create the most romantic celebration of femininity I've ever seen. I'm awed."

Oh.

Her throat tightened. It was enough to make a girl cry.

"And such a contrast to the raw power of Milano's designs," Cherry continued, sliding into her chair with a boneless sort of grace. "Also a celebration of the female form, but with a very different message."

And that was enough to make a girl want to throw things.

For once, just once, Hailey wanted to be the clear choice. The one someone wanted most. But hey, a lifetime of coming in second, third and fourth best taught a girl a few things about sticking with it.

So she kept her big smile in place and sat, not nearly as gracefully, beside Cherry.

"If you don't mind my asking, which do you think suits you best?" Hailey heard herself ask. She barely refrained from biting her lip to try to snap the words back. She'd planned to be charming, persuasive and subtle. Like her designs.

But Cherry didn't seem offended. Instead, she laughed and gave a noncommittal shrug. "I'm a multifaceted woman. Choosing isn't a simple thing. Much, always, depends on my mood."

Hailey almost pointed out that her designs suited a variety of moods, while Milano's only suited the kinkier ones. But this time she managed to keep her mouth closed.

Instead, she—finally—let herself look at Gage.

His dark eyes were aimed right at her, a small smile playing over those sexy lips. As if he were looking into her mind and poking through her plans and ideas, preparing to blow them all to teeny-tiny pieces.

Yet, she still wanted him.

If she closed her eyes, she could still taste that kiss.

Could still feel the touch of his fingers against her skin. Remember the scent of his cologne, the feel of his hair.

No, no, no. The man was a shark, she reminded herself. Not Prince Charming. He'd eat her up in one bite.

An idea which really shouldn't turn her on.

"Let's get started, shall we? Cherry's expressed her preferences between the other choices." Rudy went on to name the lines Cherry had chosen.

Hailey almost jumped out of her chair to do a happy dance when Vivo wasn't among them. They were all strong designers, but none so out there that her lingerie wouldn't complement them. Of course, none were so conservative that Milano's wouldn't work, either. But Hailey was going to ignore that for right now.

"Yours is the final line Cherry needs to review before we settle on the spring lineup," Rudy continued. Playing waiter with a dapper flair, he set a Plexiglas tray on the small table centered between their four chairs, motioned to the coffee, tea and juice as if encouraging everyone to help themselves.

When nobody did, he snagged a Christmas cookie shaped like a reindeer, bit its head off and gestured with its body. "I'd like the two of you to give a final pitch. Tell us why your design is perfect for Cherry Bella and Rudolph department stores."

"Ladies first," Gage said before Hailey could do more than take a nervous breath.

She gave him a look, intending to say something— anything—that'd put him in his place and let him know that he wasn't running this show.

But the second her eyes met his, her brain shut down. She hated that. But her body—oh, her body—it loved the results. Big-time.

Her heart did a little dance in perfect time with the nerves swirling around in her stomach. She could stare into his eyes for hours. Days, even. Nights would be even better. She wanted to see those eyes heat again, darken with desire and smolder with passion. Like they'd done when he'd kissed her.

She wet her lips, remembering his taste. The texture of his mouth. The sweep of his tongue.

"Hailey?"

"Hmm?" She blinked. Then she blinked again, her eyes widening in horror before she ripped them from Gage to focus on the man with the giant checkbook and the key to her future. "I'm sorry, what?"

"Why don't you go ahead and make your pitch."

She wanted to suggest that Gage go first instead. She wanted to ask for a bucket of ice. She could barely think straight with her brain locked in horny mode. But they were all gazing at her expectantly and she didn't want to make waves. Or worse, look as though she wasn't grateful for this opportunity.

Deep breaths and don't look at Gage, she instructed herself.

Okay, then...

She'd spent all night obsessing over this. Now that it was time to pitch it, she hoped like hell she'd obsessed in the right direction.

"Clearly you have two very strong lingerie lines to choose from," Hailey said, starting her pitch by offering Gage her first smile, then going right back to trying to pretend he wasn't there. "The question is, which one do you think is going to garner the best publicity and success for both Rudolph department stores and for Cherry Bella?

"Your theme for spring is A New You. Your strategy is to inspire makeovers, redos and taking chances. And where better to begin such a journey than with how a woman feels about herself. Lingerie goes beyond physical support. It provides emotional support. The right lingerie inspires a woman to believe in herself. It validates her femininity. Merry Widow Lingerie is more than a fashion statement. It's an empowerment statement."

Hailey paused, gauging their expressions. The interest in Rudy's combined with the agreement in Cherry's was great. But it was the concern on Gage's that rocked her. With that as encouragement, she continued her presentation. She pulled out graphs and sales figures, passed around a few samples of the merchandise in all its frothy lace beauty and put her entire heart into the pitch.

"It really comes down to messaging," she wound up. "What message do you want to send women, and what message do you think women will respond best to? I think you'll find that romance, with its empowering belief in love and happy results, will be a stronger selling point."

Pleased with her speech, and that she could sit back down and pretend she wasn't nervous enough to hurl, Hailey offered Rudy and Cherry a warm smile. Then, her body boneless, she slid into the chair next to Gage's. As soon as she did, he stood. Clearly he wanted to erase her impression as quickly as possible from the others' minds.

"Since it's just the four of us, let's be honest," Gage said in a persuasively amused tone. "We all know what sells. Especially when it comes to lingerie."

"And that is?" Cherry asked, clearly not willing to let him take the easy way through his pitch.

"Sex. Empowerment and emotions are all great between the pages of a book or at a self-help seminar. But nobody thinks that when they are buying lingerie. What women, and more importantly men, are thinking about when they look for lingerie is sex."

Hailey's mouth dropped open. It took her a solid five seconds to force it closed.

He'd thrown her under the bus. For the first time since she'd seen him all wrapped up in that green fur costume, she wanted to kick him. Gage wasn't the Grinch, she realized. He was a flat-out shark. A shark standing there in a very expensive suit, looking as though he owned the whole damned world.

"Now, as sweet and appealing as Merry Widow's lingerie is, let's face it...there's nothing that says sex like black leather." To emphasize his point, Gage lifted a presentation board from his portfolio and continued his pitch. Hailey barely heard him, though; she was too busy focusing on the photo of a leggy redheaded model swathed in leather and holding a microphone, a blatant play to Cherry.

To try to keep from hissing at being dismissed as sweet and appealing, as if those were stupid things, Hailey shifted her gaze toward Rudy and Cherry. Were they as disgusted by the hard sell as she was?

Her stomach sank.

Instead of disagreeing, Rudy was nodding away, his eyes on the leather-clad model's photos and his tongue practically draped over his tie.

And Cherry... Well, she was staring out the window, her expression as far away and morose as the gray clouds engulfing the bridge.

Gage just kept on pitching, reiterating and reframing the presentation he'd offered ten minutes before. He alternated between numbers that seemed to make Rudy drool and flattery that, thankfully, Cherry wasn't paying much attention to. Instead, the woman looked pensive as she stared out the window.

Her teeth clenched, Hailey wanted to yell *no*. They were smart business people, weren't they? Shouldn't this decision be based on an overall logic? On what fit best for the line? On the designs that'd appeal to the widest demographic?

As Gage finished his pitch, sliding the cover over his presentation board and taking a seat, Rudy's decision was clear on his face. Hailey's heart sank into her very cute shoes. He was clearly a man who'd made his fortune thinking a little south of logic.

"Well, thank you both. This was a very informative morning," the older man said. "Why don't we break for lunch now so Cherry and I can discuss this, and we'll notify you by this afternoon of our decision."

Her stomach plunged into her adorable shoes fast enough to make Hailey nauseous.

He was going to choose Milano. Despite the fact that Cherry had overruled his preference, Vivo's shoe designs, he was still going to pick the ugly leather.

And that would mean the end of Merry Widow Lingerie.

Oh, sure, she could eventually get a job doing design elsewhere. Maybe. But what about her employees? Her clients? Her dream?

She took a deep breath, trying to accept that she couldn't change the man's mind. She couldn't jump up, stomp her feet and insist he choose her. She'd tried that a few times over the course of her life, and had always been the one standing there alone with sore toes.

But…

She couldn't just let it go.

"Wait," Hailey cried, halting everyone midrise, their butts four inches from their chairs. Rudy and Gage frowned, but Cherry sat right back down, her expression warm and encouraging.

"I think he's wrong. Gage clearly has a strong grasp of basic marketing. And he's right. Sex Sells 101 is often an effective advertising ploy." She paused, letting the emphasis on the word ploy sink in. "But is that really what you want? A ploy? Gimmicks only go so far, don't they?"

She addressed that question to Cherry, who suddenly looked very tired. As if all this talking had sapped her energy.

"Gimmicks have their place," Cherry said, her shrug indicating that their place was nowhere near her.

At her words, the men settled back in their chairs. Gage's expression was guarded, but Rudy was watching his muse like a hawk.

That was her hook, Hailey knew. No matter how much Rudy might want to see women prancing down his runway come February wearing tiny strips of leather and stilettos, he'd defer to what Cherry wanted.

"Sex sells.... In this case, it'd sell to a very specific market. But you want to make this year's debut extraordinary, don't you, Mr. Rudolph? This is the first year you've ever built a line around a person rather than a theme."

"That's true. Although Miss Bella hasn't signed the agreement yet," Rudy said with a jovial sort of laugh that did nothing to disguise his concern over that detail.

"Once I know exactly what I'd be representing, I'll make my decision," Cherry said, her words friendly but firm, with just a hint of impatience. "My image, and my personal comfort levels, must be in sync with anything I do."

"Which is why Merry Widow is perfect for you," Hailey said, leaning forward and clasping both hands on her knees. "It's a line that focuses on the image of romance, of the ultimate in feminine empowerment, while ensuring you feel so real you can't be anything but comfortable."

Out of breath, Hailey forced herself not to grin. She was proud of herself. That'd sounded pretty awesome.

"I beg to differ," Gage broke in. His tone was smooth-as-silk friendly, but the look in his eyes was diamond hard. And, Hailey noted, just a little surprised. Obviously he really hadn't expected her to be any sort of competition. Just a bit of fluff, like her lingerie.

He turned to Cherry, charm oozing from every pore. Hailey wanted to hate that he could do that. But who could blame a man for being fabulous at what he did? She just wished he could be fabulous somewhere else.

Like in her bedroom.

"Miss Bella, you're a very sexy woman. Gorgeous, talented and not one to shy away from using both of those as a platform for your voice. Much like Milano Lingerie, you're distinctive, strong and bold. If anyone can showcase feminine appeal and edgy allure, you can."

Gage leaned closer to the torch singer, letting his smile widen, and laid a hand on the arm of her chair. He didn't touch her; he just suggested an intimacy, a connection.

Hailey had to actually clench her butt to the chair to keep herself seated. She wanted to leap out of her seat and smack his hand away.

You'd think her stomach would be too crowded already with nerves, panic and hurt to have room for one more nasty, balled-up emotion. But there it was, jealousy in all its hairy ugliness. "There is a lot to recommend both lines," Cherry said slowly, her gaze shifting back and forth between Gage and Hailey. "I'm not sure which I feel best fits my image."

"Isn't a better question, what message do you want to send by wearing the line?" Hailey asked before Gage could jump in with another one of those devastatingly effective innuendos. "Do your songs, does your image, equate to sex? Or to romance? Lingerie is about more than the physical act. It's about intimacy."

When the redhead's brows drew together as she considered that, Hailey took a deep breath and, ignoring her natural abhorrence for aggressive pushiness, plunged on.

"That's what it all comes down to, after all. Sex, which is strictly physical satisfaction. Or romance, which invokes the emotions, the mind and the imagination."

"There's plenty of imagination in sex," Gage said, finally dropping his charming facade to frown at Hailey.

"Sex sells for a very good reason. People like it. People want it. Sex, in leather lingerie, will appeal across the board to men and women alike. Fluff might get a few women's attention, but it won't get the men's."

"Women buy more lingerie," Hailey pointed out.

"To appeal to men," he countered.

"Romance sells much better than sex," she argued. "It sends a more empowering, desirable message and will bring in a wider customer base."

His hands loosely clasped between his knees, Gage leaned forward. He was still many feet away, but it was as if he'd moved right into her space. As if he were intimately pressing against her. Hailey's breath caught. Her body heated. She bit her lip, trying not to squirm and damning him for being able to trigger such intense sexual awareness in her body.

"Sex outsells romance. Just check the internet stats."

"Porn?" Hailey dismissed with a sniff.

"Pays well," he countered.

"Is that what Rudolph department stores is selling? Or are they focused on creating an exclusive image?"

"They're selling a trend." Gage's tone and expression were pure triumph. As if she'd just set him up to make the perfect point.

Hailey glared. She wanted to kick him for looking so smug over there, wearing his brilliant marketing-wizard face.

"Well, this has been a great meeting," Rudy interrupted before they could get to the eye-poking and name-calling portion of their argument. "The two of you have presented us with some very good reasons to consider either line. Both have great merit. But of course, we can only feature one."

Hailey ripped her gaze from Gage's smug, sexy grin to look at the man who could make or break her future. Suddenly she wanted to cry. She could see it, the decision on

Rudy's face. She'd got so close. She'd done her best and jumped way outside her comfort zone to argue for her designs. And he was still going to go with Milano?

She looked away, blinking fast to clear her burning eyes. The decorations lining the wall caught her eye. Awards. Trophies. Photo after photo of Rudy winning this or that. Many of them, she noted through narrowed eyes, at poker tournaments.

"Why don't we make a bet," she heard herself say.

"What?"

"I beg your pardon?"

"Ooh," Rudy intoned, rubbing his hands together and leaning forward. "What kind of bet?"

Hailey licked her lips, not having a clue what kind of bet. She tried to think over the roaring sound of panic rushing through her head. Taking calming breaths to try to overcome her horror at the temerity of challenging Rudolph. This man could break her. Wasn't leaving on good terms, with a possible order of future lingerie, enough? She'd made a good contact, and she'd garnered enough press and attention to possibly pull in more sales.

But a few sales and orders weren't going to be enough to get a loan the size she needed to save her business.

So stomach rock tight and nerves dancing, she wet her lips and forced herself to smile.

"Well, the question really comes down to which will be a stronger selling point for your spring line. Sex—" she bit off the word, letting it hang there for a second, then gave a deep sigh before adding "—or romance?"

Gage gave her an arch look as if to say, *didn't we already cover this?* Determined to get her point, whatever the hell it was, out before he interrupted and took over again, she sat up straighter and tilted her head toward Cherry.

"Miss Bella can sell either. But the true question is,

which one will have the widest appeal? Which one will send customers clamoring for the latest in Rudolph Exclusives? And," she added triumphantly, "which one will enhance Cherry's reputation and image in a way that benefits her career, as well?"

"I'm hearing the repeat of your sales pitch, but I'm not hearing a bet," Gage murmured.

"We each get two chances to prove our point. Sex or romance. Then Mr. Rudolph and Miss Bella decide which they think really offers the most to their prospective images."

"How do you propose we do that?"

She had no freaking clue.

But she wasn't going to let him know that.

Instead, Hailey fluttered her lashes and offered up a smug smile of her own.

"I have so many ideas, my challenge will be narrowing them down."

"We do have to get moving on this," Rudy started to say, his words drawn out and hesitant as he tried to read Cherry's reaction. "It can't go on for too long."

Trying not to let on how desperate she was, Hailey cast her mind around every idea, every argument, every possible persuasion she could offer that might get him to agree. She had nothing. Biting her lip, she looked at Cherry. The other woman didn't really want to parade around in a leather bikini, did she? It would probably chafe something horrible.

"I can give it a week," Cherry said, her eyes on Hailey. "At that point, I'll be able to let you know which lingerie line I prefer. And if I'm going to take your offered position as spokesmodel."

SON OF A BITCH.

Gage couldn't figure it out.

He'd been right there, in the winning position. They all knew Rudy was going to go with Milano.

That contract, and his freedom, had been in the palm of his hand. He'd felt bad, just a little, about playing to his strengths as hard as he had. Hailey was sweet, and clearly a talented designer. But she didn't have that killer edge that made the difference between success and luck.

Then, just when he was ready to pull out his pen and sign the contract, the pretty little blonde had outflanked him. Again. How the hell did she keep doing that? He didn't know if it was deliberate, or if Hailey was just lucky.

But now thanks to her, instead of heading up to Tahoe and mapping out the details of his brilliant kick-his-brother's-ass-and-prove-he-was-the-best business plan, he was going to be stuck pimping sex wrapped in leather for two weeks?

No way.

"I don't have another week available to negotiate this project," he said, shifting his body so he was facing Rudy. Not so much to cut the women out of the discussion as to keep Hailey from his line of sight. If he didn't see her, he wouldn't get distracted and she couldn't work her sweet magic. "And I thought you said you wanted your people moving on the advertising before Christmas. That means you don't have time to waste, either. It's not like they can whip up a brilliant campaign in a couple of days."

"You think this is a waste?"

Gage kept his grimace to a twitch, smoothing out his expression before he gave Cherry a warm smile. Her expression didn't budge. She was clearly a woman who expected to be catered to, which meant he'd just made a major misstep.

"I think your time is valuable, and that you must have more important things to do for the holidays than play…" He paused, then hating himself but knowing it had to be done, he gave Hailey an arch look. "What is it you wanted us to do again?"

She wet her lips, the move making the shell-pink flesh glisten. His own mouth watered.

He'd offered her an out yesterday. A chance to pick up a solid bevy of new clients, all ready to order. If she was as desperate as that look in her eyes indicated, she'd have grabbed his offer with both hands. She had to know her tiny company didn't stand much of a chance against an enterprise like Milano. He'd checked into her business this morning before the meeting and she wasn't heavily in debt or having obvious issues.

So it came down to one thing. There was only one reason she could have refused his offer and was pushing this silly bet idea.

Pure stubbornness.

"Maybe once we know how you think this bet will work, we can figure out the timeline," Rudy said, his tone pacifying. Not to Hailey, Gage knew. But to the lush, red-headed torch singer.

"Maybe we should just—"

"My thought is that Gage and I each take turns planning a scenario that we feel showcases the image our lingerie will offer. Mine would be to show you how romance would enhance both your reputation as a trendsetter and fashion icon, Mr. Rudolph, and the sensual image Miss Bella's built over the last few years, as well."

She tilted her head toward Gage, a lock of baby blond hair sliding over her cheek, reminding him of how soft it was. How it'd felt to tilt her face up to best receive his kisses.

Shake it off, man, Gage told himself, actually twitching his shoulders. *Don't let her get to you again.*

"And what do you suggest my scenario would be?"

"Whatever situation you think would best showcase the message your lingerie brings to the table, of course."

What message did leather panties suit?

A strip club? Bondage basement? Adult video store?

Hell, maybe she had a point.

From the look on her face, she knew it, too.

And so did Rudy and Cherry, Gage noted.

Crap.

"Not a problem," he lied smoothly.

"I like this idea. A lot, actually. And it'll only take a week," Cherry said with a languid wave of one hand, a walnut-sized diamond flashing in the morning light as she dismissed Gage's tight schedule. "But I've commitments, so my time is scarce. You'll have to plan these little tableaux for evenings when I'm not performing."

They all looked to Rudy, who ran one long-fingered hand over his bald head as he gauged Cherry's expression. When he saw her determined interest, he sighed and gave a shrug.

"Okay, then. Cherry performs four nights this week, if I remember correctly." At her nod, he continued. "That gives you three to choose among. Figure out the details and let us know by five this afternoon. If at any time either of you fails to create your scenario or in any way drops the ball, the contract goes to the other person."

He waited a beat, then stood, putting an end to the meeting.

Gage waited for the pleasantries to wind up and for the old man to escort Cherry from the room. The minute they hit the doorway, he turned on Hailey.

Damned if she wasn't adorable. Even through his irritation, all he could think of was how cute she was. And remember what she'd tasted like.

"Well, it looks like it's not quite over yet." Her voice was filled with bravado, but she'd chewed off her pretty pink lipstick and her eyes were wary. As if she wasn't quite sure what he was going to do now that they'd lost their buffer.

What he wanted to do was slide his hand up those smooth red tights, right under her skirt, and see if they were the kind that went to the waist or just to the top of the thighs. He wanted to touch her, to warm himself against her sweet little body again.

But mostly he wanted to tie her to his bed, where she couldn't cause him any further trouble. Except, he acknowledged as he shifted from one foot to the other, trouble to the fit of his slacks.

"You know what you've done, don't you?" he said, keeping his words quiet in hopes that the anger wouldn't come through. If the way her eyes widened as she leaned backward was any indication, he didn't succeed.

It didn't stop her from lifting her chin and giving him a so-what look, though. "I did exactly what I came here to do. I did my best to get this account."

Gage laughed. Couldn't fault her that.

"Sweetheart, you've got us double-dating."

7

How DID A girl dress for a date with her competition—the
sexiest man on earth—a wealthy pervert with the power
to make or break her future and a gorgeous woman who
intimidated the hell out of her?

With killer lingerie, of course.

Hopefully, killer lingerie would make this evening
magic. Parking her car, Hailey grimaced. Two days after
she'd issued the bet challenge, and it was time to rock.
She took a deep breath, the move pushing her lacy-edged
breasts tight against the sheer fabric of her blouse. Tonight was all about romance. But that didn't mean romance
wasn't sexy. To prove that point, she'd opted for exquisite
lace and satin in a delicate shade of pink under a blouse
the color of milk chocolate. Her full skirt, the same shade
of brown, hit midthigh, the better to show off the delicate
seams and bows climbing the backs of her sheer stockings.

That her thong and garter belt matched the pale pink bra
visible through the filmy fabric of her blouse was Hailey's
little secret. One that people might guess, which meant it'd
titillate and intrigue. Not scream "do me because I wear
sexy underwear"…like *some people's* lingerie.

"Miss North, you look amazing," the maître d' greeted
as she swept into Carinos, where she'd set the scene for her
special scenario pitch. It wasn't so much that she wanted

to rub in Gage's face what he'd lost by choosing a contract over her. No. Carinos was her favorite restaurant. If he ate his heart out in addition to the delicious dinner she'd arranged, well, that was icing on the cake.

"Thanks, Paolo," she responded with a warm smile, following him to the private room she'd arranged, pleased at the ambience along the way. Soft music, flickering candles, the delicate scent of roses filling the air as they skirted the main dining room and stopped just short of the atrium, with its lush display of winter roses.

"The rest of the party should be along shortly," she told Paolo, slipping him a generous tip as he gestured to the door of their private room.

"One gentleman is already here, Miss North. I'll escort the others as soon as they arrive."

Figuring that gentleman was Gage trying to get the jump on her, and wanting to be sure Paolo was waiting for Rudy and Cherry, she told him she'd seat herself. Hailey took a deep breath, mentally going over her checklist for the evening, then plastered on her biggest smile as she entered the room.

Her breath stuck in her chest.

Oh, baby, Gage was gorgeous.

The navy suit fit him to perfection. And since his back was turned while he stared out the glass wall at the flower garden, she could see how well tailored the slacks were, cupping his butt in a way that made her jealous of the fabric.

Then he turned.

And the view from the front was even sexier.

Puffing out a little breath, she forced herself to lift her gaze to his face. It was like trying to heft a very reluctant elephant over her head. Her eyes wanted to slide right back down.

"Ahh, my date." His smile was wickedly teasing and

light. But his gaze turned hot fast as he took in her appearance. "You look lovely."

Uh-oh.

The first rule she'd set for this evening was to keep a distance between herself and Gage. To stay as far away as politely possible so she could maintain control. Of her thoughts. Of her body. And of the situation.

But as he crossed the room and took her hands in his, all she could do was sigh. After all, it'd be rude to pull away.

"Thank you." She gazed up at him, her fingers itching to touch his perfectly styled hair, to muss it just a little so it fell across his forehead like it had the first evening they'd met.

Then he raised one of her hands to his lips, brushing his mouth over her knuckles. Hailey's knees almost buckled. Talk about romantic. It was as if he had magic in those lips of his.

And if he could get her all weak in the knees with such a sweet move, what else could that mouth do? She knew his kisses were hot enough to melt her panties.

Suddenly she was desperate to know how much more power he had. To feel more of what he had to offer.

And he knew it.

The look in Gage's eyes was a combination of wicked amusement and sexual heat. A promise. One she had every faith he could keep, and one she was quickly becoming desperate to feel.

"Miss North…"

Hailey's eyes dropped to Gage's mouth. Those lips were curved. Soft. Full. She wanted to taste them. To feel them trailing down her body.

"Excuse me."

"Someone wants you," Gage said, his words low and amused.

Him?

"Miss North?"

Dammit.

Hailey pulled her hands, and her body, away from Gage and turned. Face on fire, she shook her head, trying to toss off the spell, then turned to give Paolo a shaky smile.

"Yes?"

"A message for you." As polite and circumspect as if he were totally oblivious to the sexual sparks flying around the room, he stepped forward and handed Hailey a slip of paper. Then, without a word, he turned smartly on one heel and exited. Leaving Hailey alone with Gage and all that sexual temptation.

Frowning, she opened the slip of paper and read it. Her frown turned into a scowl and she crushed the note in her fist.

"What's wrong?"

"Apparently Cherry can't make it. She's not feeling well this evening. She sent the message through Rudy, who said he'd meet us in an hour and to go ahead and start dinner without him."

Damn. Damn, damn, damn.

Hailey all but stomped her foot and shook her fist at the ceiling, she was so frustrated.

She'd planned this evening so carefully. The most romantic restaurant, a private room. She'd ordered the meal, the dessert, the champagne and even picked the music, all with the idea of impressing Cherry and Rudy.

Now, neither of them was here.

Her grand plan to prove she was the best pick for the contract, *poof.* Gone. She swallowed hard, trying to get past the lump of tears clogging her throat.

"Well, I guess we can get on with the evening," Gage said, his tone close to a shrug. "Rudy will get here when he gets here."

"What's the point? I'm not trying to convince *you* of the

merits of a romantic evening," she said, jerking one shoulder in a dismissive shrug. *Be nice,* a part of her chided. He might be her competition, but Gage was still a major player who knew a lot of people. If she angered him, he could easily spread the word that she was a bitch or a diva. Or just a pain in his butt.

But for once, she didn't care about that cautioning voice. She wasn't worried about upsetting anyone. Not when she was already this upset herself.

"Look, have a glass of wine and let's eat. We might as well," Gage persuaded. "There's no point in letting this ambience go to waste. The wine is chilled. The stomachs are growling. Let's enjoy it."

Hailey looked around the room.

Ambience, indeed. A cozy table for four covered in white linen, lit candles amid holiday greenery on the table and the sideboard. Instead of the Christmas tunes that were playing gently out in the restaurant, the speakers here played the bluesy romantic tones of Cherry's music. A bottle of wine waited, as did a tray of hors d'oeuvres and fruit.

And Gage.

Looking oh so sexy and sympathetic.

She might be able to resist the sexy—and that was a huge *might*—but the sympathy in his dark eyes? Her heart melted a little; it was so unused to anyone seeming to give two good damns about her.

"Maybe we should hold the meal until Rudy joins us," she murmured, sure an evening alone with Gage was a bad idea. One that'd feel amazingly good, but still… "Wouldn't it be better to wait for him?"

"No." Gage took her hand, led her to a seat with a perfect view of the garden and held out the chair. "He said to start without him. I'm starving, so let's eat."

Hailey hesitated, then sat. Because she was starving. Not because she wanted more time with Gage. She'd been so amped over this evening, so busy planning it all, that she hadn't eaten a thing since breakfast.

"This doesn't count as my pitch for the contract. Once we eat or drink, unless Rudy or Cherry are here, the pitch is void." Determined to settle that point, Hailey gave him an intent, narrow-eyed look. "Okay?"

"You sure?" Gage leaned back in his chair, giving her a considering look that made her shiver and wish she'd worn something that didn't actually show her underwear. When she nodded, he lifted his glass of ice water with a twist of lemon and drank. "I guess we'll just have to call this a date, then."

Her eyes rounding, Hailey gulped.

"No—"

"Hey, you said it," he interrupted. "It's not for business. Which means this is a date. Just you and me and what dates are all about. Pure pleasure."

GAGE LOVED WATCHING Hailey's face. She was an open book, every emotion, every thought playing across those pretty features. Right now, her slick berry lips pursed and her brows creased, he read irritation, dismay and—yes, oh yes, baby—a whole lot of interest and sexual heat.

He figured the heated interest was enough to overcome the other dismay. And he kinda liked the irritation. It meant he was keeping her on edge. And Hailey on edge was fun. Like watching a hissing, spitting kitten.

"This is not a date."

Gage grinned. She was so cute when she was stubborn.

"Sure it is. You. Me. Candlelight dinner, all the foofy romantic accompaniments. That says date."

"Foofy?" Her green eyes slitted and she spat the word, just like the hissing kitten he'd thought her. "You call romance *foofy?*"

"Sure. It's like frosting." When she frowned and shook

her head, he elaborated. "Frosting is sweet. It's fluffy and tasty and quite often decadent. But it's not the point. The point is the cake."

"And you think leather lingerie is cake?"

"No." He waited for the stiffness to drain from her shoulders and her face to relax again before adding, "The cake is sex."

He laughed when she almost fumbled her glass of water.

"You're awfully naive for a woman who designs sex clothes."

"I don't design sex clothes. I design lingerie. Underwear, sleepwear, apparel to make a woman feel confident and attractive and empowered."

As much as he was enjoying the view of her face, those round cheeks flushed and her eyes flashing, Gage let his gaze drop.

Her see-through blouse was ruffly and full, creating a hazy distraction from the delicious curve of her breasts, highlighted to perfection in a pink bra. He had to hand it to her. Lacy and dotted with pearly things, the bra was attractive. And if it made her feel confident and empowered, well, more power to that sweet satin.

But he was thinking sex when he looked at it.

A fact he knew was clear on his face when he met her eyes again. A fact that, if the way her gaze blurred and her breath hitched were any indication, got her a little excited.

Good. He still had hope of rescuing this evening. As irritated as he was to put off his departure to Tahoe until next week after he'd nailed down winning this contract, spending more time with Hailey was a pretty good consolation.

He'd be even happier if they could spend some of that time naked. Or at least—his gaze dropped again—seeing her lingerie in more detail.

"Then I guess I'm all for empowerment if it comes in

pink satin and—" He made a show of leaning closer. "Is that lace tan or brown?"

Pink, even darker than the last blush, washed her cheeks. Gage grinned. Teasing her was fun. Something he'd never actually experienced when it came to business. Missing was that sharp competitive edge, the driving need to win. Not that he had any doubt he'd triumph when it came to the contract. But for once, it was more about enjoying himself than proving himself.

Just then, the waiter stepped in with wine and a tray.

Gage leaned back, watching Hailey relax as she chatted with the man as he poured wine, letting him know it'd just be the two of them for dinner so to go ahead and serve. He waited until the man had left before arching a brow.

"We don't order for ourselves?"

She gave an impatient little sniff, then after an internal debate that had him wondering what she was hiding, she shrugged.

"The point of this dinner is romance. Which is more than just candles, wine and music."

"I might hate whatever you chose, though," he teased.

"If you do, then I'm not very good at relaying the message of romance, am I?"

She said it as if romance was real. As if it was more than a sales pitch. He knew she was sweet, bordering on naive. But to really believe in that fairy tale? She wasn't crazy.

"C'mon," Gage said with a laugh. "It's just us. Be honest. You're not really buying into this whole romance-versus-sex thing, are you? That's only a ploy to strengthen your pitch."

Her lower lip stuck out when she frowned. He wanted to reach over and trace the pad of his thumb against it, test its softness.

"You don't believe in romance?"

"It's a device. A sales pitch." He waved one hand to indicate the room, lifting his glass of wine with the other. "It's all imagery."

He sipped his wine, then gave an approving nod, pretending she wasn't staring at him as though he'd spouted a third head and started babbling about the coming of aliens to take over the world and dress everyone in little pink tutus.

"Imagery? Romance is emotions, not packaging."

"What's its purpose?" he challenged, leaning back to rest one arm on the back of his chair and giving her a curious look. "To sell something, right? Sex, maybe? Companionship? Accoutrements like candles and wine and lingerie?"

Instead of rising to the bait and defending the fluff and froth of romance as he'd expected, Hailey just stared. Her look was intense, searching. Gage shifted, wondering if she could suddenly see through him the way he could see through her blouse. If so, he was pretty sure she wasn't nearly as intrigued by what she saw.

"Is your lingerie just packaging?" she countered. "Is it just a way to make money?"

Yeah.

That was how his grandfather had built the company. On the concept of seeing what people thought they wanted and coming up with ideas to meet those wants.

That was how Devon developed new product offerings. He looked at the ideas people thought were so appealing and made them better. Bigger. More attractive, so they'd pay top dollar.

And that was how Gage sold it. By tapping into what people thought they needed and convincing them that his product was the only one that could perfectly meet that need.

It was Psychology 101, combined with Economics and Marketing 102.

But he didn't think telling her that was going to score him any points.

So he shrugged, then shot a smile at the waiter, who chose that perfect moment to bring their food.

"Imagery is imagination, yes. It's packaging and appeal. But romance is more than that," she said as their dishes were set in front of them. His favorite spinach salad, he noted with a frown. "Romance is emotions."

"Imagery taps into the emotions. Plays them," he said, still frowning at the salad and wondering how she knew exactly what he liked. He glanced up to ask her and winced at the look on her face. Clearly she didn't think the emotions were something to be played with.

He waited for her to chew him out.

Instead, she leaned closer, resting one hand on his forearm for support as she lifted her mouth toward his ear.

"And just so you know," she said, her words a whisper of heat against the side of his head, low enough so the waiter couldn't hear, "the lace is bittersweet chocolate. You know, like frosting."

Gage closed his eyes and bit back a groan.

Every time he thought he had the upper hand, she found a way to knock him off balance.

"Enjoy," the waiter said, breaking his thoughts.

Opening his eyes, Gage watched the guy leave. In the three seconds it took him to regain his equilibrium, Hailey dug into her own salad with a tiny moan of delight.

"I'm so glad you insisted we eat," she admitted with a sheepish smile. "I was starving."

"What's for dessert?" he asked, noting that her salad was slightly different from his. Spinach, yes, but hers had strawberries, which he was allergic to. Did she know that? "Something frosted, I hope."

She laughed, looking more relaxed than he'd seen her since they'd realized they were rivals.

"You don't really mean that about romance, do you? That you don't think it's real?" she asked after a few bites. "I didn't peg you as the kind of guy who didn't believe in the softer side of love."

Another one for the imagery books. Gage shoved a fork-ful of spinach in his mouth to keep that opinion to himself.

"I think we buy into what we want to believe," he finally said. "If you want to believe that love is romantic, you look for that. If someone else thinks that sex is about physical gratification, they find images to support that belief."

"And if I wanted to believe you're a grumpy sort of emotional curmudgeon who, after being exposed to a little romance, has his heart grow three times too large, will I see that, too?" she teased, her smile bright and her eyes dancing as she referenced his Grinch costume.

"I have no doubt you could make something grow three times larger…." It was difficult, but he managed to hold back his smile until he saw that pink on her cheeks. "But I doubt it'd involve my heart. Disappointed?"

Her lips pursed, as if she was debating.

"Well, I suppose it won't jeopardize my chances of winning the account to admit that I was disappointed to find out you were my competition," she said with a little shrug. The move did delicious things under that filmy shirt, the lush pillows of her breasts moving against the satin bra as if protesting their confinement. Gage's fingers ached to touch. To see if she was as soft as she looked.

"Disappointed because you are worried I'll win?" he asked, too distracted by the view to worry about nicing up his words.

"Disappointed that it meant we can't date," she denied, just a hint of irritation. "The man I met at the party was very appealing."

It wasn't her words, so much as the snap in her tone

that grabbed his attention. Gage noted the annoyance as it flashed in her eyes, then was gone.

"But now you're wondering if that man was real." Gage frowned, wondering that, too. And wondering why he cared so much.

"You're obviously real, seeing as you're sitting right next to me all but licking—" she hesitated, took a breath that made her breasts shift deliciously again, then said archly "—your plate. The only question I have is who you really are."

Marcus Milano's son.

Devon Milano's younger brother.

The last one consulted, the one who least fit the Milano mold.

And—definitely—a man who didn't need a pretty little blonde poking into who he *really* was.

Time to change the subject.

"Isn't the more important question how you're going to pitch this romantic fluff idea of yours?" he said with just a hint of disdain. As he'd hoped, her eyes flashed and she shifted her shoulders back into combat position.

Good.

The only time he wanted her focused on him was if it included naked skin, hot tongues and the buildup to incredible orgasms.

"You're very dismissive of something you don't understand." She arched one brow, poking a strawberry with her fork and lifting it to her mouth. She didn't bite it, though. Instead, she slid the juicy fruit over her lower lip. Gage's eyes narrowed and his body stiffened.

She smiled, her look pure triumph, as if her x-ray eyes saw through the table at his burgeoning boner.

"Don't you think you're proving my point?" Gage asked, shifting in his chair. He wasn't embarrassed at his physical reaction. But he wasn't sure where she was going with this, either. Hailey had a way of leading things along, all innocent-like, then just when he was sure he'd won, she'd bat those lashes and outmaneuver him.

He had to admire that about her.

"No." She touched the strawberry with the tip of her tongue, as if testing its taste. Gage's brain shut down and he suddenly didn't give a damn whether she won or not. Just as long as she did that same move on a particular part of his body.

"Your point was that it's just about sex. That the physical act and gratification are all that matters. My point is that the packaging is what makes that act so powerful. The buildup, the anticipation. The emotional journey."

She paused to let her words sink in, then bit that strawberry right in half. Gage almost groaned out loud as his dick did a happy leap to full attention.

"You know," she reminded him softly as she licked a tiny piece of strawberry off her lip. "The romance."

"Visuals," he countered after clearing his throat. Then, always ready to play to win, he leaned closer. Close enough to get in her space. Close enough that the delicate scent of her perfume wrapped around him. And close enough to see the rapid beat of her pulse against her throat.

"Imagery is powerful. I could describe to you exactly how I want to strip those clothes from your body, what I'd like to do once you're naked and beneath me, how I want to taste you and where I'll touch." He waited, letting those words sink in. And sink they did, as she dropped her fork next to her plate and blinked quickly, looking as if she was trying to fan away that image with her eyelashes. Gage grinned. "But that's sex. Which is my point."

As if he'd been waiting around the corner for just the right moment, the waiter came in again with their entrées. Gage vowed to give the guy an extra tip for perfect timing, since Hailey now had to sit quietly, looking shell-shocked and absorbing his words instead of skipping right past them while trying to prove her point.

A point, Gage had to admit as his dinner was slid in front of him, that was pretty solid. If she was basing romance on good food and ambience, she'd have nailed it. He looked closer at the plate, noting all his favorites, from the way the steak was cooked to the type of vegetables.

"So what'd you do? Hire an investigator to scope out what I eat? If Cherry and Rudy were here, would they be having the same?"

"If Cherry and Rudy were here, their meals would fit their tastes," she said primly, cutting a delicate sliver off her chicken.

Gage glanced at the place settings, trying to see how she'd designated it so the waiter knew who got what. They all looked the same. And he'd chosen his own seat, and hers, so that wasn't it.

"Clever, but I don't see what makes the meal choice romantic. Or what it has to do with lingerie," he added, needing to remember the real purpose of this evening.

"No?" She gave him one of those looks only women could pull off. The kind that made it clear she wondered where he kept his brains but didn't hold his lack of knowledge against him since he was so damned cute. "Romance is the effort to show you care about someone else's preferences. It's putting in a little extra time to make sure they feel appreciated. Special."

"My grandma does that. Is she romancing me?"

"Does she do it in a private room by candlelight, with your favorite music in the background?"

Well, there was an image. Gage grimaced as it filled his head. Damn. She kept winning those points.

Time to turn the tables.

"So tell me, what's the point of all this romance stuff

you're so hot on?" He disguised his shift closer to her chair by filling her wineglass. "Isn't the end result the same?"

"The result?"

"When a guy romances a girl, or vice versa, the hoped-for result is sex, isn't it? Same as a woman wearing lingerie. She wears it to get—" Gage winced before a very unromantic phrase slipped from his lips and corrected "—attention. The kind that will lead to sex."

"When you're hungry, do you prefer filet mignon or a burger from the convenience store?"

Ouch.

"Then I suppose Milano Lingerie's place in that scenario would be, what? The equivalent to hunting down your own meal in the jungle and roasting it over an open fire?"

Her lips twitched and delight danced in her eyes, but Hailey shook her head.

"Oh, no. Milano's not *that* adventurous. Maybe a gourmet-catered, rich-boy frat party," she mused, tapping her finger to her chin in a way that was both adorable and amusing.

Gage laughed. She was fun. Not just fun in a cute-to-tease-and-see-her-blush kind of way. But clever. Smart and talented. Add that to a hot body and a gorgeous face, and she was trouble.

A smart man took on trouble only when he had time to deal with it. Gage had no time right now. He had a goal, a plan for his life. He didn't have time to enjoy the kind of trouble Hailey represented.

But he had a point to prove.

With that in mind, he held her gaze with his and let his smile drop. His look became intense, hot. Sexual. He let her see how attracted he was. Clear on his face, he knew, was everything he wanted to do to her, with her and for her.

Hailey's smile faded. Her eyes widened and her breath quickened. Good. She was getting the message.

"Oh, I don't know. I think this Milano can be plenty adventurous," he said quietly as he leaned in closer.

He reached under the heavy cloth covering the table and touched her knee. The soft fabric of her skirt slid temptingly between his fingers and her skin. Her eyes softened, heated. Like green glass melting into passion.

He slipped his hand under her skirt, smoothing his palm up her thigh. Delighting in the silken texture of her stocking. When he reached the top of her thigh he found lace. A band of it, separating the smooth texture of her stockings and the warm silk of her skin.

"You shouldn't…" Her words trailed off into a soft, breathy sigh as he traced the lacy edge of her stockings, slipping one finger under the smooth satin garter, then skimming it between the stocking and her warm flesh.

She was so soft.

"I think I should." He pressed the flat of his palm to her thigh, his fingers now wedged between her legs. His eyes locked on hers, silently demanding she give him room.

Her lips parted, wet and glistening, and a tiny furrow creased her brow. But slowly, so slow he wanted to groan, she unclenched her thighs and let them slide apart. Just a little. So the fit was tight.

Good.

He liked tight.

8

GAGE WAS PRETTY sure he'd just found the gates of heaven. He pressed his hand higher, rubbed his thumb over the fabric covering Hailey's heated core. It was silk, like her skin.

"What color are your panties?" he asked, not bothering to clear the husky passion from his voice.

Her eyes darted to the doorway, then back to his. She bit her bottom lip. He wanted to soothe the soft pink flesh, but his hand was busy. Instead, he arched an insistent brow.

"Pink," she whispered. "Pink like my bra. The lace is chocolate."

"Yum."

He slipped his fingers beneath the hem of those pink-and-chocolate panties. He ran his index finger along the swollen flesh he found, then gently pinched.

Squirming, she gasped. But she didn't pull away.

He shifted, so to anyone walking in they simply looked as though they were in conversation. But the move put him at a better angle, so he could use his thumb to caress her clitoris while slipping one finger into her tight, sweet core.

She whimpered.

But didn't pull away.

"I can't see a thing," he murmured, his words husky thanks to the passion clogging his throat. He had to swallow before continuing. "But I can imagine what you look like under the table. Pale flesh, blond curls. I can feel how wet you are. The images are clear in my mind. Vivid. Mouthwatering."

She opened her mouth, whether to respond or not he didn't know, because all that she offered was a low, breathy moan.

He moved two fingers in, swirling and plunging in time with his thumb's rhythm on her clit.

"I can imagine what it looks like as I touch you. My mind is painting a picture of you, naked, beneath me. Of your body straining toward mine, opening wide. Welcoming."

Her breath was coming in gasps now, even as she bit her lip as if to hold back her cries.

"Now, that's an image," he said, forcing the words out as his eyes devoured her face.

She was so damned beautiful. The flush of passion washed over her delicate skin. Her eyes glazed, lids lowered but never moving from his. Her mouth.

Oh, God, her mouth.

He wanted those lips on him.

His fingers plunged deeper. He shifted angles, pressing tight along the front wall of her core.

She tightened around him. And then, one more swirling stab of his fingers, and she went over.

God, that felt good.

A satisfaction that had nothing to do with physical release poured through Gage.

He watched her explode. Her breath came in tiny pants as her body came in tiny tremors.

Unable to resist, he leaned in to take her mouth. To taste her gasps of delight. It was as if he was a part of her orgasm. As if he was deeply embedded in the passion that engulfed her. A part of her.

It was incredible.

Then all hell broke out.

Bursting their peaceful, romantic bubble was a clash of sounds. A braying laugh. A sibilant giggle. And the sound of someone asking directions to Hailey's private room. And footsteps, clomping and rat-a-tat-tatting across the atrium's cement floor.

It was like being doused with a vat of ice water while being awoken from a very hot, wet dream by a brass band. A grade-school band, at that; one that hadn't learned all the notes.

Trying to shake off the discordant horror spinning down his spine, Gage pulled his mouth off Hailey's.

The sound came closer, in all its irritating glory.

His fingers still buried in her warmth, Gage steeled himself, gritted his teeth, then looked toward the commotion just as Rudy Rudolph swept into the room. Hanging on him like a glittering party favor was a redheaded piece of fluff who, at first glance, bore a striking resemblance to Cherry.

Gage blinked away the haze of passion from his eyes and realized the only thing the woman had in common with the torch singer was their hair color and bust size.

And Rudy's interest.

"Sorry, sorry I'm late. Candy and I got caught up at a party. You know how that goes. But I'm here now."

Indeed, he was. Thank God for the man's noisy entrance and exquisite timing. A minute earlier, and Hailey would have been midorgasm. Three minutes later, and Gage was pretty sure he'd have been sliding into her hot, wet depths.

Still, it was hard to find an attitude of gratitude when his rock-hard dick was pressing painfully against his zipper.

He slid a sideways glance at Hailey. Horror was starting to replace shock on her face. Both of which had quickly chased away that glow of desire he'd enjoyed so much.

It was as much for that, as for the fact that he had to

surreptitiously move his hand back to his own lap now, that Gage cursed Rudy.

Not that the other guy cared.

His grin as oblivious as the vacant expression in his date's eyes, the old man plopped himself into the chair opposite Gage and Hailey and threw both hands wide.

"Well? Show me some romance."

HE'D GOT HER off over dinner.

In a restaurant.

With just his fingers. And his words.

Her face was still on fire. Hailey's breath caught in her chest and she had to close her eyes against the power of that memory. His murmured suggestions echoed in her mind, making her want to squirm.

Oh, yeah, those had been some powerful words.

And then, just as she'd been ready to throw off her clothes and ride him at the dinner table, her potential boss had come in.

And Gage, damn him, had acted as if nothing at all had happened. As if he hadn't had his fingers inside her as he greeted the other man. As if she hadn't been dripping wet, hot and horny beneath his hand while Rudy Rudolph introduced his bimbo du jour. Then, while Hailey was still reeling—she didn't even know if she'd said hello—he'd claimed they were finished with dinner and suggested they leave immediately for his sexy scenario.

And she'd been too busy trying to climb out of the orgasm haze to even protest.

It was enough to make a girl scream.

And not in a good way.

"Here we are," Gage said, his words just background noise to her whirlwind of thoughts. Throughout the car ride, she'd heard him chatting with Rudy and the redhead, who were in the backseat. But she hadn't taken in a word.

The most she'd been able to do was state that her pitch would take place at another time. Just as well, since she wasn't sure she'd even get her name right at this point, let alone be able to present her argument for romantic lingerie.

Still lost in thought, she absently took Gage's hand as he helped her from the passenger seat of his car. He'd insisted on driving her to *part two* of their evening. She'd tried to disagree, desperately wanting her own car—and some time to herself. But once Rudy and Candy had decided to ride along, she'd figured it was better to just go with the flow.

Now, staring up at the building in front of them while the valet took Gage's BMW, she desperately wished she'd stood up for her choice and had a car to escape with.

Pussy's Galore, the neon sign screamed in bright orange.

"Are you sure this is how you wanted to pitch your argument for Milano designs?" she asked as they approached the rough-stone building. The red light flashing over the door spelled out clearly what kind of entertainment the Pussy Cats would be providing.

And it wasn't anything Hailey wanted to see.

"I'm sure." Gage stopped, one hand on the brass door pull, and gave her an amused look. "You're not backing out, are you? Afraid of a little adventure?"

She figured her desire to hiss and scratch could be blamed on the club he was about to drag her into. But her reaction—a nervous knot in her stomach and a feeling of nausea clogged in her throat—was definitely fear.

She slid a sideways glance at Rudy, who was pretending to read the encased poster showcasing the evening's entertainment. From the smile playing over his thin lips, he thought she was afraid, too.

His date, Hailey noted, was busy checking her manicure and clearly didn't care.

Logically, Hailey knew she could object to visiting a club called Pussy's Galore. There was nothing wrong with that. It wasn't as if she was a prude or uptight in any way. Hell, she'd just had an orgasm with her chicken piccata.

She really didn't want to go into a place that screamed sex. If a romantic setting with Gage inspired an under-the-table orgasm, who knew what inhibitions she'd toss aside in a sex club.

But she didn't want to be the one who ruined the evening, either. Nor did she want to be the one going home alone by taxi while the others had fun, with Gage charming Rudy into the contract over naked bodies.

"You're paying my entry fee, I hope," she finally said, giving Gage a sassy look. "After all, I paid for dinner."

"You made this sweet girl pay for the meal?" Rudy interrupted, pulled out of his fake perusal to frown at Gage. "That's not right."

"Romance is genderless, Mr. Rudolph," Hailey said with a shrug that conveyed she didn't play to the double standard. "And it was my point for the bet, so it's only fair that I paid. Of course, that means Gage should pay for anything we encounter in here, too."

She sure hoped the going rate for hookers was a lot more than chicken.

Ten minutes later, her wrist stamped with a go-go boot and her butt perched on a magenta fur-covered chrome stool, Hailey gave Gage an arch look.

"You said it was a house of ill repute when we pulled up." At least, that was what she thought he'd said. She'd been too busy reveling in the memory of what his fingers had done between her thighs to be sure.

"Prostitution is illegal in San Francisco," he pointed out with a grin. "This is a Kitty Cat Club. More upscale and diverse than a standard strip club. There are strippers on three stages, but there's also pole dancing, a dance floor upstairs and, in case you get any ideas, a few rooms to rent by the hour in back."

She wanted to roll her eyes and blithely dismiss the innuendo. Except her thighs were still tingling from his fingers, her panties were damp from the orgasm and, thanks to the image he'd built in her head of licking her, she didn't think her nipples were ever going to lose their rock-hard perkiness.

So instead of being hypocritical, she opted to change the subject.

"Where did Rudy and Candy go?" She'd stepped into the bathroom after they'd entered the club and hadn't seen the odd couple since.

"I'm not sure. He said something about getting drinks, and that he'd catch up with us in a minute." Gage glanced toward the back with a frown. "But he headed in the opposite direction from the bar."

She followed his gaze toward the bank of doors along the back wall, all with lights over the top, a few lit bright red to show they were occupied.

"You don't think…"

"You don't not think…" he countered, his scowl deepening. Hailey didn't figure this was the moment to point out that since Rudy was here, this did count as one of Gage's scenarios. Then she frowned, too. What if Rudy's little private party was the kind of thing that proved Gage right, that it really was only sex that mattered?

Nope, she told herself. Not going to think about that. Rudy was the pervy, have-sex-anywhere-and-everywhere-while-he-could-still-get-it-up kind of guy. This was probably just business as usual for him.

Still… Her frown deepened. It did count as one of Gage's scenarios. And maybe a successful one, at that.

"So you come here often?" she asked, wanting to distract both of them from the image of that skinny, old, bald man and whatever he was doing in the room with the red light.

"Do I look like the kind of guy who spends a lot of time at a place called Pussy's Galore?" he asked, looking a little insulted.

"Well, you don't exactly seem like the kind of guy who had to do a lot of research to come up with what scenario you thought would best prove your point about sexy lingerie." As if to echo Hailey's words, a waitress wearing a tiny blue teddy, stockings and six-inch Lucite heels approached them with a pitcher and four glasses.

"Pussycat punch," she said, setting the tray on the table between them, then poured them each a glass of the neon-pink liquid. "Your tasty treats will be out in just a second, Gage."

"Thanks, Mona."

Mona? Hailey pressed her lips together but couldn't hold back her laugh. Eyes wide and trying to look innocent, she met Gage's glare with a shrug.

"What? It's not like the reserved sign meant that this is your very own special table or that the waitress, who knows you by name, asked about your family. I believe you when you say you don't come here all the time. I really do."

His scowl deepened.

"She just might ask that of everyone," he muttered. He looked so abashed, if he'd been standing he'd have his toe scuffing the floor. Hailey told herself not to melt, but man, he was so cute.

"She'd ask about your family?" she clarified.

When he nodded, the giggles escaped like champagne bubbles. She couldn't help it.

"Look, my brother is one of the investors in this club. He's big on keeping on top of his investments and I've come in with him from time to time to check up on things."

"Of course. That makes perfect sense." Her thoughts

putting an end to the laughter, Hailey put on a serious face and nodded. "I'm sure you only visit for the articles, view the women as hardworking employees and never, ever enjoy yourself."

He shrugged.

"I did try to pole dance once." He gave her a teasing look. "You do know what pole dancing is, right?"

He said it as if she were a complete innocent. What? Wasn't it enough that she designed lingerie—a product that by its very nature demanded an awareness of sex? How did that get her a ticket to the purity princess hall of fame?

Hell, she'd just let him feel her up, and bring her down, in a restaurant on what was questionably their first date.

And he still looked at her as if she were a sweet little thing who'd run screaming at the sight of a fully erect penis.

Hailey's shoulders stiffened and her chin lifted. Was it because she was a proponent of romance? Was that why he kept dismissing her sexual savvy?

She should ignore it. She didn't have anything to prove.

But dammit, the man made her think silk scarves, whipped cream and doing it doggy style. She'd be damned if he'd dismiss her as unworthy of those thoughts.

"Let's see, pole dancing," she mused, tapping one finger on her lower lip. "Crazy gymnastic moves that require an incredible amount of upper body and core strength in order to climb a hard, phallic-shaped dance partner."

She waited for that to sink in, then leaned closer. Close enough to breathe in the scent of his soap. Close enough to see his pupils dilate and his gaze fog as the image played through his mind.

"There's something so empowering about grabbing hold of that big, hard pole and sliding yourself up and down its length." Her gaze locked on his, she pulled her glass of pussycat punch toward her and wrapped her lips around the straw. She waited just a second, watching his pulse jump in his throat, then sucked. Hard.

And that's how it's done, she thought with a grin when Gage closed his eyes and gave a soft groan. That'd show him not to dismiss her as a naive good girl.

"You've pole danced?" he clarified when he opened his eyes again, looking at her as if he wanted to cement that visual in his brain. "In a skimpy outfit?"

Hailey's lips twitched and she took another sip of the surprisingly delicious punch.

"All the way to the top. In short shorts and a cropped T-shirt," she confirmed. He didn't need to know it'd been in a gym with fourteen other women during an exercise class. Why ruin the romance or, to use his term, the image.

"They have poles in the back for customer use. Let's go." He was off his stool, his fingers around her wrist before Hailey could swallow her punch.

Freaked, she started to shake her head. It was one thing to claim she'd danced the pole. It was another to do it in front of him.

"I don't think so," she started to say.

Before she could launch her full protest—or even come up with how to do it without making him look at her like a Pollyanna again—their waitress returned with a tray covered with snack bowls. Hailey squinted. Was that cat food?

Before she could use it as a distraction to keep Gage from trying to introduce her to a dancing pole, Rudy came strutting across the room, weaving between people like a happy rooster. Hailey didn't wonder at his smile, given that he was followed by a very disheveled Candy, who was hand in hand with another woman.

"Three of them?" she murmured, a little awed.

"Gotta hand it to the guy. He's not shy about having a good time," Gage muttered back, shaking his head.

Hailey wrinkled her nose.

"I'll bet you think this proves your point." It was all she could do to slip right into a pout. Why couldn't Cherry have felt well tonight? If she'd been here, Rudy wouldn't have gone off to get off. He'd have stayed to woo his potential spokesmodel, giving Hailey plenty of opportunity to pitch charming point after charming point.

But *nooooo*. Instead, she'd said maybe a dozen words to the guy and paid a couple hundred dollars for dinner. With nothing to show for it but an orgasm.

Albeit a freaking awesome orgasm.

"I don't know if it proves my point," Gage mused. "But it definitely proves the old man has stamina."

Yeah. That was what he had. Stamina.

And a contract that Hailey wanted.

Which was why she kept to herself her irritation at Rudy's eccentric—which sounded better than *rude, inconsiderate* and *self-indulgent*—behavior and everything else about this evening all going to hell.

But now they could finally get to the business portion of the night, which was the actual point behind all this craziness. Hailey straightened her shoulders and put on her best smile. The one that didn't show how creeped out she was at imagining a skinny man in his seventies with two women who'd have to show ID to purchase alcohol, all doing sexual gymnastics in a room that looked about the size of Hailey's shoe closet.

"Rudy," she greeted when he drew closer. "Can I pour you some punch? It's delicious."

For the first time since she'd met him, the older man looked his age. Instead of bouncing on the balls of his feet, he was dragging them. His eyes were sleepy and his shoulders drooped. But his smile... Well, that was one satisfied smile.

"Gage, Hailey, this was great. Thanks to you both, I've

discovered a new restaurant and a club. But I'm tuckered out for the night, so we'll have to talk business later."

"But we're supposed to be pitching our points," she protested.

"Just one drink?" Gage suggested, who, unlike her, sounded perfectly content to write the evening off as a pitch-fail.

"No, no. It's my bedtime. We'll meet tomorrow, though. You both still have two shots to convince me. Sound fair?"

Not bothering to wait for a response, he wrapped one arm around Candy, offered his other to the blonde, gave them all a wink and headed for the door.

Hailey was pretty sure her mouth was hanging open.

So much for stamina.

Business-wise, Gage was calling this evening a total bust.

He'd set out with the intention of intimidating Hailey, charming Cherry and tossing enough sexual entertainment at Rudy that the guy didn't give this whole stupid bet thing any attention.

He'd ended up fascinated by Hailey, Cherry was a no-show and Rudy had just walked out with way more entertainment than Gage had figured on. And not one single thing had been accomplished toward the goal of being in Tahoe by the weekend.

"Damn," he muttered, dropping back onto the fur-covered stool.

"I'm sorry."

He gave Hailey a skeptical look. "Yeah? Really?"

"Yeah, really," she said, sincerity clear in those huge eyes. "It's not fun making big plans and putting everything you've got into a pitch and then having it fall apart."

Right. Because her scenario had fallen apart, too. Even though this evening had been a bust, he supposed he'd got the better end of the deal in pitching. At least Rudy had shown up for his and had enjoyed it enough that he'd remember the next day.

Her frown ferocious, like a kitten showing its claws, Hailey glared at the exit, then huffed a heavy sigh. Lifting the punch pitcher, she gestured to his glass. When Gage shook his head, she shrugged and refilled her own.

He should probably warn her that the sweet drink was eighty proof under all that sugar. Before he could, though, she drained it. The whole thing, in one swallow.

His body stirred, sexual interest once again beat out his irritation.

"Look," she said, gesturing with both hands as if to indicate that he observe, like, everything around her head. "I want this done, too. Until it is, my future is on hold."

"I'd have thought you'd want to drag it out. Put off the end until you'd got a side deal or other options." He knew it was a rude assessment, but dammit, she was right. He wanted this over with.

"Why would I want to drag this out? I have a life of my own, a business to run and Christmas is only a couple weeks away. Believe it or not, I have other things to do than hang out with an old man, his treat du jour and a no-show torch singer."

He noticed she hadn't mentioned him on that list. Because she didn't have better things to do than spend time with him? Or because she didn't see him as a major factor in her life.

"You're really looking forward to the deal being struck? Once it is, the options are done for making side deals, you know."

And she'd have no reason to spend time with him. He couldn't imagine a woman wanting to date the guy who'd beat her out of a seven-figure contract.

Date? Where the hell had that come from? He wasn't a dating kind of guy. He was a fun-for-a-night guy. Maybe-a-weekend-if-the-woman-was-wild kind of guy. But his life was business, his focus success. Women, except on a very temporary basis, didn't factor in.

And now he was thinking dating? Gage eyed the punch, wondering if the alcohol fumes were getting to him. Because he didn't think these kind of thoughts about women. Ever.

"Well, sure I'm looking forward to it. Because I'm going to win the deal."

Gage laughed and shook his head in admiration. She never gave up, did she?

"You don't really believe that, do you?" He gestured to the rooms at the back where Rudy had had his fun. "You think you made a more persuasive argument than I did tonight?"

"Maybe not a more persuasive argument, given that neither of the judges was there to enjoy it. But I do think I'll win in the long run."

"You're quite the idealist."

She shrugged, either ignoring his sarcasm or floating on too much punch to recognize it.

"I figured out pretty young that things rarely turn out the way I want right away. But if I work at them, if I push and try my hardest, eventually it all comes together."

She was fascinating. A mix of naïveté, faith, sexual moxie and determination. Throw in a gorgeous smile, her hot little body and a hell of a lot of talent, and that was one potent package. Still…she wasn't going to win.

"Are you thinking that law-of-attraction mumbo jumbo is going to help you somehow?" he asked.

"Nope. Simple optimism. I just keep believing until what I believe is real."

"And that works?"

Her smile dimmed for a second, then Hailey shrugged. "Sometimes it has. I'm still waiting for the others."

"Like?"

If that wasn't a nosy question, he didn't know what was. But he'd had his hand up her skirt already tonight. Why balk at poking into her private life, too.

"Like, you know, business stuff. I have this secretary. She's aces at her job, she's loyal to the company and she works magic with numbers. But she wishes I'd disappear."

Gage could relate. Plenty of people wished he'd disappear. But none of them had the nerve to show it to his face.

"Why'd you hire her?"

"She came with the company." Hailey waved her hand again, as if dismissing question-and-answer period, clearly wanting to make her point. "But here's the thing. Every month, every week. Every. Day," she said with extra emphasis. "She's getting closer to accepting me. To liking me. Now, would I have liked that approval and being included? Yes. Did I want to be remembered, maybe treated like I mattered every once in a while? Sure. But does it stop me from believing that I belong? That I'm important and special? Hell, no."

She pounded her fist on the table in emphasis. Gage quickly grabbed the glasses that were in sudden danger of toppling to the floor.

Frowning, he peered at her. He didn't know who they were talking about now, but he was sure it wasn't her secretary.

Another man?

A vicious clawing sort of fury gripped his guts. It took him a few seconds to realize the feeling was jealousy.

He didn't like it.

"But hey, I figure someday, she's going to adore me. Because, you know, I'm adorable," Hailey added, giggling and looking just as adorable as she claimed. And, he noted, looking as though the punch was having its effect.

He should take her home.

But first…

"When do you give up?"

Her frown was the tiniest furrow between her brows, as if that wasn't a question she let herself consider.

"If it's important, you don't give up."

"Isn't it smarter to check your ROI, and if the return isn't worth the investment, simply walk away? Quit expending energy." Gage shook his head, unable to imagine trying over and over again without success. Or only eking a few inches of success out of any given deal. He was an everything-or-nothing kind of guy, though.

"Isn't it smarter to do what you love, and believe that it's going to work out exactly how you want, than to give up on a dream and settle for less?" she countered.

Gage wanted to rub his gut at that direct hit. One she probably didn't even realize she'd made. She couldn't know how much he wanted to leave Milano. How badly he wanted to make his own mark.

Feeling his face fold into a scowl, he tilted his head toward the door.

"Ready to call it quits? I'll drive you home."

"What about my car?"

"I don't think you should be driving tonight, do you?" He arched a brow at her empty punch glass.

"I don't feel like I've had that much to drink," she said, peering into the deep glass as if measuring her alcohol levels.

"It'll hit you in about ten minutes," he guessed. Through discussing it, he shifted off the stool and, his hand on her elbow, helped her slide off her seat.

The fur grabbed the fabric of her skirt, though, holding tight so as she slid off, he got a delicious view of her thighs. And those stockings.

Hello, baby.

Tiny roses, tempting lace.

Damn, but she did have a point about how enticing that romance look was.

He was so focused on watching her legs, even though she'd freed her skirt and that beckoning juncture was once again covered, that he forgot to move, throwing her off balance.

"Whoa," she said, falling against him, her hands splayed over his chest as she righted herself. Her curves were sweet and tempting, pressed against his for just a second. Just enough to tease. But not nearly long enough for his tastes.

"I guess you're right," she said, her voice husky. Still a little unsteady, she let go of his chest to push one hand through her hair. "You're going to need to take me."

9

PUSSYCATS PACKED A WALLOP.

Hailey leaned her head against the leather seat of Gage's car and let herself float on the punch-inspired sea of relaxation.

She wasn't drunk.

She'd been drunk a few times. So she should know.

Nope. She was just relaxed.

Her body.

Her worries.

Her gaze shifted from the blur of taillights of the other cars on the freeway to the man driving.

Her inhibitions.

She wished she were drunk. It'd make it easier to do crazy things. The kind of crazy things that wouldn't be smart business decisions. The kind of crazy things that'd make the next week's competition with Gage much, much more difficult.

The kind of crazy things that'd feel oh so incredibly good. Things that followed up on the incredibly good feelings he'd given her earlier.

She'd like an orgasm where she didn't have to be quiet. She'd enjoy having one that included naked body parts. And it'd be even better if most of those naked parts belonged to Gage.

Squirming a little, she dropped her gaze to his lap, and even though it was impossible to enjoy the view since he was seated and driving, she still stared.

Because what she wanted was right there.

Barely aware of what she was doing, she reached her hand out. Maybe to touch it, she wasn't sure.

Before she could, Gage parked the car.

"Why'd you stop?"

"We're here." He tilted his head toward her apartment building. Eyes wide, she followed his gesture. They *were* here. How'd that happen so fast?

He gave her a curious look. "Are you okay?"

She took a quick inventory. Yep, still relaxed. But there was just enough horror coursing through her at the fact that she'd been about to pet his penis to assure her that, nope, she wasn't drunk.

"I'm fine." She offered him a bright smile, then gathered her purse, tucked her scarf tighter into her jacket to battle the chilly San Francisco air and reached for the door handle. "Thank you for the ride."

"I'll walk you up."

"You don't…" *Have to,* she thought, staring at the empty seat and closed door.

Well, then.

She turned to let herself out, but Gage was there, opening her door before she could fumble with the handle. He reached out to assist her from the car. Whether because he was a gentleman, or because he was afraid she'd face-plant it on the sidewalk, she wasn't sure.

"Thank you for the ride," she said, stepping onto the sidewalk with her feet, not her face. Not a hint of swaying, and only the tiniest desire to rub herself against his body. She was doing great.

"I'll see you up."

"It's a secure building." She pointed at the cameras and keypad by the glass entrance. "I'll be fine."

"I'll see you up," he repeated. Then he gave her a cute little shrug. "Hey, it's a guy thing. End of date, see lady to the door."

"This wasn't a date," she murmured. But hey, if he wanted to go inside, ride the elevator up, walk her the thirty feet, then ride the elevator back down, that was up to him.

She just wished he'd keep a little distance between them on the way. He was so close, she could smell his cologne. She could feel his warmth, tempting her to slide closer.

Suddenly nervous, she wet her lips and tried to think of something to say. But nothing came to mind.

Nope. Definitely not drunk.

And not even relaxed anymore.

In silence, she coded them into the building, then punched the button for the elevator. She gazed at the stainless doors as if her blurry reflection was no end to fascinating, trying to pretend she didn't feel the heat of Gage's stare on her face.

Suddenly, all she could think about was the treat he'd served up at dinner. That delicious, mouthwatering orgasm, brought to her by just the tips of his fingers.

It was enough to make a girl beg.

All the more reason to keep her mouth shut. Just in case.

Which she managed to do for the entire elevator ride.

When the doors slid open, she gave him a sidelong glance. Yep, he still looked determined to see her to her apartment. She didn't bother to suggest they say goodbye, and he followed her out of the elevator.

She silently led the way down five doors to her apartment.

"Well, here we are," she said in a cheery tone, pulling

her keys from her purse and giving him an *it's okay, go away now* look. "Thanks for the ride home."

"Thanks for the great double date," he shot back with a grin. Then, probably because he'd got the message from her expression, he leaned one shoulder against her door frame and got comfy.

She rolled her eyes.

"Quit saying that." She put her key in the lock and turned it, but didn't push the door open. "It wasn't a date. And if it was, it was a lousy one, given that half of our double didn't show and the other half spent his time in a room with two women whose ages, added together, still don't equal his."

"Maybe we should try it again, just the two of us," he suggested quietly. So quietly she had a feeling he was just as conflicted by all this crazy passion between them as she was.

The look he gave her was long and considering. Long enough to send the nerves in Hailey's stomach tumbling all over each other. She didn't have to wonder what he was considering. The passion in his eyes said it all.

Her chest hurt with the effort to breathe normally, to not give in to the need to whimper and beg. She stared into those dark, intense eyes, her fingers itching to touch his face. To give him back some of the same delight he'd given her earlier.

She forced herself to be practical. To think straight. In other words, to ignore the pounding desire that was screaming through her system.

"Don't you think that'd be a mistake? You know, since we're competing for this contract and all." She tried to soften her refusal with a smile, wishing like crazy she'd taken her chance with him back when he was still just the guy she'd met at the party.

Or that she was the kind of person who could separate

one thing from the other. Because she wanted him, badly. So badly, it made her ache.

"Yeah. Competitors," he confirmed, his smile falling away. The intensity in his gaze didn't. If anything, it got more powerful. As if he were through searching her mind and was ready to dive into her soul.

"Good night," he said. His words were a whisper over her skin. A soft caress echoed by his hand sweeping over her hair, cupping the back of her head.

She stared, her eyes huge, as he leaned in. Not touching, except his hand to her hair. His lips descended, his gaze never leaving hers. She sighed as he brushed her mouth with the gentle promise of a kiss.

So sweet.

Who knew he had it in him to be so damned sweet. He made her heart melt. And her resolve, dammit.

He shifted the angle, tilting his head to one side and rubbing his lips over her lower one, then taking it between his teeth to gently, oh so gently, tease.

It was as if he'd connected her to an electric wire. Sparks shot through her body, powering up every cell, sending the smoldering passion into flaming heat in an instant. Hailey gasped. Her nipples hardened and wet desire pooled between her thighs. Desire he knew just what to do with, she recalled.

She finally understood what he'd been looking for with those intense stares. The switch that'd turn off her ability to think and turn her body's need to desperate.

It worked, too.

Frantic for more, she shifted the kiss. Her mouth opened, enticing, tempting. Trying to tease him into taking more.

Gage groaned but didn't take the bait. It was as if he was forcing her to make the moves. Daring her to take the role of aggressor.

Okay, then…

Hailey swept her tongue over the seam of his lips, smiling when he opened, letting her in. She sipped, as if he were sweet nectar, until he went wild.

Then he took over.

His tongue plunged, taking hers in a wild, desperate dance.

His fingers tunneled through her hair, holding her captive to his mouth.

Yes.

Excitement pounded through her. On tiptoes, she pressed her body against his, loving that there was no give. Just a brick wall of hard, male flesh.

Releasing her hair, he swept one hand down her back, his fingers curling around the curve of her butt, pulling her closer. Hailey shifted her body so her legs were pressed against his, her core aching, needing more pressure. Needing his touch. His erection, so temptingly hard, pressed against her belly. She wanted to feel it. To see it. Oh, baby, to touch it.

She wrapped one foot behind his calf, then slid it higher, angling herself tighter against his thigh. When her foot skimmed the back of his thigh, he stiffened.

He pulled his mouth away.

Hailey frowned. Forcing her passion-heavy lids open, she gave him a confused look.

"We can't do this."

"Sure we can. If we're lying down, the height difference won't be a problem," she assured him breathlessly, releasing her grip on his shoulder to pat one hand on his cheek.

His lips twitched, but Gage still shook his head.

"We can't. You're drunk."

"No," she told him, giving her head a decisive shake. "I've already done a thorough inventory. I'm relaxed, but I'm not drunk."

"Relaxed?" His eye roll was more a suggestion than an actual move. As if he didn't want to insult her, but couldn't hold back the skepticism.

"I'm not drunk," she repeated. "I can prove it. Come inside. I'll do that sobriety-test thing."

"Why can't you do it here?"

Eyes wide with faux horror, Hailey looked up, then down the hallway.

"Here? Where the neighbors will see and start gossiping? Seriously?"

A silly argument, given that she'd just been wrapped around his body like one of those stripper poles they'd discussed. If the neighbors were the gossiping kind, that would have fueled them plenty. But Gage fell for it, nodding and then slowly—as if he were reluctant to let her go—stepping away.

Hailey turned quickly toward the door to hide her smile.

Dismiss her desire as alcohol-fueled stupidity?

She didn't think so.

This was pure determination. She wanted him, and for the first time in her life, she was grabbing what she wanted and reveling. If that reveling took place naked, so much the better. She wasn't going to worry about how it affected others; she wasn't going to let her fears stop her. She was going to enjoy every delicious second of Gage Milano tonight.

With that in mind, Hailey stepped across the threshold and tossed her purse in the general direction of the hall table. She didn't notice if the clatter meant she'd hit it, knocked everything over, or if her bag was flying across the floor.

She didn't care.

The second Gage crossed the doorway, she slapped the door shut and attacked.

With her body, wrapping it around his as tight and close as she could get with both of them in winter coats.

With her hands, skimming and skating them over his rock-hard form, reveling in the rounded muscles of his biceps under his coat, then across the granite planes of his chest.

With her mouth. Oh, baby, with her mouth. She tasted. She nibbled. She wanted to gobble him up.

For a second, a long enough second to inspire untold neurotic worries in her head, Gage was stone still. Other than the heart beating against her hand, he didn't move.

Shit.

Had she attacked too soon?

Had she misread his signals?

Had that been a pity orgasm over dinner?

Before she could do more than wonder at the depths to which her paranoid mind came up with things to worry about, Gage came to life.

He shoved at her clothes. Her hands pushing his away just as quickly, Hailey shrugged out of her coat and let it fall to the floor at their feet. She wasn't sure who pushed, shoved or pulled, but her scarf and gloves quickly fell, as well.

Their mouths slid, hot and wet, over each other. Tongues tangled in a wild dance, neither leading, both tempting.

He tasted so good.

He felt even better.

Finally, she was able to get her hands on that body. To scope out the hard planes of his chest, to feel the rounded strength of his biceps.

Hailey growled low in her throat, delighting in his shape. In the power of those muscles. He was built. He was hard. He was hers for the taking.

So took, she did.

She nipped at his lower lip, then soothed the flesh with

her tongue. Her fingers made quick work of the knot of his tie, tossing the fabric aside so she could get to his buttons. Then, oh baby, flesh.

She whimpered a little when her hands found bare skin. He felt so good.

She was so focused on his body, on discovering every little delicious bit of it, that she barely noticed how busy he was.

Not until cool air hit the naked skin of her thighs.

He'd unzipped her skirt, so it fell to the floor, billowing over her shoes. His hands skimmed already-familiar terrain, caressing her thighs there, just above the lacy tops of her stockings.

She shivered, even as heat gathered lower in her belly. Her thighs trembled a little, making it hard to balance on her high heels. To compensate, she wrapped one leg around the delicious hardness of Gage's, her heel anchored below his knee. Her core pressed, tight and damp, against his thigh.

"We should…"

"Now," she interrupted. "Here."

Her words were barely a breath, her mind a misty fog. She was pure sensation.

All she could feel was delight.

Sexually charged, edgy, demanding delight.

She wanted more.

She needed more.

Even though she was reluctant to leave the amazing hard warmth of his chest, her quest for more demanded she head south. Her hands slid, fast and furious, down the light trail of hair of his belly, making quick work of his belt.

She wasn't a fashion diva for nothing, so fast did she unsnap, unzip and dispose of his slacks. His boxers went, too, everything hitting the floor with a satisfying thud.

"Babe…"

"No," she protested against his lips, even though she had no idea what he was going to say. She didn't care. This was her fantasy and she was going to lap up every delicious drop.

With that in mind, and grateful for all the fabric on the floor to ease the impact on her knees, she dropped down in front of him.

"Oh my God," he said, his words a low, guttural groan as he stared down at her.

Loving that look on his face, appreciation mixed with fascination, coated with a whole lot of lust, Hailey held his gaze with hers as she leaned forward to blow, gently, on the impressive length of his erection.

Like a lollipop, she ran her tongue from base to top.

Gage's eyes slitted, as though he wanted to close them but couldn't resist watching the show.

The audience adding even more heat to an already-incendiary delight, Hailey shifted higher on her knees so she could wrap her lips around the smooth, velvet head of his penis. Just the tip. She sipped, swirling her tongue in one direction, sucked, then swirled it in another.

Gage's fingers tunneled into her hair, whether for balance or to make sure she didn't stop, she didn't know. She didn't care.

Her mouth wide, she took him in. Slipped her lips down the length of his dick, then back up again. Each time, she tightened her lips, until she was sucking hard, and he was squirming.

Just when his body tensed so much she thought he was going to explode, she pulled back so she was only sipping at the tip again.

"Enough," he growled, swooping down to lift her high, spin her around and pin her against the wall.

His hands raced over her body, slipping down her curves, then back up again. With his lower half pressing deliciously tight against her belly, his erection a tempting reminder of the incredible promise to come, he cupped her breasts in his palms.

Even through the heavy satin of her bra, Hailey could feel the heat as his fingers flexed and squeezed. Needing more, too impatient for him to get there himself, she reached around behind to unsnap her bra, letting the cups fall over his hands.

Gage grunted his thanks, flinging the bra away then grasping her soft, full flesh in his fingers again. His look was intent, laser-focused. As if he was getting as much pleasure from watching the slide of his thumb over her nipple as he was feeling it.

Even if he was, Hailey decided, it wasn't nearly as good as she was feeling. Her head fell back against the wall, her eyes closing so she could focus every single atom of her being on the magic his fingers were working.

He pinched her aching nipple, rolling it around gently, then swiped his thumb over its hardness. Over and over, until she was ready to scream. Heat, tight and wet, pooled between her thighs.

When she squirmed, he shifted. But not, damn him, harder against her aching core. No, he slid down.

His mouth took one nipple in, sucking gently, laving his tongue over and around the aching bud. His hand continued to work the other. Pinching, teasing.

Driving her crazy.

Hailey's fingers slipped through the silk of his hair, holding his head in place as her other hand skimmed over his chest, giving his nipple the same treatment.

He growled.

As soon as he shifted, she did, too, wrapping her leg around him again, this time closer to his waist.

Taking a hint—bless him for being so perceptive—he

released her breast, his hand speeding down her body to cup the hot curls between her thighs.

Welcome back, she thought.

Right at home, his fingers slid along her clitoris in teasing little pinches before plunging into her core.

Hailey exploded.

The power of her orgasm made her whimper at first, then as it built, she cried out, both hands fisted in his hair.

"More," she demanded, greedy and needy.

"Oh, yeah." His words were somewhere between a pant and a growl against her breast.

For just a second, Gage let her go, moved away. Before she could ask, she heard the rip of foil, felt him move away just enough to sheathe himself.

She wanted to help, but by the time she pried her eyes open, he was back in position, his hands on her hips.

Using his support, she lifted one leg up to anchor her foot behind his back. Then the other. There was something wildly erotic about trusting him so much, in believing that he'd keep her from landing on her ass.

His mouth took hers in a voracious, biting kiss.

Hailey's body started the tight spiral toward climax once again with just the touch of his tongue.

He plunged.

She shattered in another miniorgasm.

Her back slammed against the wall at the impact.

Hailey wrapped her legs tighter, no longer worrying that the sharp heel of her stiletto might be cutting into his body.

She needed him to move harder.

Deeper.

And he did.

Plunging.

In and out.

Hard and fast.

Her breath came in gasps.

Her mind swirled in a rainbow of desire, thoughts decimated beneath the power of their passion.

His moves grew jerky. Short. He plunged hard. Paused. Plunged again.

She reached low, gripping the small of his back in her hands, her feet tight against his butt, as she tried to pull him in tighter.

"Baby," he growled, plunging again.

"Do it," she demanded.

As if he'd been waiting for permission, Gage exploded. His jerky thrust sent Hailey spiraling yet again, her body splintering into a million tiny pieces of heaven.

She thought she heard him cry out. She wasn't sure, though, because her mind shut down with the power of her orgasm.

It might have been five minutes, it might have been fifty, before she settled back into her body.

It was still trembling, held against the wall by the hard power of Gage's. Tiny orgasmic quakes still trembled through her.

His breath still came, fast and furious, against her throat.

"Wow," she whispered.

"I think you took advantage of me," he finally said, his words still breathless.

Her head cuddled against his chest now, Hailey smiled.

"Ooh, poor big, tough guy," she teased, her fingers swirling through the hairs on his chest. Finally, she pulled her head back to gaze up at him. "Should I apologize?"

He looked as though he was contemplating that. Then he shook his head.

"Nah. I'll take advantage of you now. Then we'll be even."

Her giggle was cut off to a squeak when he swept her into his arms. Grinning, Hailey wrapped her hands around his neck and crossed her feet at the ankle, loving the view of her stockings and sexy shoes from up here in his arms.

"Bedroom?"

"Down the hall and to the left."

In swift, sure strides, he went that way.

She loved a man who knew how to follow directions.

Now to see what other instructions he might like to follow.

HAILEY WOKE SLOWLY, her body a melting pot of sensations. It was morning, wasn't it? From the patches of light dancing over her closed eyes, it must be. She wanted to stretch, but at the same time didn't want to move because everything felt so good.

But what might feel better was a hot, tasty breakfast of French toast and fruit. A quick mental inventory assured her that she had the ingredients to make Gage a delicious morning-after treat. Then they could come back to bed and enjoy another sort of treat. The naked sort.

And then, riding on a wave of passion and delight, they'd be able to amiably settle this whole silly competition thing. They were two intelligent, clever adults. She was sure they could figure out a way to keep that contract from being an issue. Or, more important, from keeping them off each other's naked bodies.

Finally, more to feed the desperate need to see Gage's face than anything else, she forced her eyes open. A soft, dreamy smile on her lips, she turned her head to the pillow next to her.

Ready to ask him if he liked whipped cream with his French toast, or his other treats, the question froze on her lips.

The pillow was empty.

She shifted to one elbow, looking past the tumbled waterfall of blankets tangled with her clothing from the night before.

His clothes, though, were all gone.

And so was he.

10

THIS FEELING-LIKE-a-complete-prick thing was new to Gage. He sat quietly in the corner of the meeting room, resisting the urge to hunch his shoulders, and tried to shake it off. This was a business meeting.

With a man he'd watched leave the pussycat club in the arms of two women fifty years his junior because he knew sex would hook the guy's vote.

And a woman who refused to look at him. One who was presently pretending he didn't exist, even though she'd blown his mind, among other things, the previous night, who'd provided hour upon hour of the best sex of his life, and whom he'd left without a word that morning. Why? Because he'd got a text from his brother, letting him know their father had called yet another emergency meeting.

So instead of letting Hailey know he was leaving, he'd sneaked out with his shoes in his hands.

Yeah, he was a real prince of a prick, all right.

"As you both know, Cherry's schedule has been somewhat in conflict with this little project. She'd hoped to make it here this morning, but had an unexpected doctor appointment."

"Not that this hasn't been fun," Gage said, shaking off his odd hesitation and leaning forward to give Rudy a direct look. "But how long is this going to drag out? A decision was supposed to be made by today. I don't know about Hailey, but I do know that I have a lot of other things on my schedule that need attention."

Clearly not a fan of being pushed, even when it was to keep his own word, Rudy bristled.

"If you'd like to step out of the game, feel free. That'd make this entire decision much easier."

Gage was tempted.

Dancing to the tune of an eccentric businessman with more power and money than manners was getting old.

And if he stepped off, Hailey would win the contract. Something that obviously meant a lot to her.

But he flashed back to that morning's meeting. Just him, his brother, the old man and the board of directors. All fourteen of them. All wanting to take the New Year in a different direction. None of which Gage gave a damn about, and even more, none of which had required his input. He was marketing. But the old man wanted him there as another token Milano. A show of force. A pawn.

That was another game he'd like to step out of.

And he would. Just as soon as he could do it without giving up his shares in the company or his place at the family table. Although he was willing to negotiate the latter.

"I'm not stepping out," Gage said, reluctantly giving way to the always-present nagging pressure of family obligations. "I'm simply suggesting we finalize this as quickly as possible."

Rudy's glower faded a little and he slowly nodded.

"I agree. But my arrangement with Cherry guarantees her final say in the designs she wears. If I back out, she very well might, too."

Something Rudy looked to be very concerned about. Given that the woman had barely been present so far, he probably had reason to worry.

"As happy as I am to hear that Milano is still in the

competition," Hailey said in a tone that said the complete opposite, "I'd like to make sure you're judging each of the lines fairly. After all, last night wasn't a true test, seeing as you weren't able to experience my presentation."

For the first time since she'd walked in, Gage looked Hailey full in the face. Granted, he was staring in shock at her temerity.

But damn she looked good. Her dress was green, almost as vivid as her eyes. It wrapped around her curves like a lover, sweeping from shoulder to knee with deceptive modesty. He wanted to follow the flow of the fabric, to skim his fingers along the hem, then up under that skirt to touch her soft, warm flesh.

Of course, he'd probably get his hand chopped off if he tried. But that didn't ease the need.

"What you'd have seen if you'd been present at either of our events, Mr. Rudolph, was a sharp contrast between messaging. Romance, which is all about love and happiness, promises not only fabulous sex, but of having it over and over again. That means a variety of lingerie options for each romantic fantasy." She swept her hand through the air, as if waving to a dozen invisible fantasies dancing around their heads.

Gage frowned as Rudy's eyes blurred, obviously taken in by her spiel and focusing on all his own happy fantasies.

"In comparison to the message of sex. Which, let's face it, is impersonal and can be performed just as easily in the nude as in a six-hundred-dollar leather bustier." She gave a tiny shrug, as if saying it wasn't the cost that was a drawback, but the image. "Sex is a physical sensation. Love is an emotion. And while people might be satisfied with sex—they might even crave it—it's the idea of romance and having someone worship them in a physical way that will sell you the most lingerie."

She didn't look Gage's way as she finished, but instead, Hailey gave a sharp nod, all but clapping her hands together. Her smile oozed satisfaction. As it should. Gage was ready to toss aside the leather and go for lace himself.

Then he remembered what was at stake.

"Are you saying romance equals love? You're not really using that as your selling point, are you? Because we, and Rudolph's audience, are savvier than that."

Gage wasn't proud of bashing her argument that way. But dammit, he had to get loose of Milano. He was so sick of playing his father's puppet. He needed that year of freedom, and his chances of getting it were quickly slipping away.

Clearly as impressed with him as he was with himself, Hailey made a show of rolling her eyes.

"I'm saying romance makes people feel good. When they feel that good, they are much more willing to spend money—a lot of money—on keeping the feeling."

She shifted her gaze to Rudy and tilted her head to one side. "Isn't that the point? To not only present a strong visual that will create a trend, but to get people into your store to spend money?"

"Or is it to build an air of exclusivity, something that women will aspire toward and envy?"

Gage didn't go as far as to claim that people—women especially—would pay more for the exclusive designer aura than for the feel-good romantic image.

Because from Hailey's glare, and Rudy's nod, he didn't have to.

"The real question is, which line will better suit Cherry Bella's image and enhance the message Rudolph department stores is trying to send?" Hailey put in quickly.

Rudy heaved a sigh, then watched his fingers tap the desk for a few seconds before he offered them both a grimace.

"Okay, I'm going to be honest with you both. I'm inclined to go with Milano, simply because I think the look is more cutting edge, high-fashion oriented."

Yes! Other than a slight relaxing of his shoulders and tiny twitch of his lips, Gage managed to keep his triumph to himself. But in his mind, he was already packing his bags and heading for Tahoe.

His gaze slid to Hailey, wondering if she might be in the mood for a little snow for the holidays. He frowned. Her face was like porcelain. White, stiff and brittle-looking. Did she hate losing that much? How long would she hold a grudge? Maybe he should send a car for her next week instead.

"But," Rudy continued, drawing out the word in a way that grated up and down Gage's spine. "The decision isn't mine alone."

What? No. He was already on the highway, heading up the mountain. No buts, dammit.

"Of course it's your decision," Gage said quickly, adding a man-to-man smile. "Not that Cherry's input isn't important. But, let's face it, she hasn't been in attendance for much of these meetings. Her priorities are clearly elsewhere."

The old guy pursed his lips. Gage knew that look. It was the screw-everyone, I-want-to-get-my-way-and-be-done-with-this look. He'd seen it on his father's face a million times. Usually right before he waved away every reasonable, well-thought-out and time-intensively researched argument Gage waged.

Kinda like Rudy was about to do to Hailey.

Gage glanced over at her again. Her chin was high, her smile in place. But he could see the hurt and frustration in her eyes.

Crap.

Before Rudy could say anything, and before he could talk himself out of playing hero, Gage gestured to the six-foot mock-up of Cherry surrounded by items from the various lines already chosen.

"But you've put so much time and effort into building a launch around Cherry Bella, you don't want to rock the boat," he said quickly. "She said it herself—the lingerie line is her breaking point. Can't ride roughshod over a woman's choices. You know how that'll come out if you do."

Rudy's grimace made it clear he'd paid the price for doing that a few times in his life. Big surprise.

"Okay, fine," the older man finally said with a huff. "But no more of these clever scenarios. No more romance versus sex. The two of you put together a fashion show, pitch your best spring look. I guarantee, Cherry and I will both attend and the decision will be made within an hour. We need to get on with this."

"When?" Hailey cleared her throat, then started over. "When will we need to do the show? What are the parameters? I mean, how many pieces will you want to see? The designs I pitched were exclusive, intended for your spring debut. I don't have them on hand."

Good point. Gage pulled a face. He was sure that Milano was in the same boat, although he had a hunch Devon had probably already started producing the designs, figuring if Rudolph didn't take them, someone else would.

"I have to get this nailed down," Rudy said, his usually friendly face folding into a scowl. "I can wait a week, maximum. If we can't settle this by then, I'll simply run my spring show without lingerie."

"A week it is," Gage said, his tone quick and hearty. That was six days longer than he wanted, and probably a dozen less than Hailey preferred.

"Fine. The two of you hammer out the details and email

me by the end of the day. I'll green-light it then get hold of Cherry and see you in a week."

With that, a clap of his hands and a nod goodbye, Rudy rose and strode from the room.

Gage waited for the man's size sevens to cross the threshold before turning to offer Hailey a smile.

But purse in hand and black wool coat buttoned, she was already halfway to the door herself.

What the hell?

Wasn't she going to thank him? He'd just given her another chance. Hell, he'd even gift wrapped it.

"Hailey?"

She didn't slow down.

She didn't look back.

And she definitely didn't offer a thank-you.

Seriously?

"Hailey, wait." Gage had to run to catch up with her since she wasn't slowing one bit. How the hell did she move so fast in heels that high?

"Hold up," he said, catching her arm halfway down the hallway. "I thought we'd go out, get something to eat. You know, nail down those details Rudy wants by the end of business."

His charming smile and teasing tone earned him a chilly stare. Damn. He'd known she was one of those women who needed hand holding on the pillow the next morning.

"I've plans for the rest of the afternoon," she said, pulling her arm out of his grasp. "We'll have to settle the details separately."

Awww, she was so cute.

"C'mon," he said, leaning close with his most persuasive smile. "You're just upset that I left when it was three to one in the taking-advantage department and you wanted another shot at me to even it out."

Her eyes went wide, then narrowed in glass-green slivers of fury. Then, in a sweep of those lush lashes, her expression cleared to frosty disinterest.

"You think you were that good?" she asked, giving him an up-and-down look that indicated she was trying to see what he was so proud of.

Burying his irritation, telling himself she deserved to get in a couple of digs since she was hurt, he plastered on his most charming smile.

"Baby, I think *we* were that good."

Her laugh put his charm in the fail column.

"Actually, it has nothing to do with missing out on the various delights you seem to think you are so good at," she said. Her arch look was like a rock, pounding that dagger into his ego just a little deeper. "It has to do with basic manners. If you're a guest at a party, do you walk out or do you take the time to find your host and say thank you for the good time?"

Gage tried to keep his expression smooth, but didn't have much luck holding back the scowl. Was that all she saw it as? A good time? What the hell?

First off, it'd been great. Not good.

And second, she was pissed because he hadn't minded his manners? He wanted to call bullshit on that, figuring it as a face-saving excuse.

But the chilly disdain in her eyes didn't give way to any hint of hurt, no petulant rejection. Nope, just irritated dismissal.

He didn't know how to deal with that.

"I didn't want to wake you. If I did, I wouldn't have been able to resist more." He kept his voice low, but let all the heat he felt ring out, so his words were a little husky. Unable to resist, he risked losing a limb and reached out to trace one finger along the delicate curve of her cheek.

"I knew we'd see each other today at the meeting and figured you'd appreciate some sleep."

Lame. As soon as the words were out he wanted to snatch them back. He didn't need to see her roll her eyes to know that was a suck-ass excuse.

What was it about Hailey that had him so off center? He'd never been this bad at talking to women, had never had any issue charming his way into or out of any situation that involved a female. Then again, he'd never encountered a business deal as weird and difficult to navigate as this one, either.

As the pretty little blonde glaring up at him was the common denominator, he had to figure it was her. Not him.

"Well, thank you so much for considering my needs. And now—" she shifted her arm out of his hold "—I've got an event to prepare for. I'll pull together my notes and email them to you. You can add or adjust as you see fit, then we can send them to Rudy."

In other words, she didn't want anything to do with him.

Pretty freaking insulting, considering she'd jumped his body and sexed him into an orgasmic puddle against her wall.

But if that was the way she wanted to play it?

Fine.

Without another word, not bothering to attempt an argument or another lame excuse, Gage stepped back and let her go.

Just as well. They were business rivals. One way or another, one of them—her, specifically—was going to lose. Better to let it go now, chalk it up to lust and some sexy lingerie and get his life back on track.

Still, Gage had to wonder how many times he was going to watch the sweet sway of her ass as she stormed away from him. And ponder why he liked the idea of seeing it a few hundred more times.

"HAILEY, HOW'D THE meetings go?"

"Did you wow Rudolph with your vision of romance?"

"Of course she did. Merry Widow designs sell themselves. All our Hailey had to do was show the guy the lineup, sweet-talk a little and bat those eyelashes, and boom. We're in for a Christmas treat." To emphasize that, Jackie did a little happy dance through the warehouse that sent the jingle bells on her hat, shoes and necklace a dingling.

Hailey forced a big smile on her face, sidestepped the questions and tried to make it to her office. She was waylaid again to approve a new design change, then a third time to admire the Christmas tree made of coat hangers and decorated with bras one of the team had set up in the corner.

They were all so excited.

Every face in the warehouse glowed, not unheard of on a Friday afternoon. Or with excitement over the anticipated Rudolph deal.

She'd trained them well.

Shoot for the stars, and never doubt you'll have a happy landing.

What a bunch of crap.

"I've got some samples together for the spring-line photo shoot on Wednesday," Jackie said, finally through with her dance. "I know you want to hold off to decide which pieces we're offering until you know which ones Rudolph will make exclusive. But I figured it couldn't hurt to be prepared. I've been shopping for accessories and props to go with it all."

Jackie gestured to the variety of lingerie, jewelry, shoes and pretty accoutrements spread across a long, fabric-covered worktable. "I even picked up some little goodies that I thought would go well with our Christmas pieces, figuring maybe you might want to give Cherry a little gift for the holiday."

Hailey had to blink fast to keep from bursting into tears.

Everyone was so excited. So sure they'd get this account.

Just like she'd been.

Swallowing hard to clear her throat, Hailey tried to figure out when she'd lost her hope.

"That's a great idea," she managed to say, offering a shaky smile. "Thanks for putting in the extra time."

"Oh, believe me, it was my pleasure. This is going to be the best Christmas ever," the younger woman said, all but clapping her hands together. "Don't forget, you have to do the Secret Santa drawing today, too."

"Right." More Christmas cheer. Hailey kept her grin in place as the other woman danced away.

Ho, ho, freaking ho.

As soon as she hit the stairs leading to her office, Hailey let her cheery smile drop, along with her shoulders and her hopes.

"You're late." At the top of the stairs was a loft that spanned the length of the warehouse. Between the top step and Hailey's office was what she often referred to as the dragon-guarded moat. In other words, Doris's desk. Manned, as usual, by the beehive-haired dragon. "You were due here an hour ago."

"You knew I had a meeting," Hailey reminded her in a weary tone.

"You knew it was Friday. I work half days every Friday in December."

Seriously? Knots ripped through her shoulders. On top of everything else, she needed this crap from a woman whose paycheck she signed?

"So leave," Hailey snapped, waving her hand toward the steps and stomping past the huge desk to her own office.

She didn't get any farther than tossing her bag on the chair and her coat on the floor before the dragon stormed in after her.

"You're sure in a grump of a mood. I told you going to all that trouble to try and impress Rudolph was a stupid idea."

Hailey's glower covered Doris, the woman's dour words and the entire day in general.

"I thought you were leaving. Half-day December, remember?"

"I came in to give you your messages," the older woman said with a sniff, her sky-blue-tinted eyelids lowered in a sad puppy-dog look. "Thought they might be important. One from your date last night."

Her heart tumbled, then bounced around her chest in excitement.

"Gage?"

Had he left it before or after the meeting?

Was it an apology for leaving her, naked and wanting, in her own bed?

Or another nagging reminder that they had to figure out their final pitch?

And why did she care so much?

Sure, he'd acted as if he was trying to make nice after his toss-under-the-bus attempt in today's meeting. But she'd trusted him once. She'd got naked with him. And he'd left her.

"I don't want to talk to him," she announced. "If he calls back, tell him we'll handle it by email."

Doris's pout disappeared into a look of speculation. "No. Mr. Rudolph. Isn't that who you were out with? Him and the singer lady?"

Hardly.

But Hailey just shrugged and held out her hand for the messages.

Doris, of course, didn't hand them over. Instead, she kept right on looking as though she was trying to figure out all of Hailey's secrets.

What the hell was it with people inspecting her like this? Her face, her soul, her secrets, they were her business, dammit.

"Another call, too. This one from your mom."

Like a cement block, Hailey's hand dropped to her side. Disappointment settled deep and aching in her belly. She didn't need to hear the message to know what was coming. The same thing as always.

"She said she's sorry. She's not gonna be able to do Christmas with you, after all. Turns out she got a part in a traveling theater troupe and needs to be ready to hit the road on January one."

To her credit, Doris shared the news with a heavy dose of sympathy. Even her wrinkles seemed to empathize, all curving downward with her frown.

"Anything else?" Hailey asked, trying not to feel defeated by a morning determined to kick her ass.

Doris hesitated, then curled the messages into her fist and shook her head.

"Nope. That's it."

How was that for pathetic? The woman who regularly scorned Hailey's rose-colored-glasses-wearing optimism was hiding bad news from her.

"Doris?"

The older woman's sigh whooshed through the room and she gave a jerky shrug.

"Just those Phillips brats, checking to see if you've made arrangements to pay off the business."

Hailey pushed her hand through her hair, wishing she could as easily shove away all the stress tying knots in her scalp. She wasn't ready to throw in the towel, dammit. But, inch by inch, the towel was slipping out of her grasp.

"Maybe it's time to call a meeting," Doris murmured.

Clenching her jaw, Hailey stared at the workroom floor beneath her, clear through the plate-glass window that separated the loft-style office from the rest of the small warehouse.

Below, two desks were manned by her sales team, while her marketing guru was curled up in a beanbag in the corner, laptop in hand. She could see production just beyond the curtains, packaging up the smaller orders that were going out for the holidays.

Her tiny empire, a dozen people total including her and Doris. Wouldn't calling them together for a "we've failed" meeting be tantamount to giving up? Didn't she owe it to them, to herself, to see this through?

"Next week," she said quietly, turning away to meet Doris's oddly patient gaze. "Friday at our monthly meeting. I'll either give them their holiday bonuses or give them as much severance pay as I can pull together."

A week and a half to save her business. Hailey was damned if she'd give up before she had to. Chin high, she held the other woman's gaze, waiting for the slap down.

Instead, after a few long seconds, Doris gave a jerky nod.

"I'll take a look at the books, see what's what. For the bonuses. Or just in case."

Without another word, and with those vile messages still clutched in her talons, Doris clomped out of the room.

Just in case.

Hailey sighed, sinking into her chair and dropping her face to her desk.

Maybe everyone was right.

Maybe it was time she quit believing everything in life would work out if she just held on and had faith.

After all, what'd actually turned out that way for her?

Her father still didn't consider her a part of his *real* family. Her mother blew her off with more ease than a five-year-old making a wish on a dandelion. And now her business, the one thing she'd figured she could count on because she'd built it herself, was imploding.

Tears slid, silent and painful over her cheeks.

And she couldn't do a damned thing about any of it.

11

HER PALM DAMP, Hailey curled her fingers tight. Then with a grimace she shook her hands to air-dry them, curled one again and used it to knock at the heavy oak door.

Okay, maybe *knock* was an exaggeration.

Tap. Lightly.

Still, it counted.

She had to do this. Had to give it one last shot.

She'd wallowed in misery for an entire hour. She'd eaten Doris's entire stash of cookies. And she'd watched her employees, all buoyed up with holiday cheer.

As she'd realized that whether it made her a sucker or not, she had to keep trying. Giving up, it just wasn't her.

Of course, neither were uncomfortable confrontations.

So after another five seconds of silence, she figured she'd given it her best shot and, with a relieved sigh, turned to leave.

"Hailey?"

Crap.

Forcing herself to shift her grimace into a smile—of sorts—she sighed, then turned back around.

"Hi, Gage," she said in that fake, perky-door-to-door-saleswoman tone.

He looked gorgeous. More casually dressed than she'd ever seen him, he wore a plain black T-shirt and jeans with socks. She shifted from foot to foot in her Frye boots, rubbing her gloved finger over the smooth texture of her tights below her black wool miniskirt. Clearly she was overdressed.

As usual, whenever she was around Gage, Hailey had the urge to strip off a few layers of clothes and see what they could do together, naked.

Grateful for the cold night air against her suddenly hot cheeks, Hailey puffed out a breath.

Why was she here again?

Not for that, she reminded herself.

"I was hoping we could talk. Nail down those specifics Rudy wants."

"He wanted them by five." Gage made a show of checking his watch, then gave her an arch look. "That was an hour ago."

"I spoke with him. He's fine with having the information in the morning."

"Ahh, so that's why you've been ignoring my calls and emails." He paused, probably waiting for her to look ashamed. Hailey made sure to keep her smile in place, though. She was tired of other people calling the shots, dammit.

After a second, he shrugged and asked, "Did you send a hooker to his office to persuade him?"

Hailey's lips twitched. Too bad she hadn't thought of that herself. It'd probably have taken less time.

"No. But I did promise that I'd handle everything, including getting Cherry to show up."

"Good luck with that," Gage muttered, stepping away from the doorway to gesture her inside. "Come on in. I'll make coffee."

Hailey hesitated. This was what she'd come for, to talk to him on a casual—hopefully friendly—basis. Which meant going inside.

Still, her stomach did some tumbles as she did.

"Nervous?" he teased, his eyes intent on her face.

"Of what?"

"Good question."

Hailey lifted her chin and gave him a hard look. One she hoped made it clear that she was here for business. Not to see if the sex against his walls was as good as the sex against her walls had been.

Nope. That idea hadn't once entered her head.

Not once.

Because, she assured herself, a few dozen times didn't count as once.

Still, he didn't need to know that. A man who left the morning after without a word didn't deserve any ego strokes. Or to revisit the delights they'd shared.

Dammit.

"Let me take that," he said, gesturing to her purse. She handed it to him, then slipped off her leather gloves to give him those, too.

And, try as she might, she couldn't hide her little shiver as his fingers skimmed her shoulders when he helped her out of her coat.

"C'mon in," he said.

She met his grin with a glower. Yeah. He knew what that shiver had meant.

But once she moved out of the entry and into the living area, desire took a backseat to curiosity.

Wow.

She tried not to gawk.

She hadn't been raised poor by any means.

But Gage?

Clearly he'd been raised rich.

Art, not knickknacks or decorations, but signed-by-famous-people art hung on the walls, was tucked into cubbies, hung from a corner. The furnishings were simple, leather, sleek. But it wasn't cold or, well, fancy.

She noted the pair of tennis shoes kicked off by the couch, the newspaper tossed on the chair.

It was a home.

That shouldn't appeal to her so much.

But it did.

"Is coffee okay? Or would you prefer hot chocolate? Wine? Water?" he offered, playing happy host as he moved through an arched doorway to what, if the hints of stainless she could see were any indication, was surely the kitchen.

She followed, this time not able to hide her appreciative sigh.

"Wow," she murmured. Double oven, a stove and grill, hickory cabinets and granite countertops all screamed kitchen fabulousness.

"Yeah?" He followed her gaze, then shrugged. "I guess. But I mostly order out. Coffee and scrambled eggs are about the extent of my cooking expertise."

"But you offered me hot chocolate." Something she was suddenly craving like crazy, especially if it came with whipped cream.

He lifted a brown-and-white metal tin with a familiar logo. "Heat milk, stir in chocolate."

"No whipped cream?"

His gaze heated, then did a quick skim down her body, as if debating where in particular he'd like to dollop that cream before licking it up.

Hailey's nipples tightened in a silent scream of *here, put it here.*

Focus, she warned herself.

"I wanted to get this entire matter settled, and figured it'd be easier to discuss between just the two of us." She waved her hand between them. "No Rudy, no marketing gimmicks."

No sex.

She managed to keep that last part to herself. Not so much out of concern for saying it aloud. But because she still wasn't completely sure she could—or wanted to—follow that particular mandate.

After a long look, Gage nodded. He moved around the kitchen with ease, gathering a pot, milk, grinding coffee.

Happy to leave the discussion for a bit and just watch him, Hailey settled onto an oak stool cozied up to the work counter. He moved with an economic grace, totally comfortable in the kitchen and with himself.

When he added an extra scoop of chocolate shavings to her hot milk, she tried not to drool. Especially since her mouth wasn't watering over the drink, but the man stirring the spoon.

Maybe this was a stupid idea.

Maybe she should have called instead of seeing him face-to-face. It was much easier to control her urge to lick him over the phone than it was when he was within touching distance.

"So," he asked once they were both settled into the welcoming cushions, their mugs in hand and the fireplace crackling warmly behind them, "are you going to make me an offer I can't refuse?"

"I beg your pardon?" She glanced around the room, an ode to comfortable wealth, then shrugged. What could she offer that he couldn't walk away from?

He leaned closer, the rich scent of roasted coffee and his own cologne wrapping around her like a gentle net, pulling her tight. Making her want to close her eyes and simply breathe him in.

But she couldn't close her eyes, because his were holding her captive. The dark depths promised sensual delights. A promise, she knew from experience, he could meet.

Quite nicely, too.

Hailey's pulse sped up. Her body turned liquid.

Her brain filled with visions of the two of them, their naked bodies sliding together on this couch. On that wall. On any variety of whatever flat surfaces he had in the house.

Would she do him again?

Even though her ego screamed no, for crying out loud the guy didn't even say goodbye in the morning, her body was doing the *yes, please* happy dance.

Her body was much louder, and more enthusiastic than her ego. Her body wanted to touch the hard planes of his chest again. To feel him moving inside her, pounding, throbbing. Sending her spiraling higher and higher.

A little short of breath, Hailey had to pull her gaze away from the hypnotic depths of his.

As soon as she did, logic shouldered its way in, breaking up the fight between ego and desire.

"I don't think I have anything to offer that you'd find irresistible," she stated.

"Wanna bet?" he countered, reaching out to trace his fingers along the curve of her jaw, then down the long line of her throat. The move, so soft and gentle, made her shiver.

He wouldn't be able to refuse sex, between the two of them, in exchange for stepping off the Rudolph account?

"Yeah. Right." She laughed so hard she had to set the mug down for fear of spilling her chocolate. "You'd give up a seven-figure contract for a weekend with my body?"

His eyes were hot on said body, making it difficult for her not to wiggle in place to try to relieve some of the building heat.

"I asked if that's what you were offering."

Nice double speak. For a second, just one, she wanted to say sure. To stand up, strip naked and gesture that he come and get it.

But ego, the part that was afraid he'd laugh if she did, won out. So instead, pretending she wasn't hurt by that image—or by his leaving her—Hailey gave him a sardonic look, then made a show of tapping her fingernail against her lower lip.

"Let's see. Was it only last night that you had full access to my body? Yes, yes, I think it was. And you quite comfortably walked away from it this morning, without so much as a 'see ya, babe.'" She looked him up and down then met his eyes again and arched her brow. "Did something change between now and then?"

Gage set his coffee next to her chocolate before sliding a little closer, so his hard, warm thigh pressed against hers. He ranged his arm along the back of the couch, so close she could almost feel his pulse, but not quite touching her. As if he was crowding all around her, making sure she was very, very aware of his body. But not doing anything about that awareness.

Figured.

Hailey was so sick and tired of people making promises, getting her hooked and emotionally invested, then running out on her. Was there a flashing neon sign over her head, proclaiming her a disappointment junkie?

So instead of giving in to the desire, and the heat Gage was trying to tease her with, she leaned in closer herself.

His eyes flickered, desire flaring before he banked it.

She watched his pulse jump and smiled.

Then, for good measure, she shifted again so her breath wafted over his skin, close enough to leave a haze of chocolate.

"You want to make me an offer, Gage, you go right ahead. But make sure it's one you can keep. I'm tired of being teased."

IT WAS ON the tip of his tongue to offer her anything.

Everything.

In exchange for just one more taste. One more touch. One more wild ride between her thighs.

As if magnetically pulled forward, Gage found himself bending down, his mouth ready to take hers.

And to accept any deal she wanted.

A quick flash of triumph in those green eyes served as a kick-in-the-ass wake-up.

He froze.

What the hell was he doing?

Would he give up his bid for the contract for a weekend with her body?

If the stakes had been only the contract, the answer wouldn't just be yes, it'd be *hell, yes*.

But this was his freedom, a shot at breaking away from Milano, and doing so in a way that didn't destroy his questionable family relationships.

Maybe the better question was, would she give it up for his?

"Why is this so important to you? It's just an account. Albeit a fat one, but it's not like you can't scoop up another dozen fat accounts. You've got a stellar product, a smart sales pitch, and the kudos from being considered for this are enough to parlay into a dozen open doors." Yes, he'd tried this argument once before. But he wanted an answer this time. He'd gone up against some fierce competition in the past, but never one with so much heart, so much determination to win.

Hailey's gaze held his, her eyes more serious than he'd ever seen them. It was as though someone had squeezed all of the bubble out of her personality, leaving her flat. Still sweet, still beautiful, but without the effervescence that was so natural to her.

"I need this contract," she said with a quiet shrug. The kind that said *let it go, just move on*.

But Gage didn't want to.

He wanted to know her. To know what was pushing her so hard. He wanted to know what she had to lose when he won.

"So do I," he countered. Giving in to temptation, he brushed his fingers over the tips of her hair, watching the pale blond strands slide like a silken waterfall back to her shoulder. "What else ya got?"

Her lips twitched, and after a long, considering look, she pulled away and leaned over to get her mug of chocolate again. She didn't sip, just stared into it as if searching for the right words.

"If I don't get this, I'll lose my business."

"How?" Gage frowned. "I did a check on you when I heard we were competitors. You're solid."

"On paper, with the bank, sure." Her shrug was jerkier this time, irritated. "I bought Merry Widow from my mentor three years ago. We had what you'd call a friendly agreement. We both knew the business was worth a lot more if I built it up, kept it going. So we agreed that I'd pay him a set amount each year, and at the end of five years, if I'd doubled the net worth, my debt was paid. Otherwise we'd negotiate fair-market value."

Gage's frown didn't ease, even as he shook his head.

"I don't get it. I mean, it's a crazy agreement, definitely not like anything I've ever heard before. But it hasn't been five years. You're close to doubling your net worth from four years ago so you should be fine." He ignored her look of surprised irritation that he knew so much about her. "So what's the problem?"

"I know it's unorthodox, but it was Eric's way of pushing me. Of motivating me to do my best." She smiled, as if just that memory gave her joy. Then her lips drooped. "Then he died early this fall."

"I'm sorry," Gage murmured.

She nodded, taking a sip of her chocolate. More as a

way to get hold of herself, he figured, than any desire for cooling milk laced with cocoa.

"His kids are calling the loan. Full market value, without credit for previous payments."

"They can't do that."

"Sure they can. Eric and I didn't have a contract. We had a verbal agreement because he didn't want to deal with the drama his kids would put up if they found out what a deal he was offering me."

Pissed now, Gage shook his head. She had to have a good lawyer. Someone who could put an end to the bullshit claim.

"That's crap. I'll get my attorney to look into it," he offered.

For the first time since he'd pushed her on the topic, Hailey's lips curved into a real smile and her eyes danced.

"You are so sweet. But no, it's been looked at. They're within their rights."

"That's crap," he repeated.

"Sure it is. But if I get the Rudolph contract, it'll show a solid enough income that the bank will loan me what I need to pay off the Phillips kids." She sipped the chocolate again, wrinkled her nose and returned the mug to the table. "So there you go. My reason for needing the contract."

It was pure crap. Gage didn't bother to say it a third time, though. Instead, he silently fumed. Not because her needs put him in a difficult position, although they did.

But because she'd been screwed over, royally. Because some lame ass was too worried about upsetting his kids, Hailey was in danger of either losing her business or going deep into debt. A debt that, if he'd written up the agreement as promised, she'd never have had to take on.

Damn.

Suddenly, all he wanted was to make her smile. To show her how important, how special, she was.

He didn't have words, though. And even if he did, he'd feel like a complete idiot spouting off that kind of thing.

So he offered what he had.

A soft, sweet kiss.

A promise.

To worship her.

To take care of her.

To make sure her needs, her satisfaction, were primary.

Hailey's eyes were huge as bright green saucers as she pulled her mouth away from his.

"What's that for?"

"Because you deserve to feel good about yourself."

She gave a little laugh, as though she thought he was kidding.

Then, seeing that he was 100 percent serious, her smile faded. Desire, hope and something deeper washed over her face.

"You think so?" she asked, hesitating before running her fingers, just the tips of them, along his jaw.

Gage leaned into her hand, loving the feel of her.

"Spend the weekend with me."

Her gasp was sharp. Her pulse jumped in her throat. And those glorious eyes of hers filled with questions. He didn't know the answer to most of them, though. So he lifted her hand in his and brushed a kiss along her knuckles.

"Spend the weekend with me. Let me show you how special I think you are."

She pressed her lips together, then sighed and gave him a tentative smile.

"And how were you planning to do that?"

"Like this," he promised, grabbing the invitation and opportunity fast, before she changed her mind.

Just like he took her mouth.

Fast.

Hard.

Intense.

With every bit of passion and need and desire he had for her.

Her body melted into his as he pulled her onto his lap. Her lips gave way to his tongue, welcoming him into her warmth.

And suddenly, the only thing Gage wasn't sure of was if a weekend was enough time to show her how amazing she was.

12

"THIS IS RIDICULOUS. I can't believe I let you talk me into it."
Gage huffed, giving the woman responsible a hard look.
Difficult, since she was so adorable wrapped only in one
of his dress shirts and a layer of body lotion.

Lotion he'd slicked on himself after their shower that
morning.

The memory of that soft, smooth skin under his hands,
of the slide of the thick lubricant beneath his fingers,
stirred an interest in Gage's body. One that had nothing
to do with the crazy ideas Hailey was trying to get him
hooked into.

"C'mon. It'll be fun. I can't believe you've never done
this before."

"It's not like we're talking exotic sexual positions or
kinky toys, Hailey." He hunched his shoulders, really wishing they were. In those, he had experience in spades.

"No. As fun, exciting and important as those all are—"
she paused to give him an eye roll and a teasing smile
"—this is all of that, too."

Gage sighed.

Then, showing every bit of the reluctance he felt, he
approached the corner of the room with trepidation and,
giving her a grumpy look, took the thread she'd filled with
popcorn and tried to figure out what to do with it.

"I'm supposed to, what? Throw this over the branches?"

Hailey gave him a look that said she couldn't quite believe his professed cluelessness.

"Here, do it like this," she said, showing him how to drape the popcorn-covered string.

He really should be worried, because he was starting to think she could talk him into anything.

He'd figured the fact that he had no tree was a good enough excuse when she'd asked why he hadn't decorated. But no. She'd hauled on a pair of his sweatpants, pulled on her boots and swaddled herself in one of his sweaters before hauling him down to the corner lot to choose a tree.

He'd been so entertained by the seriousness with which she studied each specimen, rounding every tree and staring at it as if coded somewhere inside was the key to Santa's nice list. Finally, when he'd tried to grope her behind the wreath display, she'd settled on a tall, skinny one, claiming it'd be easiest for them to carry back.

Carry. He'd trotted down the San Francisco streets with a woman wearing his sweats and five-hundred-dollar boots, carting a pine tree.

What else could he do once they got it inside but strip her naked and make love to her?

Now, three hours and a handful of orgasms later, she was standing there, arms akimbo, giving him the hurry-up look.

"Isn't it enough to have the tree? Why does it need crap hung from it?"

"Because it's Christmas. Hanging crap from a tree is part of the holiday fun." She finished wrapping the string of lights they'd bought along with the tree, then bent low to plug it in.

Gage tilted his head sideways, grinning. He had to admit, the decorating view was definitely fun.

"Haven't you ever had a tree before? Ever?" she asked, pausing from her study of the perfect placement of lights

to give him a puzzled look. "Does your family not celebrate Christmas?"

"Sure, we celebrate. But the tree always just sort of
showed up in the lounge—lights, balls and presents."

Depending on which stepmother was ruling the roost at
the time, it might be glinting with crystals or wrapped in
yarn. One year, it'd had tiny porcelain dolls hanging from
the boughs. That'd seriously freaked him out.

"I guess that's part of your fancy upbringing, huh?"
she teased.

"I never thought it was fancy," he said honestly, trying to hang the popcorn strands the way she had, so they
draped instead of tangled to look like something a bird
puked up. "I mean, the house was huge and there might be
a lot of social stuff going on, depending on the stepmom
du jour. My brother and I were in boarding school most
of the year, so when we'd come home for winter break,
the tree was there. Done. If we ever decorated when I was
little, I don't remember it."

Hailey paused in her adjusting and tweaking of the
lights to glance at him, those big eyes of hers filled with
tears.

"You were sent away."

"More like allowed to run away," he said with a laugh.
"Don't feel sorry for me. I loved boarding school. Anything was better than the revolving circus that was that
house's inhabitants."

She straightened, moving closer and giving him a look
so deep with compassion that Gage actually felt his heart
melt a little.

"Were you hurt there?"

His freak-out over the deep emotions she was inspir-
ing gave way to shock. "What? Hurt? Nah. It was just
crazy. My old man was a womanizer. Think Rudy, with
less money and more to prove. We used to joke that he

should lease wives instead of marrying them, since he traded them in as often as his cars."

"And that didn't bother you?"

"Why? None of them stuck around long enough to matter, so it wasn't like I missed them when they were gone."

It was only after a few seconds of silence, and his irritation with the strings of popcorn tangling together, that Gage glanced over.

Mouth open, eyes wide with sympathy, Hailey was staring at him as though she wanted to wrap him in her arms, pull his head to her shoulder and hug away all his hurts.

He figured he didn't have any, but he'd be willing to let her try, anyway.

"Don't make it into a big deal. It really isn't," he said honestly.

"What about your mom? Were you really young when she left?"

"Four and a half," he said with a shrug. "She came around a few times, I think, before she was killed in a car accident. But it's not like I grew up thinking there was a big hole in my life. It's just what it was, you know? One way or another, it was my dad, my brother and me. And a predecorated Christmas tree."

She didn't laugh.

"I'm done with the threaded popcorn," he said, tossing on the last bit in hopes of changing the subject. "Are we done or do you want more crap on the tree?"

"More crap," she said absently, handing him a stack of intricate snowflake shapes—cut from paper stolen from his office—that she'd cut out and hung on the same string she'd used for the popcorn.

"You must be really close to your brother, then."

So much for a subject change.

"At the moment, I'm almost tied. But by next year, I'll be ahead," he murmured absently.

Damned right he would. Devon had used his two-year advantage most of their life to stay in the lead, but a year off with no Milano emergency demands, and Gage was sure he was gonna sprint into first place.

"What?" Hailey shook her head. "What do you mean? Ahead?"

"You know, ahead. As in, which one of us is winning. Devon and I compete. Best grades, higher SATs, board support, bigger piece of the wishbone." He grinned, remembering. "That Grinch costume? I lost the wishbone bet at Thanksgiving and that's the price I paid. That's the kind of thing we do."

She squinted, as if trying to see through his words to the truth beneath. Why? He didn't understand her confusion.

"You're trying to tell me that the entire basis for your relationship with your brother is competition?"

Gage frowned. She made it sound so unhealthy.

"Sure."

"C'mon. No fraternal bond? No shared interests? Not even sibling rivalry?" She shook her head as if that were impossible to believe.

"Isn't sibling rivalry basically the same thing as competition?" After she gave a slow, considering nod, he shrugged and said, "Sure, we've got that. And we've got plenty of mutual interests. I check out his investments, advise him on marketing. He checks out mine, advises me on expansion options."

"That's it?" she asked.

He didn't know why she looked so horrified. Since it made him feel a little defensive, he racked his brain trying to find other examples for her.

"We aren't friends, like the kind who hang out together, but we respect each other. Family loyalty goes a long way, too. Shared life experiences, heritage, that kind of thing. But the bottom line is, we both want success. We both want to be a part of the family business, but we want it on our own, too. We both want to win."

He could see she wasn't buying his assurance that he wasn't emotionally scarred or harboring some hidden resentment of family-centered holidays. Rather than trying to convince her that, yes, he really was that shallow, he turned the tables.

"What about you? Now, granted, I was mostly focused on other things at your apartment the other night. Like your naked body and how incredible you felt under my fingers." He waited, then gave a satisfied smile when she blushed. "But I didn't see that you had a tree up."

Her expression changed, the frown seeming to turn inward before she slipped on a smile.

"I was waiting for my mom. It used to be our special tradition, and since she was visiting this holiday, I wanted to do it together. When I was little, we always decorated together as a family the weekend after Thanksgiving. After my parents divorced, I spent Thanksgiving with my father, so my mom waited until I was home and we did the tree together."

He tried to imagine her as a little girl, those flaxen curls in pigtails and some cute footsie pajamas on while she hung candy canes from the low-hanging boughs. He'd bet she'd been adorable.

"So you got to do two trees? No wonder you love this kind of thing."

"No. Just the one tree. My dad married the same year as the divorce, and Gina, my stepmom, liked to wait until closer to the holiday."

Leave it to the stepmom to shove the kid out. Gage had seen enough of it growing up to recognize the signs. He didn't even need Hailey's stiff upper lip, lifted chin or downcast eyes. And while he'd learned by seven to shrug it off, she was still carrying it around.

Time to quit bitching about the decorations, he decided. If a tree made her happy, they'd decorate. Hell, he'd take her to his father's place and she could decorate there, too.

"When's your mom arriving so you can do your tree?" I.e., how long was she available for freewheeling, wild and constant sex before family nabbed a portion of her attention?

On tiptoes, trying to wrap a thread around a high branch, Hailey went board stiff, dropping back to the flats of her feet. The snowflake was still in her hand, though. Its ripping sound was like fingernails on a chalkboard. Loud, invasive and painful. She grimaced, then crumpled the ruined decoration in her fist before shrugging.

"No mom this year. She called Friday and left a message. Something came up and she can't make it."

Did everyone let her down?

Underneath the hurt in her eyes, Gage could see acceptance. As though this kind of thing happened all the time.

"Well, hey, we'll go decorate your tree after this, okay? Just you and me. I'll bet you have actual decorations and stuff, right? So we can eat the popcorn instead of tossing it on the branches?"

As soon as the words were out, he realized he'd just volunteered to step in and play family. That was a serious thing. A way past *let's get naked and slide all over each other* thing. For a second, he wanted to grab the words back. Or change the subject. Then, as he watched her face melt into a beautiful smile, he realized he kinda liked it. Liked her trusting him. Believing in him.

"So what do you think?" he asked, gesturing to the tree. "Am I assistant material?"

"You're a great assistant." Her words were a little husky and her smile a little shaky, but—thank God—she didn't do anything crazy, like cry.

Whether because she wasn't a teary kind of gal, or because she could see how uncomfortable he was, she put on a bright face instead and looked at the tree.

"It still needs something," she decided, tilting her head to the side, as if she were critiquing an outfit about to hit the runway. Gage figured it must be a girl thing, since the tree looked fine to him. "Do you have anything shiny? Old jewelry, CDs, anything foil?"

Seriously?

He gave her a look, then glanced at the tree, then back at her. She had that stubborn tilt to her chin again, and her eyes were all soft and sweet.

Dammit.

"Let me see what I can find."

THAT WAS ABOUT the weirdest tree she'd ever seen. And given that there was one in her warehouse right now made of coat hangers and bras, that was saying something.

Gage's arms loose around her waist, Hailey leaned back against his chest and sighed.

"It's perfect," she decided.

"Okay."

"It is." Laughing, she turned in his arms, cupping her hands behind his neck and giving him a quick, smacking kiss. "You done good."

He cast a doubtful eye over her shoulder, clearly seeing the actual tree and not the sentiment hanging from its boughs.

"Okay," he said again.

Then, as if there was nothing else to say about a tree covered in foil condom wrappers, popcorn and paper snowflakes, he laughed, shook his head, then took her mouth.

Hailey let the power of his kiss take her over, pull her down, permeate her being.

Being with Gage was like being wrapped in warmth.

Not just the fiery heat of passion, although that was a constant and definitely keeping her excited.

But the laughter. The kisses. The gentle teasing and constant interest in her.

Her views. Her ideas. Her past and her present. What she wanted in the future, even. She'd never had anyone so focused on her. Just...her.

As though he really cared about her.

Breathing in deep, she pushed away the sudden tears that thought brought and focused on the kiss.

Her lips danced over his, her hands sliding gently, oh so gently, over his naked skin. Satin over steel.

They fell into the lovemaking with a gentle sigh.

Every move was a whisper. A breath of skin against skin. A tease of a kiss, a wash of warm air, wrapping them together in a sweet, dreamy sort of passion.

As Gage's body ranged over hers, Hailey stared up into the endless depths of his eyes and opened herself, welcoming him in.

As he moved, slowly sliding in and out, she held his gaze. She let everything she felt shine in her own.

The delight.

The desire.

The deep, intense emotions that she couldn't even put a name to herself.

He never looked away.

Even as she tightened, as passion caught her in its needy web, her body demanding total focus, complete attention, he still watched.

And when she went over, the desire pounding and swirling through her in deliciously hypnotic waves, he smiled.

A slow, satisfied smile.

And then with a low moan, he joined her.

Two hours later, wrapped together in front of the fire,

Hailey was still trying to come to grips with the power of their lovemaking.

Her eyes fixed on the flickering flames, the lights of the Christmas tree a soft glow against the wall, she tried to identify the feelings inside her.

Peace. Joy. Love.

Scary.

"Look," Gage finally said, shifting onto his elbow. "Next year, I'll have a lot going on. I'm going to be really pushing to get my own business solid fast. It's going to take focus and time."

Hailey froze, body and heart.

Well, at least he was being honest, she told herself, wrapping the sheet closer, trying to stave off the shivers. Still, she'd never been blown off while naked before.

"I'm going to take care of this whole thing with Rudolph, with saving your company. I don't want you to worry about it anymore," he said, his words quiet, measured. Her heart thumped a few extra beats before Hailey could catch her breath and turn in Gage's arms to face him. "I'll fix everything, okay?"

For a brief second, Hailey wanted to protest. She didn't need favors. She could win the contract on her own, without him stepping aside for her. But Rudy had already made it clear that if it were only up to him, he'd go with Milano. And she couldn't afford to put all her faith in Cherry, or to let pride stand in the way of saving her business.

"Are you sure?"

"Yeah. Totally sure."

"And the presentation on Tuesday? Should we cancel?"

His frown flashed for a second. "Nah, it's more professional to keep it. I'm sure I'll have everything taken care of, but it's a good fallback just in case, too."

Just in case.

Her heart melted, the entire world taking on a rosy glow.

He really was taking care of her.

"And us?" she asked, feeling as if it were Christmas morning and Santa had not only brought her entire list, but had doubled up on the things she hadn't even thought to ask for.

"After this deal with Rudolph is done, I want to make us a priority," he said, brushing the hair off her cheek and giving her a tender look. "It's going to be hard, but I want to make sure we get time together. It might take some juggling, maybe a few cancellations or rescheduled dates here and there. Are you okay with that?"

Hailey blinked.

"What?"

"I want us to be together. I want to build on this, to see where we go," he said, gesturing between their bodies before sliding his hand into her hair to caress the back of her head. "I want to give us a chance."

A chance.

He wanted her. Them.

Without any prodding or girlie manipulation, he'd straight-up claimed them a couple.

Hailey's smile started slow, tremulous, since she refused to cry. But then the giggles took over and she pressed her free hand to his cheek, pulling his face close for a kiss.

Then another.

And yet another, this one turning hot.

Sweet passion poured over them. She shifted, pressing his body down against the floor, the warmth of the fire flickering over their entwined forms.

Gentle kisses, soft caresses gave way to heat.

Grateful for his resourcefulness, she stretched over, tugging one of the glinting foil condom packages from the tree. She quickly sheathed him, then before he could do more than moan, she slid onto the hard length of his erection.

Together, with her taking the lead, they made slow,

sweet love again. This time, he came first. The feeling of him, throbbing and pulsing inside her, sent Hailey over, too. She collapsed, breathless, onto his chest and gave a purr of satisfaction.

"I take it that's a yes?" he murmured against her hair as they were shivering with orgasmic aftershocks.

He didn't elaborate. He didn't have to. She knew he was asking if she wanted to give them a chance.

Hailey's laugh was a whisper, nuzzled close against his throat.

"Yes. Definitely yes," she agreed.

With just the flickering warmth of the fire, and Gage's body, covering hers, Hailey drifted off to sleep. Her last thought before sliding under was to wonder if she should be happy that the contract was hers. Or terrified that she'd had to fall in love to get it.

HAILEY WAS ALMOST skipping as she made her way up the steps of the Rudolph building.

This was it. The last presentation.

She and Gage had told Rudy Friday night, before their delicious weekend together, that they'd meet on Tuesday for one final time.

Each would bring the designs they felt most represented the line, a marketing plan they planned to implement to support the Rudolph debut, and their final pitch. Even though it wasn't going to be necessary, since Gage was backing out of the contract, Hailey had still prepared as if this was the most important day of her life. And, she thought, bubbling over with optimism, it just might be.

As she exited the elevator and headed for the boardroom where they were to meet, Gage came hurrying toward her. She melted a little at the sight of him and that gorgeous smile.

"Hey, you," she said, brushing her fingers over his

cheek as if it'd been weeks since they'd been together instead of that morning. "I missed you."

"Ditto," he said with a grin. Then he tilted his head toward the double doors at the end of the hall. "I tried to reach you. Didn't you get my message?"

"No, what's up?"

"I came in early, met with Rudy." Tucking his hand under her elbow, Gage led her toward the boardroom doors as he spoke. "We're good to go. So I borrowed his boardroom to show you the setup."

Setup? He'd set things up for her?

Hailey all but clapped her hands together, she was so excited.

Together, they stepped into the boardroom. There, to one side by a set of open doors, were the samples she'd sent ahead for her presentation.

On the opposite end was a huge whiteboard. On it was a list of company names, some she recognized as huge. A marketing schematic covered one half of the board. She squinted. The schematic had her name at the top.

Trepidation started to overtake excitement in her stomach.

"What is this?"

"Rudy's going with Milano for the spring account, of course. He wanted to all along, but knew Cherry was leaning toward Merry Widow. But she's been so out of the loop, he's decided not to depend on her input any longer."

He said that as though he hadn't sold her out. As if just because Rudy would have chosen him in a head-on battle, that meant it was okay that he hadn't stepped down like he'd promised.

"You're kidding, right?"

"Nope. No joke. I got this all put together for you. You've got guaranteed orders, double the clientele as I'd suggested earlier and enough interest in your lingerie to translate into a fat load of new business." He pointed to the two-dozen names he'd listed on the board. Next to each was a dollar figure. Not shabby figures, either.

Hailey's head was buzzing.

"I put together a marketing plan for you. Now, granted, this is a first draft since we haven't talked it through and I don't have your actual figures or your business plan to integrate into it. But with it, and the prospectus I created, you have enough to take to the bank and get a big enough loan to stave off those greedy assholes."

His smile was huge, his eyes dancing. He looked as if he'd just handed her a pony covered in glitter with rainbow ribbons tied to its mane.

Instead of killing her dreams and stomping all over them.

"I can't believe you did this." Her head spinning, she shook it and hoped everything would shift. Change. Turn out to be a big fat hot-chocolate-induced mirage.

But it didn't.

Nope. Still there, on the board in bright colors, was proof that Gage had screwed her over.

And there he stood, grinning and looking as if he expected a thank-you note.

13

Hailey was pacing the boardroom, from one end piled high with lingerie samples to the other with its whiteboard and presentation details.

As gorgeous as she was, with her skirt swishing to show a tempting length of thigh with each turn, he didn't think she was happy.

"What's up?" he asked, grabbing one of the leather chairs and pulling it out from the table so he could sit.

Then he caught the look on her face.

Pure fury, wrapped in a layer of hurt.

Nope. He was better standing.

"You stabbed me in the back." The accusation was made through clenched teeth.

"What the hell?" He reared back, shocked at both the accusation and the fact that his sweet Hailey could pull together this much anger.

"I thought you said you were going to let me have the contract."

"I said I was going to make sure you were taken care of," Gage countered. "I offered this before, and now it's an even better deal. I've got a dozen stores, venues and even a TV show all lined up, each one ready to make huge purchases. The revenue in a year will be as much, if not even more, than the Rudolph deal."

He waited, sure she'd simmer down now.

But she didn't. If anything, the fury in her eyes got even more fierce.

Gage frowned, starting to worry a little. He hadn't misplayed this. He was sure of it. There was no question that he was going to have everything he wanted. It looked as though it was just going to take a few pats and soothes before he got there.

"Hey, you haven't heard the bonus yet. By getting the Rudolph contract, I get my freedom. I can take on any client I want. So not only are you getting a boatload of new clientele, you get me." His smile was pure triumph, and he held out his arms, ready for her to throw herself at him in gratitude.

She hissed. If she'd been a cat, he was pretty sure she'd be wearing his skin under her nails right now.

He dropped his arms.

"I don't get it," he said. "You want success, or do you want the Rudolph deal? Aren't you being a little shortsighted with this obsession of yours?"

"We had an agreement."

Gage nodded.

"Right. We agreed that I'd make sure you were taken care of, that you didn't lose your business."

"That's not what I agreed to."

He sighed, shoved his hand through his hair, trying to figure out where this had all gone wrong.

"I can't help what you thought," he said. "I never said I'd step off the campaign. I made it really clear why not."

"And I made it really clear what this meant to me, and why I had to get the account."

He'd be able to handle this a lot better if she didn't sound as if she was about to cry. Gage hated feeling like a jerk. Hated even more the sense that his perfect solution was turning all to hell right before his eyes.

Dammit, he wanted Hailey.

And he wanted his freedom.

She just had to get over this silly attachment to the Rudolph account, and he could have both.

HAILEY SHOVED BOTH hands through her hair, hoping that if she tugged hard enough, a solution would pop out of her head.

When she'd woken up that morning, her world had been perfect. She'd been sure her business was safe, her holidays were heading toward the most awesome of her life, and she was falling in love with the greatest guy in the world.

Hailey had a brief, pining wish to return to that moment. Whether to rejoice in its brief existence, or to slap herself for being so naive, she wasn't sure.

But the moment, and the hope, was gone.

And this was her damned reality.

"Why would you do this?"

"You always take care of everyone else. You're the fix-it girl. The sweetheart who sweeps in and makes everyone feel better. Your employees, your family. Hell, even me. But who makes *you* feel better?" Gage's grin was part triumph, part little-boy-at-Christmas excitement. "I want you to have everything, too. So I fixed it so you could."

"No, you fixed it for you," she said quietly.

"Babe, this way we both win. You get to keep your business. I get my freedom. We both get to be together. That's better than a win-win. It's a win-win-you-and-me-win."

He looked so happy, so pleased with himself.

A part of her, the part that wanted everyone happy, wanted to step forward and give him a big hug. To give him the praise and gratitude he clearly expected. But as Hailey chewed her lower lip until it felt raw, she couldn't force out the applause he expected.

It wasn't as though she wasn't used to betrayal.

It wasn't as if this was the first time someone had made her a promise, then blithely danced away from it.

But this time, it was too much.

This time, she couldn't smile and pretend she was okay with it.

Pretend she didn't mind always coming in second. Because when it came to a commitment between two people, coming in second meant coming in last.

"C'mon, Hailey, let's just move past this," Gage said, his smile pure charm.

"We can't just move past it. I can't." She shook her head. "You're like everyone else. Happy enough to say you're there for me, as long as it's convenient."

"That's not true."

In other words, he didn't want it to be true.

Hailey looked at her shoes, ready to give in. She caught a glimpse of the lingerie samples out of the corner of her eye. She was losing it. Without that contract, there was no guarantee she could keep her business. And she was about to brush that off because it might make Gage feel bad?

So she took a deep breath and met his eyes. And even though each word was painful, she forced herself to speak.

"I've spent my entire life afraid that if I ever spoke up, ever put myself and my needs ahead of my parents' self-interest, that I'd be rejected. That they'd prove, beyond just the whispers in the back of my mind, that they couldn't— that they wouldn't—set aside their own self-absorbed priorities for me."

His frown was ferocious. Whether the anger was directed at her, or at himself, didn't matter. Hailey didn't care. For the first time in her entire life, she only cared about her feelings. It was both liberating and absolutely terrifying.

"You're putting other people's crap between us here,"

he accused. "You have a good reason to have those issues. But I shouldn't need to pay for them."

"But you're doing the same thing." How could he not see it?

Gage shook his head, as if denying her words could deny the truth.

"You're saying you won't take this deal?" he asked, as if he needed to hear her spell it out in tiny letters before he'd believe it.

"I'm saying I will not take your consolation-prize accounts. They're not enough to save my business. They're not enough to pay off the Phillips kids and put an end to this drama," Hailey repeated. Then, even though it was hard to get the air past the knot of tears in her throat, she added, "And if you can't understand why, we can't be together."

In that very second, she felt so miserably selfish.

It wasn't exactly an encouraging feeling to do this kind of put-herself-first crap again, she had to admit.

"You're not thinking straight. C'mon, seriously? You'd throw us, and a golden array of contracts, over? For what? Ego?"

Nope. Not encouraging at all.

But thankfully, anger stepped in and kept the apology on Hailey's lips from spilling out.

"Ego? How is my refusing to take second—no, last place and make the best of it ego driven?"

"You just said it yourself. You have to win, so you have to have first place."

"Me?" Hailey thumped herself in the chest so hard, she almost fell over. "Are you kidding? You're the one who won't walk away from this because you're afraid to go it alone."

"Don't be ridiculous," he dismissed. He looked derisive, but his hunched shoulders and scowl told her she'd scored a direct hit. "It's not as simple as leaving a lucrative job for a start-up. If I walk out, I'm giving up my heritage. I'm giving up any future claims on a company that's been in the family for a half century."

Maybe it was because she'd never had that kind of familial obligation—and definitely never had anyone in her family feel obligated to her—but Hailey couldn't wrap her mind around it.

"You're doing a job you don't like, at the beck and call of people you say don't respect you, because…what? You're afraid you won't get your share of the pie somewhere down the road?"

"Don't try to make it sound so stupid."

"I didn't have to try."

Gage ground his teeth, probably to hold back the cussing, but couldn't keep still. He paced. He grumbled. He did everything but look at Hailey.

"I just tried to hand you the best of everything, and you're tossing it aside. You have a bad habit of that, I've noticed."

Nice way to turn it around on her. But Hailey wasn't playing that game.

"Oh, please. I've never had anything handed to me," she snapped.

"No? What about Merry Widow?"

Before she could tell him how stupid and off base that was, he continued, stepping closer, butting right into her personal space to look down into her face.

"Your old mentor gave you the business. Yes, you had to work hard. You had to make payments. But if it wasn't for him, you wouldn't have had it."

"That's not the same. He and I had an agreement. One that if he were alive would mean I could walk out this door and not have to deal with you, this stupid contract or jumping through any of these ridiculous hoops." Hailey dropped back onto her heels, a little surprised—and a tiny bit ashamed—to realize that last had been offered at a full-on scream, from tiptoes so she could better get in his face.

Hmm. Maybe she had a few issues to resolve.

"Right. You had an understanding. You with obligations on your end. Him with obligations on his end. He didn't meet his, did he?"

"He met his obligations," she retorted, biting off the words. Eric would never have deliberately hurt her.

"Why didn't he draw up a contract for the purchase of the business, then? Why do you, all of a sudden, have to fork over the remaining balance if you had an agreement?"

"Because his kids—"

"If you had a contract, they couldn't do a damned thing."

Hailey pressed her lips together, trying not to burst into tears.

She'd trusted Eric. Just like she'd believed her father when he said she was always his little girl and had faith in her mother's vow to keep their family together.

But Eric, her mentor, her friend, her confidant, hadn't wanted to put it in writing because it'd upset his kids if they found it. And he didn't want to deal with their drama, as he put it.

Hailey should have insisted.

She should have pushed.

But she'd been so grateful to have the business, so grateful to be making her dream a reality, that she hadn't wanted to rock the boat. As always, she hadn't wanted to ruin a good thing by appearing greedy.

By trying to take care of herself.

When would she learn that nobody, ever, put her needs over their wants?

"Will you please leave?" she asked, near tears.

"No. We need to settle this."

"I don't want to discuss it. I don't want to talk to you." She clenched her jaw to keep her lips from trembling, but couldn't keep the tears from filling her eyes.

"Hailey—"

"Just go. I can say my goodbyes to Rudy without you. You've done enough. You can't give up this account— even though you admit my designs are better—because you won't get your perfect outcome wrapped in a perfect ribbon and your daddy won't love you anymore. Fine."

Before he could respond, before she rushed to apologize for the unfairness of her words, she waved him away.

"Please. Go."

"We haven't settled this." Gage's hand was warm on her shoulder as he tried to turn her to face him, but she shrugged it off. "There's more between us than just some silly business issue. Don't throw this away, Hailey."

She took a deep breath, then another to try to control her sobs. She'd never felt so good as she did with him. So wanted. But she couldn't be with him. Not now. It took all her strength, but she forced herself to turn and face Gage.

"We're through. Whatever we might have had, or could have been, it's over now." She gave a tiny, helpless sort of shrug. "Call it a quirk of mine. I don't want anything to do with the person responsible for pounding that final nail in my business's coffin."

Unable to resist, she indulged herself one last time by reaching out to cup her hand against his cheek. His eyes full of anger and pain, Gage leaned into her fingers, turning just a little to nuzzle a kiss against her palm.

It was too much. Hailey had to go.

Without looking at him again, she pulled her hand away, skirted around him and ran through the open door at the far end of the boardroom so fast, she was surprised she didn't fall and break her neck.

She'd leave. Oh, God, she wanted to leave. But she had

to be a good businesswoman. Smart women didn't burn bridges. She had to say her goodbyes, leave on a good impression.

But she couldn't until she got hold of herself.

Telling herself to get a grip, the sooner she stopped freaking out, the sooner she could get the hell out of here and go home, she hurried through the small anteroom she'd left her lingerie samples and supplies in. She shut the door behind her, blocking off Gage and the boardroom.

And almost screamed, her boots skidding across the carpet as she tried to stop her forward momentum.

"Cherry?" Hailey winced. She'd had no idea the other woman was even there. After how many attempts to get the torch singer to show up and listen to one of her brilliant pitches, and she finally did. And what did Hailey do? Have a total emotional breakdown, throw over her lover and kiss her career goodbye. All in one screaming match.

Lovely.

"You're smart to let him go," the other woman said, her voice huskier than usual.

Hailey was about to agree when she looked closer at Cherry. Dark grooves circled her eyes. Her skin had a pallid cast, made all the worse by the ugly overhead fluorescent lights. Despite the misery coursing through her, it was all Hailey could do not to go over, wrap her arms around the woman and pull her into a tight hug.

"It's none of my business, but are you okay?"

Hailey waited to be rebuffed. Just because Cherry had just been privy to her personal humiliation didn't make them bosom buddies.

"I feel bad. I didn't realize how much you had on the line with this deal," Cherry said, not looking at Hailey as she ran her hand over the heavy satin of a forties-inspired nightgown.

"My future was riding on it," Hailey said quietly. Not

to add any pressure to the woman, but for crying out loud, maybe it would be nice if people started considering someone else for a change in this little scenario. Rudy was all about self-indulgence. Cherry was totally self-absorbed. And Gage? Hailey ground her teeth together. Well, he was simply greedy and selfish.

So despite her dislike for emotional manipulation, she gave Cherry a direct look. "I have a dozen people who are depending on me, on my business, for their jobs. They have kids, families to support. We've put everything into this, and I really, really think Merry Widow is the best choice for this contract."

Cherry's nod was slow, her sigh deep.

"You're right. It is best." Then, with a loud swallow, she sighed again. "Actually, I've been on the fence, but today pushed me over. I'm not going to do the spokesmodel gig."

Oh, hell.

Hailey wanted to cry.

Or scream.

Screaming would be good.

But she only screamed inside her head. Never outside, where someone might hear her and be upset.

God forbid Hailey upset anyone with her petty personal issues.

But dammit, she'd tried so hard. She'd banked everything on this. She'd truly believed she'd get it, that all she needed was to get Cherry on her side.

And now?

Now it didn't matter. Rudy had already decided on Milano. Without Cherry's vote, he'd simply do what he wanted.

Still, Hailey dropped to a chair, her butt hitting the hard wood surface with a thump.

She was done.

It was over.

"I'm sorry," Cherry murmured, her voice seeming to come from much farther away than just across the room.

Hailey shrugged. She tried to pull out her brave face. Shouldn't be hard, right? She seemed to live in it. But she couldn't. Not this time.

She tried to find some happy words to brush off the whole thing, to make Cherry feel better.

But she couldn't. Not this time.

This time, she really wanted to scream.

On the outside.

"I needed this," she murmured instead. "I knew Rudy would take the sexy sell. That was pretty much a given once Milano got mixed up in the deal. But I needed this."

"You thought I was your answer." Cherry's statement wasn't a question. It was a simple acceptance. "You figured I'd see the merits of your line versus the leather."

"Didn't you?" Hailey lifted her head from her hands to stare through dull eyes.

Cherry nodded. "Yes. Of course I did. Given the scope of the launch and the variety your designs offered, I felt yours would be the much stronger line to feature."

Hailey tried to find some comfort in that.

All her life, she'd searched for the silver lining, holding tight to it when she was being deluged by the cloud. But this time, the lining meant nothing. It could have been pure gold, and it still wouldn't have helped her.

"Why'd you drag this out? Why'd you let Rudy, let me, think you were on board? Why couldn't you have just been honest from the beginning and said you didn't want me?"

Hailey winced as those last words escaped, knowing they weren't Cherry's to own. They were more a summary of every freaking time she'd been screwed over in her life. By her mom, who was always off chasing her dream, running after the next exciting thing and too busy to care about her daughter. By her father, who'd built his new life and liked to pretend that Hailey was a part of it, but who never—ever—tried to make her one of the family. By her mentor, who'd sworn he'd file the paperwork for the business.

And by Gage, who made her feel things she'd only read about. Who made her hope for more. Hope for everything. And then who made her think that maybe, just maybe, this time she'd get it.

"It wasn't fair," Hailey finally said, for the first time in her life, letting herself express how disappointed she was.

"I thought I could handle it," Cherry said, lifting both hands in the air. "I thought I could juggle it all."

"Juggle what? Your career obligations? Your love life? Holiday shopping? What did you need to juggle here? All you had to do was make a decision, wear some outfits for a weeklong photo shoot and do one simple fashion show." Yelling the last word, Hailey realized she was standing on tiptoe in her attempt to put as much force behind the words as possible.

Cringing, she immediately dropped back to her heels.

Lovely. She'd just yelled at a very nice, very influential woman. Good thing her business was ruined. Otherwise she'd be freaking out in paranoia over the probable outcome of finally letting loose.

"I've been diagnosed with cancer. Breast cancer. Right before Thanksgiving." Cherry's voice, husky with pain, was barely audible. The redhead looked down at her fingers, twining them together then pulling them apart, then starting over again. Her swallow was audible from across the room, echoed by the sound of the outer door closing.

Gage was gone.

But Hailey could only stare, her heart devastated.

But not for herself.

For the woman sitting in front of her.

"How bad…? I mean, what's the prognosis?"

"It's metastasized." Cherry gave a shaky smile, then gestured to her ample curves. "Looks like these babies are going bye-bye. That's the oncologist's recommendation. I've been fighting it, thinking somehow, if I just believed hard enough, I could change things."

She sniffed, then lifted her shoulder.

"All my life, I beat the odds because I believed I could. I did what everyone said was impossible. My career, my recording contract, moving into the movies and modeling." She looked down at her hands again, then gave Hailey a tremulous smile. "I thought I could believe this away. Silly, huh?"

Oh, God.

"No," Hailey whispered, her throat clogged with tears. "Not silly at all."

This time, Hailey couldn't stop herself. She rushed across the room and took the other woman into her arms. Together, they held tight, tears flowing in an aching river of misery.

Talk about perspective.

14

GAGE STRODE THROUGH his father's house, anger propelling his every step.

Damn Hailey for not jumping at his deal.

Damn Rudolph for making it so easy to steal the account away from her.

And damn his father for boxing him in, forcing him into this position. All because the old man had some twisted idea of heritage. A man who, Gage realized with a growl, hadn't ever once decorated a damned Christmas tree with his sons.

He stomped into the lounge, glaring at this year's tree in the corner, then sharing that look with his brother, who was cozied up with his newspaper and a glass of brandy.

"Where's the old man?" he asked, preferring to get it all over at once.

Devon's shrug made it clear Gage's preference wasn't going to matter. "No clue. I think he might have a date."

Both brothers slanted a look at the tree. Decorated in its customary red-and-green balls, it looked like it always did when it was just the three men. Gage was sure their thoughts were in sync. If the old man was on a date, what was the tree going to look like next year?

"Did we ever decorate the tree ourselves?" he heard himself ask. At Devon's puzzled expression, he elaborated,

"I don't remember decorating. I know we always had a tree. But did we have any kind of, you know, tradition or part in it? Or was it always like the wives, simply showing up one day as a big surprise, causing an uproar for its limited time here, then the old man tossing it away when it started to droop."

Devon's smirk faded into a squint as he thought about the question.

"I don't remember decorating. That's a girlie thing, though, so it can go right there with wearing makeup and going to dance class on the list of things we're glad we missed out on."

Girlie. Right. Along with traditions, emotions and anything that couldn't be tracked on a ledger sheet.

"Today was the meeting, right?" Devon asked, as if he were reading Gage's mind. "You nailed down the deets on the Rudolph deal?"

Still staring at the tree, Gage shrugged.

"I've got a new venture I just bought into. Another club, but more S and M focused, less pussycat fluff," Devon said after a minute or so. The silence was obviously bugging him. "You want in? You can take a look at the prospectus, write up a marketing plan, make us both rich."

When Gage's laugh came a second too late, Devon scowled.

"What's the problem?"

"Do you ever get tired of chasing new ventures? Of hopscotching from project to project?"

"I'm at Milano long-term, so everything else is about short-term. That's how you should be looking at your little marketing start-up, too. Get it going, have fun with it, then once it's solid, sell it off." Devon grinned. "Should make for a fun year. And who knows, maybe you'll finally beat my side earnings. Probably not, but you can try."

Rather than incur another scowl, Gage offered up the

expected smile. But he just wasn't into it anymore. The competition, the constant searching for something new, the next big thing. He wanted to settle in, manage his business and see how far he could take it. He wanted to build some traditions, and yes, maybe even learn from a few failures.

He thought of Hailey, of her determination and drive to do everything she could to succeed. He wanted that.

Hell, he wanted *her*.

"What's your problem tonight?" Devon snapped, clearly not happy with the mood Gage had brought into the room. "Did you get the account or didn't you?"

Gage opened his mouth to snap that of course he had. Then he frowned and shrugged instead.

"I want out."

"That's the deal. You get the account, you get out for a year." Devon folded his paper in neat, tidy creases and slapped it against his knee. "The terms were clear."

"I don't care about the terms, or that offer," Gage said, realization dawning. He shoved his hands into his pockets and stared at the tree. Unable to stop himself, even though he knew he was probably cutting his own throat, he repeated, "I want out."

His brother laughed and gave him a derisive look.

"You'd give it all up? Your future? The future of any rug rats you happen to have? Don't you think your kids would someday be a little pissed to find out you threw away their heritage?"

"I'm so freaking sick of hearing about the Milano legacy. We've heard it all our lives and what's it got us? We don't have a heritage. We don't have family memories. We have a despot at the head of the dinner table and the board table, calling the shots on the business and on our lives."

Gage glanced around. "Is this heritage? We've never decorated a tree together. We've never had fun family memories. We're stockholders, assets, prime Milano resources." Gage gestured to the tree, as if it epitomized his every point. "I'd like to think that if I someday have rug rats, as you put it, they'll want more than shares in the company. They'll want holidays and traditions and cookies for Santa. They'll want more than a cold, choking tie with a million conditions on it."

"Money, success, a family name," Devon countered. "Those all buy a hell of a lot of memories and make the holidays a lot more enjoyable. All thanks to those ties you're bitching about."

"Shouldn't ties be deeper than that?" Gage growled, throwing his arms in the air in frustration. "Shouldn't they be more than a fragile thread, easily snapped because I refuse to continue giving up my own goals, my own dreams, to toe the line?"

Shouldn't they be important enough to care that he didn't want to screw over a woman who meant a lot to him, just to snag the company yet another feather for its overstuffed freaking hat?

"Well, that's an interesting take on the traditions I've handed down to you."

Shit. Gage cringed. Even Devon winced as they both shifted their gazes to the doorway.

"Dad. I didn't know you were there."

"Obviously." Marcus crossed the room to pause in front of the tree, inspecting it much as his sons had earlier, then turning to take his favorite seat by the fire. "So you want to break tradition, do you?"

Devon's look was pitying, as though he felt as if he should leave the room so Gage could be shredded in private, but couldn't resist the show. Or, if Gage were in a generous mood, maybe his brother was sticking it out for moral support. The reality was probably propped somewhere in between.

Gage met his father's stare with an unwavering one of

his own. Well, one way or another, Hailey was right. It was time to step up and stand up.

THERE. HAILEY CLAPPED her hands together to indicate a job well done and stepped back from the tree to admire her handiwork. Beads and balls and dainty lace roses, a garland of ribbon and a few scatters of crystals here and there for accent.

The perfect, beautiful tree.

She sighed, letting her smile drop.

She'd rather have the paper snowflake, popcorn and condom-covered one. Of course, she'd rather have it because it came with a very sexy, usually naked man underneath.

And with a promise.

She dropped to the couch, the tree a blur.

"The tree is lovely."

"Thanks." She offered a warm smile to Cherry, who was curled up in the corner chair. The other woman still looked fragile. As if a loud noise would shatter her. But she had an air of peace about her now, too.

Hailey figured that probably had more to do with the ice-cream sundae and Christmas-cookie binge than anything Hailey had done. But if a few hours of listening, another few of hugs and tears and a couple of vats of hot fudge had helped, she was thrilled.

"You're upset about Gage?" Cherry observed after a few minutes of silence.

They'd talked about her cancer, about the holidays, about their favorite junk food and the hottest actors. They'd covered lingerie, a mutual shoe obsession. And now, apparently, they were on guys.

Lovely. But as they'd silently established at the beginning of this bonding session, nothing was off-limits. Hailey knew it wouldn't be fair to sidestep just because she didn't want to talk about Gage yet.

But *upset* was an understatement.

Heartbroken, devastated, miserable. Those came closer.

"Disappointed," Hailey finally said. "But Gage, the lingerie deal, they're minor. Especially compared to what you're facing."

"What I'm going through doesn't mean your pain is any less, you know," Cherry chided, pushing her hand through that luxurious mane of red hair as if appreciating every strand.

"Maybe not, but it definitely puts my heartbreak and business woes into perspective."

Cherry's phone buzzed, the tenth or so time that evening. She looked at it and sighed.

"I've got to go. I have a show at eleven and my car is on its way." Cherry gave her a warm smile, then offered, "This was wonderful, though. And now we have it down pat for our next visit. First I whine, then you whine? We just keep taking turns."

Hailey laughed. Then, remembering the reason she'd brought Cherry back to her place instead of going to the other woman's—besides the ample supply of cookies here—she jumped up and, with a murmured excuse, hurried into the other room. She was back in a quick minute with a gift-wrapped box.

"I intended to give this to you after we'd signed the deal, but, well, that's out the window," she said with a shrug as she handed Cherry the beribboned gift. "It's just a little something I thought would suit you. Go ahead, open it now."

Excitement, and the special joy that came from giving a gift that meant a lot, filled Hailey as Cherry tugged at ribbon, pulled at paper. When the woman opened the box and pulled out the hand-beaded, royal-blue forties-esque nightgown Hailey had designed just for her, it felt fabulous. Even better was the wide-eyed look of amazed appreciation on the redhead's face.

"Oh, this is gorgeous," she breathed. She pulled it close, holding it against her chest as if to assess the fit. Then, with a sniffle, she lifted tear-filled eyes to Hailey's.

"It's cut to drape from the shoulders," Hailey pointed out, having to push the words past the lump in her throat. "It'll flow to the hips, then swirl to the floor. No matter what your size, it'll look amazing."

"It's as if you knew…"

"No," Hailey quickly denied. "It's simply the design. Too often, women are objectified. We're made to feel beautiful only if we fit a specific mold, if we wear a specific size. But beauty, sexuality, that comes from within. Not from what fills our bra."

Hailey sniffed, wishing she had the right words to let Cherry know that she'd always be gorgeous, always be sexually appealing.

So, instead, she shrugged and offered a smile. "It'll be beautiful on you. Always."

"I wish there was something I could do," Cherry murmured, her fingers sliding over the heavy satin, then trailing along the delicate lace. "You're so sweet, and I feel like I just destroyed your world."

"No," Hailey objected quietly. "My designs suit you, suit a woman who wants to feel beautiful, feel feminine. That's not the direction Rudy is going. Even if I'd got the deal, the message would get lost in all the sloppy sex stuff he was going to throw in there. Leather panties, dinosaur shoes. The man has seriously horrible taste."

They shared a grimace.

"You're right. Your designs make women feel great. Sexy and strong." Cherry's words trailed off and she gave Hailey a considering look.

"What?"

"Well, I know you needed the contract. And I have no idea what position your company is in now that you didn't get it. But, and I'm not saying I'm sure of this, but I was just thinking that it might be interesting if we…" Her words trailed off, her gaze intent on the nightie in her hands. After a few seconds and a deep breath, she lifted her eyes to Hailey's. "What if we did a line together? You design. I model. Through all of these pitches, I've loved your message, your passion for how romance and emotion are sexier than lust."

"Launching a line together would mean you're putting yourself, your struggle and your body, on display," Hailey pointed out quietly. She knew Cherry knew that, but it was one of those things that needed to be said out loud. A few times.

"I know. I think this might be what I need, though." The redhead arched an elegant brow at Hailey. "And maybe it can be what you need."

Could it be? Hailey's mind spun in a million directions at once, all of them excited, none of them sure.

"Together?"

"Tentatively," Cherry said, swallowing hard. "I'll be damned if this disease is going to beat me, destroy my confidence or my career. I was going to agree to the Rudolph deal because I wanted exposure."

"Our launching a line together, based on your story, might mean a lot more exposure than you bargained for," Hailey said carefully.

She didn't want to get too hopeful. She definitely didn't want to profit from the other woman's struggles. But oh, the possibilities. The idea of sharing her vision, the concept of expanding people's views of femininity and sexual appeal, it made her want to cry with joy.

Somewhere between a grimace and relief, Cherry checked her buzzing phone.

"My ride is here. I've got to go. Let's both think about this. A couple of days, maybe through next weekend. I don't want to make promises I can't keep. And you need to be sure this is enough to save your company." The redhead rose, her nightie draped over one arm and both hands outstretched to take Hailey's.

"I think this could be incredible," she murmured.

Hailey's mind was spinning. It would be amazing.

But she'd have to step up herself. She'd have to find a way to keep her business, without the Rudolph account.

But if Cherry could face this and find a way, so could she.

"I think it could be, too," Hailey finally said.

With that and one last hug, Cherry smiled and floated out of the room. Hailey grinned. The woman was pure glam, even at her lowest.

As the echo of the shutting door faded, so did Hailey's smile.

She did miss Gage.

His smile and his tight ass. His laugh and his sexy shoulders. His belief in her, his acceptance of her and his outrage on her behalf. Right up until he'd done the exact thing he was so outraged over.

She sniffed.

Still, something good had come of it all.

Optimism paid off.

Sure, things weren't turning out the way she'd expected and held out for. But they were turning out. She should be happy. She should be excited.

She'd stood up for herself.

She'd made a new friend in Cherry.

She'd found a way to save her business, and to empower someone else in the process.

But all she could think of were Gage's words. How he'd forced her to see how much damage she'd caused herself, her life and her business. All because she was always too worried about upsetting someone else instead of standing up for herself.

He was right.

And telling him off when she'd stood up for herself had felt good. Losing him hadn't. But for the first time in her life, she understood that old saying.

If you love something, set it free. If it comes back it's yours. If it doesn't, it never was.

If she was always too afraid to stand up, to take a chance that someone might leave, then did it matter if she had them in her life?

It wasn't until she felt the chill on her chin that she realized she was crying. Hailey blinked fast, wiping her face. Then, knowing she owed it to herself to make the most of the lesson—because she'd be damned if she'd lose the most important guy in her life for nothing—she picked up the phone.

"Mom? Hi. We need to talk."

HAILEY STARED AT the thick expanse of wood, alternating between wanting to turn tail and run, and puzzling over the view.

Was that a wreath hanging there?

It was round.

It was green.

It had a red bow and—she leaned forward and sniffed—it smelled like pine.

Seriously?

Gage had a wreath hanging on his front door?

It was so out of character for a man who until last weekend had never even decorated a Christmas tree, she wasn't sure what to make of it.

Maybe it'd be better if she left, thought about it for a while, then when she figured out what it meant, came back and tried to talk to him then.

Her fingers tightened on the ornately wrapped box in her hands, and, since her heart was racing fast enough to run off by itself, she gave a nod.

Yep, come back later.

She turned to leave.

Her way was blocked by a large male body.

Hailey screamed. The package flew a half foot and her feet almost slipped out from under her. Thankfully this was one of those rare occasions that she was wearing flats instead of heels. Just in case she had to run.

"What the hell are you doing?" she asked, her words a gasp.

"Coming home?" Gage said, his eyes dancing and his grin huge. "What the hell are *you* doing?"

Hailey debated.

Running now, given that it would require doing a dash around him, was a little silly. Still, silly had a lot of appeal compared to putting her heart on the line.

Her eyes eating him up as if it'd been months instead of a few days since they'd seen each other, Hailey almost sighed.

Damn, he was gorgeous.

"I brought you this," she said, holding up the gift. "So here. Merry Christmas."

She shoved it in his hands and, figuring she'd sidestepped silly, started to leave. She'd tell him all the heart-baring stuff later. When he thanked her for the gift, maybe.

"C'mon in."

Hailey winced. But her feet froze and her body, always ready to do his bidding, turned to follow. Oh, man, this was harder than standing up to him had been.

"I didn't have time to wrap yours," he said after helping her off with her coat. The feel of his fingers, lightly brushing her shoulders, burned right through her sweater.

"You got me a present?"

Hailey gave up trying to look calm and casual, dropping to the couch and staring at him in shock.

"You really got me something? But I yelled at you."

Her mother still wasn't talking to her after hearing Hailey's feelings about being dumped at Christmas. *Again.* And her father? He'd apologized all over the place, then blamed it all on her mother. She still hadn't untwisted that.

But Gage acted as if he wasn't mad. More, he acted as though he'd known he'd see her again, and that they'd be in a gift-exchanging kind of place.

It was as though nothing had happened.

Hailey wanted to grab that, to simply let it all slide. Just pretend everything was peachy, that he hadn't hurt her or screwed her over in the Rudolph deal. Act as if she hadn't said mean things and yelled accusations at him.

It'd be so much easier.

All her life, she'd gone the easy emotional route. Smiles were better than frowns, happy times preferable to angry.

But…she wanted more.

She wanted a future with Gage. To give them a chance and see where things went.

And she couldn't do that the same old, easy way.

Then he asked, "Why wouldn't I get you a gift?"

"Because we had an ugly fight."

"So? People fight. Then they make up, right? At least, that's how I've always heard relationships went."

Relationships. They were in a relationship.

Joy, giddy and sweet, rushed through her. She wanted to stop talking now. To skip right over all this soul-searching chitchat and get down to the naked makeup fun.

But they deserved more than that.

Dammit.

Taking a deep breath, Hailey looked at her hands, then met his baffled gaze.

"I don't know. I've only had one ugly fight, and it resulted in a big family rift. After that, I was afraid to fight. I was too worried that I'd lose whatever crumbs I had if I stood up for wanting more. Or that the person would walk away."

His nod was slow and considering, and the look in his eyes intense. As if he were seeing all the way into those little cubbies and closets in her brain, the ones where she hid all her secrets.

"So where does that put us? That you didn't mind losing what we had? Or that you were sure I'd stick around?"

She peered closely at his face, wishing she could see a hint of which he'd prefer she say. Then, since they'd already established that she was all about telling him like it was, she gave a little lift of her hands.

"Because you let me be me. You seemed to appreciate my strengths, my opinions. Me. I never felt like I wasn't important with you. Or that there were conditions on our being together." She swallowed, hard, then took a deep breath. Big admission time. "I wouldn't say I blew up at you for no reason. I really was angry. And hurt. But maybe, sort of, I was pushing because a part of me wondered how fast you'd walk away once I got in your face."

He arched both brows and gave her an assessing look. "A test?"

Hailey opened her mouth to deny it, then had to close it. Why deny it.

"Maybe. Sorta." She looked at her hands again, wishing she had something to do with all this nervous energy. Like run her fingers over his body, or touch his hair. But both of those actions would probably change the subject. And as much as she wanted to, she'd rather get this out of the way before they got on the subject of being naked.

"You really did offer me a better deal than I was getting from Rudolph. I could have easily taken a ledger of sales like that to the bank and negotiated a loan. Add to it your marketing package, something with such great long-term possibilities? Turning away from it was the worst business decision I could make. I accused you of putting business, your own ambitions, over what we were making together. But I was the one doing that."

Hailey winced when Gage's face creased into a ferocious frown and he looked for a second as if he wanted to hit something. What? He couldn't take an apology?

"You're killing me," he finally said, pushing off the couch to pace the room. "I had these big plans. I spent the last few days putting everything into place, fine-tuning and perfecting things. And you sweep in here with your pretty smile and fancy gift and blow it all."

She shook her head, wondering if all that humility had ruined her hearing.

"What are you talking about?"

"I quit Milano. Not a break, not a sabbatical, not a sanctioned-but-still-contracted reprieve. I quit." He threw his hands in the air, as if tossing aside his heritage, his family and his commitments. But he didn't look upset. Instead, he seemed relieved. Or maybe that was just what she was hoping to see?

"Is that a good thing?" she asked hesitantly.

"It doesn't matter now. I've busted my ass building a pitch, crafting the perfect way to show you how much you mean and how important you are, and you sweep in here and outdo me. Again. Every damned time I think I've got the upper hand, you outmaneuver, outflank and outplay me."

Hailey had to pull her chin off her chest and force her mouth closed. He was ranting, but he didn't seem upset at all. Instead, he sounded proud. As if he was thrilled with her. As if he admired her. As if he really cared.

"Oh" was all she could say.

Then, as much as she didn't want to, Hailey burst into tears.

"HELL." GAGE CRINGED.

Not tears.

Anything but tears.

"Look, that isn't a bad thing. I'm not upset about being outflanked and outmaneuvered. It's like you being on top. I like that, too."

Well, that got a smile, but didn't stop the tears.

Dammit.

Gage pulled in a deep breath. He wanted to kiss the wet tracks off her face. He wanted to distract her with a naughty promise. But he was a man who knew the importance of timing. He had to do this now. Even though it was probably going to get him more tears, he manned up and took both her hands.

"That's one of the things I admire about you," he said, keeping his words low and quiet so she had to quit sobbing to hear him. "You're incredible at what you do. You're passionate about what you believe in. And you're smart. Smart enough to call me on being a jackass. Smart enough to see my fears and push me to get over myself and go for the dream."

She sniffed, her eyes wide and wet but, thank God, not pooled up any longer.

"You think I did all of that? You actually like that I called you on being a jackass?"

"Well, I'm not saying I want it to be my new nickname or anything. But I appreciate that you see me, that you understand me. And that you believe in me."

She smiled. It was a little shaky at the edges, but filled

with so much sweetness that Gage had to smile back. Figuring he deserved a reward for not running like a sissy boy at the first sign of tears, Gage lifted her hands to his lips, brushing a kiss over the knuckles of one, then the other. She was so sweet. So delicious. Then, his eyes locked on hers, he leaned in and brushed her mouth next.

So soft.

So incredible.

Her sigh was a gentle wash of emotion. Delight and relief, excitement and joy.

All good.

But he wanted her passion.

And he knew how to get it.

Gage shifted his lips, just a bit, and changed the angle. With a barely there moan, she opened to him, meeting passion with passion. Desire with desire. And, yes, baby, tongue with tongue.

He wanted to stay here. It felt good here. Safe. No emotional risk. A part of him figured he'd already risked plenty this week. His career. His standing with his family. His heritage.

There was nothing wrong with waiting a little while before putting everything else on the line.

Then Hailey gave a tiny moan. Her fingers, warm and gentle, grazed his cheek. Slowly, as if hearing his thoughts and giving him a chance to decide, she pulled back.

Her lashes fluttered, and then she gazed up at him. Those huge green eyes were filled with so many emotions. The lust made his already-steel-hard dick happy, and the delighted joy gave his heart a little buzz. But it was the trust there, the total faith in him, that made Gage want to groan.

With happiness. And in frustration.

Because there was no way he could back down when she was looking at him like that.

"So," he started, pretty sure this was the first time in his life he'd struggled with the right words to sell his point. "I talked to Rudy this morning."

The excitement shifted in her gaze, a frown leaving a tiny crease between her brows.

Nice job, Gage thought. Maybe next he could tell her Santa was fake and that Christmas cookies made women fat. She'd probably look just as happy.

"I wanted to tell him I was off the Milano account. I couldn't throw Milano under the bus, but did suggest he take a hard look at what sexy really was to women, and to men who didn't use *Playboy* to measure their relationships."

Her lips twitched, but the frown didn't fade.

"He's sick of the whole thing. Said he'd rather the models strut down the runway nude than have to worry any more about lingerie." Gage's lips twisted in a rueful smile. "But he said he was going to think about it. That he'd probably be giving you a call."

Gage waited, ready for her to, oh, maybe throw her arms around him. Squeal with excitement. Offer up her undying gratitude and maybe a little love.

Instead, she pulled away and bit her lip before giving him a grimacy sort of look.

"You're so sweet to do that. I really, really appreciate it." So much so that she looked as if she wanted to throw up, he noted. "But I don't think Rudy is going to want to work with me."

Gage knew for sure the guy didn't want to work with either one of them. But that was beside the point.

"Why not?"

"Because I stole his star," she said, watching her fingers twist together for a second before she met his eyes with a gleeful look. "For a lot of reasons, she didn't want to work with Rudy. So Cherry and I are launching a line together."

Gage burst into laughter. Poor Rudy. Looked as though his models were going to have to strut down the runway naked after all.

"What are you going to do about the payoff?" he asked. He'd already talked to his banker, arranged for a loan if she wanted it. He'd figured on wrapping up the payoff in a bright red box, but knew she wouldn't accept it, so the loan was his backup. Just in case she wanted help.

"Well, after chewing into you, I called my mother and told her off for just about everything," Hailey said, sounding proud. "Then, figuring I was on a roll, I called my father and did the same. And then, since I had nothing else to lose, I called Dawn Phillips and told her that revised contract or not, her father and I had an agreement and I'd met it faithfully for three years. That she'd either renegotiate the terms or my attorney would be in contact and we'd settle it in court."

Gage was pretty sure his grin was wide enough to pop his ears off.

"'Atta girl. You kicked ass. I take it everyone stepped up and took responsibility?" About damned time, too.

Hailey shook her head.

"Nope. My mother cried and blamed me for ruining her holiday. My father said he'd take my complaints under consideration and discuss them with my stepmother."

Damn them. Gage was afraid to ask, but figured he'd started this so he didn't have a choice.

"And the Phillips woman?"

"Dawn?" Hailey pursed her lips before giving him a smile that lit the room brighter than the tree they'd decorated. "She agreed to the terms Eric and I had set. After I'd told her how fabulous the business was doing, and how much more money she stood to make if she let the terms play out for another two years, and then I pay fair-market value on the balance due, she saw the wisdom in waiting."

And here he'd thought he'd have to rescue her.

Gage grinned.

Once again, she'd outdone him.

He loved that about her.

"You're amazing," he said with a wondrous smile.

"I couldn't have done it without you. Without you pushing me, showing me that there's more to a relationship than convenience." She swallowed hard enough for him to hear the click, then took a deep breath and met his gaze. Her own eyes were huge. "I think I'm in love with you."

He'd never heard those words.

Ever.

Gage's heart melted. And then, like the Grinch he'd dressed up as once, it seemed to grow huge. So huge he wasn't sure what to do with it.

All he could do was pull her close.

Before his lips met hers, he whispered, "I think I'm in love with you, too."

As they fell into the kiss, the lights of the condom-covered Christmas tree twinkled.

And Gage had to admit, the holidays pretty much rocked.

* * * * *

THE NIGHTSHIFT
BEFORE CHRISTMAS

ANNIE O'NEIL

This one's for my guy. You're my Christmas, birthday and HEA all wrapped up into one handsome, blue-eyed, Scottish package.

xx Wifey

CHAPTER ONE

"OKAY, PEOPLE! LISTEN UP, it's the start of silly season!"

"I thought that was Halloween?"

"Or every full moon!"

"First snowfall?"

"Hey, Doc? Is that where your locum tenens is? Stuck in one of the drifts?"

"He won't last long in Copper Canyon if that's the case. A man needs snow tires."

"A *woman* just needs common sense! I follow the snow-plows! Got them tracked on my phone!"

Copper Canyon's Emergency Department filled with laughter. Impressive, considering they were down to a quality but skeleton staff. Never mind the fact it was almost always one of the busiest weeks of the year. The town was full of holiday visitors and the ski resort up the hill always had an emergency or six their small clinic couldn't handle.

Katie scanned the motley crew who would see her through Christmas Eve and, for some double-shifters, into the Big Day itself. Valley Hospital was no Boston General, and that was just the way Katie liked it. The facility was big enough to have all the fancy equipment, small enough to be able to give the personal touch to just about every-one who walked through those doors. And if they needed an extra hand, there were always the emergency services guys up on the mountain, willing to lend a hand. It wasn't home yet…but she'd get there.

"Thank you, peanut gallery. Time to focus." Katie tried her best to smile at the small but vital crew, all visibly buzzing with Christmas cheer. It wasn't their fault she wanted to rip every bauble, snowman and glittery snowflake from the walls. Someone else took that prize. "Thanks for wearing your red and green scrubs, by the way—you all look very…festive."

"Who doesn't love Christmas, Doc?" a tinsel-bedecked RN quipped.

Me.

"Right!" Katie soldiered on. They were used to her grumpy face—no need for Christmas to morph her into a jolly, stethoscope-wearing elf. "Just in time for the lunchtime rush, I've got our first Christmas mystery X-ray!"

A smattering of applause and cheers went up as she worked her way through the dozen or so staff and slapped the X-ray up on the glowing board with a flourish.

"Any guesses?"

"Why would anyone stick one of those up their—?"

"I know! Especially at Christmas."

"At least it's not a turkey thermometer. We had one of those last year. Perforated the intestine!"

The group collectively sucked in a breath. *Ouch.*

"C'mon, Dr. McGann, that's too easy. Give us a hard one!"

"All right, then." She turned to face the cocky resident. "If it's so easy, what's your guess?"

"Cookie cutter?"

Katie winced and shook her head.

"Nope. Good guess, though. Try again."

She joined the staff in tipping their heads first in one direction then the other. It wasn't that tough…

"Tree decoration. Six-pointed snowflake. My Gramma Jam-Jam used to have one. It was my wife's favorite."

Katie's body went rigid with shock as the rest of the staff turned to see who the newcomer to the group was. She didn't need to turn around. She didn't need to imagine who or what Gramma Jam-Jam's tree was like. She'd helped decorate a freshly cut fir in her old-fashioned living room as many times as she had fingers on a hand.

As her thumb moved to check that the most important finger was still bare, waves of emotion began to strike her entire body in near-physical blows. She willed her racing heart to still itself, but every sensory particle within her was responding to the one voice in the world that could morph her by turns into a wreck, a googly-eyed teen, a blushing bride...

Dr. Joshua West. Her ex-husband.

Well. He would be her ex if he would ever sign the blinking divorce papers!

She couldn't even manage to turn around and look at him, and yet her body was already on high alert to his presence. He was close. Too close.

She heard a shifting of feet. Maybe it was one of the nurses... Maybe it was... Her eyes closed for a moment.

Yup. There it was. That perfectly singular Josh scent. The man smelled of *sunshine*. What was *up* with that? It was the dead of winter. Freezing-cold, snowing-right-now *winter*. And yet she could smell warm sunny days and the rural lifestyle only her husband—her *ex-husband*!—could turn into something delicious. Talk about evocative! One whiff of that man had never failed to bring out her inner jungle cat. From all the excitement swing-dancing around her chest cavity in preparation for a high dive down to her...*nethergarden*...it was clear the cat had been in hibernation for some time.

Her spine did a little shimmy, as if she already didn't get the point.

She did a laser-fast mental scan of her medical books. Maybe her body was trying to tell her something different!

Frisson or *fear*?

Her tongue sneaked out and gave her lower lip a surreptitious lick.

Guess that answers that, then.

How could that rich voice of his still have a physical effect on her? Hadn't two years apart been enough to make her immune to the sweet thrill twirling along her insides every time she heard him whisper sweet—?

"Nice to see you, Katiebird."

Don't even start *to go there!* She took a decidedly large step away from Josh. *Sweet or not, they'd been* nothings *in the end.*

"Right, everybody! Let's get these patients better."

Katie clapped her hands together—more to prove to herself that she had her back-to-work hat on than anything else. That, and she didn't want anybody around to witness the showdown she was certain was coming.

The group dispersed back to their posts, with a couple of interns still marveling over the human body's ability to deal with the unnatural. Precisely what Katie was experiencing at this exact moment. Fighting a natural instinct. Every time she laid eyes on Josh it was like receiving a healing salve. Her eyes were still glued to the X-ray, but she knew if she only turned her head she was just a blink away from perfection.

She sucked in a breath. Not anymore! No one and nothing was picture-perfect. Life had a cruel way of teaching that lesson.

"Are you ever going to turn around?"

His words tickled her ear again. The man clearly didn't believe in personal space when his wife was trying to divorce him.

"Are you going to tell me what you're doing here?" Katie wheeled round as she spoke. Her breath was all but sucked straight out of her as she met those slate-blue eyes she'd fallen so deeply in love with. It had been a long time since she'd last seen them up close and personal. A really long time.

She fought the sharp sting of tears as she gave a quick shake of her head and readjusted her pose. She could do nonchalant while her world was being rocked to its very core. She was a McGann, for goodness' sake! McGanns were cool, analytical, exacting. At least that was what she'd told herself when her parents had swanned off to another party in lieu of spending time with their only daughter. McGanns were the polar opposite of the West family. The Wests were unruly, wayward, irresponsible! Invigoratingly original, passionate, loyal...

Her teeth caught her lower lip and bit down hard as her brain began to realign the Josh in her head with the one standing in front of her. Thick, sandy-blond hair, still a bit wild on top and curling round his ears, softening the edges of his shirt collar. No tie. *Typical Josh.* He rarely did formal, but when he did...

She swallowed and flicked her eyes back up to his hair to miss out on the little V of chest she knew would be visible. No hat. *Natch.* Why follow the same advice you'd give your patients? There were a few flakes of snow begging to be ruffled out of the soft waves. Her fingers twitched. The number of times she had tucked a wayward strand back behind one of his ears and given in to the urge to drop completely out-of-character sultry kisses along his neck...

No! And double, triple, infinity no! No Josh West. Not anymore!

"Didn't the agency tell you?"

The expression on his face told her he knew damn well it hadn't told her. The twinkle in his eye told her he was enjoying watching the steam beginning to blow out of her ears. Typical. He always had been spectacular at winding her up and then bringing her to a whole other plane of happy—

Stop it, Katie McGann. You are not falling under his spell again.

"Tell me what?"

"No need to grind your teeth, darlin'." He tsked gently. "It'll give you a headache."

"Headache?" Maddening and headache-inducing didn't even *begin* to cover the effect he was having on her. "Try migraine."

"Good thing I'm around, then."

He gave her one of those slow-motion winks that had a naughty tendency to bring out the…the *naughty* in her.

"Those things can knock you out flat."

An image of a shirtless Josh slowly lowering himself onto her…into her…blinded Katie for an instant. The muscled arms, the tanned chest, slate eyes gone almost gray with desire and lips shifting into that lazy smile of his— the one that always brought her nerves down a notch when she needed a bit of reassurance.

She scrunched her eyes tight and when she opened them again there it was in full-blown 3-D. The smile that could light up an entire room.

"Josh, I can't do this right now. Our locum hasn't bothered to show, and as you can see—" her arms curled protectively around herself as the sliding doors opened to admit a young man with a child "—I'm busy. Working," she added, as if he didn't quite get the picture.

Never mind the fact he'd come top in the class above hers at med school, so clearly had brains to spare. Or the little part about how she was standing there in a lab coat in the middle of an ER. A bit of a dead giveaway. *Urgh!* If she used coarse language, a veritable stream of the colorful stuff would be pouring forth! Why was he just standing there? *Grinning?*

"What's the game here, Josh? Yuletide Torture? Our last Christmas together wasn't horrific enough for you?"

His expression sobered in an instant. She'd overstepped the mark. There was no need to be cruel. They'd both borne their fair share of grief. Grinding it in deep wasn't necessary. They would feel the weight of their mutual loss in the very core of their hearts until they each stopped beating. Longer if such a thing was possible. Forgetting was impossible. Surviving was. But only just. Which was exactly why she needed him to leave. *Now.*

"Sorry, Kitty-Kat. You're stuck with me. I'm your locum tenens."

To explain why he was late for his first shift, Josh could have told Katie how his car had spun out on some black ice on the way in, despite it being a 4x4 he drove, and the all-weather tires he'd had put on especially, but from her widened eyes and set expression he could see she had enough information to deal with. The latest "Josh incident," as she liked to call his brushes with disaster, could be kept for another time.

"No. No, I'm sorry, Josh—that's not possible. We can't…"

He heard the catch in her voice and had to force himself to stay put. In his arms was where his wife belonged when she was hurting, but it was easy enough to see it was the last place she wanted to be.

He flexed his hands a few times to try and shake the urge. With Katie right there, so close he could smell her perfume… It would be futile, of course, but one thing people could always say about Josh West—he was a man who never had a problem with attempting the impossible. How else could he have won Katie McGann's heart? Cool East Coast ice princess falling in love with the son of a Tennessee ranch manager, scraping his way through med school with every scholarship and part-time job he could get his callused hands on? It was when he'd finally got his hands on her—man, they'd shaken the first time—he'd known the word "soulmates" wasn't a fiction.

"Dr. McGann?"

Both their heads turned at the nurse's call, and the strength it took to keep his expression neutral would have put a circus strongman out of work.

So. Katie had gone back to her maiden name.

Another nail in the coffin for his big plan, or just another one of Katie's ways of ignoring the fact they belonged together? That everything that had happened to them had been awful—but survivable. Even more so if they were together.

"Can you take this one? Arterial bleed to an index finger. He says it's been pumping for a while. Shannon's in with him now." The nurse held out a chart for her to read.

"Absolutely, Jorja. How long's a while?" Katie asked, taking the three strides to the central ER counter while scanning the chart, nodding at the extra information the charge nurse supplied her.

Josh took the chance to give his wife a handful of once-overs—and one more for good measure. It had been some time since his eyes had run up those long legs of hers. Too long. He'd been an idiot to leave it so long, but she had been good at playing hide-and-seek and he'd had his own dragons to slay. A small flash of inspiration had finally led him to Copper Canyon—the one place he'd left unexplored.

He stuffed his hands into the downy pockets of his old snowboarding coat, fingers curling in and out against the length of his palms. Laying his eyes on her for the first time in two years was hitting him hard. She'd changed. Not unrecognizably—but the young woman he'd fallen in love with had well and truly grown up. Still beautiful, but—he couldn't deny it—with a bit of an edge. Was this true Katie surfacing after the years they'd spent together? Or just another mask to deal with the disappointments and sorrows life had thrown at them in the early days of their marriage?

Gone was the preppy New England look. And in its

stead… He didn't even know where to begin. Was this Idaho chic? Since when did *his* Katie wear knee-high biker boots, formfitting tartan skirts in dark purple and black with dark-as-the-night turtlenecks? Yeah, they would be practical in this wintry weather, but it was a far cry from the pastels and conservative clothes she'd favored back in Boston. The new look was *sexy*.

A hit of jealousy socked him in the solar plexus. She hadn't… He suddenly felt like a class-A *idiot* for not even considering the possibility. She hadn't moved on. Not his Katie. Had she…?

His eyes shot up the length of her legs to the plaid skirt and then up to her trim waistline, irritatingly hidden by the lab coat. His eyes jagged along her hands, seeking out her ring finger. Still bare. He would never forget the moment she'd ripped off her rings and slapped them onto the kitchen counter. Throwing had been far too melodramatic for his self-controlled wife. The word "Enough!" had rung in his ears for weeks afterward. Months.

He exhaled. Okay. The bare finger wasn't proof positive she wasn't seeing someone else, but it was something. He scraped a hand through his mess of a hairdo, wishing he'd taken a moment to pop into a barber's. But he hadn't worried a jot about what he'd looked like over the past two years, let alone worried about impressing another woman. From the moment he'd laid eyes on Katie to the moment she'd hightailed it out of his life—*their* life—he'd known there was only one woman in the world for him. And here she was—doing her pea-pickin' best to ignore him.

His eyes traveled up to her face as she scanned the chart, listening to the nurse. He knew that expression like the back of his hand. Intent, focused. Her brain would be spinning away behind those dark brown eyes of hers to come to the best solution—for both the patient and the hospital, but mostly the patient. One of the many traits he loved about her. Patients first. Politics later. Because there were *always* politics in a hospital. He knew that more than most. It was why staying at Boston General hadn't worked out so well. Why a new job in Paris just might be the ticket he needed to wade out of that sorry old pit of misery he'd been wallowing in.

But he wasn't going anywhere until he knew Katie was well and truly over him. He checked his watch. Seven days to find out if she was cold- or warm-blooded. It ended at the stroke of midnight on New Year's Eve. He'd either hand her a plane ticket or the divorce papers. He sucked in a fortifying breath of Katie's perfume. *Mmm…* Still sweeter than a barn full of new summer hay.

Well, then. He gave his chin a scrub and grinned. *Best get started.*

CHAPTER TWO

"WHAT YOU GOT THERE?" Josh stepped up to the desk, shrugging off his jacket as he approached. Out of the corner of her eye Katie could see Jorja's lips reshape into an O. Josh—or rather his body—had that effect on women. It was why she'd never thought she'd stood a chance. People always mistook her shyness for being stuck-up. But Josh had seen straight through the veneer and gone directly to her heart.

He turned his Southern drawl up a notch. He could do that, too. Pick and choose when to play the Southern gent or drop it if he saw it detracted from his incredibly sharp mind.

"Dr. McGann, may I help keep you out of the fray while you sort out the big picture?"

Katie eyed him warily for a second, then made a decision. By the hint of a smile that bloomed on his lips she could see it was the one he had been hoping for.

He would stay.

Never mind the fact that showing up on Christmas Eve when they were a doctor down wasn't giving her much of a choice. She had it in her to kick him the hell outta Dodge, if that was where he needed booting. But right now there were patients to see, and pragmatism always trumped personal.

"Twenty-five-year-old male presented with an arterial

cut to the bone on his index finger." She tapped the chart with her own.

"Turkey?"

"Ham. Too easy for the likes of you."

She pressed the chart to her chest, claiming it as her own. Katie let her eyes travel along all six feet three inches of her ex. Josh had always been a trauma hotshot. And he'd always looked good. She'd steered clear of the Boston General gossip train, so didn't really know what path he'd chosen professionally after she'd left, but personally nothing had changed in the looks department. He still looked good. She looked away.

Too good.

"You're the next one down." She pulled the X-ray down from the lightboard and passed it to him with a smirk. "Make your Gramma Jam-Jam proud. You can put your stuff in my office for now—the staff lockers are further down the corridor and this patient's been waiting too long as it is."

She tipped her head toward a glassed-in cubicle a few yards away. Josh took advantage of the broken eye contact to soak in some more of the "New Katie" look. Her supershort, über-chic new haircut suited her. It sure made her look different. *Good* different, though. No longer the shy twenty-one-year-old he'd first spied devouring a stack of anatomy books in the university library, a thick chestnut braid shifting from shoulder to shoulder as she studied.

He cleared his throat. Whimsical trips down memory lane weren't helping.

"Green or red scrubs," she added, pointing to a room just beyond her office.

"You always liked me in blue."

The set of her jaw told him to button it.

"Green or red," she repeated firmly. "The patients like it. It's *Christmas*." She handed him the single-page chart with a leaden glare and turned to the nurse. "Jorja MacLeay, this is Dr. West, our locum tenens over the next few days. See that he's made welcome. His security pass should expire on the first of January."

"At the end of the day?" Jorja asked hopefully.

"The beginning. The very beginning," Katie replied decisively, before turning and calling out her patient's name.

He flashed a smile in the nurse's direction, lifted up his worn duffel bag to show her he was just going to unload it before getting to work. The smile he received in return showed him he had an ally. She shot a mischievous glance at his retreating wife and beckoned him toward the central desk.

"Don't mind her," Jorja stage-whispered. "A kitten, really. Just a grumpy kitten at Christmas." She shrugged off her boss's mysterious moodiness with a grin. "As long as she knows you've got your eye on the ball, she's cool."

Josh nodded and gave the counter an affirmative rap. "Got it. Cool. Calm. Collected. And Christmassy!" he finished with a cheesy grin.

"Says here you're double-shifting."

"You bet. Where else would a fellow want to see in Christmas morning?"

Jorja laughed. "Cookies are in the staff room down the hall if you need a sugar push to get you through the night. Canteen's shut and the vending company forgot to fill up the machines, so there might be a brawl over the final bag of chips come midnight!"

"Count me in! I love a good arm-wrestling session. Especially if the chips are the crinkly kind. I love those."

"I can guarantee you'll have a fun night…at least with most of us." She shot a furtive look down the corridor to ensure Katie was out of earshot and scrunched her face and shoulders up into a silent "oops" shrug when Josh raised his eyebrows in surprise.

"You two don't know each other or anything, do you?"

"We've met." It was all Josh would allow.

It was up to Katie if she wanted to flesh things out. He'd been the only crossover she'd allowed between personal and professional and he doubted she had changed in that department. She was one of the most private people he had ever met, and when news of what had happened to them had been all but Tannoyed across Boston General, it had been tough. Coal-pit-digging tough.

Jorja giggled nervously and flushed. "Sorry! Dr. McGann is great. We all love her. The ER always runs the smoothest when she's on shift."

Josh just smiled. His girl always strove to achieve the best and ended up ahead of the game at all turns. Except *that* night. She'd been blindsided. They both had.

He shook off the thought and waved his thanks to Jorja. First impressions? Young to be a charge nurse. Twenty-something, maybe. She struck him as a nurse who would stay the course. Not everyone who worked in Emergency did. She was young, enthusiastic. A nice girl if first impressions were anything to go by.

He'd gone with his gut when he'd met Katie. Made a silent vow she would be his wife one day. It had taken him a while, but he'd got there in the end. And today the vow still hit him as powerfully as the day they'd made good on a whim to elope. Five years, two months and fourteen days of wedded… He sighed. Even he couldn't stretch to "bliss." Not with the dice they'd been handed.

He thought of the divorce papers stuffed inside his duffel bag. There was only one way Katie could ever convince him to sign them. Prove beyond a shadow of a doubt that she felt absolutely nothing for him anymore. He gave a little victory air punch. So far he'd seen nothing to indicate she would be able to get him to scrawl his signature on those cursed papers tonight.

Just the shift of her shoulders when she'd heard his voice had told him everything he needed to know. She could change her name, her hair and even her dress sense if she wanted to—but he knew in his soul that time hadn't changed how his wife felt about him. No matter how bad things had become. She couldn't hate without love. And when she'd finally turned round to face him there had been sparks in her eyes.

Katie stuffed her head into the stack of blankets and screamed. For all she was worth she screamed. And then she screamed some more. Silent, aching, wishing-you-could-hollow-yourself-out-it-hurt-so-bad screams. There was no point in painting a pretty picture in these precious moments alone.

Seeing Josh again was dredging up everything she had only just managed to squeeze a lid on. *Just.* In fact, that lid had probably still been a little bit open because, judging by the hot tears she discovered pouring down her face when she finally came up for air, she was going to have to face the fact there was never going to be a day when the loss of their baby didn't threaten to rip her in half.

What was he thinking? That he could saunter into her ER as if it were just any old hospital on any old day? With that slow, sweet smile of his melting hearts in its wake? She'd not missed the nurses trying to catch his eye. Jorja's giggles had trilled down the hallway after she'd stomped off. Josh did that to people. Brought out the laughter, the smiles, the flirtation. The Josh Effect, she'd always laughingly called it. Back when she'd laughed freely. Heaven knew, *she'd* fallen under his spell. Hook, line and sunk. If only she'd known how far into the depths of sorrow she'd fall when she lost her heart to him, she would have steered clear.

She swatted away her tears and sank to the floor of the

supplies cupboard, using her thumbs to try and massage away the emotion. Her patient was going to be wondering where she was, so she was going to have to pull herself together. Shock didn't even begin to cover what she'd felt when Josh had walked into her ER. Love, pain, desire, hurt…those could kick things off pretty nicely.

"Of all the ERs in all the world, he had to walk into this one."

Talking to herself. That was a new one to add to her list of growing eccentricities. Maybe she should have fostered some of those friendships she'd left behind in Boston.

"Sounds like the start of a pretty good movie." Josh's legs moved into her peripheral vision as his voice filled her ears.

"More like the end of one."

"No, that's the start of a beautiful friendship."

"Well—well…" She trailed off. Playing movie quotation combat with Josh was always a bad idea.

She huffed out a frustrated sigh. Couldn't she just get *a minute* alone? She should have gone to the roof. No one went there in the winter, and she relished the moments of quiet, the twinkle of Copper Canyon's Main Street. She swiped her hands across her cheeks again, wishing the motion could remove the crimson heat she felt burning in them. Against her better judgment she whirled on him and tried another retort.

"Should I have said 'of all the *stalkers* in all the world'?"

"Oh, so going to the supplies cupboard to track down some mandated holiday scrubs has turned me into a stalker, has it?" he asked good-naturedly.

The five-year-old in her wanted to say yes and throw a good old-fashioned tantrum. The jumping-up-and-down kind. The pounding-of-the-fists kind. The *Why me? Why you?* kind. The Katie who'd shored up enough strength to finally call their marriage to a halt knew better. Knew it would only give Josh the fuel he wanted to add to a fire she could never put out.

She wasn't going to give him the satisfaction of knowing how much she still cared. That had been his problem all along. Too trusting that everything would be all right when time and time again the world had shown him the opposite was true. Who else had become an adrenaline junkie after their daughter had been stillborn? Hadn't he known how dangerous everything he'd been doing was? And she'd always been the one who'd had to pick up the pieces, apply the bandages, ice the black eyes, realign the broken nose… Trying her best to laugh it off like he did when all she'd wanted to do was curl up in a corner and weep.

Couldn't he see she had to play it safe? That losing their daughter had scared her to her very marrow? If she were *ever* to feel brave enough to move forward—let alone try and conceive again—he needed to call off his game of tug-of-war with mortality.

She scratched her nails along the undersides of her legs before standing up, using the pain to distract herself from doing what she really wanted.

"Large or extra-large?" she bit out.

"Guess that depends on if you need me to play Santa later." He grabbed a pillow from a shelf and stuck it up his shirt.

Without bothering to examine the results, Katie yanked a pair of extra-large scrubs from a nearby shelf. Not because she needed a Santa but because she didn't need to see how well he filled out the scrubs. The first time they'd met—*woof!* And she was no dog owner.

The first time they'd met… He said it had been in the library, but she was convinced to this day that he'd made it up. The day she'd first seen him—easily standing out in a crowd of junior residents, all kitted out in a set of formfitting scrubs—his eyes had alighted on her as if he'd

just gained one-on-one access to the Mona Lisa herself...
Mmm... That moment would be imprinted on her mind
forever... She'd never let anyone get under her skin—but
she'd been powerless to resist when it had come to Josh.

"Green! Good to see you remember red always makes
my complexion look a bit blotchy."

Katie blew a raspberry at him. She wasn't playing.

"Or is it that you remember green always brings out the
blue in my eyes?" He winked and took hold of the scrubs,
trapping her hand beneath his.

Just feeling his touch reawakened things in Katie she
had hoped she'd long-ago laid to rest. Her eyes lifted to
meet his. Stormy sea-gray right now. Later... He was right.
Later they'd be blue, and later still the color of flint. She
had loved looking into his eyes, never knowing what to expect, trying to figure out how to describe the kaleidoscope
of blues and grays, ever-shifting...ever true.

As the energy between them grew taut, the butterflies
that had long lain dormant in her belly took flight, leaving
heated tendrils in their wake. She tugged her hand free of
his and gave him a curt smile. Physical contact with Josh
was going to have to be verboten if she was going to keep
it together for the next eight days. It was bad enough he'd
seen her red-rimmed eyes.

She glanced at her watch.

*T-minus...oh, about one hundred and ninety-two hours
and counting!*

"Twenty-four hours."

"Beg pardon?" Josh shook his head.

Hadn't he been riding the same train of thought she had?
If she'd gone off on a magical journey down memory lane,
the chances were relatively high he'd done the same thing.
Different tracks—different destinations.

She cleared her throat. There was about half an ounce of

resolve left within her and she needed to use it. "I'm giving you twenty-four hours."

He raised his eyebrows and gave her his *What gives?* face.

"Oh, don't play the fool, Josh. You've ambushed me. Pure and simple. And on—" She stopped, only just missing having her voice break. "It's the minimum notice I have to give the agency if I want a replacement."

"What are you on about, Kitty-Kat?" He pulled himself up to his full height. Josh always played fair and he could see straight through her. This was a below-the-belt move.

She jigged a nothing-to-do-with-me shrug out of her shoulders, her eyes anywhere but on his. "If it's quiet enough we might be able to let you go earlier without telling the agency."

She might not want him here, but she didn't want to tarnish his record. He was a good doctor. Just a lousy husband. She squirmed under his intent gaze, pretty sure he was reading her mind. A sort of, kind of lousy husband.

"Don't be ridiculous. Christmas is always busy! You're going to need me. What kind of man would I be, leaving you to deal with a busy ER all on your own?"

"That's terribly chivalrous of you, Josh. I'm going to need a doctor—yes. But I don't need *you*." She looked at her watch again, not wanting to see how deep her words had hit. Laceration by language was *way* out of her comfort zone—but tough. Josh had pushed her there—and she had an ER to run.

"Sorry, I've got to get to this patient."

"Yup! I'm certainly looking forward to mine!" He mimed snapping on a pair of gloves with a guess-it's-time-to-suck-it-up smile.

If she was feeling generous, she had to give it to him for keeping his cool. Assigning him a rectal examination as a "welcome gift" was not, she suspected, the reunion he had been hoping for. Then again, finding out her es-

tranged husband would be her locum for the next week
wasn't much of a Christmas present for her, so tough again!
Hadn't two years' worth of sending him divorce papers
given him enough of a clue?

"Uh… Kate?"

"Yes?"

"Are you going to move so I can get my patient's Christmas ornament back on the tree?"

"Yes!" she blurted, embarrassed to realize she'd been
staring. "Yes, of course. I was just…" She stopped. She
wasn't "just" anything. She stepped back and let him pass.

"I'm happy to see you, too, Katiebird," he said at the
doorway, complete with one of those looks she knew could
see straight through to her soul.

She rubbed her arms to force the accompanying goose
bumps away.

"Me, too," she whispered into the empty room. "Me,
too."

"Hello, there… Mr. Kingston? I understand you've got a
bleeding—" Katie swiftly moved her eyes from the chart
to the patient, instantly regretting that she'd wasted valuable time away from her patient.

Unable to resist the gore factor, the young man had lowered his hand below his heart and tugged off the temporary
tourniquet the nurse had put in place. Blood was spurting
everywhere. If he hadn't looked so pale she would have told
him off, but Ben Kingston looked like he was about to—

Oops!

Without a moment to spare Katie lurched forward, just
managing to catch him in a hug before he slithered to the
floor.

"Can I get a hand in here? We've got a fainter!"

Katie was only just managing to hold him on the exam
table and smiled in thanks at the quick arrival of— Oh. It
was Josh. *Natch.*

He quickly assessed the situation, wordlessly helping Katie shift the patient back onto the exam table, checking his airways were clear, loosening the young man's buttoned-at-the-top shirt collar and loosening his snug belt buckle by a much-needed notch or two as she focused on stanching the flow of blood with a thick stack of sterile gauze.

"Got a couple extra pillows for foot elevation?"

"Yup." Katie pointed to the locker where they stored extra blankets and pillows. "Would you mind handing me a digital tourniquet first? I'll see if I can stem the bleeding properly while he's still out."

"Sure thing." Josh stood for a moment, gloved hands held out from his body as they would be in surgery, and ran his eyes around the room to hunt down supplies.

"Sorry, they're in the third drawer down— Wait!" Her eyes widened and dropped to Josh's gloved hands. "Weren't you in the middle of…?"

She felt a sharp jag of anger well up in her. *Typical, Josh!* Running to the rescue without thinking for a single moment about protocol! Was simple adherence to safe hygiene practices too much to ask?

"Done and dusted." He nodded at the adjacent exam area. "He's going through the paperwork with Jorja." He took in her tightened lips and furrowed eyebrows and began to laugh. Waving his hands in the air, still laughing, he continued, "You didn't think…? Katie West—"

"It's McGann," she corrected quietly.

"Yeah, whatever." The smile and laughter instantly fell away. "I always double-glove during internal exams. These are perfectly clean. You should know me better than that." His eyes shifted away from hers to the patient, the disappointment in his voice easy to detect. "You good here?"

She nodded, ashamed of the conclusion she'd leaped to. Josh was a good doctor. Through and through. It was the one thing she'd never doubted about him. He had a natural bedside manner. An ability to read a situation in an instant. Instinctual. All the things she wasn't.

She slipped the ringed tourniquet onto the young man's finger and checked his pulse again. It wasn't strong, but he'd be all right with a bit of a rest and a finger no longer squirting an unhealthy portion of his ten pints of blood everywhere. He'd need a shot of lidocaine with epinephrine before she could properly sort it out, so she would need to wait for him to come to. Being halfway through an injection wasn't the time when a patient should regain consciousness. Especially when Josh was leaping through curtained cubicles, coming to her rescue. She jiggled her shoulders up and down. It wouldn't happen again.

"Are you nervous, Doc?"

"Ah! You're back with us!" Katie turned around in time to stop the young man from pushing himself up to a seated position. "Why don't you just lie back for a while, okay? I have a feeling your finger didn't start bleeding half an hour ago, like it says in your chart, Ben."

He looked at her curiously.

"Is it okay if I call you Ben?"

"You can call me what you like as long as you stitch me up and get me outta here, Doc! It's Christmas Eve. I've got places to go…things to do—"

"Someone to drive you home?" Katie interrupted. "After your fainting spell, I don't think it's a good idea for you to get behind a wheel."

"And I don't think it's a good idea for *you* to boss someone around on Christmas Eve!"

Katie backed away from Ben as his voice rose and busied herself with getting the prep tray ready. Emotions ran high on days like this. Especially if the patient had had one too many cups of "cheer." Unusual to encounter one on the day shift, but it took all kinds.

"Cheer" morphed into cantankerous pretty quickly, and

Ben definitely had a case of that going on. She stared at the curtain separating her from her colleagues, knowing she'd be better off if there was someone else in the room when she put in the stitches.

She sucked in a breath and pulled the curtain away. "Can I get a hand in here?" She dived back into the cubicle before she could see who was coming. Josh or no Josh, she needed to keep her head down and get the work done.

"Everything all right, Dr. McGann?"

At the sound of Jorja's voice, Katie felt an unexpected twist of disappointment. It wasn't like she'd been hoping it would be Josh. Her throat tightened. *Oh, no...* Of all the baked beans in Boston Harbor... Had she? *Clear your throat. Paste on a smile.*

"Yes, great. Thank you, Jorja. Nothing serious, just thought we could do with an extra pair of hands now that Mr. Kingston here has rejoined us."

Josh tried his best to focus on the intern's voice as he talked him through how he saw things panning out on Christmas Eve based on absolutely zero experience, but he couldn't. All he could hear was Katie, talking her patient and the nurse through the procedure in that clear voice she had. The patient had definitely enjoyed a bit of Christmas punch before he'd arrived, and Josh didn't trust him not to start throwing a few if he was too far gone.

"Hey." He interrupted the intern. "What did you say your name was again?"

"Michael," the young doctor replied, unable to keep the dismay from his face. He'd been on a roll.

Tough. Fictional projections weren't going to help what was actually happening.

"Michael, what's your policy on patients who've had a few too many?" He mimed tossing back some shots.

"Oh—each ER head is different, but Katie usually calls

the police." He looked around the ER as if expecting to see someone stagger by. "Why?"

"Just curious." He gave Michael's shoulder a friendly clap with his hand, hoping it would bring an end to the conversation. "Thanks for all the tips," he added, which did the trick.

He tuned his hearing back into the voices behind the curtain where Katie was working. The patient was young and obviously a gym buff. As strong and feisty as she was, Katie was no match for a drunk twenty-something hell-bent on getting more eggnog down his throat. Drunk drivers on icy roads were the last thing the people of Copper Canyon needed on Christmas Eve. Or any night, for that matter.

"Okay, Ben, you ready? I'm just going to inject a bit of numbing agent into your finger."

"What *is* that?"

Josh inched a bit closer to the curtain at the sound of the raised voice.

"It's a small dose of lidocaine with epinephrine," Katie explained. "It will numb—"

"Oh, no, you don't!" The patient—Ben, that was it— raised his voice up a notch. "I've been on the internet and that stuff makes your fingers fall off. No *way* are you putting that poison in me!"

Josh only just managed to stop an eye roll. Self-diagnosis was a growing epidemic in the ER…one that was sometimes harder to control than any actual injury.

"I think if you read all of the article you'd find that's more myth than reality."

Always sensible. That was his girl!

Ben's voice shot up another decibel. "Are you telling me I'm a *liar*?"

"No, I'm saying digital gangrene is about the last thing that's going to happen if I—"

"You—are—not—putting—that—sh—"

"Hello, ladies." Josh yanked the curtain aside, unable to stay quiet. "Need an extra pair of hands?"

"No," Katie muttered.

"Yes," Jorja replied loudly over her boss.

"They're trying to give me gangrene!"

"Really? Fantastic." Josh rocked back on his heels and grinned, rubbing his hands together in anticipation. "I haven't seen a good case of gangrene in ages." He flashed his smile directly at Katie. "Are you trying to turn Mr. Kingston here into *The Gangrene who stole Christmas*?"

Everyone in the cubicle stared at him for a moment in silence.

"The Grinch!" Josh filled in the silence. "Get it? Gangrene? Grinch?"

There was a collective headshake, which Josh waved off. "You guys are hopeless. They're both green!"

Jorja groaned as the bad joke finally clicked.

"Well," he conceded, "one's a bit more black and smelly, and isn't around for the big Christmassy finish, but, Ben, my friend…" Josh took another step into the cubicle, clapping a hand on the young man's shoulder from behind and lowering himself so that he spoke slowly and directly into the young man's ear. "I've known this doctor for a very long time, and if she needs to stabilize the neuronal membrane in your finger by inhibiting the ionic fluxes required for the instigation and conduction of nerve impulses in order to stem the geyser of blood shooting from that finger of yours, she knows what she's talking about, hear?"

Ben nodded dumbly.

"Right!" Josh raised a hand to reveal a set of car keys dangling from his fingers.

He saw Katie's eyebrow quirk upward. He would have laid a fiver on the fact she was thinking he'd taken up pickpocketing to add a bit more adrenaline to his life. He'd win the bet and she'd be wrong. He'd just seen enough drunks in his Big City ER Tour. The one where he had done everything but successfully forget the brown-eyed beauty standing right in front of him.

He cleared his throat and stepped away from Ben. "You owe Dr. We—Dr. McGann an apology. And while you do that—" he jangled the keys from his finger "—I'll just be popping these babies over to Security until we get someone to pick you up."

Ben opened his mouth to object, his eyes moving from physician to nurse and back to Josh before he muttered something about being out of order, his mother's stupid car, and then, with a sag of the shoulders, he finally started digging a cell phone out of his pocket.

"Excellent!" Josh tossed the keys up in the air, caught them with a flourish, gave Jorja a wink and tugged the curtain shut behind him before anyone could say *boo*.

"Well…" Josh heard Jorja say before he headed off. "He's certainly a breath of fresh air!"

Katie muttered something he couldn't quite make out. Probably just as well.

Josh grinned, his shoes glued to the floor until he was sure peace reigned behind Curtain Three. He heard Katie clear her throat and put on her bright voice—the one she used when she was irritated with him.

"Now, then, Ben, if you can just show me that finger of yours, we can get you stitched up and home before you know it. Jorja? Could you hand me some of the hemostatic dressing, please? We need to get the wound to clot."

Josh began to whistle "Silent Night" as he cheerily worked his way back toward the main desk. Job. Done.

"How long do you intend to continue this White Knight thing?"

Josh's instinct was to smile and tell her he would wield his lance and shield as long as it took for her to see sense and come back to him. Longer. Until the day he died, he would protect Katie. He'd taken a vow and had meant it.

He had broken part of it, and he was going to spend the rest of his life making good on it. Even if that meant walking away, no matter how hard it hurt.

But this was work. Personal would have to wait.

"Where I come from, people stick around to help one another when the going gets tough." He laid the Tennessee drawl on as thick as molasses. It always got to her and this time was no different.

He watched as her hands flew to her hips in indignation, then shifted fluidly into a protective, faux-nonchalant crossing of the arms. Her eyes widened, the lids quickly dropping into a recovery position. One of her eyebrows arched just a fraction before her face became neutral again. But she couldn't keep the flush of emotions from pinking up her cheeks.

He shifted his stance, ratcheted his satisfaction down a couple of notches. He wasn't playing fair. He knew more than anyone that teamwork in an emergency department was something Katie valued above all else. Unless, it seemed, it came from him.

He stood solidly as she gave him the Katie once-over. He wouldn't have minded taking his own slow-motion scan over the woman he'd dreamed about holding each and every night since she'd told him in no uncertain terms she'd had enough of his daredevil ways. He'd have to play it careful. Divorce rules shifted from state to state, and he hadn't checked out Idaho. If she'd moved to Texas he would have shown up a lot earlier. No need to wait for a signature there. As it was, he thought two years had given them each more than enough time to know they were meant for each other. Given *him* enough lessons to know she'd been right. He'd suffered enough loss to know it was time to change. Move forward—whatever shape that took.

"Where are you staying?"

Unexpected.

"Here." He pointed at the hospital floor.

There went that eyebrow again.

"Locum tenens wages aren't enough to get you a condo?"

He shook his head. "I didn't know how long I'd be stay-ing."

She refused to take the bait.

"Usually housing comes with the contract."

What *was* she? The contract police? Or... A lightbulb went off... Was she trying to figure out where he'd be laying his sleepy head? Was she missing being held in his arms as much as he had longed to hold her? Truth was, he never bothered with separate housing on these gigs. Hos-pital bunks suited him fine... Friends' sofas sufficed when he was back in Boston. Home was Katie, and it had been two long years...

He heard the impatient tap of her foot. Fine...he'd play along.

"Not this time of year. And it was too short a contract for me to put up a fight."

Katie's jaw tightened before she shifted her chin up-ward in acknowledgment of the obvious. She knew what he meant. The locals had dibs on all the affordable properties. Everything went to the top one hundred highest-paid, most famous, with the biggest bank account, et cetera, et cetera. Life in Copper Canyon was a heady mix of the haves and those who *worked* for the haves.

Mountain views, private access to the slopes, sunset, sunrise, heated pools, wet bars, ten thousand square feet minimum of whatever a person could desire—you name it, they had it. Copper Canyon saw most of America's glit-terati at some point, on the slopes or at one of the resorts... if, that was, they didn't have a private pad.

"You staying at your parents'? I remember them having a pretty plush pad out here and not using it all that much."

Risky question, but he couldn't imagine why else she would have moved here. She walked over to the board and began erasing patient names and rearranging a few others.

"They're usually at the Boston brownstone or in the Cayman Islands, right?"

"Jorja? Could you make sure the tablets are all updated to reflect what's on the board? We've got quite a few changes to note," Katie called over her shoulder to the main desk.

"Sure thing, Dr. McGann. On it!"

Josh leaned against the wall, one foot crossed over the other, hands stuffed in his pockets, happy to just watch her play out her ignoring game. He threw in an off-key "Rudolph the Red-Nosed Reindeer" whistle for good measure.

"And let's pop something different on the music front, Jorja. Some *nice* carols."

Josh grinned at Jorja, dropped her a wink and dropped his whistle simultaneously.

"They just don't stop, do they? Your parents?"

Only the squeak of the whiteboard pen could be heard over the usual hospital murmur.

Wow. Having a conversation with a brick wall would have yielded more return.

"The indefatigable McGanns! That's how I always thought of them."

Katie's lips tightened. She didn't do chitchat. Especially when it came to her parents. They were the source of any well-packed baggage Katie had hauled around through the years. Parents who'd discovered they hadn't really been up to parenting so had handed it over to nannies and boarding schools to do the work for them. They were harmless enough folk at a cocktail party, but he knew their lack of interest as parents hurt Katie deeply.

"I'm not staying there this week."

Interesting.

"I always stay at the hospital over Christmas," she volunteered hastily, with a quick pursing of her lips. "My parents have come in to ski for the week—"

Josh snorted and was relieved to see Katie join in with an involuntary snigger.

"Well…at least they'll look fabulous in their ski gear before they hit the cocktail circuit."

Her eyes flicked away with a shake of her head. She must have remembered she'd told herself not to enjoy being with him.

"It's easier not to get stuck in a storm if I'm here."

Wow! Two whole sentences! They were on a roll. He kept his ground. Nodded. Tried not to look too interested. He'd learned long ago that it took a lot to get Katie talking, but once you opened the floodgates…

"So…where are you really staying?"

Bang goes that theory.

"Honestly, Kit-Kat. My plan was to just stay here."

Her brown eyes were briefly cloaked by a studied blink. Then another. Her lips twitched forward for a microsecond in a moue. Was that a response to his being there? Had an image of the two of them wrapped together as they'd always been in bed flashed across her mind's eye as it had his?

He cleared his throat and shifted his stance. "Casual" was getting tough to pull off. What he wouldn't give to take the two steps separating them and start to kiss those ruby lips of hers as if each of their lives depended on it. It felt as though his did, and standing still was beginning to test his fortitude.

"I see." She abruptly turned to face the main desk, where Jorja was checking in a new patient. "We'd best get you to work, then."

Fair enough. *She wasn't saying no.*

And… A smile began to tug at the corners of his mouth. Depending on how you looked at it, Katie was saying *yes.* Yes to his staying. Yes to his being in the hospital. Yes to their being together.

Okay, it was a bit of a leap, but he was willing to take the risk. In for a penny and all that…

He pushed away from the wall and took a step behind her when she turned back to face the board, unsurprised to see her shoulders stiffen...then relax when he kept just enough space between them for her to know he wouldn't do what he'd always done before their lives had been ripped in two.

He closed his eyes and pictured the scene. She'd be studying something—anything—an X-ray, a chart, the wall—it didn't matter. He'd step right up behind her, arms slipping round her waist, hands clasped against her belly, his chin coming to a rest on her pillow of chestnut hair or slipping down alongside her cheek for a little illicit nuzzle or to drop a kiss on her neck...

He heard her sigh at the exact same time he was blowing out a long, slow breath between his lips. *Oh, yeah*. They were on the same page all right. It just hadn't been turned for a while.

"Hey, you two—you're in for the Secret Santa, right?"

Josh and Katie both whirled round to see a grinning Jorja holding out a Santa hat with folded pieces of paper being rapidly jiggled around.

"Count me in." Josh reached into the hat and grabbed a bit of paper. If he was going to show Katie he knew how to settle down, enjoy small-town life... "Who doesn't love a bit of Secret Santa action?" He turned to Katie. "That is if it's all right with the boss lady?"

"Who am I to curtail your holiday cheer and our small-town ways?"

And they were back in the ring! Three years ago the idea of going back to his small-town roots would have made him run for the hills...or the bright lights of Manhattan, more like it. But after he'd quit Boston for Manhattan, Chicago, Miami, none of them had stuck. Not one had sung to him. Nothing worked without Katie.

"I'm just a small-town boy, and nothing says home

like…" His eyes sought hers and in that instant he was sure each of them knew what he might say.

"Like what, Dr. West?" Jorja pressed.

Katie. It had always and only been Katie.

"Like having an opportunity to put down roots! In the form of a Secret Santa. I just love a good old-fashioned round of Secret Santa."

Too emphatic?

He felt Katie giving him a curious glance. *Good.* He wanted her to see the changes. Maybe not all of them. The pins in his leg could wait. And the scars along his hip and spine. It wasn't looking like she'd be ripping off his clothes for a moment of unchecked ardor anytime soon, so he was good with that. But he'd been careful that she didn't see him walk too much. She'd know. She'd definitely know. And she'd never come back to him then.

"Dr. McGann? Are you taking part in the draw?"

Jorja waggled the hat in front of his wife's face. She might be a good nurse, but that girl sure didn't read body language all that well.

He watched Katie put on her bright face and return her focus to Jorja. "Of course. In for a penny…"

Josh felt Katie's eyes land on him as the words came out of her mouth, her hand plunging into the hat blindly to grab a bit of crumpled paper.

She remembered. They'd both said it. A lot. Especially in the early days of their marriage, when they'd needed every penny to repay their medical-school bills, making their own way after just about the best elopement a couple could ever have had when Katie had decided her parents didn't deserve to put on a society wedding. A church full of her parents' business associates and bridge pals mixing with his ruckus of a family, who would show up to a black-tie event wearing their funeral clothes? No, thanks.

His lips twitched as her eyes stayed locked on his.

They'd spent just a few hundred dollars on rings, the honeymoon, and a huge chocolate cream pie that they'd set between them at a roadside diner and eaten in one go… Then, not too long after, they had been putting down deposits on cribs and—

Josh raked a hand through his hair and looked away first. It was still hard to go there. Still impossible to believe they'd really lost their little girl. That sweet little baby who'd never even had one chance to look into her parents' eyes…

"Right! You said you wanted me to get to work." He craned his neck to look around at the waiting room and stuffed the bit of paper into his lab coat pocket. "Who's next?"

Katie had to shake her head for a minute before she could think clearly. Having Josh here was like receiving a physical assault of emotions she hadn't wanted to feel again.

Pain…

She unnecessarily scrubbed her hands through her super-short hair, having forgotten, just as her eyes connected with Josh's, that she didn't have a ponytail to curl her fingers through anymore. *Yup.* The pain she could certainly do without.

Fear.

That Josh would be safe. That he'd come home from his latest escapade unscathed. That he would come home at all. Bearing another loss in the wake of their stillborn baby girl…wondering if he'd well and truly be there for her if they decided to try and conceive again… No. She just hadn't been able to do it.

Desire.

The desire felt good. *Too* good. And it was too much of a link to the pain and the fear. A trilogy of Josh, all wrapped up in a gorgeous sandy-haired, blue-eyed package she had never been able to resist. But she had to. For her sanity, first and foremost. For her heart.

"What do you think? You happy to let me go with the photocopy girl?"

"Beg your pardon?" Katie forced herself to focus on the words coming out of Josh's mouth about a patient newly arrived from an office party gone wrong. Photocopies. Bottoms. Broken glass.

His front tooth was still crooked. She'd always liked that. The imperfection made him more…perfect. Hmm… Maybe she shouldn't focus on his mouth. His eyes—definitely blue-gray in this light. Flinty? Steel-blue. Was there such a thing? And with little crinkles round the edges. Those were new. Sun, maybe? Or just the passage of the two years they'd put between them?

It might have felt like an eternity, but two years wasn't really that long. Then again, they'd been through a lot. But Josh had always seemed impervious to it all. Definitely a glass half-full— That was it! *Glasses.* He probably just needed glasses. Typical Josh to put practical needs like getting his eyes checked on hold. She tilted her head to the side. They *were* kind of sexy. The crinkles…

Nope. *Nope.* Still not hearing words. Still not focusing. What about the little bridge between his eyes? That was just like anyone else's. Just part of someone's face. A plain old face just like any other doctor in any other hospital. With a nose and high cheekbones and two perfectly formed… *Argh, no!* And she was back to his lips.

"Apologies, Dr. West." She put on her best interested face. "I didn't quite catch that."

A low laugh rumbled from his chest. Josh knew damn well she'd been ogling him and he was loving it. From the first day he'd draped a stethoscope round her neck, he'd known he had the power to cut straight through her prim-and-proper exterior and bring out the hidden tigress in her. The one she hadn't known existed. Bookish only children who preferred the company of their elderly nannies weren't obvious contenders for being horny minxes aching to see how it felt to be scooped up in a single swoop, her legs wrapped round his waist, his hands cupped on her—

"...derriere."

"Beg pardon! What was that again?"

This time Josh didn't even bother going for subtle.

"Katie, do you just wanna sneak off and make out for old times' sake while the anesthetic gets to work?"

"What? *No!*" She shook her head, sending a horrified look over her shoulder to see if anyone had overheard him. "No!" she added, with a look. She didn't *make out* with people. Let alone with the one man on the planet she needed statewide clearance from if her brain was ever going to work properly again.

She forced herself to play a quick game of catch-up.

"You say she broke her office's copy machine by sitting on it? Why on earth was she doing *that*?"

"You never butt-copied—?" Josh stopped himself, his smile shifting from astounded to tender. "It's something that happens when an office party gets out of hand. This gal clearly likes to get her cray-cray on."

"I have *no* idea what crayfish have to do with it."

"Crazy!" Josh laughed. "Cray-cray is crazy, if you're down with the kids—know what I mean?" He struck a pose for added emphasis.

Katie sniffed. She could do zany. If she put her mind to it. But photocopying her butt? That was just ridiculous. The germs on one of those things should be off-putting enough!

"Well, you two sound perfect for each other."

Katie saw the sting of hurt her words caused and wished she could yank them straight back. Josh might do wild but he also did wonderful. If only he hadn't kept pushing the boundaries after their loss. If only he'd convinced her he could play things safe—even for a while—they might...

"I best get on, then."

Katie watched as Josh turned and made his way toward the curtained cubicle where his patient was waiting. There was something…different about his gait. Something different about *him*. He'd changed. Really changed. Her teeth caught hold of her lip and gave it a contemplative scrape.

Changed enough to hear what she had to say?

A series of loud guffaws burst from the curtained area where Josh was de-sharding his patient's booty.

No. Same ol' Josh! Some stray Christmas spirit must have sneaked into her coffee that morning. No one changed *that* much. She would just see through the time they had to work together as professionally as she could. No point in reopening old wounds. She'd borne enough hurt for a lifetime.

She scanned the board and picked a good old-fashioned broken arm. Some enthusiastic decorative touches to a snowy rooftop, no doubt. Fixing. Setting. Repairing. That was what she did. It was how she survived.

Once again she shook on her bright smile and pulled open the curtain.

"Right! Mr. Dawsen, I understand you've broken your arm?"

CHAPTER THREE

"I'LL JUST BE in the residents' room—cool?" Josh popped a finished chart onto the RNs' central desk, flashing a smile to the two nurses trying to untangle a set of twinkling lights. A patient's or some late decorating? They paid him no attention, so he hightailed it down the corridor, hoping for a few moments to regroup. It was time to pull up his socks and tell Katie the truth. The real reason he was there.

She'd yanked six of his safety-net days out from under him, unwittingly putting all his partridges in the one pear tree. It was do-or-die day *now*. For a man who didn't plan much, he had definitely planned this out. A whole week to gauge her mood…time to maybe inject a bit of romance into snatched moments alone. But with this stupid twenty-four-hour thing she showed no sign of shifting from, he had to get a move on. They were just a few hours away from midnight, and once that clock pinged upon the Christmas star, his time would be well and truly running out. Josher-ella was going to have to get a move on.

He looked at his backpack, slung on the back of the lone chair parked across from the bunk he'd thrown himself on for a catnap. He wouldn't have been surprised if the sheaf of official papers lurking in the side pocket had taken on a life of their own, unzipped the bag and come out and danced at him like an evil sugarplum fairy…or whoever the evil one was in *The Nutcracker*.

He cursed silently. He'd once loved Christmas and all the schmaltzy, cheesy, sentimental stuff that went along with it. When they'd lost their daughter just a few days before the holiday, it had sucked the season dry of any good feeling. He wanted that back—and the only way to get it was to woo his wife back into his arms. And if this was the season for miracles he was a first-rate candidate.

Otherwise…? Otherwise he would have taken the job in Paris when he'd got the offer. Moved to France to study with the most elite team of minimally invasive fetoscopic surgeons? Hell, yeah! It would have been a gargantuan leap forward for his career. He'd spent the past two years doing locum residencies in every single obstetrics unit he could. He would never know why his little girl had been stillborn—but if he could help other women he'd be there.

But his heart wouldn't be. And to end up in the City of Love without the woman he adored by his side would have been pointless. Not to mention the fact that Dr. Cheval insisted on total focus. No distractions and no demons. Right now Josh was hauling those things around big-time.

When the job offer had come, he'd seen it as life's way of grabbing him by the scruff of the neck, giving him a right old shake and demanding, for once, that he take responsibility for everything he had done. Own up to how his behavior had driven his wife away. And after she'd gone he'd pushed at life a bit more. A *lot* more. Life had pushed back, and now he had the metal infrastructure to prove he hadn't come out the winner.

He gave his head a good old scratch, shooting a look up to the heavens to see if there were any clues there.

Mistletoe.

Of course. *Love.* The high-voltage current he'd felt the first, second and every other time he'd laid eyes on his wife was electric. But going to the city where hand-holding and kisses on bridges and feeding each other delectable morsels of…

Hey! Now, *there* was an idea. He and Katie had always enjoyed a good picnic. Out on the common—or on a bench if it was pouring down—regardless of the sideways glances they'd received from passersby. It was what supersized umbrellas were made for, right?

A smile lit up his face. He'd do a Christmas dinner picnic! The smile faded just as fast. The canteen was closed. The way the snow was coming down meant leaving the hospital would be a challenge. Or just plain stupid. He'd already done stupid…

"Hey, Dr. West." Jorja poked her head round the corner with an apologetic expression. "Sorry to ruin your break, but we've got mass casualties coming in!"

Adrenaline shot through him and he was up and out of the bunk before Jorja had even removed herself from the door frame.

"What happened? How many? Do we have enough on staff? Is there any chance of diverting any of the patients to another hospital?"

Jorja's eyes widened, along with her mouth. Streaks of red began to color her cheeks.

"Uh…" She pushed at the floor with the stub of her toe.

"Sorry, too much television! I forget Copper Canyon is totally different from what you get out east."

"There are two. Patients, that is. With gastro. Dr. McGann is already down there."

Josh's heartbeat decelerated and he tried not to laugh. Much. The poor girl looked mortified. He slung an arm around her shoulders and tugged her in for a half hug as they made their way out into the main corridor. "Hey, Jorja, don't you worry. I can adjust my big-city ways…"

The words stopped coming. What the heck was he doing, bragging about his big-city machismo when he'd grown up in a town with two unlit junctions? Junctions where he'd been guaranteed to see his math teacher or his father heading off to the cattle markets. There was no hiding anywhere in that place if you stuck around—which was why he'd loved losing himself in the big city. And then he'd met Katie…like an angel he hadn't known he'd needed to meet. Found him. That was what she'd done. She had found him. Shown him how important it was to be grounded.

He looked straight up, silently cursing the invisible heavens. She was his lighthouse, his beacon, his…whatever analogy best fit the scene. She was his heart. His soul. And if he didn't get a move on he was going to lose her for good.

"Uh… Dr. West? Are you trying to…?" Jorja was shifting underneath his arm, turning toward him, shifting her gaze upward as well.

Damn. Mistletoe.

Katie heard them, then saw them. A twist of nausea squirled around her stomach as she took in the nervous laughter, the awkward shuffle of feet and the chins tipping up toward the ceiling. Jorja had practically covered the hospital in mistletoe, so it was hardly surprising that the one person who would find a way to put it to use was Josh. He had always been a flirt. It was his nature. To charm, to delight, to dazzle.

She turned away quickly, not wanting either of them to see the hurt in her eyes, the sheen of tears she'd only just managed to check when she'd spotted them. The last thing she was going to do was stick around and watch her husband kiss someone he'd only just met!

At least she knew Josh showing up out of the blue wasn't some clever plot to see *her*. It was a fluke. A needle-in-a-haystack chance of Yuletide torture. *Just terrific.* She'd spent two entire years patching the shredded remains of her heart together, and just when she'd come to terms with her play-it-safe, hiding-out-in-Idaho lifestyle, Josh had parachuted in and undone years of exacting damage control.

Adrenaline began to surge through her. She tugged at the high ribbing on the neck of her sweater, suddenly wishing she had scrubs on. Why hadn't one of her patients thrown up on her? Then she could have missed this nauseating scene of mistletoe magic. She checked herself. Wishing patients ill wasn't her style, and thankfully the two gastro cases had turned out to be overindulgence rather than food poisoning.

Who ate massive portions of something called Chocolate Decadence and *didn't* expect a sore stomach? People who weren't careful. People who were reckless. People who made decisions on a whim—like Josh.

She made a beeline for the doctors' locker room and grabbed her winter coat before pushing through the heavy door into the stairwell and pounding up step after step toward the roof, letting out an involuntary wail of relief when she found it was empty.

Silent screams into blankets while trying to retain her control were one thing—but seeing Josh with another woman… Words couldn't even describe how much it had hurt. Throat-scraping wail after howl poured out of her throat as the snow bit at her cheeks and the wind swirled through her hair and into her tear-blinded eyes. Why had Josh—of all the people in the world—had to show up? Hadn't he done enough harm? It was worse than shock. It was Shock and Awful.

Chest heaving from the effort of purging her sorrow, Katie forced herself to take more level, steadier breaths. Knowing a chill could turn into pneumonia in the blink of an eye at this time of year, she excavated a woolly hat from the depths of her pocket. She hadn't let those Girl Scout sessions go to waste.

Prepared at all times. Self-contained at all times. She tugged on her hat and scowled. Which one had she left out?

"And a smile in the face of adversity."

Katie's frown deepened. She turned this way and that, taking in the roof as though she were a child stuffed into an over-thick snow outfit. The urge to throw a tantrum was welling within her again. Twice in one day? Must be a record! Maybe she should have gone the bad-girl route as a kid. It might have garnered her a bit more attention from her parents.

She harrumphed. Unlikely.

She pulled out her phone and trawled a finger along the not-very-long list of names to see if there was anyone on there she could talk to. Colleague. Colleague. Colleague. Mentor. Nanny.

Alice Worthing! Her shoulders softened. She had absolutely *loved* her Irish nanny. Alice was the only person she'd told in advance of her elopement, and the second she'd seen the twinkle in the dear woman's eyes, she'd known she was doing the right thing.

Wow—had they both been wrong!

She pushed at the phone symbol anyhow. It would be nice to hear a friendly voice on Christmas Eve.

After a couple of rings she heard laughter and then the lilted *hello* she knew so well. Fifteen years in the US, married to an American for ten of them, and her accent hadn't changed a jot.

"Hello? Is anyone there?"

Katie started. "Sorry, Alice. It's me, Katie Wes—Katie McGann."

"Katie! My sweet Katie. Darlin', how the devil are you? It's been so long. *Too* long! What is it? Over a year now since you went out west. Are you all right, love? Is everything okay?"

"Yes. Fine." She kicked her boot into the thick rooftop snow.

"Well, that's a lie and we both know it."

Katie smiled at the phone, double-checking that she hadn't video-dialed her friend by accident.

"It's just—I—um—wanted to wish you a merry Christmas."

"Well, that's a lovely sentiment, Katie, but why not tell me the real reason you called?"

"I'd forgotten how quickly you see through me." Katie grinned, now wishing she *had* video-called Alice.

"Well, you and I both know how precious life is, so come on—spit it out."

"Josh."

"Oh, Katie, no—nothing's happened to Josh, has it?"

"No! God, no!" Katie felt surprised at how glad she was that was true. She might not want to be married to him, but she couldn't bear the thought if… "He's shown up at the hospital as my locum."

Another round of laughter followed as Alice called out to her husband, saying Josh had found Katie. She heard the click of the receiver as Alice's husband got on the line.

"So he finally tracked you down, did he?" James's deep voice rumbled down the line. "He tried to plumb us for info but we didn't breathe a word. We knew you wouldn't want us getting involved. Want me to come out and beat him up for you?"

Katie knew he was joking, but James had always been very protective of her. Her relationship with her own father had never been a close one, so she liked James's concern.

"What sort of nonsense are you talking, man?" Alice hushed him. "Josh's dead romantic. Always was. A bit wild, but showing up on Christmas Eve and all…"

"It wasn't exactly as if they left things on a good note," James riposted.

"Yeah…well…" Katie's mind whirred, trying to catch up with everything as Alice and James bantered. "He came and asked you where I was?"

"Course he did. The boy's mad for you. Always was."

Then why was he trying to kiss Jorja?

Katie and Alice talked for what felt like hours. They had a lot to catch up on. But as the roar of doorbells and barking dogs started to drown out their voices, Katie knew she had to let Alice get back to her own life. She tipped her head to see if she could differentiate between clouds and the falling snow.

"Sorry, Katie. Our little girls' choir has just shown up to sing carols. Please forgive me but I need to go. You'll sort it out for the best. You always do. Lots of love."

"Oh! How is Catherine?"

"She's grand, darlin'. Must dash, but call again soon!"

And the line went dead.

Katie didn't know if she felt better or worse for having made the call. A thousand questions and no answers added to her frustration. She kicked a satisfying lump of snow up into the glowering sky and watched it float back down to the rooftop.

The helicopter hadn't been used in a while, and from the looks of things, the crew hadn't been up yet with the blower. The snow was a good foot deep where she was standing. The drifts were deeper over by the edges. A good three feet by now. Maybe deeper. Winter had started early in Copper Canyon, and no matter how hard they tried to stay on top of the accumulating snow, they couldn't. Which, in this case, was all right. Because it was…beautiful.

She felt the fight go out of her. Maybe that had been her problem all along. Trying too hard to control things. Josh. Herself. She'd even broken down the seven stages of grief, giving herself a month to go through each stage, fastidiously identifying and eradicating anything that would hold back her progress to—to what, exactly?

Josh's angry words came back to her in echoing anvils

of self-recognition. *Micromanager. Risk-averse. Exacting perfectionist! Control freak.*

The last one wilted her shoulders into a hunch against the buffeting wind. She looked around the roofscape again, as if it would conjure Josh up from the lower reaches of the hospital so he could call her out himself. Except the only voice she heard those words in was her own. *She* was the one who had shaken off the rest of the words he'd said and turned those remaining into insults. The words she wouldn't let herself remember?

Gorgeous. My love. Sweetheart. Angel. Darlin'.

She blinked away the sting of tears. When things had been good between them, they had been, oh, *so* good. Josh had given her reserves of strength she hadn't known she had. Lit her up like a…oh, the irony…lit her up like a Christmas tree!

She blinked again, feeling a tear drop this time. She swiped it away and tried to shake off the memories. She was in a new place now, and up until the start of this double shift on Christmas Eve, things had been pretty good. Well… She tugged a foot through the snow and stomped toward the roof edge.

Neutral.

How pathetic was that? Even *she* had to snicker at herself. To aspire to have a *neutral* day? Wow! That elite education she'd aced had *really* prepared her for life. She scrunched her eyes tight and forced herself to open them with the promise of seeing something that made her smile.

Not too far away the twinkling lights of Copper Canyon's main street were glittering away like a perfectly decorated window display. The town council always did well. Never too opulent, never mistaking the decor for any holiday other than Christmas. At the far end of Main Street, where the two-lane road split and circled round the town's green, an enormous evergreen twinkled and shone like a bejeweled Fabergé egg through the fat snowflakes swirling around it. At the base of the tree, Katie could make out the lit outline of the bandstand, its columns rising in twisted swirls of red and white lights.

She reached the edge of the roof and eyed the drift. Higher than she'd thought. Enough snow to cloak the thick safety barriers she knew ran around the edges. She should make a note to hospital admin that they really must be raised—

She checked herself. As far as she knew, she was the only one who was mad enough to come up to the roof in the middle of a snowstorm.

See, universe? Katie McGann can be just as much of a nut burger as the rest of them!

She gave the elements a satisfied grin as she pulled her emergency pair of waterproof mittens from the inner pocket of her down jacket.

Well…pragmatism *was* useful. And it was hardly a storm. A bit of wind. Thick latticed snowflakes big enough to catch on her tongue. She eyed the split-level roof just below her. The empty administrative offices…

She pushed her lips in and out as she considered. Without snow…? Maybe a six-foot drop. With snow…? Hmm… two feet of emptiness before she hit several feet of fluffy virgin snow. Her mind shot back to the rare trips up to her late grandparents' cabin in Vermont, where she, Alice and her grandmother had made endless snow angels.

"Always room for more angels to look out for us." That was how her grandmother had put it. So when she was upset and there was some snow to hand…snow angel. Magic recipe for a better mood.

Would it be fluffy enough to…? *Yeah…why not?* She could throw caution to the wind as easily as the next person…right?

She opened her arms wide, eyed the tilt of the snowdrift, turned around and began to press her weight into her heels. She wobbled for a moment…regained her footing…then reasoned with herself that this was precisely the sort of litmus test she needed to pass in order to prove she could well and truly survive without Josh…beyond *neutral*.

She sucked in a breath and smiled—at the world for just being there and being all snowy and twinkly so that she could make a snow angel when she sure as hell needed one.

As she shifted her heels along the edge again and raised her arms, the door to the stairwell burst open. Josh was calling out her name at ten decibels. His face was a mix of horror and fear when his eyes lit upon her. He called her name again, the vowels bending and elongating in the wind.

"Kaaa-tieee!"

Their eyes connected in a way they never had before. For the first time she saw he had been through it, too. The harrowing, mind-numbing pain of loss. And in that moment she wished back the two years they had spent apart.

Josh watched in horror as Katie's arms windmilled for balance. His eyes raced down her legs as she shifted her heels to regain traction on the icy ledge. Each micro-move she made became overexaggerated with her fruitless efforts to stay upright. Their eyes stayed locked as she completely lost her footing and fell helplessly back into the void.

Never in his life had he felt such searing pain. He had thought the grief at losing his daughter was the worst thing he could have lived through, but losing Katie as well would kill him.

An infinity of darkness spread out before him as he shouted and stumbled toward the edge, not even sure he was making a single sound above the howling in his skull.

Katie's comprehension of the world shifted as her body lost its fight with gravity. Apart from the terror she'd seen in her husband's eyes, she suddenly understood what he meant about the freedom in letting go. Just the release of falling backward was exhilarating.

She opened her throat and screamed as sensations hit her in surreal hits of slow-motion recognition. The breeze swept past her cheeks. She blinked away a snowflake. With the surprise of the fall she'd lost her sense of where she was actually falling. It might have gone on forever.

The sky was astonishingly textured with clouds and the odd hit of stars… When was the last time she'd just looked up and enjoyed the sky?

Before she could take it all in, she hit the powdery snow with a fluffy *ploof!* and lay utterly still as her breath came back to her.

A dim awareness of sound came to her. A male voice. *Josh!* It had to be Josh. Her mind whirled into catch-up mode, her eyes widening as she realized what she was hearing.

"Katie! No!"

Ragged. Rough. Grief-stricken. Why was Josh so upset? She was just making a snow angel, for heaven's sake.

His face appeared over the edge, his features etched with anxiety.

"I fell."

"Yes!" The air came out of his mouth in thick, billowed huffs of breath. "Yes, you did."

"It's nice down here." She saw the sheen of tears rise in his eyes before he had a chance to disguise it as something else. Josh had never been a weeper. He swiped at his eyes with his sleeve. Maybe she'd been mistaken.

"Are you all right?"

Katie could tell Josh was trying to keep his voice under control. Behave as if he saw his estranged wife fall off the edge of a building every day. It suddenly struck her that his reaction was utterly different from what she would have expected. The old Josh would have just leaped over the edge and joined her. Pulled her into his arms and then, after a deep, life-affirming kiss, would have made snow angels with her. Right?

"Katie?" Josh knelt on the ledge and began to scan her acutely for injury. "Are you okay?"

"Pretty good." She moved her arms and legs just a little bit, suppressing a surprise hit of the giggles as she did so. Nothing hurt. She'd landed on an enormous pillow of snow, for heaven's sake! "Actually..." She met his eyes properly this time. "It was pretty fun."

"Fun, huh? Is that what you think? Near enough giving me a heart at—?"

He stopped himself and she watched silently as Josh re-arranged his features into a long, studied look before visibly deciding to swallow whatever lecture he'd been about to give. She knew the expression well...and it gave her a hit of understanding she hadn't known she needed. It was the look Josh must have seen on *her* face time and again after they'd lost their baby girl and he'd come back from yet another high-octane experience.

Josh looked away from Katie and gave the vista a scan. The early-evening gloaming left hints of light on the tips of the mountains...gave the glittering Main Street more of a festive punch. His lips thinned as he slowly inhaled and exhaled, trying to get his racing heart under control.

His relief at finding Katie alive and well was morphing into anger. How *dare* she do this? Take such a huge risk? Didn't she know how precious she was to him? His anger welled up further into his chest, searing him from the inside out. *How dare she?*

"A thank-you for stopping you killing yourself might be nice."

"Killing myself?" She pushed herself up to sit and squinted at him through the falling snow. "You think if I—Katie West—Katie McGann," she corrected herself, annoyed, "was going to do something so stupid as to kill myself I'd do it by jumping two feet into a snowdrift?"

"That was difficult to see from the doorway." Josh cleared his throat again and swore under his breath. "So you weren't—?"

"Of course I wasn't. I was just…" She let herself plop back into the lightly compacted drift. "I was just trying to make a snow angel."

She spoke softly. More truculent than apologetic, but, hell, he'd take it. She was alive. That was good enough for now.

He tipped his head to the side and eyed her. "You only make snow angels when you're upset."

"No, I don't!" she shot back, her eyes anywhere but meeting his.

Yup! She was upset. He knew his arrival had upset her, but he hadn't thought launching herself into a snowdrift four floors off the ground would be her response. Maybe he should have called. Scheduled lunch. Done something normal, like she'd been begging him to do all along.

He knelt on the ledge and hitched up his bad leg before slipping over into the snow mattress Katie was pillowed in. He winced. The old-timers were right about feeling the cold differently once your body had proved itself fallible.

He gave her a grumpy glare and flopped down onto the snow beside her, where they lay in silence for a few moments. He'd thought he'd lost her just now. Lost the love of his life.

Okay, firebrand…cool your jets. You've both had a shock.

He shot a sidelong glance at Katie and saw her all wide-eyed and… *Seriously?* Was she *grinning?* That grin near enough sucker punched the rest of the breath out of his chest and he only just managed to reel in the angry words.

His emotions were running so wild it was impossible to tell if he should just whip out those stupid divorce papers and give her his signature right now. Then maybe they could both get on with their lives.

He swiped at the snowflakes clustering on his lashes. There was no way he could move on. Not like this. Not yet. And if Katie didn't give a monkey's about him she wouldn't be flinging herself off the sides of buildings on Christmas Eve. So…it was a silver-linings moment. A weird one. But a moment to count himself lucky. Blessed.

It didn't stop him from needing to expunge a bit of "grumpy," though.

Eyes rigidly glued to the heavens, he leveled his voice before starting. "Well, isn't *this* cozy?"

"That's one way of putting it," Katie grumbled.

"This a new Idaho thing? Hurling yourself off the side of buildings without an audience?"

"Something like that."

"Any reason in particular, or did whimsy just overtake you?"

"Yeah," she bit back drily. "That's how I roll. Got it in one, Josh. Crazy Katie West, hitting the fast lane again!"

"West?" He tried not to sound hopeful.

"Whoever."

He let the words settle for a moment. It took one to know one, and she was calling him out. She always read life's instruction book. He barely looked at the book's cover before flinging it away and just going for it. Especially once he'd met his wife. With Katie by his side he had felt invincible.

"It was pretty reckless." He couldn't stop the words choking him as they came out. He sounded like his dad.

"Yeah? Well, the fact you couldn't see the four-foot-deep drift of snow I was aiming for probably gave you the wrong idea. I calculated the risk in advance and determined there was little to no damage that could come to a girl trying her best to have a little *alone time* and make herself a blinking snow angel! And if you want to talk about reckless, you'd better be careful with Jorja. She's got a reputation."

Josh pushed himself up on his elbows and gave her his best *what are you talking about?* look. "Jorja?"

"Yes. Jorja." Her voice went singsong as her hands started to make the beginnings of angel wings in the snow. "Josh and Jorja, sitting in a tree…"

"What are you talking about?"

"The mistletoe?" Her arm movements widened and her legs joined in, occasionally giving his own hand or leg a bash as she worked out her frustration on her snow angel.

"You think I made out with Jorja under some mistletoe?" His voice rang with pure incredulity.

"I *saw* you!" Katie all but snarled.

"No, you did *not!*" Josh retorted, dredging up his best five-year-old's retorts. "You might've seen me standing there—but dodging mistletoe in that hospital of yours is as easy as avoiding patients!"

"Which—by the looks of things—you're doing a pretty good job of. You were hired to work—not to gallop round like an errant King Arthur, swooping up damsels in distress at every hint of a berry! You're a doctor, if my memory serves me correctly! Shouldn't you be behaving responsibly for once? *Doctoring?*"

Katie's words hit him with rapid-fire precision—her body was moving as quickly as she could speak. Josh had never seen her like this—in full flow. Her arms and legs swinging hither and yon. It was going to be one hell of a snow angel.

He couldn't let her words go. Wouldn't stay silent. He was hurting, too. Always had. Putting on a brave face had been the hardest thing he'd done, but he'd thought that was what she'd needed from him.

"You're the one in charge, Katie. Shouldn't you be down there, bossing people around? Making sure everything's in order? Everything in its right place?"

Again and again he'd bitten back words like these in the depths of their grief. But this was Last Chance Saloon time.

Despite the widening shock in her dark eyes, the words continued to fly, unchecked, past his lips.

"C'mon, Katie—you always seemed to know what was best for me. What would you advise? What would you suggest I do now?"

"What—what do you mean?" She pushed herself up to stand, distractedly brushing the snow off her clothes, discomfort taking the place of fury.

"You're really good at laying down guidelines. Heaven knows how they're getting on down there without little Miss Perfect dotting the 'I's and crossing the 'T's. How would you *recommend* I comfort myself after seeing my wife take a swan dive off of a building?"

He was all but shouting, rising to his full height before they both awkwardly swung themselves over onto the roof, then stood for who knew how long like two cowboys frozen in a standoff.

"I wasn't—" Katie finally broke the silence then stopped herself, unable to resist glaring at him while she tried to regain her composure. Her common sense.

They'd had a variation on this fight a thousand times and she didn't have it in her to have it again. Didn't want to. She'd seen the fear in his eyes and she'd never meant to be cruel to him. Not then. Not now. But this very moment was proof positive that they couldn't be together. Not when they couldn't even bring a bit of good out of the other as they had once done. They needed to wrap this up. It was the only way to go forward.

"Why are you here, Josh? What exactly is it that you want?"

"You," he answered. "I came here because I want *you*."

The air between them grew electric. With unspoken words. Unspent desire.

His blue eyes told her a thousand things at once. Gone was the recrimination. The anger. In their place was the heady, crackling energy that had never failed to draw them together. Katie hadn't realized how much she missed Josh on a physical level.

He didn't wait for an invitation.

Two of his long-striding steps and he'd pulled her up and into his arms. All thought was gone. She was reduced to sensation only, such was the power of his touch. She felt his lips against hers, both urgent and tender. Her every pore ached with the immediacy of her body's response to his touch. Winter jackets, woolen hats, leather gloves—none of the clunky gear of the season detracted from the pure, undiluted hunger Katie was experiencing.

Somewhere out there in the far reaches of her mind she knew she should be pushing him away. Knew she shouldn't be returning hungry kiss after kiss, each one filled with two years' worth of need. His hands cupped her jaw as the kisses grew deeper still. A low moan met one of his as they pressed tightly against the other. Everything felt familiar and new—as it always had—but their connection was... It felt unbreakable. Timeless.

Had she been wrong to send him away?

A vibration jostled at her waistline. Her pager.

Another one sounded. Josh's.

She pulled back, wondering if her mouth looked as bruised with kisses as Josh's did. Her fingers fumbled with the pager, her eyes still glued to her husband's face.

He was part of her. She knew that now. Making him leave had been ridiculous. No amount of time or distance could sever the ties between them. But what they had wasn't healthy. Wasn't meant for long-term—especially if she were ever, one day, to hold a baby of her own in her arms.

"Multiple injuries. We'd better get down there."

"What?" Katie shook her head clear of the "Josh and baby" fog.

"Read your pager. Ambulances are due in a few minutes."

"Right. Yes." She grabbed her phone from her pocket, relieved it hadn't been lost to the snowdrift in her snow-angel frenzy, and punched out the numbers of the ER desk. "It's Dr. McGann. Are the teams setting up the trauma units?"

Josh watched as Katie listened, responded, thumbed away the stray wisps of lipstick from around her mouth and tugged her clothes back into place. Moment by moment she became Dr. McGann again. This reinvention of herself who was all business. The Katie he'd first met. Not the one who came alive each time they touched or when their eyes lit upon the other. *This* Katie's eyes were near enough devoid of life. His heart ached to put back each and every spark he knew lay dormant within them. Now wasn't the time.

He shifted his hips. His body was trying to fight down the force of desire kissing Katie had elicited in him. She felt good. Ridiculously good in his arms. It made the idea of Paris even more insane if she weren't by his side.

The peal of ambulance sirens became faintly audible.

If he'd had a spare half hour he would have made a snowman up here and then kung fu'd its head off. It would have been satisfying. For about a second.

He shook his head and took up the pace Katie was setting to the roof door. At least he knew work would keep him distracted for the next hour or five, depending upon how bad the traumas were. Snow and automobiles? The onset of darkness on Christmas Eve, when everyone's expectations were just a little bit higher than any other time of year...? Yeah. It wasn't going to be pretty. Not in the slightest.

CHAPTER FOUR

KATIE STOPPED IN her tracks. Now, *this* she certainly hadn't expected. The first ambulance had pulled into the covered bay with a horse trailer attached to it, and the crew, along with the help of a teary girl dressed up as the Virgin Mary, were unloading a donkey.

"Can you help Eustace, please?" the girl wailed when her eyes lit on Katie.

Eustace the donkey?

"Ooh! A nativity donkey!" Jorja appeared alongside Katie, rubbing her hands together and blowing on them as her feet sashayed her from side to side.

"I think we'd better take a look at *you* first." Katie's eyes were on the girl who, through the folds of her costume, was clutching her side. "What's your name, hon?"

"Maddie."

"What a lovely name! Is there anyone you can leave in charge of the—Eustace—while we bring you inside?"

"No!" The girl's eyes widened in fear, and as she and the donkey stepped into the bright light of the ambulance bay outside the ER, Katie could see she also had a cut on her forehead over what appeared to be a growing lump. "I am not leaving Eustace. He is my best friend and we have to get to Bethlehem tonight!"

"Maybe we can find a hitching post for Eustace."

"But he's bleeding!"

"What have we got here?"

Josh's voice shot along Katie's nervous system as she approached Maddie. Her fingers flew automatically to her lips, and she wished the remembered pulse of their kisses weren't so vivid. She pushed down the thoughts and forced herself to focus. A Mary intent on getting to Bethlehem and a donkey with quite a serious cut to his haunch. Hospital protocol to adhere to...

A lightbulb went off. Josh's passion for medicine had come about by fixing the local wildlife and working under the wing of the country vet on the ranch his father had managed. It wasn't really playing by the rulebook, but... Were there different rules at Christmas? Or at least a bit of Yuletide flexibility? The emergency vets were on the other side of town, and using ambulances to tow livestock trailers had already been done—

"What do you say we pop you on a gurney, Maddie? Out here? That way Dr. McGann can take a look at you and I can stitch up... What did you say your pal's name was?"

Mind reader.

"Eustace!" Maddie replied with a broad smile, then another wince.

"Eustace! I had an Uncle Eustace, and he was as stubborn as a mule. Did you say your Eustace was a mule or a donkey?"

"A donkey! Can't you tell the difference?" Maddie giggled through her pain.

Katie couldn't fight the smile his words brought. Josh's way with patients—especially children—had always been second to none. He still had the magic touch. Something she'd worked hard at and never fully achieved. Especially after the baby.

The thought instantly sobered her. They had two or even three more ambulances due in from the same crash, so they needed to get down to business, bedside manner or no. Maddie's parents, or whoever had been driving the truck pulling the trailer, must be incoming. Otherwise they surely would have shown up with Maddie and Eustace.

"Jorja, can you—?"

"Already on it!" the nurse called, halfway through the electric doors.

"Hey, fellas!" Josh was signaling to the ambulance drivers to move the livestock trailer outside of the bay so the other ambulances would have room to pull in when they arrived.

Katie's two interns had appeared, with a gurney each, and Jorja had shouldered an emergency medical kit.

"Where would you like this one, Dr. McGann?" asked Michael. She smiled gratefully at the curly-haired intern and pointed over to a well-lit spot by the sliding doors. He was quiet—very committed and ultraserious. Birds of a feather. They got on well.

"Make sure those brakes are on." She pointed at the gurney wheels. If they needed to whisk Maddie inside for any reason, they could—but out here they needed to be as safe as possible.

"Where are your parents, honey?"

"Be careful with his halter." Maddie's eyes were glued on Josh as he expertly knotted Eustace to a pillar, petting and soothing the donkey, who seemed also to have fallen under Josh's spell. *Dr. Doolittle strikes again!*

Maddie threw tips at Josh for keeping Eustace happy, her fears about his welfare quelled by his verbal updates. Katie gave an internal sigh of relief. If Maddie had been in that livestock trailer when the crash happened, she was bound to have had a heck of a knock, and inspections for broken ribs were less than fun. If she was properly distracted that would help.

"We're going to put a little numbing agent on Eustace's rump, here. Is that all right, Maddie? Do we need your parents' permission to go ahead and give him stitches?"

Katie shot him a look. She received a nod of response.

One that said he knew what was going on and was playing the Distraction Whilst Gathering Information Game.

"Michael," she whispered, "can you get me some scissors, please? We need to cut these off." Katie needed to get the layers of robes off Maddie without moving her ribs. If she lifted the robes off over the girl's head and there had been any acute breaks or internal injuries, the movement might make things worse. Broken ribs were one thing… Punctured lungs were a whole new kettle of fish.

"Dr. McGann." Shannon, her other intern, tapped her on the shoulder, magically appearing with a pair of scissors in hand. "A second ambulance is five minutes out. They've got a male patient presenting with suspected fractured wrist and extensive leg injuries and another young adult male presenting with a broken nose and other minor injuries from an air bag."

Katie nodded whilst deftly dividing the robes of Maddie's costume. The girl's face was growing paler, and the sooner she could get her lying down for an examination the better. "Want to give me a hand here, Shannon?"

"Sure, but don't you want me to do the incoming—?"

Shannon was always keen to be first on scene for whatever "A-list" injuries came through the emergency room doors, but Katie had been very careful to divvy them out between her gore-hungry intern and Michael, whose "ladies first" attitude Katie hadn't quite figured out. Nervous or just genuinely polite?

Tonight wasn't about politics, though. It was about priority.

"If you could help me get Maddie out of these robes and then make sure there are two triage areas prepped, nurses on standby with gurneys and a couple of wheelchairs, that would be great. There doesn't sound like much the EMTs won't be able to handle in terms of stabilizing. Let X-Ray know someone will be on the way up."

Shannon's lips pursed in disappointment, and Katie

knew better than to think the evening would run smoothly. If you relaxed, things went south. That was how it worked in an ER. That was how it worked in life.

"Ouch!" Maddie gasped and wobbled.

Katie and Shannon each reached for an elbow as the last of the biblical robes dropped away. Maddie's hands flew to her side, where blood was seeping through her shirt, and Eustace brayed softly, as if he knew his owner was in pain.

"You cut my robes?" Maddie was properly tearful now.

"Easy there, boy. I just need you to stay steady," Josh was saying.

"It's all right, honey. We can get those stitched back up for you—no problem."

Katie's eyes flicked back to Josh as he made a general callout for an electric shaver. The donkey's winter coat was making the topical numbing agent less effective, and she could tell he was trying to play by the rules as much as possible. They could use xylocaine without too many questions. But proper injectable painkillers…? Less easy to explain where vials of lidocaine were—much less to write up a chart for Eustace. Off the books was best—even if it bent the rules.

Katie thought for a second of stopping him. This was how doctors got fired. Risks. She never took risks. Josh never needed to think twice about it.

"Nurse!" he called, without looking up from what he was doing.

Katie flinched infinitesimally as Jorja appeared by Josh's side in an instant. He had said it was all a mistake. The mistletoe mishap…

She pulled her gaze back to Maddie, whose eyes were widening at the sight of the blood on her white shirt.

"It's all right, Maddie. Let's get you up on the gurney, honey." She looked at Michael, who had arrived back at Maddie's other side. "On three." They eased Maddie up and onto the gurney on her count. "Right! Let's check you out. I'm going to have to lift up your shirt, and it's pretty cold out here. Are you sure you don't want to go inside?"

"No!" There was no mistaking the determination in the girl's voice. "Where Eustace goes, I go." She twisted suddenly, trying to get a better look at her pricked-eared pal. Her eyes tightened with pain. "It hurts to breathe."

Fear suddenly entered the little girl's eyes. She couldn't be more than eleven…but Katie was sure an old soul was fueling her.

"Lie down again, hon. I think you might've bruised a couple of ribs. Michael, could you get me a couple of blank—?"

"Already on it, Doc."

Katie rucked up Maddie's shirt, relieved to see the bleeding was from a gash and nothing more. But in a dirty livestock trailer? They'd have to put a booster tetanus shot on the girl's tick-list as well.

She tried to go for Josh-casual. "Say, it looks like you and Eustace are both going to be getting stitches tonight."

A grin lit up the girl's face. "Really?"

Hmm… Josh-casual obviously works.

A sting of guilt shot through her at the words she had flung at him when things had seemed too dark to continue. *Reckless. Unthinking. Careless.* Maybe his laissez-faire attitude had been to soothe her. To comfort her in a time of great sorrow.

She swallowed hard and continued her examination of Maddie.

"That hurts!" Maddie yelped.

"That's your rib cage acting up. Where exactly were you when the accident happened?"

"With Eustace."

Katie's eyes widened, her suspicions confirmed. *Well, that was just about as health and safety unconscious as things got.*

"And your parents let you ride in there?"

Maddie's eyes began to dart around the covered area. "Not exactly…"

"Who was driving the tow vehicle?"

"My bro—" She reconsidered giving the information, swallowing the rest of the word. Tears sprang into her eyes. "Am I going to get in trouble?"

"No, honey. Of course not. But riding in trailers with live—with Eustace—isn't really legal."

"Are my brothers going to jail?"

Katie's eyes shot across to meet Josh's, but he was one hundred percent focused as stitch after stitch brought the sides of the cut on Eustace's rump neatly together. She had always loved watching Josh's hands at work. They were large, capable hands. The intricate work they completed with skillful dexterity always surprised her.

Just as easy to picture him whipping a lasso into action as he had when he was a boy as it was to see him deftly tying a miniature knot at the end of a row of immaculate stitches as he was now.

"Probably best if you keep pneumonia out of the symptoms…"

Josh didn't look up as he spoke, but he had always had a second sense for when Katie's eyes were trained on him. She stiffened. It wasn't often he had to remind her to keep her eye on the ball. The role reversal didn't sit well.

"Maddie?" Josh raised his voice a bit. "Eustace is doing pretty good, here. Mind if I snaffle him some carrots from somewhere, then let him have a bit of a lie-down in the trailer?"

"That would be nice." Maddie sniffled, her fear and pain visibly kicking up a notch. "There are carrots already in the trailer."

"Michael." Katie snapped into action. "Let's tuck these blankets round Maddie and get her a tetanus shot before bringing her up to X-Ray, please, to check on her ribs. Maddie, honey, Michael's going to need your parents' phone number so we can get in touch—just to okay any treatment you're going to need, all right?"

"You're not going to let them arrest my brothers, are you? We just wanted to get to the nativity early!"

Tears began to pour out of Maddie's blue eyes and Katie's heart all but leaped to her throat. There was such love and protectiveness in her words. "Why don't we take things one at a time? We'll call your parents, sort you out, and then deal with everything else as and when it happens."

"Do you think there will be an angel looking after my brothers?"

"Dr. McGann?" Jorja stuck her head through the sliding doors. "That second ambulance is incoming."

"I sure do, Maddie," said Katie. And she meant it. "This is Michael—Dr. Rainer. He's going to take you up to X-Ray. We'll see you in a little bit, all right?"

"Okay…" The young girl snuffled. Her head turned to find Josh within sight. "Thanks for looking after Eustace."

"You bet, kiddo. It was my pleasure." Josh flashed her one of his warm smiles and gave her arm a quick squeeze before Michael and a nurse wheeled her off to the ER.

The wail of the sirens grew louder and Katie ripped off her protective gloves, quickly wiggling her fingers into the fresh pair one of the nurses handed her. If she'd thought things had been busy earlier, they were going into full-time Christmas Eve Crazy now the sun had set.

"Teenage male, presenting with multiple leg injuries and compound fracture to the wrist."

"Got it." Josh helped unload the gurney along with the EMT. This was Chris, Maddie's older brother.

Josh took in the EMT's rattle of information as he scanned the teen's face again. Chris couldn't have had his first whiskers for long, let alone gained much experience behind the wheel in a snowstorm.

A nurse met him at the doors and took over as the EMT

finished reeling off the treatments Chris had already received. His injuries were severe. Compound fracture to the femur. Possible compression to the ankle. Severe dislocation of the knee. And who knew what muscles and ligaments might have been torn or burst? He'd be off that leg for months. Minimum. From the looks of the blood loss and extensive damage, the boy would need to be in surgery sooner rather than later. No time to wait for parental consent.

"Right, we'd better take a look at the mess you've made of yourself."

"Where's Maddie?" The boy's eyes were wide with panic.

"It's all right, buddy. Maddie is up in X-Ray. Looks like you messed your leg up pretty well."

"Where's my brother? Have you seen Nick? Where's Maddie? Is Eustace all right?"

A gurney went past with one of the interns at the helm. The keen one. Shannon…? Didn't matter.

"Hey, bro!"

Another teenage boy called from a gurney as he was wheeled past. Blood was smeared all over his face and winter coat. This was obviously the one with the broken nose.

"You haven't given them Mom and Dad's number, have you?" he shouted, before his gurney turned the corner to one of the triage areas.

"No way—what do you think I am? An idio—? *Ow!*" The scream Chris emitted filled the corridor, and just as quickly as the howl of acute pain had taken over the soundscape, it disappeared as Chris lapsed into unconsciousness.

"Anyone think to check on the femoral artery?"

Josh didn't know why he was asking. There was blood everywhere, the EMTs were long gone, and the nurse had been with him for no more than a few seconds.

"Let's skip triage and get straight up to surgery—"

"Only for a handover." Katie's voice broke in.

"This guy's going to bleed out if we don't get him on a table fast. And who knows what sort of filth is in that leg? Time's against us, Katie."

"Yes, it is. And that's why we're going to let one of the orthopedic surgeons cover this one. They're already prepping the room."

Josh nodded curtly. He thrived on make-or-break surgery, and if there was one person in the world who knew that was true of him, she was standing right there looking the picture of officiousness.

"We need you in Trauma, Josh. There are more patients incoming. The rescue crews only just opened up the car that got hit by the snowplow."

"Understood."

And he did. Katie did prioritizing. He did gut instinct. It was why they had always worked together so well. The yin to the other's yang. Sure, there were fiery moments— but balance always won out in the end.

Well… He watched as she flew past him into one of the cubicles, where a patient could be heard arguing with one of the nurses. He scrubbed his jaw hard. Balance hadn't *always* won out in the end.

He gave the nurse on the other side of the gurney a tight smile.

"Let's get this whippersnapper up to surgery so we can get back for the incomings."

"You bet, Dr. West."

"Mrs. Wilson goes into Three and Mr. Wilson into Four." Katie was issuing directions faster than a New York traffic cop in rush hour. She was in a fury. The Wilsons had been the hardest hit but had been the last to be brought in.

"It took the fire crew a while to dislodge their car from the snowplow."

"One more patient incoming!"

Michael was hurtling down the corridor with a gurney. Gone was his quiet, serene demeanor. He looked near wild with panic. For an instant Katie thought the gurney was empty and that her reliable intern had all but lost the plot entirely—until she saw the tiny figure lying on the gurney. A little girl. She looked about three.

The same age her daughter would have been if she had lived. The hollow ache of grief began to creep into Katie's heart. Josh appeared on the other side of the gurney. *Great. Just what she needed.* The one person in the world who could make these feelings multiply into Infinityville.

"What have we got here?"

"Three-year-old girl presenting with abdominal bruising and pain, blood in the urine, internal bleeding—suspected trauma to the left kidney."

Michael rattled out a few more details as they raced the gurney toward the trauma unit.

"Can we get her into OR Two with Dr. Hastings?" Katie kept her eyes trained on Michael. This was a nightmare blossoming out of control.

"Nope. He's busy with an emergency appendectomy."

This little girl couldn't wait. If her kidney was bleeding out, she needed surgery immediately or she would die. Her eyes flicked from Michael to Josh.

"What about Dr. Hutchins?"

"They're all busy, Dr. McGann." Michael churned out the information, oblivious to the emotional storm brewing between Katie and Josh. "We've prepped OR Four for you. Do you need me to assist?"

Katie's eyes widened. She blinked, doing her utmost to wear her best poker face. All the other surgeons were busy. She'd have to do it—keep this child alive. She felt her hands go clammy as they clutched the side rails of the gurney.

Her heart rate quickened and she knew if she looked into a mirror right now she would see her pupils were dilating.

"Are you up to doing a nephrectomy?" Josh's voice was low. Not accusatory—the tone *she* would have used for someone out of their depth. Safety was paramount, particularly with lawsuits swinging like an evil pendulum above their every move these days.

"Of course!" she bit back.

Josh accompanied her, uninvited, into the lift on the way to the surgical ward, dismissing Michael from gurney duty with a smile.

"It's a routine surgery. I did one last week."

But not on a child...a little girl. And not with you here.

Katie didn't dare meet his eyes. If she was going to keep it together to save this little girl's life, a shot of Josh's deep blue eyes was exactly what would have calmed her three years ago. That time had long passed. Even so, she could almost see her heart pumping beneath the scrubs she'd tugged on after Snow-Angel-Gate.

She couldn't help herself. As the doors slid closed and the pair of them were left alone with their tiny patient, she lifted her eyes to meet his. They said everything she had wanted to see in them when they'd lost their little girl.

I'm here for you. You can trust in me. Let me help you.

"Don't worry. I've got this." Katie ripped her eyes away from his. "You should go back down. If anything major happens in the ER—"

"If anything major happens in the ER," he interrupted, "they will page us. I'm staying with you."

"What are you saying, Josh?" Katie couldn't keep the disbelief out of her voice. "Are you saying I'm not up to this?"

"No," he began carefully. "I'm saying you've had a long day, a couple of shocks, and whether you like it or not, you need me by your side. I'll just stay for a minute or so—until you get going."

The elevator doors opened before Katie could reply. Which was just as well. Because what could she say other than *You're right*?

She had struggled over the past three years, doing operations that reminded her of her little girl and the life she might have had. Earlier on she'd deftly handed over any critical surgeries on young children to her colleagues. Just being responsible for the delicate life of a child had been too overwhelming—her own body had proved she didn't have what it took to care for one. But in the past year she'd taught herself to close down—to behave like the clinician she was.

But with Josh here...? Game-changer. She had to prove to him she was over it. Over *him*. That she had moved on from the loss of their child.

Elizabeth.

Elizabeth Rose West.

A beautiful name for their darling little girl, who was nothing more than a statistic now. One out of seventy mothers give birth to a stillborn baby in America every day. The volume of that annual loss was almost too much to bear. She'd never even bothered to check the statistics on failed marriages in the wake of such a loss. Just shut it all out and moved away.

Katie gritted her teeth and gave her head a quick shake. Cobwebs and history didn't belong in there now. This child's life depended upon clear, swift thinking.

The anesthetist met her at the OR door for a quick handover. "A necrotomy?" He tipped his head toward the little girl.

"'Fraid so." Katie tried to keep her tone bright.

"Well, you did a great job with the last one—no reason this should be any different."

"Thanks, Miles. I appreciate it."

"Well, if you'll both excuse me, I'll go in with the patient and get the anesthetics in order."

"Sure thing. Oh! This is Josh. He's—" *Er...my husband, and I still love him, and...*

"Dr. West." Josh jumped in to rescue her. Again. "Locum over the holiday period. I would shake hands, but—" He gestured at the gurney he was trying to navigate into the OR.

"Miles Brand. Good to meet you." He took over moving the gurney, along with a nurse who had materialized from the OR. "Let's get this girl inside and on the table, shall we?"

"I'm going to scrub in while she's prepped," Katie said needlessly after he'd left.

"I'll join you," Josh offered with a soft smile.

An encouraging one. One she should graciously accept. Because what was happening right now was ticking all the I'm-Not-Ready-For-This boxes she'd systematically arranged in her brain's no-go area.

"Thanks."

They pushed into the scrub room together, shoulders shifting against each other's as they had back in the day.

Josh allowed himself a millisecond of pleasure before he realigned his focus. Covert calming. It was his specialty.

"What's the layout here?"

"Near enough the same as Boston," Katie answered, pointing out the shelves that held surgical caps and masks.

Their eyes met as she tugged on a standard blue surgical cap.

"Where's the one I got you?" It had been covered in wildflowers. What she smelled of, he'd told her when she'd unwrapped it.

"In the wash."

Her eyes flicked away and he knew she was lying.

He tried not to notice her tying on her face mask in an

effort to hide the painful thickets of emotion she was stumbling through.

Never mind, sweetheart. I feel it, too.

Stepping up to the sink, they both let muscle memory take over. The warm, steady flow of water was the predominant sound in the room as he and Katie took a good five minutes to systematically wash and scrub, first their nails, then their hands, which they held above the level of their elbows to prevent dirty water from dripping onto them.

Josh hit the taps with his elbows when they'd both finished. Katie nodded at the stack of sterile hand towels—one for each arm.

"You sure you're good?" He handed her a towel.

"Medicine is the only thing I *am* sure of these days."

Two nurses pushed into the scrub room with gowns before he could reply. There was room for hope in her response. Room to believe he was right to have sought her out. His lips parted into a smile for which he received a quick, grim nod.

Fine. He felt he'd been thrown a buoy. He could work with a nod.

She could do this, Katie silently assured herself. She'd done it before, and she would do it again.

"Arm," instructed the surgical nurse.

Katie stuck her arm into the sterilized blue sleeve and made a one-eighty twist to fully secure the surgical gown around her, finding herself standing face-to-face with Josh while his gown was tied. He arched an inquisitive eyebrow.

Are you ready? it said.

She arched one back. Hadn't they been through this?

"Left hand, please, Dr. McGann."

She lifted it up and widened her eyes to a glare. Why didn't he stop *smiling*?

"And the right."

Katie raised her hand, holding her arm taut as the nurse tugged on the glove. The other nurse was clearly pleased she had won Josh in the surgeon crapshoot.

"Thank you, Marilyn. Merry Christmas to you."

"Merry Christmas to you, too, Dr. West." The nurse giggled.

Katie frowned. How on earth did he know *Marilyn*?

She had half a mind to step across the small room and lick Josh's gloved hands, rendering him unclean for the surgery.

Childish? Yes. Something the head of the ER should do right before surgery? Probably not.

There was a life to save—and she was going to be the doctor who saved it.

CHAPTER FIVE

"ARE YOU DOING it open or laparoscopically?" Josh kept his voice low and steady. Curious.

"Open."

Katie's eyes flicked to his as he skirted the periphery of the surgical team gathering in the OR.

"Unusual."

Not for his girl, but he knew she was always at her calmest when she talked systematically through her surgery.

Katie nodded. Blinked. His heart skipped a beat before she responded in a clear voice.

"Not in a trauma like this. Laparoscopically is better for routine."

She wasn't saying anything he didn't know, but with a team of people in the room, communicating with a nod or a look wasn't good enough. Everyone had to be on the same page or mistakes would be made.

"There is potentially a lot of other damage in here, and we're better off with a clear view of what we're dealing with."

"Rib removal?" one of the surgical nurses asked, indicating that she wanted to have the correct instruments to hand.

"Hopefully not, but one could've been broken on impact. We'll have to check."

Katie was grateful other members of the OR team were chiming in. She knew Josh's steady, careful breakdown of the steps in the guise of "reminding himself" was to keep her mind off the tiny body lying on the operating table. Josh could have done this surgery in his sleep. So could she. And he was just reminding her of what was true.

"A partial nephrectomy with so much damage could lead to the need for another surgery," Katie continued. "I don't want that for her. I won't know until I see the damage, but radical is the best option to keep things minimal for—"

"Casey," volunteered one of the nurses as the little girl's body was stabilized for Katie to make the first incision. "Casey Wilson's her name. The parents sent up her information when you were scrubbing in."

Perfect. A name. Just the way to keep it clinical.

Her grip tightened on the scalpel. "I'm preparing to make the incision."

"The bruising certainly indicates massive trauma."

"The EMTs said the snowplow hit her side of the car. She's lucky to have survived at all."

Katie shook away this new piece of information as she made an eight-inch cut from the front of the girl's soft belly to just below her small rib cage. Her mind began to take over, and her heart beat with a steadier cadence. A clock could have marked time with her breaths.

Massive trauma to one kidney. The other, thankfully, was untouched.

She switched instruments and began to cut and move muscle, tiny pieces of fat and the collection of tissue that held the kidney in place. It was steady, systematic work. A glance at the stats here. A minute cut and stitch there. Updates from the nurses. Eyes fastidiously avoiding the tiny little girl's head, just beyond the surgical drape. A vague awareness of Josh moving opposite her at the surgical table.

As she guided her hands through the surgery, it hit her how quickly she'd lapsed into deriving comfort from Josh's rock-solid presence across the table from her. From the moment before she'd stepped into the OR, when fear had threatened to compromise all that she worked so hard for, even the tiniest of tremors she had felt in her hands had left her. And something deep within her heart told her it was having the man she'd once believed to be the love of her life with her.

She flicked her eyes up to meet his. Blue, pure, unwavering. He nodded before returning his eyes to the operation. There was severe bruising along Casey's rib cage—no doubt from the seat belt—but the kidney seemed to have taken the bulk of the trauma. Katie worked her way around the tiny organ, taking particular care to properly clamp and seal the blood vessels before ultimately and successfully removing the kidney.

Textbook.

"You want me to close?" It was an offering, not a doubt about her ability.

Katie shook her head. "I'm good." She'd made it this far. She was going to see it through.

Again, muscle memory took over as she pulled the surgical area back together, minus the small kidney, with a series of immaculately executed stitches. She ran the nurses through the aftercare before allowing herself another glance across the operating table.

"See?"

Josh's blue eyes twinkled at her. Katie could tell from the crinkles round them he was smiling.

"You did it."

"You ready for Secret Santa?" Jorja, despite nearing the end of a sixteen-hour shift, seemed just as sprightly as she had when Josh had first met her.

Was she rechargeable?

"Sure thing."

"We're all meeting down at the central desk at midnight." Jorja's hand shot up to cover her mouth as she stifled a yawn.

Ah! She was human.

Josh kept a good arm's length between them as they walked down the corridor toward the ER. He didn't want any more misunderstandings under the mistletoe. He'd tried dating a couple of times after he'd decided the only way forward was moving on, but had never got past ordering a drink before faking a pager call. Cheap trick, but faking affection would have been worse.

But that didn't mean he couldn't be chatty.

"This was a long shift for you. A double?"

"No longer than yours."

She nodded her head in acknowledgment. "I do it every year." She continued when Josh raised his eyebrows. "So I can be with my family on Christmas Day."

"Oh, right! So you're a local?"

"Yup." She nodded, her voice swelling with pride. "Born and bred Copper Creeker. All six of my brothers and sisters, too."

"Six!" Josh couldn't keep the surprise out of his voice.

"Yup!" Jorja chirped again. "It means the turkey has to be absolutely ginormous—so my brothers have started deep-frying it outside to keep the oven clear for Mom."

"Sounds good."

Jorja brightened. "Want to come? You're welcome. Everyone brings a boyfriend or a girlfriend."

Josh widened the gap between them. "Oh, no. No, thanks. Not for me. I'm on shift. Thanks, though."

Jorja's smile faltered a bit. Josh scrubbed a hand through his hair. She was a nice enough girl, but… But he already had a girl. The girl of his dreams. And he was a little busy proving to her how indispensable he was.

"It was a lovely invitation—it's just…"

"Don't worry." She stopped to pick a piece of errant tinsel off the floor and wove it round and round her finger, turning it pale, then pink again…pale, then pink.

"I'm sorry, Jorja." Josh checked an instinct to reach out and give her shoulder a comforting squeeze.

"I saw how you looked at Dr. McGann when we were under the mistletoe."

This time Josh really *was* surprised. He didn't know he'd been that obvious.

"You two know each other from before, don't you?"

That was one way to put it.

"We met in medical school."

Jorja discarded the tinsel in a bin and gave a wistful sigh. "It's always the good ones who are taken!"

Responding to that might be awkward.

"Hey!" The young woman's features brightened again as she tugged her errant ponytail back into place. "Who'd you get for your Secret Santa?"

"Isn't that supposed to be secret?"

"Yeah—but wouldn't it be fun if you got Dr. McGann?"

Josh considered for a moment and then lifted an eyebrow to indicate that, yes, there just *might* be some fun there…

"Here!" She dug into her nurse's smock and pulled out a crisply folded bit of paper. "I got Dr. McGann. Who'd *you* get?"

"Didn't you get her a present already?" Josh fought the urge to seem too keen.

"Oh, I just snagged a plateful of my grandma's Christmas cookies. She makes an amazing selection. Snickerdoodles, gingerbread men, buckeyes, peppermint crunch—you name it, she makes it."

"She sounds like my Gramma Jam-Jam! Never met a Christmas cookie she didn't like."

Her passing had been like losing a limb. Another loss he'd had to deal with without Katie by his side. It struck him that this mission was about more than trust. He'd known the second Katie had laid eyes on him that she still loved him. What they had was chemical. No amount of spreadsheets or flowcharts or "stages of grief" steps were going to take the connection they had away.

But this little reunion had brought more questions than answers so far. He knew in his heart that she could trust him. But when he'd needed her most she'd upped and left. Could he trust her to stick by him if things got tough again?

"Dr. West?"

Josh could see Jorja was talking to him, but did he have a clue about what? Not one.

Jorja threw her hands up in the air. "Typical man! Concentration factor...nil! No wonder I can't get a boyfriend. I can't even get a male to *listen* to me, let alone like me."

She swatted his arm, bringing his focus back to her. Again. *Oops.*

"Sorry, Jorja—I didn't quite catch what you said."

"Yeah," she deadpanned. "I got *that*. I was asking who your Secret Santa was so we can trade. If you still want to."

"Well...it sounds like—" he dug his scrap of paper out of his lab coat pocket and read "—Dr. Michael Rainer is going to be one lucky guy...having a plate of your grandmother's cookies all to himself."

"Michael..." She said the intern's name as if she were tasting it and wasn't entirely sure what she thought of it. Then clearly a decision was made. "Michael." She said it again, this time looking as though she'd just enjoyed a delicious bite of peppermint candy.

Josh grinned. Michael might have to watch himself around the mistletoe. He threw an arm round the nurse's shoulders and gave her a quick squeeze. This Secret Santa swap could be just what he needed.

Katie nodded at the cleared ER board with a satisfied smile. It probably wouldn't last long—but even a few moments of clean board always lifted her heart.

"Someone looks happy. Did the surgery go well?"

Michael appeared at her side, giving her a little jump.

"Yes." Katie nodded, feeling the weight of the success lighten her heart. "Yes, it really did."

And it meant more than anyone will know.

Well. One person would know.

She heard Josh's laugh before she saw him—and the hit of response in her belly shifted the charge of success into something more electric. It didn't take a doctor to know it was pure unadulterated attraction. It was adrenaline from the surgery, she reasoned. It would pass.

"Right!" Katie went into efficiency mode. "We've got both shift groups together. Quick reminder: Secret Santa gifts go into lockers, please—not here in the reception area."

A nurse guiltily tucked the foil package she'd been edging onto the counter back into her pocket.

Katie gave her lower lip a guilty scrape with her teeth. She hated being a Scrooge, but this *was* a place of work.

"Good work on clearing the board after a pretty hectic run. A couple of patients are in Recovery after surgery, but there's no one unexpected in Intensive, thanks to you all."

A smattering of applause filled the area around the central desk. The staff looked tired, but triumphant. Shannon—her keenest intern—for once looked as if she'd had enough. Michael still looked doggedly studious, but she could see the fatigue in his eyes when he pulled off his glasses and gave them a rub. A few of the nurses were hiding yawns. Most of them, actually.

They'd all been through the wringer and Katie didn't feel any different.

Despite her best intentions, Katie locked her eyes with Josh's. She might not have made it through surgery without him by her side and he knew it. It made her feel vulnerable and protected at the same time. The look in his eyes made her breath catch in her throat. Pure, undiluted love.

Saying goodbye at the end of this shift was going to be harder than she'd thought.

Her eyes widened, still holding the pure blue magic of Josh's gaze. *She hadn't called the agency for a replacement!* And, realistically, was there going to be a locum tenens out there in the mountainscape of Copper Canyon— or anywhere in Idaho—willing to tear themselves away from whatever they'd planned to do with their family over the holidays?

When she and Josh had had the holidays off they'd been inseparable. In more ways than one.

She hunched her shoulders up and down. She was just going to have to suck it up. Getting a replacement for Josh at this juncture was about as likely as Santa Claus walking through the sliding doors.

"Where *is* he?"

A huge gust of wind and winter storm burst into the waiting room, along with a bearded man dressed in full Santa regalia with a rosy-cheeked Mrs. Claus following in his wake.

"Where's my son?" the bearded man roared again.

Temperatures often ran high in the ER, and it looked like Santa's temper was soaring.

"What's your son's name, sir?" Josh was by his side in an instant—with a mix of concerned doctor and *Watch yourself, Santa* in his tone and body language. Josh was tall, and he had the confident carriage of a rodeo cowboy. Santa, however, seemed immune to what had all but buckled her knees.

"Klausen. Check your list, Doc. Check it twice if you have to!"

If Katie hadn't been so taken aback by Mr. Klausen's arrival, she would have tittered at this similarity to a certain red-suited fellow who, by all accounts, should be pretty busy shooting down chimneys about now.

"Chris Klausen," the man bit out.

His tone was so sharp Katie choked on her giggles.

"I've seen the trailer in the parking lot. It's the busiest

night of the year and I *know* they've got Eustace in there. The nativity was a shambles!"

"Dad?" Maddie appeared round the corner, a bandage on her head, her arms wrapped protectively round her ribs and a slightly fearful look on her face. "Mom?"

Katie stepped toward Maddie—ready to intervene if things grew more heated.

"Maddie!" Mrs. Klausen rushed to her daughter's side. "What happened? We just got the call that there was an accident."

The tension eased from Katie's face as the anger obviously born of fear for their children turned into protective hugs and kisses.

"Where are your brothers?" Her father pushed her back to arm's length. "I'm going to wring their necks!"

Then again...

"Dr. McGann, I was the one who brought him up to—"

Katie waved Michael to silence. They didn't need to hear the gory details out here with a crowd gathering.

"Sir, perhaps you'd like to follow me?" The last thing the couple's son needed, still in Recovery from surgery, was his father dressed as Santa shouting at him.

"You all right?"

Josh's voice trickled along her spine as she felt him approach. He was doing it again. White Knighting it in the face of adversity. She was glad he couldn't see her face as she pressed her lips together. Hadn't she just proved she could hurdle her demons in the OR?

Not without Josh by her side.

"Would you like to come with me, Mr. and Mrs. Klausen?" Katie put her hand up in an *I got it* gesture to Josh and snapped a glare back at Jorja, who was busy choking down her own case of the giggles. Most likely born of nerves, but inappropriate all the same.

"What for? Show us where the boys are, Maddie, and we'll get on our way."

"I think it would be best if we had a chat before you saw your boys." Katie was solid now—shifting her gaze from one rosy-cheeked face to the other.

"Maddie…" Josh put a protective arm around the young girl's shoulders. "Why don't we see if we can track down some gingerbread?"

"All right," Mr. Klausen grumbled, his attention fully focused on Katie. "Let's hear how naughty they've been."

Katie led the way into one of the comfortably furnished family rooms the hospital had created for delivering tough news. She and Josh had been led to one like it after the postmortem on their little girl.

No discernible evidence to indicate a problem. Just one of those things.

The words had sat in her heart like an anvil. If there had been a reason, she could have *done* something. Fixed it. Not felt the living, breathing, growing terror that she had no control over what might happen if they tried again.

"So what've they done? How's Eustace?"

"Your donkey is fine, sir." Katie's eyebrows lifted in surprise at the parent's priorities—but you never knew a person's history. Never knew how someone would respond in times of extreme stress.

"One of our surgeons had to give him a few stitches—"

"He was *hurt*?" Mrs. Klausen's hands flew to her mouth in horror. "Eustace!" She exhaled into her cupped hands. "Eustace… We've had him longer than the boys! Our first baby."

Okay. Well, that explained that.

"Your son Chris has some pretty serious injuries. Maybe we should sit down so we can talk through them before I take you through to Recovery."

"Recovery?" Mr. Klausen's face was twisted in incomprehension. "What do you mean?"

"He's really been hurt?" Tears sprang to Mrs. Klausen's eyes.

"Yes." Katie shifted her tone. The Klausens would need a gentle touch now that the fog of displacement was beginning to clear. Rage, anger, even disbelief were common when the worst thing that could happen to someone actually happened. Particularly when it came out of the blue.

"Why don't we all take a seat and I'll talk you through the surgery Chris has had? Then we'll get you up to see him and Nick, who is with him, as soon as possible. No doubt seeing you both will be the perfect medicine."

She hoped no one could see the fingers she crossed in the depths of her lab coat.

Josh eased the locker open with yet another surreptitious over-the-shoulder check that he was alone. Subterfuge hadn't been his initial plan of attack, but it seemed alone time with Katie was going to be hard to come by, so he was going to have to find just the right pocket to tuck his wrapped present into.

He was hit by Katie's scent in an instant. She'd always smelled like fresh linen with a teasing of vanilla. He gave himself a moment to close his eyes and take a scented trip down memory lane.

A noise further down the corridor jarred him back into action. Winter coat or…? What was that? In the very back of her fastidiously tidy locker, behind the hanging lab coats and winter wear, was a grainy black-and-white printout. The image of their little girl hit him straight in the solar plexus. If kissing Katie on the roof had brought back everything good about their marriage, seeing the last fetal scan they'd had of their baby girl brought back the blackest.

"What are you doing?"

Josh whirled around at the sound of Katie's voice, the sheen of emotion blinding him for just an instant. His hand shot protectively to his hip. He'd turned too sharply. Abrupt turns always gave him a stabbing reminder of how far he'd pushed the envelope. Why Katie had asked him to leave. Why he was here.

To make a smart move. For once.

Katie's eyes flicked from his hip to his eyes. He saw the questions piling up in her deep brown eyes and the flicker of her decision not to ask.

"What are you doing in my locker, Josh?"

He heard the tiniest of wavers in her voice—but her body language told another story. Hands curled into fists on her hips. Mistrust laced through those dark eyes of hers. Her chin tilted slightly, as if daring him to confirm all her worst fears.

He'd gone too far. Just as she'd predicted.

"Even angry, you are the most beautiful woman I've ever seen."

She stepped back, shocked at his words. He was a bit, too, but he meant them. Her face still carried the broad features youth afforded. Full lips. A cute little gap between the two front teeth that had rebelled against the years of expensive orthodontics she'd once confessed to enduring. It made for a slightly crooked smile that lit the world up when she unleashed it. Something she wasn't even *close* to doing now, from the looks of things.

"Josh…" Her smooth forehead crinkled. "Are you all right?"

"I—uh…" He swung his gaze back to her locker, still holding the wrapped package in his hand. The pendulum of Tell or Don't Tell bashed the sides of his brain.

You were right. I should never have taken up motorcycle racing.

You were wrong—you always needed me.

He thrust the tiny package forward so it sat between them like a buffer against all that was going unsaid. "I know it was supposed to be secret, but… Merry Christmas…"

A rush of emotion crossed her face, darkening her eyes so that they were near black.

"I didn't… I don't have anything for you."

"Well, it was the luck of the draw that I got your name in Secret Santa." He hoped the white lie wouldn't come back to haunt him. "It's not exactly as if you were expecting me to turn up in Copper Canyon, now, is it?" He laughed softly, hiding a swipe at his eyes with a scrub along his forehead and a finger-whoosh through his hair.

Her expression softened.

"Are you going to unclench that thing or do you just want me to guess?"

He released his grip and let the small box rest on his palm. His eyes narrowed a bit as he watched her reach out to take it. The paper was crumpled. Worn, even. He'd wrapped that thing up the day after she'd thrown it at him and told him she'd had enough. Waiting…waiting for the perfect moment.

He cleared his throat when her fingers gained purchase on the box, her skin lightly skimming across his. He couldn't even remember how many times he'd imagined this moment. Her response would trigger a chain of events that would either make or break him.

She withdrew the box from his hand. He felt the absence of its weight and her touch instantly. Maybe ignorance *was* bliss. As long as he didn't really know how Katie felt about him, he could believe there was hope. Believe he'd never have to put his signature to that ragged pile of papers he'd been dragging around in the same backpack as the little box she was now slowly unwrapping.

The dawning of recognition wasn't far off. He'd used the same box the rings had come in. Placed them—engagement and wedding—side by side. The rings they had bought with downright giddy smiles wreathing their faces and the last handful of notes and coins they had between them.

There were only two other times when he'd seen her smile as much. Their wedding day and the day they'd found out she was pregnant.

Katie's expression became unreadable. That hurt as much as no reaction. There had once been a time when he could have told anyone her mood before she'd walked into a room. They had been *that* connected. Genuine soulmates.

"Oh…" It came out as a sigh. "Josh…" Beads of tears weighted her lashes as she held the box open, her eyes fastened to what lay inside. "I can't do this. Not right now. I just can't do this."

She turned on her heel, all but knocking Michael off his feet as he entered the locker room.

"Everything all right?" Michael pulled off his glasses and gave his eyes a rub.

"Yeah, sure." *No.* "She probably just got paged or something."

"Mmm…"

Michael seemed to take his response at face value, which came as a relief. Fatigue hit him like a truck. Heavy and unforgiving.

"Say, Dr. West… Would you like to have a coffee or something later?"

"What? Tonight?"

"No, no. Just before you hit the road again."

"Like a debrief?"

Michael's forehead scrunched. "I guess…"

"Sure thing. Just grab me next time you're free."

He gave him a gentle back-slap as he pushed the door back into the corridor open, smarting at Michael's words. The icing on the cake! So much for his fairy-tale moment when Katie slipped her rings back on her finger and his life became whole again.

He fought the urge to punch the wall. *It* hadn't done anything wrong. *He* had. He'd made a complete hash of giving

Katie the rings and now Michael wanted an exit interview. Fan-freakin'-tastic.

His eyes shot up. *More mistletoe.* Merry Christmas, everyone!

CHAPTER SIX

"DR. McGANN, WOULD you mind signing these…? Hey, are you all right?"

Jorja skidded to a halt, openly gawking at Katie. Her go-to neutral face obviously wasn't cooperating tonight.

"Of course," Katie answered briskly. "What can I do for you?"

"Before I go I just need your signature on these release forms for Mr. and Mrs. Wilson."

"The parents of the little girl? The one who had the nephrectomy?"

"Yes, that's the one. Luckily they just had a few cuts and bruises. Nothing serious. So they want to head up to the Pediatric recovery ward. Hey!" Jorja's face split into an impressed grin. "I heard you aced that baby!"

Katie's heart tightened at the choice of words, but she couldn't stop a shy smile in return. She *had* done well. And Josh had been right. She didn't need to be pinned down by her grief. Just needed to learn from it and move on. Eyes forward was a lot healthier than always looking over your shoulder at the past.

She scribbled her signature on the forms and told Jorja where the Wilsons would be able to find their little girl. They must be frantic to be with her. Hold her small little hands. Kiss those soft cheeks of hers.

Katie's fingers tightened round the ring box in her pocket.

"I'm just going for a quick power nap. Are you off for the night?"

"Yup—me and my five thousand relatives are meeting up at Midnight Mass. Spouses, girlfriends, boyfriends, uncles, aunts—you name it. And little ol' me. Late, as usual, and all on my lonesome!"

"There's plenty of time for that." Katie smiled and gave the nurse's arm a squeeze. She was pretty, vivacious, and would be a great catch for the right man. One with lots of energy. Heaven knew, her brothers were busier than an online dating agency trying to find her a beau, if all the staff-room gossip she'd caught was anything to go by. "You have a good time with your family, Jorja."

"You too, Dr. McGann." Jorja's eyes widened as her lips opened into a horrified O. "I mean—keep manning the ship like you always do! It's what you always do, isn't it? Meticulous Dr. McGann!"

Jorja's face contorted into an apologetic wince as she thudded her forehead with the heel of her hand.

"Stop while you're ahead?" Katie suggested.

"I think that's best." Jorja pulled Katie in for an unexpected hug with a whispered "Merry Christmas" before skip-running back down the hall to the main desk, her tinsel scarf trailing behind her like a glittery red boa.

Katie stood and watched her for a moment, slightly envious. Not of her youth—she was only a few years older—but of all that was yet to come for her.

She eased open the door to the residents' room, grateful to see the two beds were empty, and dropped onto one of them with a sigh of relief. Double shifts were never fun—but today had been particularly taxing. Physically and emotionally she'd been through the wringer. Seeing Josh...?

That alone was enough to send her into a tailspin. But on Christmas Eve… The night they'd lost their baby girl…

She twisted the small box round and round in her fingers until finally daring to open it again. The night she'd hurled her rings at him… Well…sensibly placed them on the counter—hurling things had never been her style… That night had been like ripping her own heart out.

She fumbled in her other pocket and pulled out her phone. Yes, it was super-late—but if she knew Alice, there would be no begrudging an after-hours call.

The phone rang a couple of times and Katie grinned, remembering the silly ringtones Alice had kept putting on her phone when she hadn't been looking.

"Hello, angel…" a sleepy Alice answered.

"Hi—sorry. I know it's late, but—"

"It's all right, darlin'. I'm just watching the dying embers of the fire. What's that little scamp done now?" Alice cut to the chase.

"He gave me back my rings."

Katie heard Alice rearrange her position on the sofa, or wherever she was. "What? For good?"

"Well, I presume so." She hadn't got that far yet.

"On bended knee? Or with a scowl in a *Here, let's have done with it* kind of way?"

"Well…" She'd been so annoyed at seeing him in her locker it hadn't even occurred to her that there might have been a plan. "There wasn't a bended knee—but there wasn't a scowl either."

"So," Alice said in her perfunctory Irish way. That meant any number of things, and in this case Katie was guessing it meant *What the hell are you going to do now?*

"I don't want to give them back." The words rushed out before she'd had a chance to edit them.

"In a good way? Or in a *Fine, you've done your business now let me get on with mine* kind of way?"

Katie laughed. She loved this woman. There were incredibly few people she'd let into her heart…well, okay, Alice and Josh were really it…and she'd missed speaking with her.

"I was sorry to cut you off earlier."

Alice didn't wait for Katie to explain herself.

"I know it's a hard day for you, and there was me prattling on about my daughter and all. It was thoughtless. What you both went through, losing Elizabeth like you did…I can't begin to imagine."

"It wasn't thoughtless." And Katie meant it. "It's…it's life. And other people have it."

"What? Are you saying to me you *don't* have your own life?"

Um…a little bit?

"No."

"My goodness. Is that Katie McGann all grown up now? Are you telling me you're done hiding away in your idyllic mountain village, pretending you're the only one to have ever gone through something awful?"

"Say it like it is, why don't you?" Katie muttered.

Alice let her stew for a moment.

She looked down at her hands and realized she'd been fiddling with her rings during the call and had unconsciously slipped them back into their rightful place. On her left hand's ring finger.

"Well?" Alice had never been known for her patience.

"I've not been hiding. I've been…thinking."

"Thinking about getting on with your life or thinking about hiding away there forever?"

"Thinking about letting go."

"Of what, exactly?"

Katie lifted her hand and eyed the rings in the half dark. "Fear?"

"That's a good way to start the New Year, love." Alice's voice was soft, but then it took an abrupt turn. "But don't go hurtling yourself off of a mountainside with a couple of fairy wings for support."

Katie laughed again.

"I will be sure to have on full reflective gear and the entire mountain rescue crew on standby if I ever do such a thing."

"That's my girl. Now, let me get some sleep and I'll speak to you soon, all right? I love you."

"I love you, too. Merry Christmas, Alice."

"And to you, angel. And pass on my love to the rascal, won't you?"

Katie nodded and said goodbye. She rolled onto her side, putting her left hand in front of her face, flicking the backs of the rings with her thumb again and again, even though she could see they were right there.

All the emotion she'd been choking back throughout the day abruptly came pouring out of her in barely contained wails of grief. If she was going to let go of fear, she was also going to have to let go of the sorrow that the fear had been protecting. Sorrow over the family she would never have. The child she had only held once. The husband she loved so dearly that the thought of losing him all but crippled her.

She was so consumed with heartache she barely registered the door opening and the arrival of a pair of male legs appearing by her side. She rocked and cried as a pair of familiar arms slipped around her, holding her, soothing her.

Josh.

Of course it was. He knew her better than anyone. Knew she would need him.

After all this time apart, he was finally there for her in the way she had longed for. Present. Still.

He slipped behind her on the bed and gently pulled her into his embrace so that she could curl up in a tight little ball, chin to knees, arms tangled through his, fingers pressing into his shoulder as if her life depended upon it.

There were no whispered placations. No *There, there* or *It'll be all right.* They might love one another, but how could he assure her about a future they would never have? Neither of them knew if anything would be all right…if they'd have the big family they both longed for. If they'd be together at all.

When at long last she was all cried out, Josh eased them down into a seamless spooned embrace. For a moment she thought to fight him. *How could she trust this? This deep, organic comfort she had longed for during those cavernously dark days?* The weight of her fatigue decided for her. She was so tired, and lying there in his arms…the one place she'd always found comfort…she began to feel the release of dreamless sleep overtake her.

It would be all right. Just this once.

It was Christmas.

Her body instinctively snuggled into his. She heard his breath catch as her own steadied. With his arm as a pillow, she became tuned in to his heartbeat, to that warm, spicy scent she would know until the end of time, to his strength. Her own body hummed with a growing heat. A sense of familiarity and comfort.

One night.

There'd be no harm in that. Right? Just one night before they said goodbye forever.

She felt his fingers stroke along her cheek, then slip down along her arm so that their fingers were intertwined. It was what she needed. To simply…*be.* Without hope or expectation. Just some peace. Some sleep. Some long-awaited comfort in her husband's arms.

Josh moved his hand along an upward curve. What the—? He waited another moment until his brain caught up with his hand. It wasn't a pillow he was caressing. It was his wife. And that sweet scent wasn't hospital antiseptic… It was the ever-mesmerizing Essence de Katie.

He nuzzled into her neck, instinctively tipping his chin to drop a kiss onto her shoulder. He stopped himself, then decided just to go for it. It was Christmas Day and Katie was asleep.

His lips sought and found a bit of exposed shoulder in the wide V-neck of her scrubs. Mmm…just as he'd remembered. Silk and honey.

Katie rolled over to face him, eyes still closed, an arm slipping round his waist. He couldn't tell if she was still asleep or not. When they had been together, the night had always found them tangled into one pretzel shape or another. Just so long as they were connected, everything had been all right.

A little sigh escaped her lips and he couldn't resist pressing his own lips to that beautiful mouth of hers.

She responded. Slowly, sleepily at first, but with growing intent as their legs began to tangle together in an organic need to meld into one.

He felt Katie's hand slip onto his hip and under his scrubs. Their kisses deepened. He couldn't believe how good it felt to feel her hands on his bare skin. Especially, he realized with a smile, when the cool silver of her wedding rings intermingled with the warmth of her fingertips.

Her fingers slid along his hip and up his spine, causing him to jerk back sharply when her fingers hit his scars. She didn't need to know about the accident. Not yet.

"Josh?"

Katie remained where she was but he could feel her heart rate escalating.

"Are those—?"

"It's nothing." *It had been huge.*

"It didn't feel like nothing." Katie's eyes blinked a couple of times before refocusing more acutely on him. He could almost see the wheels whirring in her mind to make sense of what she'd felt.

"Merry Christ— Oh, my gosh, I'm so sorry!"

Josh felt Katie shoot out of bed at the sound of Michael's voice and a blast of light. For a moment he couldn't understand why the intern looked so embarrassed. He was too busy trying to figure out how to explain to Katie what she'd discovered.

"I'll just—leave you to it, then… Uh…" Michael wasn't moving, so why on earth was he—?

Wow. Did twenty-eight-year-old men still blush?

"Merry Christmas, Michael. You're up with the lark."

Katie was tugging her scrubs top down along her hipline. Ah…the slow dawn of recognition began to hit him. No one knew they were married. No one knew Dr. McGann was Katie West. *His* Katie.

"Not really, Dr. McGann. It's nine o'clock."

"What?" Katie shot Josh a horrified look.

He just grinned. He hadn't slept until nine o'clock since… That wasn't a tricky one to figure out.

"My shift started at *seven*. Why didn't you page me?"

"Oh…" Michael began awkwardly. "Jorja said you looked really tired last night, so I left a note with the morning shift to let you sleep in."

Michael nervously shuffled his feet, still unable to connect his gaze to Katie or to Josh, who thought he might as well stand up and be counted.

"Right. I see…"

Katie didn't really seem to know what to do with the information. Or how to explain being discovered in the arms of a man she wasn't meant to know.

"Well, let's get going, shall we?"

"Merry Christmas, Michael," Josh contributed merrily. If he was going to fake it about having been critically injured, he might as well go the whole hog and rustle up some fake Yuletide jolliness.

"Uh… Merry Christmas…"

Katie steered Michael away from the room without a backward glance.

Josh huffed out a mirthless "Ho-ho-ho…" and plunked back down on the bed. *Merry Christmas, indeed.* It shouldn't have come as a surprise. Shouldn't hurt so much. A psychiatrist would have a field day with them. No fluid Seven Stages of Grief for the Wests! No, sir. Just a tangled mess of How-the-Hell-Did-We-End-Up-Like-This?

He scrubbed at his thickly stubbled jaw. It had been a long time since he'd thought of himself as a plural. They had both been bulldozed by shock. At least they'd done *that* by the book. He'd skipped the next few stages and gone straight to testing. Testing limits. Pushing boundaries. Trying his best to show Katie there was still so much life to be lived and all along only succeeding in pushing her away. Making her more fearful than he had ever thought she could be.

From everything he'd seen, she was still sitting pretty in the snowcapped Village of Denial. As long as she didn't see him, everything that had happened could be her own little secret, locked away wherever it was she locked things up.

His heart ached for her, and at the same time he wanted to roar with fury at how fruitless blocking out the past was. *Hmm…good one. Anger.*

Okay. He'd probably hit that one a few times, too. Depression? Didn't really compute. He simply wasn't that kind of guy. There were too many good things in life to counterweight the sorrows. Otherwise—what was the point?

Bargaining?

Maybe that was what being here was. If he won Katie back then his life would feel complete again. Just like in these last few precious hours. The first time he'd held his wife in his arms for two years. The first solid sleep he was guessing either of them had had since the split. The first time he'd let himself really believe they might be together again.

If he didn't believe…?

Nah. He wasn't there yet. No point in accepting things you didn't know the answer to.

"Dr. West! Good of you to finally join us."

Katie was back to her crisp efficient self. Surprise, surprise.

"Granny dump in Four."

She handed him a file without a second look. *Wow. Talk about terse!* Even at her most efficient Katie was never rude. Her heart normally bled for the elderly people families dropped off in the ER on Christmas Day so they wouldn't have to look after them on the holiday. It happened a lot in the city. Had to be pretty rare out in these parts.

He watched her reorder a few files, the crease between his eyebrows deepening. Katie knew exactly how Josh felt about caring for the elderly, given he had been near enough raised by his grandmother, with his parents so busy on the farm. He clamped his teeth together to bite back a snarky comeback. He'd expected more from her. Maybe she *had* changed and he was the last one to see it. The last one to accept the truth. They were different people now.

He shook his head. This sat wrong. At the very least she should have opted to tell him the condition the so-called "dump" was for.

He glanced at the chart.

"Peripheral edema." The notes went on to say the patient was complaining of swollen ankles and feet. Could be anything. Ankle sprain, obesity, osteoarthritis—and so the list went on, all the way up to congestive heart failure. That would have to be one cold family to drop their grandmother off at the ER, without so much as grandchild in tow.

"And what have *you* got this fine Christmas morn?"

Josh asked Katie, thinking he'd make a stab at civility. It wasn't like they'd spent the night wrapped in each other's arms or anything.

"New bride having a panic attack." Her eyes flicked to his. "Trying to live up to unrealistic expectations."

He turned and went to Exam Four. She was obviously in a mood. He'd already opened up about his expectations. She'd felt his scars. Thought the worst. Maybe this was her way of saying all bets were off.

He stopped just before entering his cubicle and turned, catching a glimpse of Katie's hand as she went into the cubicle beside him.

Ha! He just resisted throwing a punch up into the air. She still wore the rings. Hadn't sent him to the scrap heap just yet.

A grin lit up his face. Maybe it *was* going to be a merry Christmas after all.

"Now, Mrs. Hitchins, is it? I'm Dr. West. I understand you're not feeling at your best?"

"I don't think this is working."

The young woman sitting on the exam table lowered the paper bag she'd been breathing into when Katie entered.

"Is she going to be all right? Is she having a heart attack?" asked the young man beside her, presumably her husband. His face was laced with anxiety.

Katie pulled her stethoscope from around her neck and gave the couple as reassuring a smile as she could muster.

"I understand you've got your in-laws visiting for the first time, Mrs. Davis?"

"My family. Yes." Her husband answered for her. "Emily had just put the roast in the oven and then my mother, who has *always* made our Christmas dinners in the past, started asking about what Emily's family ate for Christmas. The next thing I knew, she was hyperventilating, saying she could hardly see… My mother kept offering to take over in the kitchen, and that's when Emily really took a turn. Is she going to be all right?"

Katie took Emily's vitals while he spoke, gently encouraging the twenty-something newlywed to return the paper bag to her mouth, assuring her husband they would do everything they could to help his wife.

She could hear Josh merrily chatting away with the woman next door. He was obviously bringing out the best in her from the sounds of their joined laughter. She would have expected nothing less. He had a wonderful way with grandmothers. Everyone, really. *Why had she been so sharp with him?* He didn't deserve to be sniped at when all he'd done was show her kindness.

What were those scars all about?

She forced herself to tune back in to her patient's husband.

"I'm happy to call my mother and tell her to take over. My mother does a *perfect* Christmas dinner. Doesn't she, Ems?"

Emily's breathing suddenly accelerated, and her eyes dilated as they darted from her husband to Katie.

"Deep breaths, Emily. Keep the bag up. *Deep* breaths. Mr. Davis—do you mind if I have a moment with your wife alone?"

"Are you sure there's nothing—?"

"Absolutely. If you could just take a seat in the waiting room, I'll be with you in a few moments."

After her husband had dropped a nervous kiss on his wife's head and left the cubicle, Emily's breathing changed. Lost its harsh edge. Katie rubbed her hand along Emily's back as she might a small child and kept repeating her mantra.

"Breathe slowly. Deeply. Count to three…count to five… deep and slowly…"

It was what had got her through her first few attacks after she'd left Josh. Part of her had actually been shocked that she'd done it. It had been so out of character! She'd checked into a hotel when her car had all but run out of gas and had just sat at the end of the bed and shaken for who knew how long?

She gave her head a little shake. This wasn't about her. It was about Emily and a mother-in-law whose son seemed to have problems letting go of the apron strings.

"First holiday meal for the in-laws?" Katie asked gently, lowering herself into the seat beside the exam table and making a Christmas-tree doodle on the corner of the chart.

Emily just nodded. Tears springing to her eyes.

Katie tugged a tissue out of the packet she always had in her lab coat and handed it to her.

"Would it be safe to say this is the first time you've ever experienced these symptoms?"

Another nod and a sniffle. A tear skidding down her cheek.

Katie stood and patted the empty space on the examination table. "Mind if I join you?"

Emily shook her head and Katie scooched up onto the table, her feet crossed at the ankles.

"I remember making my first—my *only*—Christmas dinner for my in-laws. I was a wreck!" She laughed softly at the memory. "My husband's family loved their food and they were happy slaves to their long-established Christmas traditions. And, of course, there was Gramma Jam-Jam's unbelievably perfect cooking to contend with. What I *didn't* realize was that most families *don't* buy the entire meal in from a fancy grocery store and heat it up."

She laughed again before going on, pleased to see Emily's breathing was becoming more regular as she spoke.

"I mean, I obviously knew people made Christmas dinner—it was just that my family never had. And when I volunteered to cook for my husband's family, I didn't realize what I'd gotten into until they started sending me emails about how they liked three-peak dinner rolls, whatever they were, homemade cranberry sauce—but only if there was orange zest and no orange pulp—mashed potatoes—but made with a ricer, which made no sense at all. And lots of butter—salted."

She held up her fingers and added another memory. "A big enough turkey so that there'd be enough leftovers for sandwiches to see them through at least the next week. There I was, a grown woman, and I'd never so much as *peeled* a potato, let alone mashed one."

"At least they ate the same thing!" Emily cut in. "David's family don't eat a single thing my family does. Beef instead of turkey, because they feel the one at Thanksgiving is enough. Roasted potatoes instead of mashed. Which is just *wrong*." She reeled off a list of her family's specialties before giving Katie a wide-eyed look. "What's Christmas without turkey and stuffing?" She spread her hands out wide in a *what gives?* gesture. "I mean—I've never, *ever* had Christmas without turkey and stuffing! It's like a sign that this whole marriage was never meant to happen!"

"Hey," Katie soothed. "Marriage involves a whole lot of things we don't think about when we say our vows. But you can *do* this! Think about your guy. Maybe he's been pining for beef each Christmas he's spent with your family? Embrace the changes as learning opportunities. Doesn't mean they have to be *your* things."

She took both of her patient's hands in her own and gave a decisive nod. "How 'bout this? When your in-laws leave, why don't you make a turkey for New Year's? Just the two of you. Stuffing. Mashed potatoes. The whole nine yards."

Emily sniffled, swiping at her tears to reveal a hint of a smile, giving Katie a nod to continue. Not that she would have been able to stop her. She was on a roll now. Her own marriage might be in tatters, but she damn well wasn't going to let *this* pair of young lovers fall to bits over a piece of roast beef!

"Have your *own* traditions! My husband and I made ours. Pancakes on Tuesdays after a double shift. Grilled cheese sandwiches with pickles and tomato soup on Valentine's…"

Katie felt a flush of pleasure begin to color her cheeks at the memory of the goofy traditions they'd made up through the years, then sobered. She was at work here—not on a magical trip down memory lane.

"You know what, Emily? If your mother-in-law is so desperate to cook…let her! Have your husband drive you home via a restaurant and get a to-go bag filled to the brim with turkey sandwiches—then put your feet up and enjoy letting someone else cook dinner. I bet you've spent days making the house and everything just perfect?"

Emily nodded, the light shadows under her eyes offering the proof that Katie wasn't just making a stab in the dark. "I do feel pretty tired."

"Okay! Why not go home, play the sick card? Put your feet up and enjoy the day with your husband. Play a board game and enjoy the aromas wafting from the kitchen. And in a few days…when they're gone…pull out your apron and make exactly what you want—just for the two of you. It sounds to me like you know how to cook! That's more than *I* could ever do!"

"The grilled cheese sandwiches?" Emily grinned at her.

"Burned at the corners, gooey in the middle. My specialty." Katie smiled back, giving her patient's knee a knowing pat. Family life could be tough. And the holidays could make it tougher.

"Don't give yourself such a hard time, Dr. McGann."

Katie started when Josh poked his head into the exam area, with his own patient grinning up at him adoringly from her wheelchair.

"I have it on good authority that your husband thinks your cooking is fantastic."

He dropped her a wink and pushed Mrs. Hitchins away, leaving Katie at a loss for words.

"He's cute. If your husband is anything like *him*…" Emily gave a low whistle of appreciation.

Katie briskly jumped off the exam table. Her husband was *nothing* like the Josh who'd just strolled past as if they hadn't just spent the past two years apart. This guy seemed reliable, steady…*present*. Someone she could trust *not* to scale sheer cliff faces or zip wire across the Grand Canyon. *That* was the Josh she knew. This guy…? He might have some scars she didn't know anything about…but he was here for her exactly when she needed him and she hadn't even known it.

"So!" Katie picked up Emily's forms. "I'm going to make a note that you were suffering from mild hyper-ventilation. Effectively you had an in-laws-induced panic attack—but we won't put that down," she added conspira-torially. "It is not uncommon this time of year. If you like, you can tell your family it was exhaustion. But you know how to fix it now…right?"

"Step back, take a look at the big picture and remember I married the guy I love?"

Her words bull's-eyed Katie right in the heart.

She'd never done that. Taken a step back from it all. The grief. The sorrow. She'd never remembered to take in the big picture. She'd just pushed Josh away as hard as she could. Even put a mountain range between them!

Images of her heart soaring over the Rocky Mountains with a goofy pair of fairy wings pinged into her head.

For a smart woman, she was feeling like a first-class ding-a-ling.

How could you hide from what was alive in your heart? Especially if it was love? Had time finally given her the perspective to see the situation for what it had been? Awful, *awful* luck.

"Exactly." Katie forced a smile. "You married the guy

you love. Now, get out there and go hunt down some turkey sandwiches!"

Emily gave her a tight hug and all but bounded out of the cubicle, tugging on her jacket as she went to find her husband.

The unexpected flush of emotion at their encounter made Katie pause. *Whoo!* She needed a few extra seconds for private regrouping.

So…if Emily was The Patient of Christmas Past…

Had she been so blinkered about Josh's adrenaline-junkie ways that she'd forgotten to look at the big picture? To look at *him*? He had been grieving, too. Maybe his relentless drive to cheer her had been the same desperation *she'd* been feeling for him to weep with her. Sob his heart out as she'd done, hidden away in the back of her closet so no one could hear her mourn.

There just wasn't any way to prepare for a loss like that, let alone know how to react. Had *she* been the one to react poorly? To lose sight of what was important?

The weight of the realization nearly buckled her knees. *What had she done?*

The iron taste of blood in her mouth brought her back to the present. *Hey! Let's just add a self-inflicted bloody lip to the mix.* Precisely the Christmas look she'd been hoping to present to her patients. To Josh.

She needed a Christmas cookie.

Stat.

If she got to the staff room fast enough, there just might be a few left after Jorja's grandmother's annual Christmas bake-fest.

CHAPTER SEVEN

"SOMEONE'S GOT THE MUNCHIES!"

"Hi, Michael." Katie guiltily swiped some crumbs away from her lips as she swallowed down an unsuspecting gingerbread man's leg. His head and arms had already been snapped off and munched. "Sorry, I was just…"

Just trying to drown my sorrows by massacring a gingerbread cookie?

Not strictly what you wanted your boss to say.

"Don't worry. I've already eaten a dozen. Maybe more."

The unexpected hint of a wicked smile crossed his face and brought out one on her own. She had a soft spot for Michael. Hair always a tousled mess. Ink marks regularly dabbing his cheeks. He'd joined the internship later than most medical graduates, having taken a year out to work with a charity in South America. Methodical. Steady. He was a serious guy. Not to the point of being humorless, but it was nice to see a smile on his face.

"Lucky you—getting Jorja as your Secret Santa."

"Yes! Yes, it was most excellent. A real surprise. Incredibly generous."

And a really effusive thanks for a plate of cookies Jorja hadn't even baked herself.

Katie looked up from her cookie to give Michael a closer look and was surprised to see a hint of color pop onto his cheeks. Did he…? Could he really…? Bouncy, gregarious

Jorja? Who wore costumes on any given holiday? Well…
Katie had been all but surgically attached to her books at
university and Josh-the-Gregarious had certainly brought
her out of her shell. Maybe Jorja brought out the hidden
Romeo in Michael.

Katie felt her beeper buzz and tugged it off her scrubs
waistline.

911—suspected cardiac arrest.

Katie didn't bother to wait for Michael's response.

The patient was her father.

"Who does a woman need to call to get a cappuccino in
this hospital?"

Josh knew that voice. He knew it very well. And he
knew the bottle blonde coiffure that went along with it.

"Mrs. McGann?"

"Josheeee!"

Katie's immaculately turned out mother twirled around
on her heels with the style and panache of a nineteen-fifties
screen legend, holding her hands out in a wiggly fingered
show of delight before planting a big lipsticky kiss on his
cheek. Nothing had changed there, then.

"What are you doing here, Mrs. McGann?"

And…why don't you find it strange that I'm here?

"Oh, Josh…"

Sheree McGann placed a perfectly manicured hand on
Josh's forearm. She was as touchy-feely as her daughter
was reserved. No apples had fallen near *her* tree.

"It's Randall. He's gone and had a blasted angina attack
and he didn't have any of his squirty stuff left so we could
finish—you know—*business*."

She raised her eyebrows and smiled when he made the
connection.

"Josheeee…" She gave his arm a squeeze. "I would just
murder for a cappuccino. Any top tips from an insider?"

She dropped him a knowing wink, but before he had a chance to answer, Katie skidded to a halt alongside them. Perfect timing? Or damage control?

"Mom! Is everything all right? Where's Dad?" Katie shot him a wary glance while she waited for a response.

"Katie, darling! You didn't tell us Josh was back in town. *Naughty* girl. It does explain why you've turned down our invitation to stay at the condo whilst we're here. Now, what does a girl have to do to find a barista on Christmas morning?"

"I bet we can rustle something up for you, Sheree."

Katie's blood ran cold, then hot, then cold again.

This isn't happening! This isn't happening. No, no, no, no, no, no. No!

She squeezed her eyes tight shut. Then opened them.

For the love of all the Christmases past and present... please be gone!

She eased one eye open. Nope. They were both still there. Josh and her mother, nattering away like a day hadn't passed since they'd seen each other last. At Elizabeth's funeral. That was the last time they'd all been together. At least her parents had managed to make good on *that* promise.

"Oh, Josh!" Sheree gushed. "It is *so* good to see you again. I kept telling Katie to stop hiding you away in all of those specialist hospitals and to join us up here in the Canyon. What did she do to finally lure you to our little mountain retreat?"

"Mom!"

Katie blanked Josh's wide-eyed expression. So she hadn't strictly told her parents she and Josh were no longer together? So what? They'd never been close. On top of which, shouldn't her mother be behaving a bit more as if her husband was having a heart attack?

"Where's Dad?" She wheeled on Josh. "Are you—is *someone*—looking after my father? I just got a 911."

"That was me, dear. I wanted to get back home as soon as…"

Her mother's voice trailed off and she pulled back to view her daughter at arm's length.

"Oh, honey. Couldn't you have made a bit more of an effort?" Sheree tsked as she top-to-toe eyeballed Katie with obvious disdain at her choice of scrubs and trainers. "It's *Christmas*."

Katie crinkled her nose and shook off her mother's comment. Typical McGann reaction. Ignore the real problem and focus on something superficial.

Fine.

She obviously wasn't going to get any sense out of her mother, whose breath smelled as though she'd already hit the wet bar. Mimosas or martinis? She leaned in for a sniff. Mimosa. Her eyes flicked to the clock. Eleven-thirty.

Well. It *was* Christmas.

"Where's Dad? Is he okay?"

"Oh, honey. He didn't have a heart attack. He was just behaving like his usual greedy guts self—eating too much foie gras last night—and he's out of his whatchamacallit… Nitro-something-or-other."

"Nitroglycerin?" Katie crinkled her nose. "You didn't tell me Dad was on medication."

Katie's mother gave a tiny shrug and continued speaking as if Katie hadn't said a word. "Remember what a little piggy he is, Josheee? You know, we were both just talking about you, and I said to him—"

"Why don't we all go see him together? I think I overheard Dr. Vessey saying *she* was doing a preliminary check on an angina case in Two."

Josh smoothed over his mother-in-law's ruffled feathers with the promise of a shot of espresso somewhere in the near future in exchange for a few moments with her husband and daughter.

"Oh, your father won't like that. That's why we had the girl at the desk send out the 911. You know him—refused the wheelchair, staggered in like a drunken pirate, insisting on seeing his little girl. He won't be treated by anyone but you, Katie."

"But—" Katie's face was wreathed in confusion.

"You know your father, dear. You always were his favorite."

"I should think so, Mother. I *am* his only child," Katie ground out, looking a little less like a glowering twelve-year-old.

Josh's grin widened. He was enjoying every single second of this. Not the part about his father-in-law staggering into the ER bellowing to see his daughter before his heart gave out…but all of this complicated, messy family stuff? This was a side of the McGann family he'd never known existed. And on top of everything, Katie hadn't told them they weren't together anymore. It was like fifteen Christmases all rolled up into one!

Out of this world. Heart-thumpingly out of this world.

"Shall we?" Katie bit out, clearly displeased with the notion of the proposed family activity.

Josh tucked his mother-in-law's hand into the crook of his arm as Katie stomped off in the lead.

"Temper, temper!" Sheree stage-whispered.

Katie's shoulders stiffened, but they weren't rewarded with the glare Josh was fairly certain would be playing across Katie's face. She could have whipped round and stuck her tongue out at them for all he cared.

Deck the halls with Katie's white lies, tra-la-la-la-la, la-la-la-la!
She's not told her parents she left me, fa-la-la-la-la!
Merry Christmas to me!

Maybe that dream of running off into the sunset hand in hand with his wife hadn't been so silly after all. And…seeing as it was winter…sunset came early this time of year!

Katie unceremoniously yanked back the curtain to her father's cubicle, shooting Josh a *back off, pal* look as she did.

Then again…

"Hi, honey! Will you tell this kid to stop it with her tests, already? I told her my daughter and son-in-law would sort me out. I want Copper Canyon's best."

"I'm a fully qualified intern—" Shannon began, before her reluctant patient gave her a dismissive pat on the hand.

"They're here now, honey. Thanks for being so attentive. I'm sure you've got a great career ahead of you." He dropped her one of his aging soap star winks in lieu of a wave farewell.

Katie shot an apologetic look at Shannon, indicating that she could leave. She had this one. Josh received a similar look, but it was a bit more of a bug-eyed *Scram, pal!*

"Oh, don't go, son!" Her father held up a hand in protest. "Josh, Katie's mother and I have been asking ourselves why you and Katie haven't come up to the house yet. Heaven knows we've had no luck getting Katie up this season—as per normal. Where's she been hiding you anyway? It's been—has it been *years* since we've laid eyes on you? Sheree, honey—when was the last time we saw Josheee here?"

"Dad! Can you stop jabbering for a minute, please? I just want to listen to your heart."

Katie fastidiously avoided Josh's twinkling blue eyes, blowing a breath or two onto her stethoscope before positioning it over her father's heart.

Randall McGann's words were like music to Josh's ears. *They really don't know. Katie hasn't told them.*

He ran the words over and over in his mind like a healing mantra.

A few seconds of silence reigned before Katie's mother jumped in.

"Darling, I think your father just needs a refill of his medicine. This little incident started when we were in the middle of a…a *bedroom workout*." Mrs. McGann's voice slipped into a slinky-dinky tone appropriate for a perfume commercial and her husband gave a knowing chortle. "If you know what I mean."

"Gross." Katie shook away the mental image building in her head. "Mom. Just… Can we stick with the facts, please?"

"What, honey? Your father and I were having sex. You and Josheee still have sex, right? It's what loving couples do?"

"Mom!" Katie's eyes darted to Josh and then assumed a full glower on her mother. "Can we *please* just…?" Katie huffed out a sigh. "Dad. Can you tell me what sensations you experienced?"

"Well, your mother was in the middle of a new trick she read about in a magazine, and I was just on the brink of having a wonderful—"

"Whoa! Whoa! Still too much detail. Let's just stick with your heart. The pains in and around your heart."

"Well, I didn't have the shooting pain down the arm that says you're having a heart attack, if that's what you're after, honey."

"Dad!" Katie's exasperation was growing. "I need details. Did you experience shortness of breath? Sweating? Did you lose consciousness—?"

"Uh… Katie, would you like *me* to do the examination?" Josh only just managed to keep the corners of his mouth from twitching into a broad smile. "I think you might be a bit too close to the patient. Your questions are coming out a bit more Guantanamo than—"

"This is *hardly* an interrogation, Josh!" Katie bit back, fastidiously keeping her eyes glued to her stethoscope.

"And I am *perfectly* capable of assessing an angina attack, thank you very much!"

"*Honey!* Is that *any* way to speak to your husband on Christmas?"

"Mom, he's not—" Katie froze.

This could be interesting.

Josh quirked an eyebrow. Her parents, for once, were silent. What to do? Break some pretty painful news to Mr. and Mrs. McGann on Christmas Day or come to his wife's rescue? The wife he really wanted back in his arms.

He held up his hands in mock surrender.

"Confession time! I'm not really supposed to be here."

"Ooh, you old rascal." Randall threw a high five at him from his hospital bed. "Did you fly in special, just to make sure our Katie's Christmas was a bit more naughty than nice?"

"Dad!"

Katie could not have looked more horrified than she did now. Josh couldn't help but laugh. He might be having the best Christmas of his life, but he would put money on the fact this was very likely Katie's worst.

The smile dropped from his lips.

Second worst.

There would never be a Christmas more devastating than the one they'd had three years ago.

"Nope. Sorry. Nothing quite so thrilling. I just meant I'm on shift, and my boss here—" he nodded at Katie "—would probably like me to see some of the patients I hear building up in the waiting room. Lovely to see you both."

Katie exhaled a sigh of relief when Josh left the cubicle.

"Okay, Dad. Will you hush for a moment and let me get through this exam?"

"As long as you promise to bring Josh over for dinner. Tonight."

"I can't tonight—I'm on duty."

"On *Christmas*?"

"Mom! People don't have health problems just during office hours."

"Tone, Katie! Your mother's had a rough morning." Her father gently chastised her. "Tomorrow, then. Or how 'bout New Year's Eve? That'd be fun. See in the New Year together as a family."

Katie looked at him dubiously. Since when did her parents give a monkey's if they did *anything* as a family?

"Surely the hospital doesn't have you working round the clock?" Her mother added to the appeal.

If only she could!

Her father crossed his arms across his chest. "Sheree— get a yes out of our daughter and promise not to cook."

"Honey—we'll get delivery. I know an excellent Korean barbecue here in town. They do the most delicious ginseng pork—"

"New Year's Eve—fine! Okay? I will bring Josh and we will have dinner with you. Now, can you just *hush* for a minute so I can see how clogged up your arteries are?"

Her father, duly chastened, nodded his assent whilst making a *zip it* gesture on his lips.

Case. Closed.

"You can clear the mistletoe poisoning and the burned fingers from the board."

"Both of them?" Katie's eyes widened in surprise but she whooshed the eraser over the names on the whiteboard.

Josh couldn't tell if he'd startled her or if she was amazed he'd seen two patients to her one—albeit particular—patient.

"Yup. The mistletoe-berry-swallower had to revisit the berries, if you know what I mean."

"Induced vomiting with charcoal?" She gave a shiver at his grossed-out face.

"Not quite the lump of coal Santa had in mind—but, yes.

We ran an EKG, did some blood and urine tests and apart from discovering that the hallucinatory effects of mistletoe aren't just a myth, and seeing the magic of receiving fluids through an IV, I think he'll be okay. Michael's just signing him out."

"The little girl with the burned fingers?"

"Minor. But each and every finger. Her teenage cousins were having a contest to see how many votive candles they could put out in three seconds. She came first."

"Nothing like the holidays to bring out the best in a family!" Katie intoned, her eyes still solidly on the board.

"Speaking of which—is everything all right with your father?"

Josh thought he'd better test the waters before going in for the proverbial kill. Telling Katie how much he loved her. Inviting her to Paris. Asking her to renew their vows.

"If being blackmailed into having dinner at my parents' on New Year's Eve is your idea of 'all right,' then yes."

"That should be fun for you!"

"Well, you're coming too, so you can wipe that smug look off your face."

"Ah!" His heart gave a satisfying thump. She hadn't called a replacement.

"Is that a good 'Ah!' or a bad one?" She frowned.

His eyes did a quick dart down to her hand. Yup! The rings were still there. His eyes flicked back up to Katie's.

"Your mother's not cooking, is she?"

"No way!" Katie looked horrified at the thought. "I don't think Dad even lets her heat things up for him anymore. He had food poisoning three months ago, from something she insisted she'd had in the oven all day. Turned out she'd only had the lightbulb on, and had put on the grill at the last minute to sear it and cover up the mistake."

"Maisie's on Main?"

Josh had stopped at the local diner on his way to the hospital when he'd arrived in town. Damn good toasted cheese sandwiches. They'd even put in the dill pickles when asked.

"Nope. Korean. Mom's into 'Asian trilogy ingredients,' whatever those are."

"Aphrodisiacs, I'm guessing."

"Joshua…" Katie's voice was loaded with warning.

"Uh-oh!" He put on a mock dismayed face. "You only ever call me Joshua when I'm in trouble. What did I do?"

Katie maintained a neutral expression on her face, but the tone of her voice spoke volumes. "Don't. Even. Go. There."

"Which 'there'?" He tried to joke. "The embarrassing fact your parents are still heavily sexed up and you act more like a parent than they ever did? Or the very interesting news that you haven't told them you've been asking me for a divorce for the past two years?"

"Holy cow!"

Michael popped up from underneath the central reception desk, much to Katie's obvious horror.

"You two are *married*?"

"No!"

"Yes."

Katie's negative response was drowned out by Josh's emphatic affirmation.

"Not that we're telling anyone—are we, Katie?"

"Uh…" Michael's eyes shifted from one to the other, as if he were expecting one or both of them to sprout wings. Or horns. "I'll just leave you two to it, then…" And he promptly bolted from the desk toward the staff room.

"Now look what you've done!" Katie's expression was one of pure dismay.

"What *I've* done? Are you *kidding* me? All I've done is everything you've asked of me for the past three years, Katie."

Whoops. Not quite the love-heals-all-wounds tack he was hoping to take.

"Everything but one!" She furiously obliterated her father's name from the whiteboard.

Josh's heart plummeted to his guts, then rebounded with a fiery need to lay his cards on the table. Katie didn't need to know he'd almost died. Didn't need to know he was being offered the chance of a lifetime in Paris. Didn't need to know a single one of those things to know if she loved him. But she *did* need to know them if they were to go forward truthfully. With trust.

He steadied his breathing before he began speaking, but the moment the words came out, he knew he should have walked away. Thrown a snowball. Pulled her into his arms under some mistletoe and showed her the other side of his love. Something—*anything*—to temper the volcanic strength of rage and sorrow he felt at what had happened to them.

"Is that really what you want? You honestly want me to sign those papers? Or do you just like holding it over me so we can both pretend *I* was the one who pushed *you* away after Elizabeth died?"

Josh could have punched himself in the face when he saw the look on her face.

There had been no need to be cruel. It was just that it hurt so *bad*. A physical pain compounded tenfold when he saw the tears spring into Katie's eyes before she turned on her heel and strode away.

It was time. Every pore in his body was rebelling, but the decision he'd needed to make since his arrival had been made.

CHAPTER EIGHT

NOT EVEN A snow angel was going to help dilute the bad mood Katie was in. A good stomp around the corridors of the hospital might do her good. Instill a bit of calm now that… She checked her watch… Nope! Wasn't over yet.

She glanced out the window… A perfectly beautiful white Christmas. If this day would just hurry up and be over, the little gremlins of Christmases Past could just go back to where they came from! She checked her watch again, tapping the surface of the glass as if the hour hand would suddenly leap forward.

Nope! Time didn't really seem to be playing ball today. Not in the slightest.

She kicked her pace up a notch. Including stairwells, she could get in a good three-mile walk. All she needed was to keep her pager from…

Zzzzt! Zzzzzt!

…going off.

She turned her race-walk into a run toward the surgical recovery ward. Was it the little girl she'd operated on yesterday? Casey Wilson? She offered up silent prayers as she kicked up her pace. Of all the surgeries in her entire career that needed to come out golden… *Please, please, please…*

If she could just block out the fact that she might not have made it through Casey's surgery without the sandy-haired, blue-eyed boy she'd lost her heart to way back in the innocent days of her junior residency…

She swiped at the tears cascading down her cheeks. Try harder. Block harder. *Shut him down.*

She was going to have to. Lives depended upon her ability to focus and to block out the pain that would drive her wild if she let it surface. Block out the need to be held in her husband's arms and have him tell her everything would be okay when she knew it wouldn't be. Couldn't be.

Where had those scars come from?

Run. Work.

Run faster. Work harder.

She reached the recovery ward breathless, more from fear than exertion. Was Casey all right?

"Hey, Dr. McGann." One of the nurses looked up when Katie approached the desk. "Sorry to set off your pager like that. It's just the Wilsons. They wanted to thank you for everything you did for Casey, and no one down in Trauma knew where you were."

"Oh! Good. That's all right." Katie's heart was still thumping away as she registered the nurse's words. "Fine. Good. Um…"

She saw Casey's parents through the glass door of the recovery room their daughter was in. Faces soft with pride and affection. She felt a swell of pride and a stab of loss squeeze all the breath out of her.

She and Josh could have been those parents. That family. Would most likely have been home with their little girl right now instead of haunting the corridors of the hospital, sniping at each other.

She could see it so easily. The three of them gathered round their Christmas tree, decorated with a mix of preschool decorations and generations of hand-me-down ornaments. A fire crackling away and all three of them sitting together in a sea of wrapping paper, gifts and laughter…

"Can you just let them know I stopped by, got their message, but had to dash? Apologies."

"They're just right—" The nurse looked at her strangely as she angled her pencil in the Wilsons' direction.

"Sorry." Katie faked getting another page. "Gotta dash! Give them my best." She threw the words over her shoulder but kept moving. Away from the memories. Away from the pain.

T-minus I don't think I can do this much longer.

Katie rattled through the days and hours on her fingers and clenched them into fists. Didn't matter.

Too many. That was how many more hours she had with Josh.

She swept past the patients' rooms, hoping to find somewhere else to burn off her excess energy before returning to the ER.

"Merry Christmas, Dr. McGann! Can we offer you some eggnog?" A familiar rosy-cheeked woman caught her by the elbow before she flew past another recovery room.

"Mrs. Klausen?" Her eyes widened at the scene playing out before her. "What's going on here?"

A small card table had been set up next to her son Chris's bed, and the other children—Maddie and Nick—were busy hanging up stockings along the curtain rail. Mr. Klausen was poised to start carving an enormous roast turkey.

"Well, we couldn't let Chris be here all alone on the big day, could we?" Mrs. Klausen asked.

Katie scanned the family, each sporting an atrociously jolly Christmas sweater, faces wreathed in smiles. The delicious scent of turkey floated toward her as Mr. Klausen began slicing the large bird. Gone were the recriminations. The threats to wring necks, revenge plans for Eustace's injuries. There were just faces glowing with happiness. An overall sense of contentment that only being together as a family could bring.

"Join us!"

"You shouldn't be all alone on Christmas Day!"

"Eustace sends his love!"

"Can we at least give you a sandwich?"

A sting of guilt at her brisk treatment of her own parents hit her. It deepened as she wove Josh into the equation. She'd all but built a physical wall around herself to distance her from the things—the people—she thought had hurt her most in the wake of Elizabeth's death. But if she came at it from a different angle...?

Her parents and Josh were warriors. Relentless, driven, undeterred warriors. Carrying wave after wave of love with them.

Flawed? Hell, yeah! But who wasn't? She doubted Santa would have a long enough scroll if she were to start cataloging the ways she might have dealt with her grief in better ways. Been a better daughter to parents who clearly weren't the picket-fence type of mom and dad.

A more loving wife.

"Dr. McGann?" Maddie broke into Katie's reverie. "Are you all right?"

"Yes," Katie responded after a moment. "You know... would you mind if I took that turkey sandwich to go?"

"Truce?"

Katie approached Josh, who was doing his best sit-like-a-Buddha on a gurney he'd wheeled into a quiet corner.

"Truce?"

She tried again, her voice sounding more uncertain the second time.

Josh only just stopped himself from making a snarky comment about not knowing they were at war. But if he stopped and counted just how many scars he'd taken on in the past three years—both figurative and literal—maybe they had been. Heaven knew Katie had been nursing her own wounds, and these past two days had done nothing but reopen them.

He shifted across when she turned and pressed her hands against the gurney to hop up alongside him.

"Want some?" Katie offered when she'd settled.

Josh warily eyed the sandwich she waggled within his eyeline. He wouldn't have blamed Katie if she had laced the thing with strychnine, the way he'd spoken to her last.

"A peace offering." Katie held out a triangle of sandwich on the flat of her palm. "C'mon." She nudged him with her knee. "Go halvesies with me. I'll take a bite first, to prove I didn't load it with mistletoe berry sauce!"

He grinned. *Mind reader.*

He angled his head to take a surreptitious look at her through narrowed eyes. When she'd plunked herself down beside him on the gurney, he'd figured minimal eye contact would be the best way to go, but now that she was here... sandwich in hand... She took a smile-sized chomp of the thick sandwich and made a satisfied *"Mmm..."* noise.

He exhaled slowly. No doubt about it. No matter the time, date, place...no matter how angry he was or wasn't... she still took his breath away. If this were the olden days, there would be a kiss on her cheek, a hand slipped round her shoulder or her waist, a cheeky tickle somewhere or other and laughter. By God. He missed the sound of her laugh.

"Truce."

He put out a hand and received half of the turkey sandwich in his palm.

"It's from Santa."

"Really?"

"Sort of," Katie continued, almost shyly. "Remember the Klausens?"

"The 'I'm going to wring their necks when I get my hands on them' Klausens?" Josh held back from taking his first bite.

"The very ones. They're feasting it up on the recovery ward. Mashed potatoes, sweet potatoes, turkey bigger than an emu, stuffing—the whole kit and caboodle!" Katie took another chomp and grinned before her tongue slipped out to swoop up an escaped bit of cranberry sauce.

If this were the olden days, he would have licked that off, then hung around for a bit more lip-lock. He shifted again. For another reason this time.

Sweet dancing reindeer, who made this girl so sexy?

He thought back to this morning's escapade with her parents and felt the corners of his lips twitch before giving in to a full-blown grin. They might be the most surreal parents he'd ever met—but they were a good-looking couple. A good-looking couple who'd created one spectacularly beautiful daughter. A daughter who clearly didn't keep her parents up to date with everything in her life.

"Any chance you want to talk me through why you haven't told your parents we're not—?"

"Nope," she cut in, as if she were dodging questions about ditching school for the afternoon. "Aren't you going to eat that?" Katie popped the rest of her sandwich into her mouth, her fingers automatically reaching toward his untouched triangle.

He took a huge bite, smiling as he chewed, eyes hooked on hers. This was nice. And in the best possible way nice. He slipped his fingers through hers, eyes glued to the snow falling outside the window they were parked across from, not wanting to break the spell. This was more than he had hoped for. Just a few moments to sit and eat a turkey sandwich on Christmas Day with his wife.

He felt a tiny little squeeze from her fingers to his, and out of the corner of his eye he saw Katie lean her head back against the wall and close her eyes, a soft smile playing across her lips. His thumb shifted along her ring finger. His grin widened. Yup. Still there.

He took another bite. It was a helluva sandwich.

"I'm on my pager if you need me. And you know Maisie's number is just on the—"

"Go!" Jorja insisted, her finger pointed firmly at the exit. Katie obeyed.

The instant she turned the corner outside the ambulance bay, she felt her step become a little bit lighter. She tilted her head back and let a huge snowflake land and melt on her tongue.

It was the first time she'd stepped outside the hospital for four days, and the crisp air gave her an unexpected shot of energy. She needed a little reflection time in advance of New Year's Eve, and seeing as it had crept up on her all of a sudden, she was stealing an hour or two of alone time.

The truce she and Josh had been observing had given her some much-needed time to regroup. And the steady flow of patients had kept them both busy enough not to have to talk about things. Sometimes you needed that.

She stood still for a moment, not wanting to hear the crunching of her boots on the snow, and listened to the perfect wintry silence Copper Canyon did so well.

Maybe "silence" wasn't the best word to describe it. Perhaps...peaceful winter wonderland soundscape? Her eyes scanned the hillside—the trees and houses still twinkling away with all their holiday lights. The wind wasn't strong, but there was the occasional creak and shiver of the evergreens as they rocked back and forth with the soothing cadence of a cradle.

She resumed her journey toward Main Street. The call of one of Maisie's grilled cheese sandwiches had grown too loud to resist. There was only so much hospital canteen food a girl could take, and she wasn't technically due back on shift for a few hours now.

With everything that had happened over the past few days, Katie found herself looking at the picture-perfect town with fresh eyes. She'd always been a big-city girl. Moving out here two years ago had been less by design and more a matter of the most convenient way to put as much distance as possible between herself and Josh as she could.

Now that he was here, she realized how little of it she had actually *seen*. Her parents' condo. Maisie's. That was about it. It was all she had been able to handle. How her mother—who only came out here once or twice a year—knew about a Korean restaurant that did home delivery was beyond her. Had she lost all curiosity about the world around her? Or just needed things to be as straightforward as possible?

Probably the latter. It was as if grief had physically filled her up and rendered her incapable of living in a big city. Too frenetic. Too much to process when she could barely take on board what was happening in her own life. And now…? Now she was getting better. Able to take on a bit more razzle-dazzle in her day.

Ready for Josh?

She opened her arms wide, as if to ask the small town what it thought. *Was* she ready? *Could* she consider life with her husband again? Or was all of this just life's way of wrapping up their marriage in a gentler style?

Her feet picked up the pace, as if leading her to the answer. Within a few minutes she found herself outside Maisie's big picture window, trying to decide whether to laugh or cry. Sitting in her favorite booth was none other than Josh West. She could only see the back of his head. He looked bent in concentration over something. The menu? She doubted it. He walked into a diner and ordered one thing and one thing only.

Maybe that had changed.

She moved toward the door, then hesitated. Something about seeing Josh sitting there felt big. Momentous, even. Magic Eight Ball spooky.

Maybe just a quick walk round the block would help

her. If he was still there when she'd done a lap, she'd go in. If not…?

She'd cross that doorway when she came to it.

Josh couldn't believe he'd actually done it. Put his signature on the divorce papers. He'd wanted to see what it looked like. Having his name there in black and white. Well… Black typeface and blue ink from the pen he'd sweet-talked from the waitress. He wondered if she would have handed the thing over if she'd known what he was going to sign.

Just looking at the Petition for Divorce made him wish he hadn't ordered anything to eat. Hadn't pushed his curiosity so far.

Nausea welled deep within him and he sucked down the rest of his ice water to try and rinse the taste away. His head began to shake back and forth. It looked wrong. Both their names on those papers. It *was* wrong. The best place for these papers was in a shredder or on top of a roaring fire.

The past few days working alongside Katie had been good. Really good. But she had shied away from any heart-to-heart business. Which was fair enough, but he was beginning to feel the strain. Two more days and he needed to call the hospital in Paris with an answer.

"Can I fill you up there, hon?" The waitress reappeared with a jug of water and Josh guiltily stuffed the papers into the inner pocket of his coat. No need to make her complicit in his need to experience everything firsthand.

"Mind if I join you?"

"Katie!" Josh's eyes near enough popped out of his head as his wife appeared behind the comfortably proportioned waitress.

"I see you've found the best grilled cheese in town." She slipped into the booth after making a *may I?* gesture and receiving a mute nod of assent.

"There are other places that serve them?"

"Not with pickles." She smiled, then conceded. "Not really. I can't imagine a Korean grilled cheese sandwich."

"Kimchi and Swiss on rye?"

They laughed, then fell silent. Josh linked his eyes with his wife's, wishing he could dive into them and find all the answers he needed.

"Are you stalking me?"

Katie screwed up her face in consternation. "No…this just happens to be the only place to get a good sandwich at—" She glanced at her watch. "At seven-thirty at night on the thirtieth of December."

"So you weren't worried I'd left town without signing your papers?" The words came out bitterly. He took another deep swig of ice water, feeling a shot of iceberg zap straight to his temples as he did.

"Oh, Josh." Katie's voice grew heavy with sorrow. "Do we really have to do this?"

He suddenly felt fatigue fill him like cement.

Yeah. We really do.

"What?" He maintained eye contact. She wasn't going to dodge him now. "You mean talk about why you walked out on me two years ago and why the only contact I've had from you is through a lawyer. Hell, yeah, we've got to talk about it, Katie! That's what adults who love each other do."

Her breath caught, as if she were going to contest him, and a moment passed before a sad smile hinged her lips downward. "Not in my family."

"Well, I'm not your parents. I'm your husband. And the second you ran off to marry me in Niagara Falls I became your family. Doesn't that count for anything?"

"Of course it does—*did*—Josh. It's just…" She shook her head at him, her eyes pleading for him to stop pressing.

"Just *what*?" He stopped himself just short of pounding the table with his fist. If he was going to hand over those papers, he had to know why.

"I just thought it would be easier if I went back to the

way things were before I met you." Her shoulders slumped and she looked away.

Josh's body straightened with a lightning bolt of undiluted indignation. "What does *that* mean?"

"It means that before I met you I was used to having no one to rely on. I didn't *need* anyone to get by."

"Is this because your parents weren't around?" he asked, already knowing the answer as dawn began to break in his thick-as-a-coconut husk of a head.

"Weren't. Aren't. Never will be," she droned, her fingers methodically folding a napkin into an ever-diminishing square.

"Why on earth would you have thought that about *me*?"

"Because you weren't there!"

"Of course I was."

"'I'm going up to the slopes with the guys, Katiebird.'" She mimicked him. "'Off to the track for a few rounds of speed cycling.' 'Heading up to Maine for the switchbacks.' 'Want to jump on the back of my motorcy—?'"

"Okay, okay." He held up his hands. "I get it." And did he ever? Especially when she got to the motorcycle part.

"And I guess…" She trailed off, her eyes filling with tears as she began micro-squaring another napkin.

"Hey…" He reached across the booth and stroked her cheek with his fingers. "What did you guess?"

"I guess I was scared that if—"

Her voice faltered and Josh took hold of her hand, rubbing the back of it with his thumb. Seeing her like this was torture.

"What were you scared of?"

"Josh!" She tugged her fingers through her hair in despair. "For a doctor, you really are thick as two planks, sometimes. Didn't you *see* it? I was terrified to get pregnant again because if losing one child had pushed you that far away, what would happen if I lost another? Or lost *you* to one of your crazy escapades? I just couldn't bear the thought of losing you, so I made the decision that I thought was best for both of us."

The words flew out as if they were all attached to the other in a long string.

Josh couldn't even speak. It hadn't occurred to him for a New York second that Katie had let him down. If anything, he'd felt he'd let *her* down. He was the one person who had been able to draw her out of her shell, make her laugh like a hyena, smile so broadly movie stars would have envied her...

"You know what, Katiebird?" He drew his finger along her jawline and kept it there when their eyes met. "If brains were leather I wouldn't have enough to saddle a June bug."

He felt her chin quiver. Tears...or a snigger?

"I have no idea what that means." She lifted her tear-beaded lashes to meet his gaze.

"I'm saying I don't have the sense Mother Nature gave a goose!"

"Cute Southern colloquialisms aren't helping to make what you're trying to say any clearer, Joshua West." But Katie giggled as she spoke.

"So you think I'm cute, do you?" He jostled her knee with his under the table.

"Maybe a little bit," she eventually conceded.

"Oh, really? And just how big is this little bit of cuteness you are affording me?"

"Maybe this much?" She allowed a pinch of air to pass between her fingers before closing them tight.

"That's pretty cute, if you ask me. My mama said I grew up on the far end of the ugly stick. Never said which end was which, though..." He picked up Katie's hand and put her fingers in a slightly wider pose. "Now, I don't want to go tootin' my own horn, but wouldn't you say *this* much is a bit more accurate?"

Katie gave him a sidelong glance, then burst into hysterics. His laughter was soon intermingling with hers, and it was only when their guffaws began to die out that she realized the handful of other patrons in the restaurant had been caught up in their chortle-fest as well.

"What are we doing here, Katiebird?"

"Apart from ordering grilled cheese sandwiches?"

"Yes, Katie," he replied good-naturedly. "Apart from that."

"Tying up loose ends?"

He shook his head at the same moment as she made a face at her own suggestion. It didn't sit right.

"Clearing the air?" he offered.

"Getting our facts straight," she said with a definitive nod, as if the matter were settled.

"Hi, hon—the usual?" The waitress appeared by their table.

"Yes, please, Eileen." Katie smiled up at her.

"You know—we *do* have a Brie and cranberry special on for the holidays."

"No, thank you."

Katie and Josh recoiled and responded as one, much to Eileen's obvious amusement.

"Funny how the only two people I've ever met who like dill pickles in their cheese sandwiches are sitting together." She gave the pair a *go figure* shrug and turned back to the kitchen without waiting for an explanation.

Josh looked over at his wife, saw her cheeks a bit flushed with emotion. It wasn't peculiar at all… They were the only thing she'd known how to cook when they'd met, so they'd eaten them. A lot.

"Have you already eaten?"

He nodded that he had, but didn't move. "Have you ever known me to turn down a chance to steal some of your dinner?"

She grinned and shook her head. He would stick around. Show his wife he was a changed man.

"Well, then. Prepare to defend your pickles!"

* * *

"Dr. West—" Michael ran to the door to catch Josh before he went to warm up the pickup. "Are you still good to meet up for that coffee?"

"Absolutely." Josh nodded, yanking up the zip on his snowboarding jacket before he hit the automatic doors. "Is it something we can chat about here at the hospital?"

"Uh, well…" Michael sent an anxious look over his shoulder back to the main reception desk, where Jorja and a couple of the shift nurses were laughing at who knew what. "Maybe not?"

Ding! Girl trouble.

"Got it." Josh put out a hand to fist-bump but Michael just looked confused. He lowered his hand. "I'm out to-night—but maybe sometime tomorrow?"

"Yeah!" Michael's grin widened. "That'd be great. Thanks, Doc." Michael raised his hand, then turned it into a fist, making a sort of weird revolution-style gesture.

"Tomorrow," Josh said with a grin, taking a hit of cold as the double doors parted to let in a blast of icy air.

He'd need a few minutes to get the truck ready in this weather. Beautiful to look at. A monumental challenge if you weren't where you were supposed to be.

"Are you ready for this?" Katie hauled herself into the truck and slammed the door against the cold wind.

"As I'll ever be."

Katie gave Josh a sidelong glance as he turned down Ol' Bessie's radio.

"It was a whole lot busier today than I thought."

"New Year's Eve!" Josh singsonged. "All the ailments people didn't want to pay heed to on the big day and the day after—and the day after that—building into a mother lode of excess straight up to the point of no return."

"I know," Katie agreed rigorously. "No amount of 'all things in moderation' speeches seem to stop everyone from going overboard on the holidays, and this year was no different!" she finished indignantly. Then she thought a moment.

Except on one front.

It was the first time she'd worked her way through patient after patient, case after case, and come out the other end feeling a sense of being whole again. Complete. She didn't need to visit Neurology to know what was going on. The wounds she'd thought she'd stitched together hadn't been ripped open when her husband had arrived in Copper Canyon. They had never been fixed in the first place— just hidden away and stuffed in a faraway corner that was too hard to reach. Leaving Josh behind was never going to bring Elizabeth back. Or her old life.

Who knew having Josh here would be more healing than she ever could have imagined it to be?

She couldn't help running her hands along the dashboard. "Check out this old jalopy! Still keeping her pristine, I see."

"Yup. I keep waiting for some movie producer to pull me over and offer me a million dollars to put her in a film, but it still hasn't happened."

She gave a barely contained snort. Ol' Bessie was the one thing in Josh's life he took care of, keeping her immaculate. She shook her head. That wasn't fair. He'd always taken care of her. But after Elizabeth...?

Her rigid belief that he'd gone off the deep end had shifted in the past few days. Maybe pushing life to the extreme had been his way of grieving. His way of trying to help her see the light at the end of the tunnel. She swallowed away the sting of tears and ran her finger along the trim of the red leather bench seats.

"Remember what you said to me on our first date?"

"You can sit here, right next to me." His hand patted the bench seat. Josh needed no time to remember.

"We hadn't even shared a soda or anything together."

"A *soda*?" Josh guffawed. "We weren't *twelve*, Katie-bird."

She'd felt twelve. All nerves and jittering expectations of the unknown. But when he'd looked at her...

Mmm...things had started pinging inside of her that she'd never known existed. Sparks, tingles, heated shivers—the whole bag of clichéd responses—each and every one of them feeling utterly fresh and new.

So when they'd discovered they both had some time off, and he'd asked her if she wanted a day out in the countryside, she'd pulled together all her courage and said yes.

Josh had been everything she'd admired in a man and in a doctor. He'd been a year into his residency, having just blasted through his junior residency, and she'd been on the first stint of her rotational internship. He'd had confidence, an infectious laugh, a genuine connection with his patients...and a drawl from somewhere down South that had lit her up like a—she smiled—like the big ball in Times Square on New Year's Eve.

Josh barked a laugh into the cab—with a puff of breath that disappeared shortly after.

"What?"

"You barely even acknowledged me when I held open Ol' Bessie's cherry-red passenger door for you. Me being all gallant and gentlemanly, and your big brown eyes were fixed on the dash, the road, the crazy bright scarlet, orange and yellow blur of the leaves we were flashing past as we left Boston. I thought I might've woken up with the chicken pox or something and not noticed."

He glanced over to see Katie smile at the memory and he patted her leg.

"But three days later you didn't stop talking, did you?"

She shook her head no. It was true. And he was the only thing she'd had eyes for.

She looked across at his hands—one loosely resting on top of the steering wheel, the other holding on at three o'clock. He looked relaxed enough, but she could see his thoughts were about as busy as hers were. On her parents? On the rings she still hadn't managed to take off her finger?

She kept her eyes on his hands, wondering how much the past couple of years had truly changed him. She still hadn't worked up the courage to ask him about those scars. What if what he had been through made him someone she could no longer truly access? That was what it had felt like in that awful dark year. Why would he risk his own life again and again when they'd just lost their tiny precious baby?

Josh would argue that no one changed—they just became more of who they had always been, just a bit smarter about things.

She'd changed. She was sure of it.

Her head tipped against the cool of the window. If she was brave enough to ask, Josh would probably say she hadn't changed—she'd just reverted back to the introvert he'd pulled out of her cocoon that magical first year in Boston. Her butterfly year.

"Are you having an entire conversation in your head again?"

Katie couldn't help but give him a congratulatory laugh. "Got it in one!" Then she surprised herself by chasing it up with a wistful sigh. She'd forgotten the comforting side of having someone know her inside and out.

"Something like that. Remember when—" she started, then hesitated. Memory lane could be a rough road to travel. Especially this time of year.

"The apples?" He shot her a quick look, before refocusing on the road.

How did he do that?

"Yes…the apples. What was it—three or four bushels we took down to your grandmother's for canning?"

"I think it was more like five. You were on a high-speed race—dodging all of my clumsy attempts to catch you up in a sexy clinch—so I did the only thing I could!"

"Oh, yeah? And what was that?"

"I had to win you over with my apple-picking prowess!" He dropped her a quick wink, his eyes barely leaving the road as he did.

"Ha!" Katie barked out. "Don't be ridiculous. I didn't know you were trying to kiss me."

"Course you did, Katiebird." His voice was soft now. Gentle. "You were just scared of what would happen once I caught you."

She had been terrified. Her whole life she had always been in control. Of everything. It had been easier that way. Easier to understand why her parents had never been around. Easier to zone in on a high-stakes medical career, knowing she could harness her mind and shape her ability to learn into an aptitude to heal. If she let herself fall for Josh, it would be a whole different ball game. Whole different park. She'd known then that she would never be able to control her heart once she gave it to him. And from the increased hammering she was feeling in her chest, it still held true.

She narrowed her eyes and slid them over to the driver's side of the cab to take in Josh's profile. Her tummy did its usual trip to the acrobatics department. Gold medalists had nothing on her!

All of a sudden she hurt inside. Hurt so much she could actually put a name to it. *Regret.* She regretted making Josh decide between adrenaline fixes or her. Regretted packing her bags and hightailing it without even scribbling a note to explain. Leaving him to grieve on his own.

She twisted the rings on her finger. She still hadn't quite managed to put them back in their box. The rings she had accepted with a vow to love Josh until her very last breath.

"I don't think I've ever seen Gramma Jam-Jam look

more surprised than when we pulled into the drive." Josh's quiet voice and soft laughter broke into the silence filling the cab.

"What?" Katie exclaimed, tucking a foot under her leg on the bench seat as she turned to face him. "You told me she was expecting us."

"You believed me?"

"Of course I did!" Katie insisted. "People don't just *spontaneously* drive down the Eastern Seaboard to their grandmother's to can and preserve and…"

"Uh-huh?" Josh started nodding, the smile on his face growing. "It's coming to you now, isn't it?"

Little ding-ding-dings of recognition started going off in Katie's head, and her eyes widened as each detail began to slip into a new place. "She set me to peeling and coring all of those apples, saying she needed your signature on something down at the bank in town. It was a Sunday."

"Yes, it was. We couldn't believe you fell for it, what with you being a highfalutin valedictorian and all!"

"*You* were a valedictorian!" Katie protested, fingers digging into the leather seat as Josh took a right turn onto the small lane that brought them up the side of the mountain to her parents' place.

"Doesn't count as much when you're in a class of one hundred in a town that wasn't too much bigger." He reached across and gave her leg a squeeze. "Lucky for me you were too blinded by my good looks to pay any attention."

"Ha! As if!" Katie lied.

"Don't go playing coy with me, Katherine McGann."

He withdrew his hand and Katie immediately slipped her own over the spot on her thigh to keep the warmth in.

"Well…that might've been a little bit true. And when your grandmother assigned someone a task—you did it!"

"That is most definitely the truth! Gramma Jam-Jam was a tough taskmaster!" Josh's laugh ended with a sigh.

"I am really sorry to hear she's passed."

"Yeah…well…" Josh drove on for a while before filling the cab with a big laugh. "Lucky for me she had no problem with white lies if the intent behind them was loving."

"What do you mean?"

"Once you were peeling all those bushels of apples, she and I set off like wildcats, scraping the shelves clean of jars, pie tins and whatever else I needed to bribe my grandmother into helping me win your heart."

"She did that, sure enough."

"She did…?" Josh's voice deepened with emotion. "Or I did?"

"Both of you," Katie answered hastily. Then, "You did." It was the more honest answer. "Of course you did."

Her mobile phone jangled, breaking the weighted atmosphere in two.

"It's my mom. Sorry." She winced apologetically as she pressed the button. "Hi, Mom—what's up?"

Josh couldn't make out what Katie's mother was saying, which didn't much matter as everything rattling round his head was making a big enough racket.

Katie still loved him. His wife still loved him.

Was that enough to bring them back together or had time just been too cruel? Maybe knowing she loved him would be salve enough for him to carry on. Go forward. Let each of them get on with lives that could never be the same if they were together.

"You *forgot*?"

Katie's voice had careened up a few octaves.

"Mom, not even five days have passed since you asked us. How could you forget?"

She listened in silence, then gave a brusque "goodbye" before jabbing a finger at her phone to end the call.

"Typical."

"What?"

"My parents are out tonight."

"Better offer?"

"Something like that."

"Are they in town?"

"They're at someone else's condo in the complex. 'Too good an invitation to refuse.'" Katie expertly mimicked her mother's mid-Atlantic accent, then huffed out an exasperated sigh. "I don't know why I let it get to me. Why I didn't *expect* it! You'd think after thirty-one years of being dodged by my own parents I'd be used to it."

"Is that how you see it?"

"That's how it *is*! Whenever I really needed them to just *be* there—nothing else—there was always an excuse. Always something 'too good to miss' for them to go to."

Her words hit home. He wondered if things would have been different between them if he'd let Katie go through a phase of wallowing in dirty pajamas, with a sink full of dishes growing God knew what kind of mold. It had killed him to see her so low, and he'd all but turned into a parody of himself to try and cheer her up.

It was also pretty obvious that Katie had learned some less-than-awesome tricks from her parents. Leaving him on his own when he'd begun to run out of false cheer and had needed her most.

His shoulders sagged. She hadn't known. He'd had just as thick a veneer of protectiveness over his emotions as Katie had over her numbness. Grief had rendered them both loners. She hadn't been avoiding him for the past two years out of malice. It had been out of grief.

"They should've had to apply for a license," Katie grumbled.

"What kind of license?"

"A baby license."

"What do you mean?"

"You have to get a dog license, don't you?"

"Yes…"

"Well, there are countless people out there in the world who actually want children and don't get them—and my parents have a child and don't give a flying pig!"

Josh took his eyes off the road, reaching out to put a hand on Katie's leg.

When he felt the front wheels of the truck start to skid, he instantly regretted not giving the road his full attention. Black ice. He resisted putting his foot on the brake. Drove into the skid. Everything the rulebook said.

"Josh!"

He fought the urge to overcorrect. And still the truck slid. He reached out his arm to brace Katie against the crash. She had on her seat belt but she would always be his responsibility. And in the blink of an eye, that lightning flash loss of control ended in an abrupt thud and a jerk as the truck lodged itself into a roadside snowdrift.

"Are you all right?"

They spoke simultaneously.

"Yes. Are you?"

It happened again.

They both laughed, their breath huffing out into the cold cab of the truck in tiny clouds of confirmation that they had both made it. They were okay.

Before he thought better of it, Josh unbuckled himself and his wife, pulling Katie into his arms, holding her tighter than he ever had. He felt her arms come together round his waist, slipping up along his back and pulling him close. Despite the layers of winter clothes, he could have sworn he felt heat move between the two of them, tightening the bond of connection he had feared was severed.

"That was a bit scary." Katie's muffled voice came from the crook of his neck, where she had nestled.

"It was a bit, wasn't it?" He stroked his hand along her hair, giving in to the desire to weave his fingers through it, enjoying the sensation of silk against skin. "We're all right, Katiebird. We're all right now."

Talk about a loaded statement!

He tugged her in a bit closer, not having a clue *what* they were. Together? Apart? Wrapping things up for good or starting afresh?

Whichever way the wind blew, he would be forever grateful for having her in his arms right now. Feeling her nestle into him a bit more, not pushing him away, hearing their breathing steady a bit. The skid and the jolting snow-drift stop had been a shock. Not a horrible one. But one that needed this sort of quiet recovery time.

He was surprised to discover that his fingers had taken on a will of their own and had shifted beneath the pash-mina Katie had tied loosely round her neck. They were slipping up and along her neck, just to the base of her hairline, massaging away any stress or worry. As his awareness of her response to his caresses grew, so did the depth of their breathing. They weren't in their own worlds any longer.

Katie felt Josh spread his fingers wide along her back, fluidly changing the movement into slow circular caresses. Each change of pressure quickened her pulse. The ache of desire overrode her need to intellectualize the moment. She tilted up her chin and after a microscopic hesitation her lips met his.

The explosion of sensation all but overwhelmed her. Heat, scent, taste… Everything was accentuated. Her heart-beat accelerated as the fulfillment from each kiss deepened. Josh's touch felt simultaneously familiar and forbidden. Fa-miliar after the years of shared history. Forbidden because of the deep well of pleasure she felt at his touch. Pleasure she didn't feel she deserved.

As their lips touched and explored, Katie felt as though her body was going through a reawakening. Where she had felt exhausted and dark, she now felt charged and vi-brant. Where she had felt deep, weighted sorrow, she now began to feel possibility and renewal. Where she had felt numb…she now felt love.

Her fingers pressed into her husband's shoulders as their breath intermingled in searching kiss after kiss. When it seemed as though time had all but stood still, she felt him pull back. She felt the loss of his embrace instantly and it struck her how time and again over their courtship and marriage Josh had been nothing short of her pillar of strength. Almost shyly, she looked up to meet his blue eyes.

"Look at us, steaming up the windows like a couple of high school kids." Josh's voice was light, but the mood in the truck was laden with meaning. Past, present, future… too much to think about. Too much to consider.

Katie suddenly began to feel claustrophobic in the cab. "We should probably see if we can get the truck out of the drift in case anyone else comes along this road." She pushed open the door, surprised to find it resisting.

"I think we're wedged up against the bank. Come on out my side. We'll have a look."

Josh was reaching across her as he spoke, flicking open the glove compartment, raking around by touch as there had never been a cab light in the old truck. She drew back in the seat, surprised at how Josh's touch suddenly had become something to avoid. Having his warm body all but wrapped around her just moments ago had been like accepting a vital life force, but now that her brain had taken a few moments to play catch-up, she was treating the poor man like he was toxic. It wasn't fair. To either of them.

He tugged a flashlight out of the glove box, clicking the beam off and on as he pulled back into the driver's seat. "Guess that's us in action."

His voice sounded unchanged. Had he not noticed her flinch at his touch, or was he choosing to ignore it—his modus operandi of The Dark Days.

"Can we just get out of here?" Katie knew she sounded

impatient, but she didn't have the wherewithal to edit herself. "I feel like a sitting target."

In more ways than one.

"Not a problem." He stepped aside as she clambered out of the truck—a bit less gracefully than she'd intended, but suddenly a deep breath of icy air was paramount. She let the sharpness of the cold hit her lungs hard—hold her static for a moment and then release her with a billow of breath.

"You all right?" Josh's voice was all concern, but his focus was on the front of the truck—the front half of which was soundly encased in the snowdrift, as if it had been put there before the winter had begun.

She mumbled an affirmative, working her hands round herself and giving her arms a rub as she looked around at the quiet lane, surprised at how much she could see without streetlights. It was snowing lightly. And it was peaceful. So incredibly quiet and *peaceful*.

In any other circumstances it would have been romantic. She silently chided herself. Less than a minute ago it had been romantic! Passionate, even. How could five days have changed how she saw the world? As she thought the words, she knew they were ridiculous. Ten minutes could have an impact. Even less and your life could change forever. For better…or for worse.

She heard Josh crunching through the snow around the truck. "What's the damage?"

"Doesn't seem to be too much wrong with the truck— but I doubt we're going to get out of here without a tow truck. Unless you feel like digging it out of this eight-foot snowbank?"

"Seriously?" *Okay.* Her voice really couldn't have gone more high-pitched than it just had. Dogs would be howling soon.

"Sorry, Katie." Josh shrugged. "This gingerbread truck has well and truly crumbled."

"I don't know how you do that." Katie shook her head.

"What?"

"Not go mental over Ol' Bessie being near enough to-taled."

"Accidents happen. Life goes on." He shrugged it off.

Cool Hand Josh! One of the many reasons why she had married him. Her very own cowboy—calm, cool, and kicking the back tires on his truck.

"Does that make it work faster?"

"Yes," he answered drily, giving the tire another kick just to prove to her that the total opposite was true.

Katie couldn't stop a burst of giggles from burbling forth. His eyes met hers—and the familiar deep punch of connection put her insides through another spin cycle.

Okay, girl—time to decide if we're playing hot or cold. Time to stop playing.

"What are you doing here, Josh?"

"I could ask you just about the same thing, Katiebird." He leaned against the back of the pickup, one leg crossed over the other—his body language as stress-free as if he were talking about a bowling league.

"I *live* here." Her emotional temperature shot up.

"No, you don't." He tilted his chin up in the classic guy move. "You hide out in your parents' chalet—where, I would put money on it, you haven't done a single thing other than unpack your clothes."

Guilty.

She clamped her lips tight. What *was* this? A standing-up psychoanalysis session?

"When anything approaching life comes to your door, you hide out in your work, just like you've always done."

"No, I don't!"

Wow. Good comeback. Someone has playground patter down to a fine art.

She threw in a glare for good measure.

"Look, Katie. I don't want to fight."

"*I* don't want to fight!" she shouted back. Hmm...

Maybe she did. And why not? They were stuck out here in the middle of nowhere, with nothing but a truck stuck in a mammoth snowdrift, and…and… Inspiration hit. She scooped up a handful of snow faster than she'd ever done, crunched it into a ball and threw it at him. It landed on his chest with a satisfying thud.

"Feel better?"

"A little."

She sniffed, thought for a moment about using her sleeve, then sniffed again. Usually she was the one who got to play the grown-up. What was up with this role-reversal thing?

Another little marker went up in her Things-That-Are-Different-About-Josh list.

"Should we get a tow truck out here?"

"I'll call. What road are we on again?" She hadn't been paying attention. She'd been too busy making doe eyes at the man she was meant to have hardened her heart to.

"You're going to laugh."

"I doubt it." Being petulant wasn't making much of an impact on her grinning husband.

"Guess."

"No."

"C'mon, Katie. What do you *think* the road's called?" He drew her name out all slow and Southern-style, as if he were skittering the vowels down the back of her sweater with a revitalizing handful of snow. Verbal retaliation for her juvenile attack?

"I don't know. Rudolph Place?"

"Christmas Lane."

"It is *not*!" she retorted, swiping at the air between them.

"Sure is." He looked at his phone screen, where she could see him increasing the size of their location on his map app. "And if my map-reading is still as good as it was in the Scouts…we've got Christmas Farm up ahead, about a mile. Unsurprisingly, they sell Christmas trees."

"You can tell that from a map?"

He turned the screen so she could see it. A little bubble ad had popped up over the satellite image, with "Christmas Tree Farm" on it and their opening hours.

Ah. So he wasn't all-knowing. Just *mostly* all-knowing.

An image of an admissions form pinged into her mind. "That's where the Klausens live! I thought they'd made that up."

"You doubted the rosy-cheeked and extremely jolly Mr. and Mrs. Klausen's good word?" Josh teased.

"Yes." She scrunched up her face. "But you always knew I was a Scrooge."

"I knew nothing of the kind, my little Katiebird."

She didn't say anything in return. Couldn't. He knew more about her than anyone in the world. He'd been the only one she had well and truly let in.

"Look—there's a chapel just a couple of hundred yards down the road. We can hang out there. Safer than here in the pitch-black. Have you called a tow truck?"

Katie shook her head and blew on her fingers. "Let me grab my bag. I've got an automobile emergency services card in there."

"Prepared for everything, aren't you, Katie?"

"What's that supposed to mean?" She wheeled on him, handbag swinging around and banging into her hip as she struck a defensive pose.

It wasn't her fault she had had to behave as a grown-up for most of her childhood, let alone after the death of their daughter, when Josh had rediscovered his inner teenager.

"Nothing," Josh replied, fatigue suddenly evident in his voice. "It didn't mean anything. Should we start walking to the chapel while you call them so we don't get cold?"

Katie rang the company, only just managing to keep the bite out of her voice when she discovered they were short-staffed and the wait would be a while. Everyone had bad days. She and Josh were no different. And compared to what they'd been through in the past, this was a doddle.

They crunched along the side of the road in silence, Josh holding no particular path with the beam of his flashlight. It illuminated an icicle-laden tree here. A slushy puddle there. A thickening of the snow in the air all around them. The silence of the snowy night began to close in on Katie. More accurately, the silence between *them*. Between her and the man she had thanked her lucky stars she'd met all those years ago.

Without warning she suddenly flung herself into a snow-drift and began moving her arms and legs as rapidly as she could. She needed a snow angel—and fast.

Josh had been so wrapped up in his own thoughts he'd walked on a few steps before realizing Katie was no longer by his side. When he turned round, he hooted with unchecked laughter. There was his proper-as-they-come wife, looking like a frenzied wild woman. This was going to be the least peaceful snow angel ever created. Snow Tasmanian devil?

Katie abruptly stopped swinging her arms and legs, her eyes locked on Josh so intently it felt like a make-or-break moment. He opened his mouth, then shut it again.

Katie's hand shot out. "Aren't you going to help me up?"

"Of course."

He reached out his arm and felt himself being yanked into the snowdrift. His boot slipped on a skid of snow Katie had smoothed into angel submission and he fell with a thud onto his bad hip.

Containing the howl of pain was impossible.

"Josh!" Katie pushed herself up, a horrified expression playing across her face. "Are you all right?" She began issuing instructions. "Lie back. Breathe steadily. Follow my finger."

He batted away her hand. "I'm fine." He was still hurting and just needed a minute.

"Josh!" Katie's voice broke as her fingers ran along his
cheek. "I'm so sorry. I didn't mean to hurt you."

"You didn't."

Yes, she had. But not in the way she thought.

He could be mean right now. Cruel. Because that was
what it had felt like when she'd left him. Just about the
cruelest thing anyone had done. But he'd known Katie
hadn't left to hurt him. She'd done it to save herself. Save
herself from a man who'd seemed intent on self-destruction. And here was a sign of that self-destruction for her
to bear witness to.

Terrific. Everything going according to the Great Win
Back Katie Plan? That's one big fat tick.

He smoothed his hand along his hip and gave it a rub,
made sure everything was still in place. Ditto for the knee.

"Help me up?"

"Of course." Katie scrambled to her knees, shifting a
shoulder under his to help him up from the snow. "What
happened there?"

"Just lost my—" He stopped himself. No more lies. "I
had an accident."

He felt Katie tense beneath the weight of his arm, but
she just mmm-hmm'd him and waited for him to continue
as they both pushed upward.

He took his arm off her shoulders when they were standing and gave himself a little wriggle of a once-over. Head,
shoulders, knees and toes all in working order. Haphaz-
ard as they were.

He tipped his head in the direction of the chapel. "Shall
we get in the warm?"

"Do you need a hand?"

He couldn't tell if she was furious or concerned. Probably both.

He shook his head and they walked on in silence. Josh concentrated on working the kinks out of his hip as Katie visibly struggled with the thousands of questions that were no doubt playing through her mind. She'd begged him again and again not to get hurt. Told him that she didn't have the strength for it. And here he was—giving her evidence that her decision to leave because he was too hell-bent on pushing the envelope had been the right one.

"So…" Katie prompted, unable to wait anymore. "This accident. Was it a bad one?"

"Something like that," he admitted, ignoring her exasperated sigh. "I'll tell you everything you want to know. I just need to sit down for a minute, all right?"

The chapel came into view as they turned the corner. It was a pretty little thing. Clapboard, white as the snow, with a green trim, he thought, though it was difficult to tell in the dark. Twists of fairy lights had been spun round the two evergreens flanking the front door to the chapel, and there was enough snow on the steps to tell him no one had been inside for the past few hours. A large and intricate star was shining at the very top of the church. He would have laid money on it being visible near enough everywhere in the valley.

Katie stepped up onto the entryway first and gave a relieved smile when the door opened. "Thank goodness for small-town security systems."

"I don't know if Gramma Jam-Jam even had keys."

"She had neighbors. Same as keys. Were you…?" Katie hesitated.

He shook his head, knowing where the question was heading. "I wasn't with her. One of my biggest regrets."

A huge mistake not worth making again.

"I'm sorry," Katie said with genuine feeling. "I know how much you loved her."

"Yeah, well…I seem to be chalking up valuable lessons left, right and center these days."

They stood face-to-face, there in the quiet of the church, their eyes saying more to each other than they could ever say aloud. Love. Pain. Regret. Josh could have ticked them off one by one and kept going. He hadn't been joking. All he needed to do now was prove he had learned from those mistakes.

"Let's go light a couple of candles."

"What?"

"C'mon. Over here." He tipped his head toward the far corner. "Let's go light candles for Gramma and Elizabeth. We've never done that together."

Katie eyed the end of the church where the candle table stood, her head making the tiniest of shakes back and forth.

He wove his fingers through hers. "C'mon, darlin'. Isn't it time we sent our little girl some light—seeing as we're together? Sent her a blessing at Christmas?"

"I don't *want* to say goodbye!" Katie's words all but echoed through the small church.

Josh pulled her into his arms and held her tight. "It's not goodbye, Katie. I didn't say anything about goodbye." He pressed a soft kiss onto her forehead before holding her back at arm's length so he could look at her. "Think of it as her mother and father saying hello. Letting her know we'll always love her."

Katie began to nod her head. Slowly at first, and then in a pronounced yes. She would never, ever in her heart be able to bid her daughter farewell. But hello? She could say that again and again. And yet without Josh she hadn't been able to say anything to her daughter. It hadn't seemed possible. And now here he was—her big ol' country husband—making the hardest thing in the world one of the simplest and most beautiful.

Hand in hand they approached the small table. Josh lit a candle for his grandmother, and then both of them lit Elizabeth's. As the flame flickered and gained purchase, Katie felt an emotional weight shift from her chest—the light of the flame was offering her a lightness of spirit she wouldn't have believed possible.

The moment lengthened and absorbed them both in its glow. Katie tipped her head onto Josh's shoulder and felt his head lightly meet hers. They'd both lost their little girl. It was right that they were doing this together.

As they watched the candle flicker and flit alongside the one meant for the woman who would have been her great-grandmother, Katie could almost picture Gramma Jam-Jam up there in heaven—wherever *that* was—teaching Elizabeth how to make apple pie. As she swiped away a wash of tears, she was astonished to realize there was a soft smile on her lips.

Was this what it took? Being together with Josh again? Josh, who *still* hadn't told her why he had howled like an injured wolf when he fell into the snow.

"Right!" Katie clapped her hands together a bit too loudly. "Shall we take a pew? Hear all about this big bad accident of yours?"

Josh's heart squeezed tight as he heard her trying to lighten the atmosphere. He was surprised she wasn't a fuming ball of I-Told-You-So.

He wandered a few aisles down and chose a pew, patting the space next to him for Katie.

She sat down next to him, but kept her eyes on the front of the church, where garlands were still strung across the apse. A simply but beautifully decorated Christmas tree twinkled away in the half-light.

"It was a motorcycle accident."

Katie sucked in a sharp breath and tightened her jaw. If the light had been better, he would have seen if those were tears that had sprung to her eyes or if it was just the wintry light.

He reached across to take her hand, and though she didn't turn to meet his gaze, he was relieved to feel the soft squeeze of her fingers. He had to keep reminding himself…she cared. She loved him. She might not like him very much—especially right now—but she loved him. It was worth fighting for.

The words began to pour out. "It was meant to be a Saturday-morning ride. Just a few guys out for a run—before traffic built up."

"But…?"

"But it got competitive. The roads were tricky. In the mountains up north of Boston."

He saw Katie wince. She knew the ones. They'd used to take breaks up there whenever their hectic hospital schedules would allow. When she'd finally taken those first days of maternity leave.

"We were riding the switchbacks and a logging truck came down the center of both lanes. It was veer or—"

He didn't need to paint the full picture. She was an intelligent woman. Move or get mashed was what it had boiled down to. And he'd moved.

"No one else was hurt, so there was that to be thankful for, and one of the guys was an EMT—he made sure I kept my—"

"Kept your what?" Katie whipped round to face him, tears streaming down her cheeks.

He brushed them away with a thumb. "My left leg. It's good. He knew every trick in the book. I hit some dark moments during recovery, and going through airport security is a bit of a bells and whistles affair these days—but I'm all good, Katie. I'm here."

"How long were you in the hospital?"

Josh sucked in a breath as he did the mental arithmetic. "About seven months. Maybe eight."

"ICU?"

"For a lot of it."

"Internal damage?"

"Some."

Katie's fingers flew to her mouth. *Josh could have died.*

He could have died and she would have been none the wiser. She'd left no address, no clue as to where to find her. Strict instructions with Alice never to speak of him again. Nothing. For a moment she thought she was going to be sick.

"What happened when you got out?"

"I roomed with a few guys. Doctors. Long enough to know what an idiot I was to let you walk out the door."

"And your motorcycle?" She registered his words, but needed more facts.

"Hung up my helmet, sold the Jet Ski, my snowboard— you name it. I realized life was a bit more important than what I'd been calling living after you left." He laughed. "You'll love this."

Her eyes widened. What exactly would she love about her husband's traumatic motorcycle accident and harrowing recovery?

"I've taken up yoga."

He watched her take in this new slice of information then reshape her face into something a whole lot happier.

"You're going to *yoga class*?"

All right. It was a tone of pure disbelief. But he'd take that over a telling-off for the motorcycle crash any day of the week.

"Three times a week. Sometimes four!"

"In Boston?"

"No, Katie."

He cleared his throat. Spilling this piece of news was going to be almost as rough as telling her about his accident.

"What?" She poked him in the arm. *"What?"*

She poked him harder when his eyes started taking an unnecessary journey round the small church. It was clapboard. There were pews. And a Christmas tree. *C'mon, already!*

"I can tell when you're holding back information. Where have you been? What happened to our—the house?"

"I rented it out."

"What? Why?" She pulled her hand out of his, clasping her two hands together over her heart.

"Are you kidding me?" Now it was Josh's turn to look astonished. "Live there without you? Sit in those rooms knowing the chances of you walking back through the front door were nil to—?" He sought for a word that meant less than nil and threw his hands up in the air instead. "There was no chance of me staying there once you walked out that door, Katie. Absolutely none."

She suddenly missed her nickname. It had rankled when he'd first used it, but now...why wasn't he? *Wasn't she his Katiebird anymore?*

Her stomach churned and she could feel her hands shake even though she was pressing them tightly together.

Was he finishing things between them?

She blinked and stared, her body and mind not comprehending what exactly it was Josh was saying to her. She felt the backs of his fingers shift away a stray lock of hair, then give her cheek a gentle stroke, and she watched his lips as he continued to speak.

"My life was with you, Katiebird, and then you—you left. What else was I meant to do?"

Katie's eyes shifted back up to Josh's and she just stared at him, hands still clasped as if they were the only things holding her thumping heart inside her chest. *She had left him.* She'd thought of it as saving herself, but in doing so had she destroyed Josh? Her eyes took in his beautiful face, the strong shoulder line, the chest she'd used as a pillow more than once.

The pounding in her heart began to drown out what Josh was saying. She could see him speaking, but the words weren't computing.

Okay. Regroup.

Katie ripped through the index cards in her mind to make sense of things. Reorder what she had believed to be true. Reimagine the last two years.

It hit her—almost physically—that what had enabled her to run away was the knowledge that Josh would always be there. In her mind's eye she had vividly kept Josh on the porch of their sweet little house, with its tiny little porch and tinier backyard, where their daughter would be old enough to ride on a swing about now. How they would have got a swing into the backyard was beyond her, but if anyone in the world would go to any lengths to make his little girl happy, it was Josh.

Leaving had been self-preservation for her—but in saving herself had she destroyed Josh? She swallowed. This was going to be so much harder than she'd imagined.

"If you haven't been in Boston, where have you been?"

CHAPTER NINE

JOSH TOOK KATIE'S hand between both of his and tugged it over into his lap, forcing her to scooch in closer to him. Were they going to do this? They were going to *do* this. There would be a serious amount of beans spilled tonight.

They both felt her pager go off at the same time. Mutual looks of dismay passed between them as Katie pulled back and unearthed her pager from beneath the snow coat, the sweater and finally her tank top.

She took a glance at the small screen, then immediately dialed in to the ER. A few "Yup…yup…" then a rattling of satellite coordinates and a "Got it…" later, she stuffed the phone back into her bag.

"We've got to go." Her expression was pure business now.

"Tow truck should be here any minute."

She shook her head. "No. It will take too long and we have to go by helicopter anyhow. Did you notice an open field near where the truck hit? We're going to have to meet it there in five."

"Helicopter? We?" he repeated, as if he hadn't heard either of the words before.

"We are going on a helicopter to help a woman give birth on a gondola."

"A *gondola*? When did Copper Valley become Venice?"

Katie snapped her fingers before tugging up the zipper

on her winter coat. "Earth to Josh! The gondolas that go from the ski resort down to Main Street! Copper Canyon's ingenious way to transport its punters to and from the valley has broken and there is a woman in labor. You've got to help her."

"Me?" Now Josh was fully alert.

"Yes," Katie answered perfunctorily, turning toward the door. "I don't do deliveries. Not since…" She skipped over the explanation. "A tree hit the power lines and took out the power for the gondolas. They're trying to get a generator up there, but that could take hours—"

"Wait a minute," he interrupted. "How are you suggesting I get myself up to this gondola if it's dangling somewhere between Copper Peak and the Valley?"

"You'll get winched down."

"No." Josh shook his head. He wasn't being contrary. He just couldn't do it.

"They're short-staffed at the hospital, Josh. You've done a run in Maternity. You did more winchman training than anyone I can call. Who else do you suggest perform the obstetrics on this?"

"You." There wasn't even a hint of a waver in his voice. "You're stronger than I am."

"And with the metalwork in my hip and leg, I *don't* get winched into airborne gondolas. I'm not up to the gymnastics. *You* are."

"But—!" Katie didn't even know how to finish her protestation. Every rug she'd believed had been cushioning her feet just a few days ago was being ripped out from under her.

"But what, Katie?"

Josh had her full attention now. Medical emergencies were not something she was wishy-washy about, and something wasn't sitting right.

"I haven't been able to do a delivery since—"

There was no need for her to finish the sentence. They both knew what she was talking about.

"Right." He took her hand in his and headed for the door, already hearing the distant hum of the helicopter on approach. "Today's going to be the day that changes."

Ten minutes later Katie and Josh were watching the ground disappear beneath them as they hustled themselves into flight jumpsuits, secured their helmets and rapidly scanned the small body of the search and rescue helicopter the hospital shared with the emergency services. Bare-bones equipment and no spare staff. It was suck-it-up-and-get-on-with-it o'clock.

Katie had been in the helicopter loads of times over the past year—but tonight everything was blurring. Katie the control freak had…lost control.

"Dr. McGann, we're about four minutes out. How are your headsets working?"

"I can hear you," she confirmed to the young pilot. Jason. His name was Jason. She knew that. She knew *him*. All of this was familiar. Just not the part about going to help a woman give birth in a broken gondola, hanging who knew how many meters in the sky—?

"Dr. West?"

"I'm ready if you are."

Josh's words were meant for the pilot, but Katie could feel his eyes all but lasering through her.

"Jason, what's the word from the crew who are working on the gondola? No chance of getting them down the normal route?"

"'Fraid not, Doc. It's midway between the resort and the valley—right over the Canyon. So we're looking at maybe…" He paused to calculate. "We're looking at a one-thousand-foot drop."

"Three hundred meters…ish. Not too far." Josh's eyes twinkled, making the number seem less horrifying.

His face told a completely different story from the man who had given up speed thrills for yoga. *This* was the sort of rescue he was made for. During their residency he had all but wrestled his way to the roof every time there'd been a helicopter callout. Adrenaline junkie or not—he was the person she was going to have to put all her trust in today.

Tomorrow? There wasn't time to go there.

She let Josh's steadying voice trickle through her headphones and into her heart as he rattled out statistics and tips. It was obvious what he was doing and she wasn't going to stop him. He was pulling out his "Calm Down Katie" arsenal.

"Want to talk through scenarios?"

"A lot of this is dependent upon that door being open, Doc," Jason piped in.

"Isn't there an emergency release inside?" Katie's heart rate spiked again.

"Yes—but I'm not sure they would've figured it out. From the phone calls, they are sounding pretty stressed."

"How long has the mother been in labor?" Josh's voice cut through to the quick of the matter.

"They reckon she started about three, maybe four hours ago?"

"Dilation?" Katie only just stopped herself from cringing as she waited for the answer.

"Not a clue. We're both going into this dark, Dr. McGann. Speaking of which—there are night-vision goggles. You both should put them on."

"What about once we lower Dr. McGann down? How will they work in the snow?"

"Not good." Jason didn't mince his words. "There's a couple of head torches. Better bring those down to work in the gondola."

"Hang on!" interjected Katie. "Aren't we going to strap her into the stretcher and bring her straight up?"

"All depends upon what you find, my love."

Josh leaned forward, elbows on knees, bright blue eyes glued to hers, his fingers making a lay-them-on-me gesture. She complied, slipping her hands across his broad palms, but part of her wanted to do nothing more than retreat. Trust a man who had pushed life so far he'd nearly died?

His fingers wrapped round hers, heat shifting from his hands up into her body. And then the lightbulb pinged on with full wattage. She loved Josh. Heart and soul. The last few days had reawakened that knowledge in her beyond any reasonable doubt. But he was the same man who had tested her and tested her when she had been beyond fragile. Did loving him mean putting away her fears from the past and learning to trust again?

"If you look up to your right, you can see the gondola— Wait. I think there are two. That might be the reason for the accident."

Katie and Josh shifted in their seats, craning to see what Jason was describing.

"Is anyone talking to the couple?"

"Someone at the hospital, I think. Want me to patch you in?"

Katie nodded, before remembering she needed to confirm verbally. Josh had shifted across the helicopter floor and started organizing the winch clips.

"What are you doing?"

"Getting you clipped up and ready to go down." Josh dropped her a fortifying wink. "You've got this, my little multitasker. You can listen and clip up at the same time."

And so she did. As her fingers busied themselves with the spring-gated hooks that would secure her rescue kit and the stretcher, she tuned in to the voice of a man describing his wife's labor pains to— Who was that? Jorja? Jorja was on the other end of the line. Good. She was solid.

Katie listened, methodically tugging her straps into place, checking and double-checking the hooks and clips, until she heard the words "I can see something—but I don't think it's the baby's head. Is that all right?"

"It sounds to me as if your baby is in the breech position, Mr. Penton." Jorja confirmed Katie's suspicion.

"We're just about there, Dr. McGann. You ready to go?"

Her eyes met Josh's. Heaven knew what he saw in there. Eight years of shared history? Three years of pain? Whatever it was, it spoke to him deeply. A sheen of emotion misted his eyes for a millisecond, and then just as quickly he was back to business.

"I've got enough fuel to hold here for ten to fifteen. If you think you're going to be any longer, let me know ASAP—so I can get back and refuel."

"Right." Katie put on her medical tunnel vision. Fifteen minutes. Breech birth. In a gondola stuck over a canyon in the dead of winter. Piece of cake.

She looked down at the gondola they were hovering over—high enough not to rock it, low enough to see the door was being jacked open, inch by painstaking inch. She needed to get down there—and fast. If the wind hit and the gondola started to tip—

No. It wasn't worth thinking about.

"Let's do this." Katie nodded to Josh, who set the winch in motion.

Being lowered to the gondola was half-surreal, half-ultra-real. The cold bit at her cheeks, and when she would have expected her heart rate to career into the stratosphere…it slowed. Everything became a detail—as if she were in a film and watching her own life frame by frame. The silhouette of the mountain. The snowflakes. Her breath condensing on the lip of her winter jacket.

She could hear Jorja offering Mr. Penton reassurances while his wife roared at the hit of another contraction in the background.

It streamlined her focus. If ever there had been a time she needed to give herself a pep talk—this was it. This was what she knew. Medicine. She had this one. Never mind the fact she hadn't assisted in a birth in three years. She'd gone to medical school for over a quarter of her life. This was the stuff legendary dinner party stories were made of! The day Katie West delivered a baby in a gondola!

Josh's voice crackled through the headphones to say Katie was nearly there. A sudden urge overtook her to climb right back up that winching cable and crawl into his arms. Seek the comfort she'd so longed for. She didn't want to do this. Couldn't. *He* was going to have to. She'd just stretcher the poor woman up, they'd winch her quickly into the helicopter and Josh could deliver the baby. He'd always been brilliant with obstetrics. He could be brilliant tonight.

Another female bellow of strength and pain and the sound of impending motherhood filled her headphones.

She couldn't go back up. And yet…

She looked down.

Hmm…vast chasm courtesy of Mother Nature, or get into that gondola and conquer three years' worth of fears?

The winch cable continued lowering her, oblivious to the high-stakes tug-of-war occurring between her heart and her mind, bringing her to a smooth halt opposite the gondola door.

All she had to do was unclip herself and…

Katie lodged a booted foot in the small opening Mr. Penton had managed to cleave with his hands. Three years of fears it was.

"Everything all right in here?"

Nothing like starting off with a bit of small talk when you're hanging outside a gondola!

"Not exactly!" howled his wife from the floor, her hand on her husband's ankle. "Mike, honey, we need to get this baby out of me before I rip your leg off!"

The thirty-something husband threw Katie the pained expression she'd seen on many a father-to-be. Times ten.

He was still straining to hold the doors open the handful of inches he'd managed. Katie braced her knee against the opposite door and took hold of the exterior handle. She wasn't there yet.

"Mrs. Penton? My name is Dr. McGann. You can call me Katie if you like. Or anything else that suits. But I need to borrow your husband for a few more seconds. We need the door open wide to get me and my gear in. If you could scooch yourself as far away from the door as possible…"

Adrenaline took over. That and eight years of education and a residency that had made her one of the best.

She locked eyes with Mike. "Fast and strong. Let's get these doors open and your baby out. On three—I'm going to push with my foot and you push the opposite door. Okay?"

She counted. They pushed. And with an awkward swing of her kit and the stretcher, Katie got the equipment in— only to have the doors snap shut behind her with her cable still attached. The roar of blood in her ears threatened to overwhelm her. Spots flickered across her eyes. She had maybe six to ten inches of cable between her and the door. The gondola rocked and Katie felt herself tugged and slammed against the glass-fronted door.

Make that zero. And add a bloody nose to the mix.

"I'm going to guess that wasn't meant to happen." Mike's quiet voice was barely audible above his wife's deep pants.

"It's okay." *No, it's not!*

She flicked on her head torch. *Please, please, please let the winch clip be on this side of the door!*

"Get. It. *Out!*"

"Lisa, babe. It's going to be fine. Just push a little harder," Mike coached.

"No!" Katie wrenched her head around, swiping the blood from her face. "Don't push until we see what's going on—all right?"

"What would be *all right* is to be in a warm hospital bed—like *someone* promised me!"

"Well, how did I know they were going to take so long to make the molten chocolate cake *someone else* insisted upon ordering?"

"Whoa!" Katie interjected. "Time for everybody to take a deep breath."

Including me.

"Everything okay down there?"

Josh's voice gave her a shot of Dutch courage.

"In some ways. Others…not so good."

"But our baby's going to be all right, isn't he?" Mike sent her a pleading look as his wife repositioned herself in between contractions.

"I'm really sorry, Lisa, but this is going to take just a little bit longer than you'd like."

"Katie? What's wrong?" Josh obviously had his mind-reading button on high alert.

"Mike. I'm going to need you to pry the doors open again. They're trapping the cable that has me linked to the helicopter."

"What the—?" She tuned out the expletives coming from the pilot's microphone.

"Katie—you have got to get that door open. The winds are picking up and we can't hold her steady."

"Tell me something I *don't* know," she ground out, taking in the fact that her release hook was inches away—on the other side of the door.

"Get this baby *out of me*!"

Short-circuit and potentially kill everyone on the helicopter and the gondola…or get a grip. Those were the options.

"Katie, my love, you can do this."

Josh's voice, soft and steady, trickled through her headphones.

"I'm right here. I'm not going anywhere."

Her decision was made.

"Mike. Your job is to get these doors open again, and

I'm going to unclip myself the second you do." Her eyes hooked his. "It's vital we do this now. When I'm free I'm going to help your wife. If you need to use the stretcher to keep the doors pried apart—do it. If you need to rip one of these chairs out to keep them apart—do it. If I can't get to your wife I cannot help your baby. Do you understand?"

"Katie? Have him tie you to a chair before you do anything," Josh directed.

"Grab that rope. Tie me in and tie for yourself as well—*Ow!*" Her face hit the glass again.

"Katie?"

"Fine. I'm fine. Mike's on the case. Aren't you, Mike?"

"For the love of Pete! *Move*, honey!"

Lisa's voice snapped Mike out of his daze, instantly shifting him into a man of strength and action. Ropes were taken from Katie's kit and turned into lassos round the gondola's chairs.

"We've got maybe ten more minutes of fuel, Katie."

"On it. You should have the cable in less than a minute."

"How long do you think it's going to take to get her stretchered?"

"A few minutes."

"I need to push!"

"Don't push, Lisa. *Whoa!*" A rush of freezing air hit Katie's face as Mike yanked open the door, the movement nearly tugging her out of the gondola but for the rope holding her to a chair. She shot a grateful look up to the helicopter holding her husband.

"Just unclipping now, and then I'm going to have a look."

"You're clear?" The pilot hardly waited for the confirmation to leave her lips before peeling off a few hundred meters.

"Right. Lisa—mind if I take a look?" She received a nod as the poor woman tried to control her pain.

"What's it like, Katie? What are you seeing?"

Josh's voice took away the edge of postcrisis that was

beginning to creep in now that life-and-death decisions were off the book.

"We've got about eight more minutes of fuel, Katie."

"Can you see my baby?"

For her anyway.

Now that the focus was rightfully on Lisa, Katie could hear fear taking over the roars of the woman's bravura.

"Let's take a look. I can see his— It is a he, right?" Katie received a pair of nods from the parents.

Damn. A tiny baby's buttock was just visible at the birth canal. A breech birth. At the hospital? Not a problem. Whip her into the ER and give her a C-section. In a freezing-cold gondola, hanging above one of the nation's steepest canyons...

"He's not in the best of positions for a natural birth."

Thank heavens for understatement.

"But everything will be all right, won't it?"

Katie froze. They were the words that had played through her mind again and again when the doctors had first told her they were having trouble finding her daughter's heartbeat.

"Will Huckleberry be all right?"

Huckleberry?

"Don't promise them anything, Katie."

Josh's voice appeared in her head. It was hard to tell if it was real or if she'd summoned up what he might say if he were there.

"Just tell them you will do everything you can."

That's what the doctors had said to her and Josh.

Huckleberry?

Apprehension was replaced by a need to fight the giggles. Inappropriate! *You're a doctor—act like a doctor!*

"What position is she in, Katie?"

Josh was in her headset for real this time.

"We're going to do our best to turn this little guy round."

"That's my girl," Josh encouraged softly. "Are you all right getting the mother into the basket?"

"I need to push!"

Katie began raking through her medical supplies kit. "Fight it, Lisa. Fight it as hard as you can."

"Katie?" The pilot's voice came through as she was tugging on a pair of gloves. "I'm sorry—we're going to have to refuel. I don't think we're going to have enough time."

"I don't think I can hold off much longer..." came Lisa's strained voice.

"Are you kidding me?" Katie demanded.

"I thought you said you could help." Lisa's voice was little more than a whimper now.

"Sorry. I was talking to the pilot." Katie forced herself to speak calmly. "The helicopter needs to go back to Copper Canyon. It means we'll most likely be delivering your baby here and then getting everyone back to the hospital. Mike, can you grab those heat blankets and lay them out on the floor here? We need to get a clean area for Lisa. Keep everyone warm."

"Back as soon as we can. We'll switch to your cell phone if we lose contact," Josh assured Katie. "I love you, Katie-bird. You can do this."

She let Josh's words swirl around her heart as the rest of her body prepared for action. The amount of complications that could stack up against them weren't worth considering. There was only one good outcome here, and the growing fire in Katie's belly told her to start fighting for it.

"I'm going to massage your belly...see if we can shift the baby round."

"Huckleberry," prompted Lisa.

Katie managed a nod. Naming a baby before it came out was dangerous. Naming a baby something that gave your doctor the giggles...? *Awkward!*

"I'm not feeling much of a shift here." She racked her brain to try and remember as many variations as she could.

"I need something for the pain!" Lisa panted. "I had it all planned out. An epidural, some lovely music, soft cozy blankets."

"I've got the music right here, honey. On my phone."

"Why don't you put your playlist on and I'll get you something to see if we can relax the uterus."

Katie's mind went blank as she stared at her medical kit.

"Josh?" She felt like she was speaking to the universe.

"Yeah, babe. I'm here."

Her shoulders dropped an inch in relief. Josh still had her back.

"Talk me through."

"You don't know how to *do* this? I thought you said you were a doctor!"

Mike could not have looked more horrified. Lisa was too busy fighting the onset of another contraction to care.

"You *are* a doctor, and you *can* do this."

Josh's voice came through loud and clear. Katie repeated the words in her head as if she were on automatic pilot.

And Josh continued to speak—a blond-haired, blue-eyed angel in her ear—enabling her to respond, to act, to react. First they worked their way through the basics—blood pressure, heart rate of the baby and the mother, checks for bleeding.

"Do you have an IV of fentanyl in your kit?"

"Yes." Katie reached for the bag, then chose the vial instead. "I think we're going to have to get her on her hands and knees. The massage isn't shifting the baby's position."

"Good thinking."

Josh fell silent while Katie explained to Lisa about the injection of painkiller. It would decrease the likelihood of having to treat her newborn with naloxone for respiratory depression after delivery—but it would need to be given again if the pain increased.

"Right, Lisa, can we have you on your hands and knees, please?"

Mike helped his wife roll to her side and press herself up.

"Good. Now, can you drop down onto your forearms?"

"Why?"

"It's going to elevate your hips above your heart. That's a great way to encourage your baby to shift position on his own."

"Huckleberry, you mean," Lisa pressed as she dropped to her forearms with a huff.

"Yes." It was all Katie could manage. Naming a baby before it was born was too much for her to take on board right now.

"Have a feel and check the heart rate again," Josh instructed after a few moments had passed.

"I think it's working!" Katie couldn't keep the joy from her voice.

"Great. Katie—I think we're going to land in a second. We'll be out of contact for a minute. But I will call you, and you can put me on speaker if you like."

"No, don't worry," Katie answered as the infant inside Lisa's womb turned into a little acrobat. "I think I've got this one."

She tugged off her helmet and poured her entire store of concentration into Lisa and her child. They were going to *do* this. And when they did she was going to turn her life around. Just because the helicopter needed to refuel it didn't mean Josh was leaving her. He'd made it more than clear over the past few days that he had come here for *her*. To see if what they had once shared was worth salvaging. A year ago she might not have been ready. Wouldn't have been able to see the possibility. Now…? Now she wanted that man back in her life, and she was hard-pressed to keep the smile of realization off her lips.

As the medicine began to take effect and the baby shifted position, Lisa called out that another contraction was on the way.

"Great. Good!" Katie responded confidently. "Mike,

do you want to rub your wife's back? Because I think it's time to push."

"Really?"

"Really."

There was a head full of red hair at the entrance to the delivery canal, and in just a few…

"C'mon—you can do it. *Push!*"

And there he was, landing in her hands as if it were any old day. Huckleberry Penton. He was beautiful. Ten fingers, ten toes, a mouth, two ears…as perfect a baby as a family could hope for.

"You've done it, Lisa," Katie said unnecessarily as she cleared away the mucus from the little boy's mouth and nose, making way for a hearty wail. "Turn around real careful now—he's still attached to your umbilical cord."

Katie swiftly gathered together a sterile drape and a heat blanket to swaddle Huckleberry before double-clamping and cutting the umbilical cord between the two clamps. It was cold in the gondola, and the last thing this little one needed was pneumonia.

She dried off his head, resisting the urge to give him a kiss, and handed him to his mother. She kept the swell of emotion she was experiencing at bay by focusing on the postnatal checklist. She gave Lisa a gentle uterine massage, leaving the rest of the umbilical cord in place and checking that the rest of the placenta did not need to be immediately delivered. It would be safer to do that in the hospital.

"Shall we get an IV into you? It'll help replace all those electrolytes you've been losing and make sure you don't dehydrate."

Tears sprang to her eyes when she lifted her gaze to the couple, saw both sets of eyes wide with wonder, delight. They hadn't heard her. The only thing they could see or hear was their newborn baby boy.

Katie was astonished to realize the tears trickling down her cheeks were happy ones. She was genuinely happy for them. Not that she'd wished anyone ill when she and Josh had lost Elizabeth…but it had been tough to see parents with a newborn. More than tough.

It came to her that this was what she'd been waiting for—the desire to try for another baby. Three years ago she wouldn't have dreamed of getting pregnant again. *Ever.* Two years—she'd become numb to the ache to be a mother. But being with these two—being with her husband…could she really have the strength to try again?

The lights in the gondola suddenly flickered into life and almost instantly a hum could be heard, accompanied by a slight jerk as the gondola slipped into action.

"Hold on for the ride!" Katie grinned, but the smile instantly slipped from her face when she saw the expressions on the Pentons' faces.

"Um… Dr. McGann…?" Mike began, making a little dabbing gesture with his hand around his nose area. "I think you might need a little cleanup."

Katie's hands flew to her face. Her nose! With everything that had happened she'd completely forgotten her blood-smeared face.

She grabbed for a packet of antibacterial wipes and gently swabbed at her lips and cheeks, happy to note that there was a big grin on her face it would be near impossible to wipe away.

CHAPTER TEN

"QUIT PACING."

"I'm not pacing," Josh retorted, feeling about ten to Jorja's twenty-five years as he did so.

He'd been ramped up for going back in the chopper to get Katie down from that blasted gondola, but when the generator had unexpectedly kicked into action they'd been told to stand down. Now he was ready to lay everything on the line. See if it was time to hand over the signed divorce papers and try to find a way to move on or—and here was where it got tricky—see if there were some way—*any* way—he could get the real life he wanted back with his wife.

So sitting down, standing still, anything stationary was not an option. Pacing like a caged beast was a bit more like it. He'd just do it in front of the patient board to make it look a bit more…functional.

"The ambulance should be here any minute," Jorja finally allowed.

"And she's in it?"

Jorja looked at him like he was crazy. "Of *course* the woman who just gave birth in a freakin' gondola on New Year's Eve is in it! What are you? Nuts?"

"I meant Dr. McGann."

"Oh," Jorja replied. Then visibly experienced a hit of understanding. *"Oh!"*

Josh narrowed his eyes. "You've spoken to Michael, haven't you?"

"I work with him—of course I've spoken to him." Her eyes flicked back to the files she had been ignoring.

"About Katie—Dr. McGann..." Josh tried to give her his I'm-Not-Messin' look, failing miserably, from the looks of things.

"Sorry, Dr. West. Nothing's secret for long in a small town. But your business is your business. If you want to spend New Year's Eve trying to convince Copper Canyon's most unavailable doctor to go out with Michael so that *he* can get fired for inappropriate behavior and *you* can get his job—be my guest." She folded her arms defensively across her chest. "And good luck tryin'," she added, quite obviously not meaning the last bit.

Ah. Wrong dog, wrong tree.

If he hadn't been so stressed he would have laughed. He'd have to remember to meet up with Michael for that coffee. He owed him for the red-herring behavior. *Hang on a second!*

"Jorja, are you sweet on Michael?"

"I have no idea what you're talking about," she replied primly, giving a stack of patient files a nice clack on the countertop as she did.

"Jorja and Michael, sitting on a—"

"Dr. West!" Jorja put on her most outraged face. "I'll have you know my brothers are all taller than you." She sized him up quickly, to make sure she'd been correct. "And stronger. I will *not* have my name tarnished in such a way."

"Shame..." Josh leaned against the counter, thoroughly enjoying himself now. "I think you two would make a cute couple."

"You do? I mean..." She quickly dropped her happy face and went for nonchalance. "That's interesting. I've never given it much thought."

"Why don't you ask him out for a coffee? The diner makes a mean cup."

The ambulance crew burst through the double doors, pushing a gurney with Lisa on it, holding her baby tightly in her arms, and her husband by her side, sending a mix of anxious and proud looks at anyone who was looking while the EMT crew hurriedly rattled off handover information to Michael, who had appeared alongside them from the ambulance bay.

Jorja gave her cheeks a quick pinch, even though they didn't need any extra pinking, and flew out from behind her desk with a chart to assist.

They all passed him in a whirlwind of activity, leaving the waiting room entirely empty of people save a weary-looking mother with a pile of knitting well under way as she waited for her skateboarding son to get his leg put in a cast after inventing a whole new style of ice-skating.

No Katie.

Josh looked round the waiting room to see if it would give him an answer.

No dice.

Just the clickety-clack of the mother's knitting needles and the low hum of a television ticking off the New Year's Eve celebrations around the world.

He took a few steps closer to see if… Was that…? *Huh.* Paris. He glanced at his watch. That would have been over hours ago. Ah—there was London. He'd clearly hit the replay… Yes, there was the Statue of Liberty…and cut to Times Square…

New York City was moments away from dropping the gong on the New Year. That gave him a paltry three hours. He'd promised himself he'd have this sorted by midnight. He didn't know if he was Prince Charming or Cinderella in this scenario—but whatever happened, he was going to cross everything he had in the hope that Katie was up for a bit of glass-slipper action.

* * *

Katie sank onto the bench in the locker room, relieved to have found the place empty. She'd left the EMTs and Michael to sort out the Pentons and had taken a fast-paced power walk round the hospital, sneaking in at the front door in the hopes of just a few more minutes to regroup before she saw anyone—*c'mon, be honest!*—before she saw Josh again.

If the past few days had been an emotional roller coaster, the last few hours had been... She looked up to the ceiling for some inspiration... *Seismic.* Everything she had held to be true over the past two years had been a fiction. A way of coping with the tremendous loss she and Josh had suffered. But ultimately she had been hiding. And not just from her husband. She'd been hiding from life.

Her right hand sought purchase on her ring finger. It surprised her how much relief she felt at finding the rings still there. Side by side. First one promise and then another. Promises she'd blamed Josh for breaking when maybe all along *she* had been the one who had let him down.

He had changed. She could see that now. But she still wasn't entirely sure what sort of future—if any—he was offering her. He'd said he had come here to Copper Canyon to find her, but to what end? Another chance? Another child?

She opened up her palms and imagined the weight of the newborn she'd just held in them. Tears welled. Could she do it? Maybe she had changed too much. Become too clinical. Or had her time away been more about healing than hiding? Josh's surprise appearance had definitely taught her one thing—there was always room for another way of seeing things.

She glanced at her watch. Three hours and counting. What would this New Year hold in store for her?

She slowly unwound the scarf Josh had twirled round her neck before she'd descended to the gondola, then pushed herself up and opened his locker. His winter coat was hanging on its hook. She folded the scarf and put it in his pocket—but when it was obvious the wool wrap wasn't going to fit, she tugged it out again. A few pieces of paper fell to the floor with the movement.

She knelt to pick them up, eyes widening, stomach churning as she took in the contents of the paperwork.

She shouldn't have looked.

A sour sensation rose from her belly as she absorbed the writing on the letter, the airplane ticket and—her hand flew to her mouth, hoping to stem the cry of despair—the divorce papers.

Signed.

Unsealed.

About to be delivered?

She felt herself going numb. How could she have been such an idiot? Josh was here to give her the signed divorce papers. Why else would he have a job offer and a ticket to France falling out of his pocket? The whole "making peace" thing had just been a ruse to make himself feel better.

Running away again suddenly seemed too exhausting. She pulled her feet up and curled into a tight ball on the bench, no longer interested if anyone saw her. Two years of holding it all together, pretending she was nothing more than a dedicated physician—no personal life, no history, just medicine. And now everything she'd sought to keep under control was unraveling from the inside out.

She lay on the bench, her cheek taking on the imprint of the wooden slats, and for once she just didn't care. Her body was too weighted with the pain of knowing that her life wasn't going to be about suppressing anymore. It was going to be about letting go. She lay perfectly still for she didn't know how long, just thinking. Because once she started to move it would be the start of an entirely new life.

One without the baby she'd had to say goodbye to sooner

than anyone should have to. One without the family she'd always dreamed she'd have. A life without Josh. Her sweet, kind, loving husband who had brought out a spark in her she'd never known she'd had.

A surge of energy charged through her, making a lightning-fast transformation into a burning hot poker in her heart. She felt branded. Marked with the painful searing of anger, sorrow and indignation. She'd been such an *idiot* for thinking Josh had changed. It was all she could do not to ball her hands up and try to knock some actual sense into her normally oh-so-logical head. She'd actually believed that he was here to try again—to start anew. To try to make that family they had both ached for. And…for the most tender of moments…she had believed she could do it.

A primal moaning roar left her throat as she pushed herself up and shook her head. Maybe she could shake out everything that she didn't want to carry into the future. Turn into a whirling dervish and spin everything away. A human centrifuge. It would be hard—and by heavens it would hurt—but she could clear her system of Josh West again. And this time for good.

She glanced at her watch, surprised to see how close to midnight it was.

She needed air. Light. Cold. Anything to remind her that she was vital. Alive. Just one tiny thing to show her that she would survive this.

Josh pushed the plug into the extension cord, not even daring to look for a moment. He knew this was a make-or-break moment. He shifted his chin along his shoulder until he could catch a glimpse of his handiwork. It was cold, but with the wind dying down, the stillness added a strange sensation of otherworldliness to the twinkling lights he'd laced into hearts and trees and stars, to the lengths of decorations he'd stolen from the nurses' lounge.

Perfect. Even if he was a caveman in the home-decor department, he'd done a pretty good job of gussying up Valley Hospital's roof. Now to rustle up something poetic to say about—

He whirled around at the sound of the roof door slamming open.

"Can't a girl get a *single* moment alone?" Katie looked little short of appalled to see him standing there. "What *is* all this?" she snapped.

"Oh, just a little decorating…" Josh started—not altogether certain his words were even being received by his wild-eyed wife.

"All I wanted to do was make a snow angel. One tiny little freakin' snow angel to prove that the world *is* nice, and good things *can* happen, and what do I get instead?"

She didn't wait for him to fill in the answer to what was obviously a rhetorical question.

"*You!* The one person I loved the most in the whole world, leaving me again. And just when I thought we were beginning to repair things."

"Wait! What?" Josh strode up to Katie, hands outstretched in a *What gives?* position. "What are you talking about, Katiebird?"

"Oh, don't Katiebird me." She all but spit at him.

Josh had never seen her so riled, and the force of her anger nearly pushed him back. *Nearly.* He ground his feet in and pressed himself up to his full height.

Tough. It was less than an hour to midnight and he was damned if he was going to hit the New Year without finding out if he had a future with his wife. Her face told him everything he'd feared—but he wasn't going to let go of this one without a fight.

He held his ground. "What exactly are you talking about?"

"I'm talking about the divorce papers."

He raised his eyebrows. "You mean the ones you've been sending me by special delivery for the past two years?"

"I mean the signed ones in your locker."

Her stance was defiant but he could see the hurt in her eyes. He wished he'd never put a pen to those damn things. It was the type of thing a trip to the stationery store could never fix. That type of ink was indelible.

His voice softened. This wasn't going remotely the way he'd hoped, but at least it was as painful for her as it had been for him to see his name on those pages. "I thought it was what you wanted."

"I did too," she said after a moment, her booted foot digging a sizable divot in the snow.

"And now?"

"Now it looks like what I think doesn't matter." A guilty frown tugged her lips downward at his raised eyebrows. "I found the job offer and the ticket to Paris. The one-way ticket."

"Oh, you did, did you?" Josh found himself needing to suppress the grin splitting his face in two.

"Yes. Or should I say *oui*?" Katie couldn't meet Josh's eyes but she kept on talking. "Looks like you've gone and done what I haven't been able to do."

"And what's that, then?"

Josh took a step closer.

Katie put her arm between them.

"You've been able to move on. Get past everything we've been through." She lifted her gaze to finally meet his, her tears only just resting on her lids. They'd spill any second now. She tipped her head back to buy herself a few more moments of dignity, if that was what you could call standing on the roof of your place of work and hollering at your husband—ex-husband—for doing exactly what you'd asked him to do.

"When you were busy rifling through my things—"

"I wasn't rifling. I was—" She stopped to search for a

less invidious word than "rifling," accidentally biting the inside of her cheek in the process.

"Uh-huh? What *were* you doing?"

The twinkle in Josh's eyes stirred something within her. She knew what it was, but it was embarrassing to admit it considering the turn of events.

Lust. She just wanted to rip his clothes off and have her wicked way with him.

Would that *ever* go away? She stared at him, her body itching to stomp her feet or jump up and down. Anything to stop the skittering of goose bumps working their way across her body. Wow, did she *ever* need to make a snow angel!

She shifted her eyes up to the heavens. How the heck was she going to carry on with her life when she still fancied the pants off her husband?

"Did you happen to see the ticket beneath the ticket?"

"Um…what was that?"

Best not to appear too keen to have gotten the wrong end of the stick.

"Katie McGann." Josh stepped forward and took both her hands in his. His blue eyes were like sunshine, and a halo of twinkly lights lit him up from behind.

Oh, no, no, no, no… This can't be goodbye. Is this really goodbye?

"I came back here to do one thing and one thing only."

She couldn't speak. The other side of her cheek was being chomped on. Hard enough to draw blood.

"I came back here," he said in his soft, beautiful drawl, "with the sole intent of seeing if you would consider becoming Katie West again."

She blinked a snowflake out of her eyelashes. The rest of her body was frozen in place.

"Katie?"

"Yes?" Her insides had started doing a June-bug dance.

Her outsides still weren't up to much more than providing a landing zone for the supersized snowflakes.

"I am presuming you heard what I just said."

A little furrow was beginning to form between the one pair of eyes that could light up a room. What made them so *bright*?

"Yes, I did," she managed to croak out.

"And are you planning on drawing out the torture, or are you going to tell me what you think of the idea?"

"What? About Paris? That job offer sounds pretty amazing. Groundbreaking surgical techniques? Champagne? I bet it's practically free over there. And the architecture! The Eiffel Tower versus Main Street and grilled cheese sandwiches?" She squawked out a mysterious sound that was meant to say *No-Brainer*, wondering why on earth she was trying to talk him out of staying when all she wanted to do was to tip back her head and scream *Yes! A thousand times yes!*

Josh rocked back on his heels and gave her comments some thought. Katie's stomach began to lurch as her heart plummeted.

Why had she opened her big mouth?

"A chance to work with the world's best prenatal surgeon? It's a once-in-a-lifetime offer," he admitted, before a near-wistful look added a glint to his eyes. "And I *do* love those baguettes. Especially when they're all crunchy on the outside and that gooey cheese they have is just dripping out over the edges."

"You've already *been* there?" Katie's dog-whistle voice sprang into the stratosphere, her game face all but disappearing as she spoke.

"How else do you think I got the offer?" He thumbed away another snowflake. "But then I got to thinking. Do I sign those damn divorce papers you've been sending me, move on—or do I try to win back my girl?"

Katie swiped at a couple of snowflakes that were tickling her nose, too heartbroken to speak. He'd signed the papers and he had a ticket to Paris. Why did he have to be so *nice* about it all? Where was the adrenaline junkie she'd hardened her heart to?

"All of which is a really long-winded way of saying—" he paused to run the backs of his fingers across her cheeks before tucking her hair behind her ears "—there are *two* tickets to Paris in my locker."

Her heart gave a particularly large thump.

"I'm guessing you didn't see the second one."

"That would be a fair guess." Her voice broke with relief. Josh wanted to be with her. He wanted to start again!

The questions began tumbling out in a torrent. Would this really be a new beginning or would they fall into old patterns? Had he really thought through where he wanted to be, what he wanted to do?

She sucked in a breath, closed her eyes and asked the one that scared her the most. "Do you want to try for another baby?"

She felt his breath upon her lips as he spoke. "More than anything in the world."

Their foreheads tipped together and her breath intertwined with his. "Even if it's the scariest thing in the whole wide world?"

"Even if it's the scariest thing in the universe." He pressed a soft kiss onto her lips. "And I promise to be by your side every step of the way."

"Here in Copper Canyon?"

"Wherever you like." He started pressing kisses onto each of her cheeks, her eyelids, the tip of her nose. "We *do* have two tickets to Paris if you'd like to go check it out."

Her eyes flicked open. A penny dropped. "Joshua West—you aren't chicken to go to Paris all on your lonesome, are you?"

"Ha!" A cloud of breath hid milliseconds of acknowledgment. "As if. But it would be much easier to go into the big new world of surgery with my brave and talented wife by my side. If she's interested in giving up her job here at Valley Hospital, that is, for one in Paris…"

"Oh…I don't know. The boss here is pretty hard-core."

Josh grinned broadly. "I hear she has a heart of gold."

He dipped his head to kiss his wife again. It was a kiss filled with the deep satisfaction of a man who had found his way in the world again. Katie returned each and every one of his kisses with all her love. As they sought and answered each other's caresses, they pulled back for a second to grin when the church bell began to toll midnight.

Katie's heart felt full to bursting. Everything was going to get better now—the healing had begun and the New Year couldn't start at a better time or in a better place…right here in her husband's arms.

EPILOGUE

"DID YOU GET to the bakery?"

"Hello to you, too, my little Katiebird." Josh paused to drop a kiss onto his wife's forehead. "And, *excusez-moi*, but I think what you were trying to say was did I get to *la patisserie*."

Katie couldn't help but laugh at her husband's exaggerated French accent. Tennessee meets Paris was an interesting combo. Not that *her* accent was all that hot. Just mastering the medical vocabulary had been enough of a challenge. But they had both impressed not only themselves but their new colleagues as well. Sure, they both might sound like yahoos from America—but nearly a year in Paris had changed everything.

"I thought I'd go for something different, seeing as it's the holiday season."

"And Emmy's birthday," Katie added, as if either of them needed reminding.

Together they turned to beam at their daughter, her face covered in spaghetti sauce after Katie's unsuccessful attempt to get some of her dinner inside the cheeky nine-month-old. With a head of jet-black curls and a pair of bright blue eyes, she was a reflection of the pair of them.

"So?" Katie prodded. "What'd you get?"

Josh pulled out a box from behind his back. A box that

wasn't nearly big enough for the kind of birthday cake she'd had in mind.

"What's that?"

"Not what you had in mind for our cherished daughter's birthday?"

She resisted sticking out her lower lip in a pout. *Just.* "Depends… Is this one of those 'good things come in small packages' deals?"

"In a way…" Josh held up the small box and waggled it in front of his wife's eyes. This was fun.

Who was he kidding? There hadn't been a moment in the past year when the smile had been wiped off his face. The world's longest honeymoon, he had billed it. And a move to Paris. His wife back by his side. A daughter to crow over whenever he wasn't learning about mind-blowing surgical techniques with his new mentor.

"Want to open it?" He held up the package when Katie snatched at it.

"You know I do—I need cake!"

"Need or want?" he teased.

"Both."

He handed the box over, watching with bated breath as Katie ripped it open with the glee of a five-year-old.

The myriad of expressions playing across her face as she took in the contents of the box only broadened his grin.

"This is a napkin from Rooney's…" Her big brown eyes met his.

"Best chocolate cake in Copper Canyon," they recited in unison.

"Um…" Katie looked up at him quizzically. "I hate to point out the obvious, but there isn't any cake *in* here, buster."

"What's below the napkin?"

"Oh, my gosh…" Katie's cheeks pinked as she lifted the tickets out of the box. "Are we *really*?"

"I think the first place our baby girl should make a snow angel is in Copper Canyon. Don't you?"

Katie rose up on her tiptoes and gave Josh an appreciatively lingering kiss.

"I couldn't agree more, my love. Christmas in Paris and New Year in Copper Canyon. Doesn't get much better than that, does it?"

"So long as I have the two of you, Katiebird, I have everything I need." He gave her another kiss and dropped a wink in their daughter's direction. "But some of Rooney's finest chocolate fudge for our daughter will be the icing on the cake."

* * * * *

'TWAS THE WEEK
BEFORE CHRISTMAS

OLIVIA MILES

For my darling little girl, Avery.

May you have a dream, and may you never
stop reaching for it.

Chapter One

"Looks like a storm's about to roll in."

"So I heard," Holly Tate murmured distractedly. Furrowing her brow, she studied the reservation list and then glanced at the hands of the old grandfather clock at the base of the stairs. There was still one guest unaccounted for, and the dining room would be closing in fifteen minutes. Well, she'd have the chef hold a turkey sandwich and a slice of apple pie. She could always send it up to the guest's room upon check-in, just as a courtesy. Exceptional customer service was something she took seriously, and while a few minor complaints were inevitable, The White Barn Inn had yet to receive a bad review on any travel website Holly knew of. The repeat customers she saw year after year—and the referrals they provided—always filled her heart with a sense of pride and warmth.

"They say we should get three or four inches tonight," the assistant manager and housekeeper, Abby Webster, continued. "Steady through the morning and afternoon, but the Nor'easter's expected to hit tomorrow night."

Holly finally glanced out one of the tall, lead-paned windows that framed the front door. Large flakes of snow were falling steadily on the vast stretch of lawn that separated the old mansion from the main road. There would be no sense in asking the handyman to clear the path; it would be covered again in half an hour. It would have to wait until morning.

"We're still waiting on one guest," Holly informed her friend. Though she was Abby's employer, the two women were also good friends. Life at the inn was quiet and occasionally confining, resulting in long days, weekends, and holiday hours. After leaving Boston five years ago to transform the large historic home she had inherited from her grandmother into a bed-and-breakfast, Holly had retained fond memories of riding bikes or lining up at the candy store on Main Street with Abby during her annual summer visits to her grandmother's house in Maple Woods. Having lost touch years before, the friends had picked up where they had left off and grown even closer since.

"Do you want me to stick around until he arrives?" Abby asked halfheartedly.

Holly shook her head. "You go home to that handsome husband of yours," she said. "Besides, I don't want you driving in this kind of weather at night."

"The streets should be plowed by the morning." Abby stifled a yawn and pulled her red wool pea coat off the wrought-iron rack next to the front desk. She shrugged herself into a hand-knitted creamy wool hat and wrapped a matching scarf tightly around her neck. "Don't stay up too late."

"Have a good night," Holly called after Abby, pulling her cardigan tighter around her waist as a cold gust of wind rushed through the open door. The flames that were burning high and steady in the fireplace in the adjacent lobby flickered precariously. Holly wove her way through the oversize sofas and chairs, pausing to plump a pillow and refold a chenille throw, and then added another log from the neatly packed pile at the side of the brick hearth.

She checked her watch again. Ten minutes until the kitchen closed. Stephen, the chef, would be eager to get home, especially in this weather. Inside the dining room, another large fireplace crackled invitingly, casting a warm, golden glow on the four couples hunched over their desserts and savoring the last sips of their red wine. Conversation was low and intimate, and Holly silently crossed the polished floorboards to the kitchen where inside a clattering of pots and pans posed as a sharp contrast to the serenity of the other areas of the inn.

"We've got a straggler," Holly said, grabbing a Christmas cookie from a tray and taking a bite.

"Those are for the guests!" Stephen chided, throwing a white dishtowel over his shoulder.

"You know me." Holly laughed. "I can never resist your gingerbread. Besides, it's only a few weeks out of the year, so I'm entitled. I'll hit the gym in January."

"Sure you will." Stephen smiled, knowing all too well that this was not true. Holly had only been saying this every Christmas season since the inn had officially opened for business four and a half years ago, and she still had every intention of following through—if she ever managed to find the time. Running the inn had become her life and she poured everything she had into doing her job well. There was little time for anything else. Or *anyone* else, as Stephen also liked to point out.

"Do you mind putting together a tray before you go? A turkey sandwich and a slice of pie would be perfect."

"Are we sure this person is even going to make it in to-night?" Stephen pulled a loaf of sourdough from the bas-ket on the counter and began slicing two thick pieces. "It's getting bad out there."

"Maybe not, but even if he's already tired from a long drive, he might want a little something." Holly perused the variety of cookies and plucked a dried-cranberry-and-nut variation off the platter. She took a quick bite, casting a furtive glance in Stephen's direction. *Delicious.* "Besides, this particular gentleman is staying in the Green Room."

"Ah," Stephen said, laying a wedge of cheese on top of a round of heirloom tomato. Every room in the inn was named after the color of its walls, and the Green Room was the best suite in the house, right down to its king-size bed, steam shower and private balcony. Abby liked to joke that it was named the Green Room because it reeked of money, but Holly had chosen the color specifically because of the way the leaves from the trees grazed its third-floor win-dows in the spring.

"I should go and see if he's arrived yet," she said, dust-ing the cookie crumbs off her hands. "Thanks again for putting something together."

"No problem," Stephen said. "See you tomorrow af-ternoon."

Holly retraced her steps to the front lobby, noting with a stir of childish glee the way the holiday lights, wrapped around garland framing each window, glowed like stars in the dimly lit room. Standing just to the left of the mas-sive Christmas tree was a tall man hunched over the thick doormat, stomping the snow off his feet. His slightly wavy brown hair was wet and slick, and the shoulders of his black cashmere coat were dusted with fine white powder. *At last!*

"Welcome to The White Barn Inn," Holly said cheer-fully, watching in slight dismay as the melting snow spilled over onto the cherry wood floors. She darted to the small reception desk to grab a rag, and returning quickly to the scene of the crime, she sopped up as much of the icy water as the cloth would hold.

"I'm afraid I've made a bit of a mess."

"Oh, no…it's fine," Holly said easily, still fixated on her task. "Just a little water, no harm done. There." Once satisfied that the damage was under control, she stood to formally introduce herself to the latecomer and found herself face to face with a shockingly handsome man.

"Sorry again." The guest grinned sheepishly, gesturing to the snow melting off his weather-inappropriate shoes. His turquoise eyes flickered with boyish charm.

Holly struggled to compose herself, finally finding her voice. "Good to see you arrived safely. These roads can be treacherous if you aren't used to them."

"No, I'm fine," the man said mildly. He swept a hand through his damp hair and followed her over to the reception desk. "Believe it or not, there's a country boy hiding under this city slicker." His grin widened.

"That makes us opposites, then. I was born and raised in Boston. I've been in Maple Woods for five years now and I'm still terrified of driving in the snow, especially at night." Holly smiled.

"I'm Max, by the way. Max Hamilton. I'm booked for the next two nights. But then, you probably knew that."

Holly accepted Max's hand into her own, alarmed by the chill of his palm. The man must be freezing. "I had an inkling," she said, noticing how his skin warmed slowly from the heat of her own. The subtle intimacy made her feel instantly connected to him. "I'm Holly. Holly Tate."

"Pleased to meet you, Holly Tate."

Sucking in a nervous breath, Holly fished through the drawer for the key to the Green Room, noting the slight quiver in her hands, but happy for a diversion. Finally locating the familiar green keychain, she handed it over to its temporary owner and went through some of the routine information about the inn. The sound of her voice, on autopilot, filled the room, but her attention was on anything but breakfast hours or turndown services.

It had been a long time since she'd had the pleasure of being in the company of a man as attractive as Max Hamilton, and her stomach fluttered as she looked him over. She estimated him to be in his early to mid-thirties—unmarried, she noted with a flip of her heart as he signed the registration book, left-handed, and devilishly handsome. Something about those electric blue eyes and that broad, kind smile made him instantly appealing.

"I'm past check-in, aren't I?" Max looked slightly alarmed at the realization. "I hope they didn't keep you at work on account of me."

Holly took in the friendly twinkle of his eyes and genuine, lopsided grin and felt herself inwardly melt. "Don't worry about it," she said. "And besides, they didn't keep me at work. I own the place."

Something in Max's demeanor shifted and the glint of his eyes turned murky for one quick, telling second. Holly wasn't surprised. No one expected a woman in her late twenties to be the proprietor of this establishment. She was often met with disbelief when she revealed this fact.

"Surprised you, didn't I?" she smirked, coming around the desk.

Max curled his lips into an irresistible smile. "You definitely did," he said.

Max Hamilton wasn't sure what to make of this revelation. What a strange profession for a woman as young as Holly. An *innkeeper?* In this remote little town? He had assumed that the owner of this quaint establishment would be an elderly retired couple, not the sexy young thing that stood before him.

He'd have to rethink his strategy.

"So you own all this?" he asked, gesturing to the lobby and the rooms beyond. It was clear that a lot of attention had gone into the furnishings and decor. The house was built in the colonial style, traditional with white siding and black shutters, but large and substantial. Coming up the main drive, he'd noticed the wreaths hanging from each window by a thick crimson ribbon, the inviting lanterns the hugged the front steps, the pine garland that wrapped the awning posts. Sweeping his gaze over holiday decorations that seemed to fill every inch of the foyer in which they stood, he had to wonder if that red front door had been painted especially for the holiday. Probably, he decided.

"That's right," Holly nodded and then stopped herself suddenly. "Well, almost. My family's been leasing the land for three generations, but I've been saving toward buying it when the lease is up."

Max raised an eyebrow. "That's a pretty substantial investment."

"You'd think so, but not in a small town like this. The Millers were the original owners of the land back in the early nineteen hundreds and the family has stayed in town for the most part. George Miller is the current owner now and he and his wife have no real use for the land, so luckily we've managed to come to an agreement."

"So then you were right the first time you answered my question," Max continued. "You really do own all this."

"Not yet," Holly corrected. "The lease was for ninety-nine years. It was a Christmas gift from my great-grandfather to my great-grandmother. It expires next week."

"And then?"

"And then hopefully everything can be signed and sealed." Holly smiled, bringing a soft blush to her otherwise creamy complexion and a spark to her hazel eyes.

Max shifted his weight from his left foot to his right, unable to match her visible excitement. He grimaced at the water seeping from his black leather loafers onto the polished floorboards. "I'm doing it again," he warned, glancing at Holly from under the hood of his brow.

Holly laughed at his expression, saying, "Oh, I'm being rude…babbling about the history of the inn when you've had such a long trip and probably want to get settled."

She bent down to pick up his luggage, but Max immediately stopped her. "I may be your guest for the evening, but I'm also a gentleman."

Holly's pale cheeks flushed with pleasure and she refused to meet his eye when she said, "I'll show you to your room, then. Follow me."

Gladly, Max thought, fighting off a suggestive smile. He did as he was told and followed her up the winding staircase to the second floor landing, and then up yet another set to the third floor. He couldn't resist taking in the curves of her figure, the slim waist and flare of her hips under her form-fitting black skirt. Her rich, chestnut brown hair brushed her back, swaying slightly against her narrow shoulders, and he traced his gaze down the length of her long legs as she carried herself silently up the red carpet-lined stairs, careful not to disturb guests who, it seemed, had already turned in for the night.

"Here we are!" she announced breathlessly, catching his eye. Max noticed how large and round her pupils were in the dim light, how her hazel eyes had darkened to moss, interrupted by flecks of amber. Her cheeks had a slight rosiness to them, and her lips were wide and tinted with the faintest touch of ruby lip gloss.

"You honestly planned to carry my luggage all this way?" Max grinned and reflexively winked.

Holly bristled and tucked a loose strand of hair behind her ear. For the faintest hint of a second, Max wondered if this was such a good idea, after all.

As a major retail owner and developer, Max and his team had pinpointed Maple Woods as the ideal location for the next major upscale shopping mall in their portfolio. The demographics were strong, and the location roughly half-way between New York and Boston made a compelling argument. He'd driven through Maple Woods and the four neighboring towns three times each in the last two months, and the thirty acres of land housing The White Barn Inn was the best site.

He'd come to Maple Woods tonight with his render-ings in hand, along with substantial market and financial research to back up his pitch, prepared to meet with the planning board and make an offer to the owner of the inn that couldn't be beat. He'd assumed the owner would be a retired couple, happy to trade in long, relentless days of serving others for a life of comfort and financial security.

He had assumed wrong.

The owner of the inn was this bright, cheerful, drop-dead gorgeous creature. And something told him she wasn't going to walk away quietly. The owner of the land, on the other hand, could most likely be bought. There was no way Holly could top his offer, and George Miller would have to be a fool to turn down what Max was prepared to offer him.

Max rolled his luggage to a stop beside an oversize arm-chair near the far window. Looking around the perfectly appointed room with the white trim and soothing sage-green-painted walls, it was becoming increasingly clear that Holly had invested a lot of time and money into what had probably been a very old home in need of substantial work. The inn could hardly be pulling in enough to make her rich. And that only led to one conclusion.

She loved this place. She wasn't going to go down without a fight.

Unless, Max thought, *I manage to convince her otherwise.*

Holly's nerves were getting the better of her. She didn't know what to talk about with Max—his easy charm and sparkling blue eyes disarmed her—and she rapidly ran through the one subject she knew best. Her inn. "Unfortunately, dinner service has already ended, but I went ahead and had the chef make up a turkey sandwich for you. It's quite good, I can promise you that. Freshly baked bread and local produce. We use only free-range poultry. We bring in homemade pies daily, and there's apple on the menu for today if you'd like dessert. If you'd like to go ahead and get settled, I can bring it up to you. Unless…is there anything else you need? Hot tea, perhaps? Cocoa? A glass of wine?"

Stop rambling!

Max's lips twitched but he said nothing. Seemingly entertained by her formal hospitality, his eyes gleamed merrily. Holly had to admit it felt strange to be talking to a guy not that much older than herself in this manner. She wasn't used to having guests like this; her usual weekly crowd consisted of married couples of all ages looking for a quiet and temporary escape from the hustle and bustle of their hectic city life.

Standing alone with him in the Green Room, Holly's eyes were instinctively drawn to the large bed between the two French windows draped in heavy Jacquard fabric. The crisp white duvet was soft and billowy and the feather pillows were plump and inviting. Holly couldn't help but imagine Max later climbing into this very bed, and she suddenly had a strange longing to curl up into it herself. It had been a long day and Max was a welcome surprise.

"Nice bed."

At the sound of Max's voice, Holly snapped her gaze to him, her heart skipping a beat at his heated stare. She quickly composed herself, thinking of something to say about the linens or pillows, and then gave up. A look of naked amusement had taken over Max's blue eyes. His lips curled conspiratorially.

"A glass of wine sounds great, actually," Max finally said, casually changing the subject and releasing Holly from her misery. "Am I allowed to go into the lobby to eat, or do I have to stay in my room?"

Holly took a second to absorb the question, still recovering from her earlier embarrassment, and burst into laughter. Max stood before her in wide-eyed, mock innocence, still bundled in his coat, looking every picture the mischievous school boy just waiting for an opportunity to taunt the teacher.

She really was acting like a prim headmistress. Knowing the other guests were all tucked in for the night, Holly decided she'd had enough of the uptight pleasantries. It was time to go off duty and enjoy the rest of her evening with something other than a good book for a change.

And what better way than with this devastating charmer?

"I'll allow you to come out of your room if you promise to behave," she chided. As soon as she saw Max's surprised reaction, she immediately regretted her words.

He flashed an openly suggestive smile and his eyes smoldered with interest. "And what happens if I don't?"

Rattled, Holly frantically searched for the best way to get the conversation back on track. "Then you'll go to bed hungry."

"I never go to bed hungry," Max said confidently, a

cocky smirk forming at the proclamation. He shrugged out of his coat and flung it on the armchair, his lightweight wool sweater revealing a broad chest and strong arms. "Come on," he said, motioning to the door. "You've made that turkey sandwich sound too good to resist."

Descending the stairs single file, Holly was grateful that there was no chance for Max to see her face, which burned with a mixture of pleasure and humiliation. What had gotten into her? She was a proper businesswoman. This inn was her pride and joy. Maintaining utmost professionalism was something she drilled into every member of the staff, and she herself practiced what she preached. Yet here she was positively *flirting* with her highest paying guest of the night. It was shameful!

As they neared the last landing, Holly took three deep breaths to compose herself, determined not to give in to her growing attraction for her newest guest. But as her foot reached the ground floor and she turned to face him, her heart disobeyed and lurched with excitement.

"I'll just go to the kitchen," she said tightly. "Why don't you go ahead and make yourself comfortable in the lobby, and I'll bring everything over to the coffee table near the fireplace?"

She turned on her heel and headed to the dining room, which she already knew was empty. Often a guest or two would stay downstairs well into the night, reading a book, or lingering over a glass of wine. But not tonight. Tonight it was just Holly and Max.

Holly and Max. Has a nice ring to it.

Just as quickly as the thought formed, Holly pushed it aside. She had to get herself under control. This man was her guest. He was a paying customer in search of hospitality, not a date.

Max was hot on Holly's heels. "I'd rather put myself

to use and help you, if you don't mind. Besides, I've been sitting for the past five hours. The drive from Manhattan took a lot longer than expected and it would be nice to stretch my legs."

Holly's stomach somersaulted as she led them into the kitchen. He wasn't going to let her out of his sight. Not that she minded. Not in the least.

"So what brings you to Maple Woods?" she inquired, glancing behind her.

Max stood in the entry to the kitchen, his broad shoulders filling the door frame in the most manly and thrilling way. Holly was not used to being alone in this room with any man other than Stephen, and that was different. Stephen was five years younger than she and madly in love with his college sweetheart; he was the kid brother she never had. Max, on the other hand, was anything but familiar.

"Oh, just business."

Business in Maple Woods? On December 19? Holly frowned. Few people came to this small town to conduct business, much less the week before Christmas, but she knew better than to press. Max was being overtly vague and he was, after all, her guest. Most likely personal business, she surmised. He probably had a relative in town that he was visiting for the holidays.

From the industrial-size refrigerator, Holly retrieved the sandwich Stephen had made earlier. She placed the chilled plate on the tray and set about cutting a large wedge of pie that was resting on the butcher's block. "Do you think this will be enough?" she asked over her shoulder.

"More than enough, thank you." Max ventured farther into the room and Holly felt her skin tingle. "Now what can I do to help?"

She chuckled nervously. "Oh, just make yourself at home. You're the guest."

"Nonsense," Max said firmly. "I've kept you up late, it's the least I can do. Now tell me. Where do you keep the wine?"

Well, wasn't he smooth? Holly smiled and resigned herself once more to his natural confidence. He had a real knack for taking control of a situation, and she liked that in a man. With any other guest, she would be appalled to even allow them entrance to the kitchen, but Max was right. It was late. No one was around. And besides, she was starting to have fun. More fun than she probably should have under the circumstances.

"The rack is just behind that pantry door. And the glasses are in the cabinet above the sink."

Max strode to the wine rack and casually stuck his hands in his pockets as he perused the selection. After a brief deliberation, he made his choice then crossed the room to the cabinet to fetch a glass. With one hand gripping the stem of a second glass he arched an eyebrow and asked, "Will you be joining me?"

Holly hesitated. He was her guest. A handsome one, but a paying one just the same. She should make a polite excuse. She should leave him to enjoy his evening in peace. But one curl of those magnificent lips was all the encouragement she needed.

She picked up the tray and shrugged with a smile. "Why not?"

"So tell me more about the inn," Max said. He took a hearty bite of the turkey sandwich, noting that Holly was accurate in her description. Turkey sandwiches usually bored him, but this one was a step above the norm. Like everything else in this place, it seemed. "How did you come about running it?"

"This was my grandmother's house, actually." Holly

toyed with the stem of her wine glass and forked a bite of pie from the slice on her plate. "When she passed away a little over five years ago, I inherited it. It was much too big for me to live in and since I don't own the land I wasn't in a position to sell. I had been working in a hotel in Boston as the special events manager at the time, and I knew this place would make a fantastic bed-and-breakfast."

Max nodded, absorbing the information and wondering just what to do with it. Perhaps there was a chance that Holly would be eager to move on with her life. A woman of her age and position would surely want to move back to the city at some point. What kind of life would a small town like Maple Woods hold for her? She didn't appear to have any money of her own other than the revenue from the inn. Max was an astute enough businessman to gauge the earnings of this place, and they were hardly a reason to continue. No, she was running the business for one of two reasons: either she had no other options, which would be great, or because she loved her job.

Max studied her from across the coffee table, noticing the way her rosy, plump lips twisted into a proud smile as she described the renovations that had gone into the house before it could be established as an inn. She gestured with her hands when she talked, underscoring her passion for the place, and despite the trepidation that stirred in his belly, Max couldn't help but smile as he listened.

God, was she gorgeous. Now, sitting across from her in the dimly lit room, he was able to take the time to really look at her properly, and he found her more alluring than he had even first thought. Draped at her shoulders, her hair appeared darker in this light, and an auburn glow was cast on it from the golden flames crackling in the fireplace. Her deep-set eyes were alive and innocent, twinkling with unabashed excitement as she spoke so passionately about everything that had gone into transforming the original property.

"I'm probably boring you," she said with only a slightly apologetic smile.

"Not at all," Max assured her. "It's nice to see a person so accomplished and passionate."

Holly's cheeks burned at the compliment and Max shifted uneasily. It was time to call it a night.

Standing, he heaved a deep, long sigh, but at the sight of Holly standing to collect the plates, his worries shifted to something softer. "Let me."

"No, no," she insisted, brushing away his hand. The plates were already loaded onto the tray and Holly stood straight to lock eyes with his. "Don't worry about it. I have to go by the kitchen anyway to get to my room."

Her room? Max's stomach tightened with realization. The thought of it hadn't even occurred to him, but of course it made sense. Holly lived here. This wasn't just an inn; it was her home.

"I guess this is good night then." She stared at him expectantly, a sweet smile on her lips, which were now the center of Max's focus.

Before he could do anything he would most certainly regret, Max stuck out his hand, accepting Holly's slim palm into his own. He held it there for a moment, watching as her eyes clouded in confusion, deferring to him as her guest, or perhaps, waiting for him to take the lead. He swallowed hard.

"Good night, Holly."

Holly gave a small smile. "Good night, Max."

Reluctantly, he released her small, warm fingers and shoved his hands deep into his pockets. The memory of her touch burned his palm. The fact that he hadn't wanted to release it made his stomach turn with unease. He turned quickly and walked through the lobby to the stairs, which he took two at a time all the way to the third floor, not daring to turn back once.

Downstairs in this giant house, a young, beautiful woman was cleaning up the dishes from the dinner she had thoughtfully planned just for him. She was probably eager to rest up for another day of working hard at a job she loved.

She had no idea that as of Christmas Day, he would be the sole owner of the property, and that by the first week of January, The White Barn Inn would be torn down.

Chapter Two

The dining room was already buzzing with cheerful conversation by eight o'clock the next morning. There was nothing like a dusting of fresh snow to excite even the calmest of her guests, Holly had noticed over the years. With Christmas already in the air, today was no exception.

Holly smoothed her winter-white cashmere sweater at her hips and glanced around the dining room once more. It was silly, she knew, to be so nervous over the thought of seeing a man—and one of her guests at that—but she couldn't deny the quiver that zipped down her spine every time she caught a glimpse of a newcomer through the dining room door. He'd be arriving any minute, she was certain, and the anticipation was starting to gnaw at her. She wasn't quite sure she had ever taken so much time in deciding what to wear to breakfast before, but the little sleep she'd gotten the night before had allowed ample time for hemming and hawing. And primping.

Ridiculous! She scolded herself once more. Max was her guest. A friendly one, yes. A handsome one…absolutely. A charming one… Holly closed her eyes to capture the memory of that lopsided grin. But a guest nonetheless, she reminded herself firmly. And a guest that would be on his way back to the city tomorrow morning.

"Miss Tate."

Holly turned at the sound of her name and smiled pleasantly at the familiar guest from the Blue Room. "What can I do for you, Mrs. Adler?"

"Have you heard any news on the storm, dear?"

Evelyn Adler was one of Holly's favorite guests. She and her husband came twice a year—once in the winter and again in the summer—and Evelyn always requested the Blue Room, claiming it accentuated her eyes. While slightly eccentric, she was well-liked by all members of the staff, and Holly had personally come to see the Adlers as a Christmastime staple.

"I checked the local news this morning," Holly informed her, "and they're still expecting two feet tonight."

"Oh dear." Evelyn's brow creased and her mouth thinned as she turned to look out the window. The snow was falling steadily, coming down in small, persistent flakes, forming a fresh dusting on the white blanket that had accumulated overnight.

Holly felt a flicker of worry as she considered the encroaching storm and the effect it would have on her guests and the Christmas traditions she had put such effort into planning. She did her best to mask the concern and said with forced brightness, "I hope it won't keep you from enjoying some of the activities we have scheduled for the day. Ice skating on the pond, the indoor campfire with s'mores and of course, your favorite—the morning sleigh ride."

Evelyn managed a smile. "I do love a good sleigh ride."

"Wonderful. Just gather in the lobby at nine and be sure to bundle up," Holly said, but her guest had turned her attention away, her sky-blue eyes roaming to the right of Holly's shoulder with sudden interest.

"My dear," Evelyn said as she wrapped a hand around Holly's wrist. "Who is that *man?*"

Holly glanced over her shoulder to see Max standing near the doorway studying the breakfast buffet. Her pulse quickened as her breath caught in her chest. *Pull it together, Holly!*

Turning back to Evelyn, she mustered a fragment of composure. "That's one of our guests, Mrs. Adler."

"I've never seen him before!" Evelyn murmured, her eyes fixed on her subject matter.

Holly suppressed her amusement when she noticed Nelson Adler shake his head slowly over his wife's innocent enough behavior from his vantage point near the hearth. She said to Evelyn, "He just arrived last night."

Evelyn's eyes flashed with curiosity and she darted her gaze back to Holly. "Alone?"

Holly chuckled at the insinuation and, with the hand that wasn't still in Evelyn's determined grip, waved a playful finger at her beloved guest. "Now don't you be getting any ideas into your head, Mrs. Adler."

Evelyn's sharp eyes glistened at the accusation. She opened them wide, innocently explaining, "I'm just saying that if he's alone…and you're alone…well, do the math, dear."

Holly tossed her head back in laughter, noticing with a slight jolt that she had inadvertently caught the attention of Max himself. Lowering her voice, she decided to put a polite end to the topic. "Enjoy your breakfast, Mrs. Adler. And remember, nine o'clock in the lobby for the sleigh ride."

Evelyn reluctantly moved aside, disappointment written all over her face as she pulled her attention away from Max. She glanced back hopefully a few more times as she returned to her table and her eternally patient husband who stared at her over the rim of his reading glasses, shaking his head once more in mock annoyance before burying his nose in the newspaper.

Left on her own again, Holly did her best to ignore the less than subtle gestures Evelyn was making from her corner, which included larger-than-life head nudging in Max's direction and mouthing of the word "adorable" with increasing passion. *As if I need to be told how gorgeous he is,* Holly thought. It was only when Nelson gave his wife a sharp look over the top of his paper that Evelyn lowered her eyes and focused on eating her breakfast.

Drawing a deep breath for courage, Holly squared her shoulders and quickly plotted her next move before turning around and facing Max. She'd have to say hello to him; there was no room for being coy. He was her guest and she would have to treat him as such. He was no different than... well, than Evelyn Adler herself!

"Good morning," Holly said, her voice softer than usual from the sudden tightening in her chest. She forced a shallow breath and smiled up at Max, her heart warming as the corners of his eyes crinkled into a smile.

"Good morning." His voice was deep and smooth, and something in the low tone left her with a sense of suggested intimacy, as if Max felt they were in on some special secret together. Locking her gaze for enough time to make her heart sprint, he finally motioned to the buffet. "This is quite a spread."

Holly exhaled a burst of pent-up air and with a humble shrug said, "Oh, it keeps the guests happy."

"I can see why!" Max grinned, helping himself to a plate. She gazed at the buffet, trying to see it through Max's eyes. Platters of steaming cinnamon French toast, poached apples with vanilla syrup, fluffy scrambled eggs, sliced tomatoes, and crisp asparagus spears were lined side by side on the antique farmhouse table. At the end, tiered trays held fresh buttermilk scones and wild blueberry muffins, as well as several carafes of strong coffee.

"You have quite a talented chef," Max said as he added a scone to his heaping plate.

"I actually do the breakfasts," Holly muttered, averting her eyes and bracing herself for his reaction. She busied herself by straightening a set of napkins as the heat of Max's stare burned her cheeks.

"You *made* all this?"

Holly shifted her gaze to his shocked face. He was looking at her as if she were half-crazy, as she knew he would. It must seem like a lot to take on—a whole lot—but Holly loved it and she would have it no other way.

"I'm an early riser," she explained as the flush of heat crept around the back of her neck. Realizing her excuse was rather lame, she added, "And I like to cook. It's the only time of day I can, since Stephen, our chef, takes over lunch and dinner service."

Max's aquamarine eyes sparked with interest. Speechless, he surveyed the buffet once more with an appraising raise of his brow. "Well, I'm impressed."

Holly smiled to herself at the compliment. She'd been making breakfast for so long, she had stopped thinking of it as anything more than functional. It was an activity she intrinsically enjoyed, and with the number of guests at one time usually being not more than ten or sometimes twelve—and sometimes as few as four, but thankfully, never less than that—she had become a master of preparing meals for a crowd of this size. It *was* arranged nicely, she supposed, and one might go so far as to find it impressive.

Especially a bachelor, she couldn't help but hope.

"Sit wherever you'd like," Holly said. She glanced at a few tables by the window and caught a glimpse of Evelyn Adler watching the interaction with a tickled smile on her lips and a sheen to her eyes that was brighter than the flames in the fireplace. "Maybe this would be a nice spot," she suggested, pointing to a table farther from Evelyn's access.

Max pulled out a chair and sat down as Holly filled his mug with coffee. "If you're around today, we have some festive activities planned," she said.

Max tipped his head. "Festive activities?"

Holly felt her cheeks flush once more, but she bit back the wave of embarrassment she felt when she saw the twinkle in Max's blue eyes. He was messing with her—looking for a reaction—just like the boys on the elementary school playground. Not that she wasn't enjoying the game…too much.

"Everything's detailed on the chalkboard in the lobby," she said as she started to walk back to the kitchen to refill the carafe. Not quite ready to let him out of her sight just yet, she instinctively paused and tilted her head. "Maybe I'll see you later."

Max grinned. "Maybe you will."

What the hell was he doing? Max sampled a forkful of eggs and chewed thoughtfully. *Maybe I'll see you later. Maybe you will.* What was he thinking, carrying on with Holly in this manner? It was completely inappropriate given the circumstances, and yet…he seemed incapable of restraining himself.

Max ripped off a chunk of scone and crammed it into his mouth hungrily. He sighed in defeat. Delicious. Of course. He took another greedy bite and washed it down with a swig of coffee so smooth and strong he was already hoping for a refill. He wanted to hate this place, and he was finding it downright impossible. From the goose down comforter to the Egyptian cotton sheets to the scented soaps to the gourmet food to the gorgeous proprietor…there was nothing to dislike about The White Barn Inn.

And that was just a shame.

Max swallowed another bite of his scone and sipped at his coffee. Allowing his scope to widen, he scanned the room, noticing an older woman near the window smiling at him. Unsure of what to do, he gave a tentative smile in return and to his surprise, the woman winked and gave a little flutter with her fingers.

Max fought back a smile as he tucked back into his scrambled eggs. Avoiding the gaze of the silver-haired woman in the corner, he focused on the other guests, feeling oddly cheered by the soft tinkle of Christmas music that lent a subtle backdrop to the buzz of the dining room.

What had gotten into him? He loathed Christmas. He couldn't stand those twinkling lights or the smell of pine. And yet here he was feeling downright merry.

Something was very wrong here.

He was out of his element and he wasn't thinking clearly, it was as simple as that. He hadn't had a vacation in too long. He was getting swept away. Yes, that was it. It had to be. But he had a job to do, a purpose for being here, and he needed to focus. He wasn't here to flirt with the locals or get caught up in…*festive activities*. The sooner he got out of this town and back to his regular life in New York, the better he'd feel.

But even as he processed this reassuring thought, his stomach rolled with uneasiness. He was struggling to convince himself. And that was a problem. A big one.

As he ate, he scanned the business section of the local

newspaper. It was a far cry from the national news he was used to reading—the biggest story, it seemed, was the rebuilding of the town's library, which had apparently been damaged in a fire several months ago. Max leaned into the paper and squinted with concentration as he reread the article more carefully for a second time, his pulse quickening as he realized the importance of the story and the implications it could have on his purpose in Maple Woods.

It was just the leverage he needed.

Sensing that Holly wasn't going to be emerging from the kitchen any time soon—and that it was probably for the best that she didn't—Max folded the paper under his arm and wandered through the lobby, up the stairs and back to his suite. It was early, but he wasn't one to sit around waiting. He'd go into town, feel out the locals, and then make his pitch to the mayor.

But even with his new information, something told him this wasn't going to be as easy as he had previously thought. And Holly was only part of the problem. There were several moving parts that needed to fall into place, and if one of the necessary parties couldn't be swayed—or bought—then the plans for the shopping center would collapse. A year's work down the drain. They'd be back at square one, trolling Connecticut and Massachusetts for a new plot of land for the project and Max already knew from his own research that no other location would do. The few other options he had considered were too small, too far from major highways, or too close to other competing shopping malls. The land that housed The White Barn Inn wasn't just ideal, it was really the only choice. Anything else would be a far second—the profit wouldn't be the same. The chance of securing tenants would be too risky. The sales projections were too shaky. It would cost them…too much to even think about. It was Maple Woods or nothing. He *had* to make it happen.

Shaking off his own misgivings, Max changed into a suit and tie, grabbed his blueprints and thick folder stuffed with financial papers and locked the suite door behind him. Back downstairs, he crossed to the front door and yanked it open. A strong, arctic wind slapped him in the face and he reflexively recoiled and pulled his collar up around his neck.

Only two hours north of Manhattan and he was pathetically ill-prepared. He made a mental note to buy a scarf when he got into town. And some gloves.

"The drive's not clear yet," a familiar voice behind him said. Max turned to face Holly standing in the open doorway, shivering at the cold.

His brow furrowed. "Oh."

"Hank just got in," she explained. "He's going to plow it now."

Max closed the door. *So much for his plans.* "How long will it take?"

Holly's hazel eyes flickered in surprise. "Eager to get away, are you?"

Realizing he'd spoken too sharply, Max offered a smile. "Sorry, I just had some business to take care of in town."

Holly narrowed her stare suspiciously. "We'll have you in town shortly. Doubt anyone's there yet at this hour anyway. Things move a little slower in Maple Woods than they do in the big city."

Max glanced at his watch. She had a point.

"It will probably take about half an hour to clear the drive, so if you want to go sit by the fire, I can have someone bring you a cup of cocoa."

Admitting defeat, Max realized it was hardly a compromise to relax for a bit in the warmth of the inn. A fresh waft of cinnamon filled his senses, bringing a resigned grin to his face. "How about another cup of that coffee instead?"

"Cream?"

"And sugar."

Holly smiled and patted his arm in a reassuring manner. Feeling instantly foolish, Max stomped the snow off his loafers—boots were another purchase he'd need to make— and shrugged out of his coat. Sitting in one of the leather club chairs by the fire, he pulled out some financial projections and studied them.

"You weren't lying when you said you were here on business," Holly observed a few minutes later as she placed a steaming mug of coffee on an end table.

"Bad habit," Max shrugged, quickly closing the folder. "I've got a lot going on back at the office. And I've never been good at sitting around and waiting."

"Or relaxing?" Holly arched an eyebrow.

Max held up his hands and grinned. "I stand accused. Guilty as charged."

Holly tipped her head thoughtfully. "Christmas is only five days away. I would think business would be slowing down."

"Business never slows down. Not for me at least." He stirred the cream in his coffee and noticed the steady stream of guests filing into the lobby. "But then, I guess the same goes for you."

Holly smiled as she turned toward the gathering crowd. With a shrug, she said, "Yep. But I wouldn't have it any other way."

Max dragged in a breath and rubbed the back of his neck. If she kept talking like this, she was going to make things a lot more difficult than he preferred.

He watched Holly retreat to the end of the lobby and fall easily into conversation with a middle-aged couple. She looked nothing short of gorgeous this morning, with her chestnut hair cascading over that creamy sweater that— even from this distance—looked so soft it was practically begging to be touched. Surely a woman as beautiful and sweet as Holly couldn't be without a handful of men lining up and hoping for a date. She'd talked unabashedly about the inn all through their conversation the night before, but she hadn't mentioned if there was someone special in her life. It didn't appear there was, but Max intended to find out just to be sure.

Holly was exactly the kind of woman he imagined himself marrying—if he ever intended to get married, that is. And he didn't. Marriage didn't work—he'd lived long and hard enough to know that—even if he wished it did. The older he grew, the more he found himself wondering if maybe…but he always came to the same conclusion: nope, not for him. Some memories were too deep. Some facts were just facts.

So no, he didn't have any intention of settling down with Holly, but he wasn't going to let that stop him from getting to know her a little better. And besides, if he managed to win her over, maybe Holly wouldn't think twice about giving up this place and moving to the city herself.

"Drat!"

She'd done it again. Holly grabbed an oven mitt and threw all her upper-body strength into moving the enormous stainless-steel pot of hot chocolate to the back burner just before it boiled over. Flicking off the gas to the stove, she grabbed a ladle from the ceramic pitcher on the counter and began filling a dozen red thermoses with the bubbling concoction. She'd managed to save it just in time, and the aroma of freshly melted dark chocolate mixed with heavy cream was heaven for her senses. She—and more often

Stephen—made this treat in batches during the fall and winter seasons, but despite years of practice, she almost always got so busy talking to a guest that the simmering pot would slip her mind. Today that guest had been none other than Max Hamilton. Of course.

Pulling a jar of homemade powdered-sugar-coated marshmallows from a shelf, Holly dared to steal a glance out the window above the sink. The snow was still falling steadily, but it was the threat of more that worried her. She'd overheard more than one guest grumble about the impending storm and the road conditions, and two others who were scheduled to arrive today had cancelled their reservations. With all the energy she'd poured into the holiday week's events, it would be a shame to see none of it come to fruition.

Her heart ached a little when she considered her real concern. She couldn't bear the thought of being alone at Christmas.

"Hello, hello!" Abby burst into the kitchen, all rosy-cheeked and bright-eyed. Snowflakes still spattered her eyelashes and she blinked rapidly to melt them.

"Hey there!" Holly brightened at the sight of her friend, comforted with the knowledge that she could at least spend the holiday with Abby and her husband Pete. She was their token charity case, she liked to joke. But the joke was becoming old. And she herself was becoming tired. Tired of being alone in this world. Tired of watching life pass her by. All she wanted was a family of her own. Was it really too much to ask?

Hard work usually eased the pain and kept her from thinking of how different life could have been and should have been, but Christmas brought a fresh reminder. It was her favorite time of the year, but it would be even more magical if she had someone special to share it with her.

"Um, Holly?"

Holly finished placing a marshmallow in each thermos and found Abby leaning against the counter and staring at her expectantly. "Yes?"

"Who is that *guy?*" Abby practically hissed the last word of her question, and the gleam in her eyes said everything.

"He's our VIP."

"Green Room?"

"Yep." Holly heaved a sigh. It seemed everyone was as smitten with Max as she was. Chances were there were many more women back in New York with the same intentions.

"What do you know about him?" Abby reached for a lid and screwed it on top of a thermos.

"Thanks…I don't know much about him actually. But we did—we did have a nice chat last night. He's very nice."

"Holly!" Abby squealed and did a little dance on the floorboards. "How long were you planning on keeping this from me?"

"It's nothing," Holly said, instantly regretting she had said anything at all. She was building this up to be more than it was. Max was her guest. And he would be leaving tomorrow. *If not sooner,* she thought, turning to the window with a sinking sensation. "He's nice. That's all."

"No, that is not all!" Abby insisted. "And besides, a man like that is not *nice.* Nice is not an appropriate adjective at all."

Holly snorted. "No? Do you have a better term then?"

"Dashing. Dapper. Completely irresistible."

Holly smothered a laugh and shook her head. "Come on," she said, picking up the rattan basket now loaded with the thermoses. "We've got a group eagerly waiting for a sleigh ride and we don't want the hot chocolate getting cold before we're even outside."

Holly pushed through the kitchen door with Abby in tow, crossed through the dining room and ventured into the lobby, where nearly every guest was now gathered in their winter best around the roaring fire, awaiting the morning's activity. Evelyn Adler had bundled herself into a royal-blue coat with a black fur collar and matching hat. Ever the lady of the house, Holly noted with a smile.

She set the basket on a table near the front door and peered out the window for a sign of the stable manager, Rob, and the horse-drawn sleigh. She searched farther out to the white barn at the north end of the estate, finally capturing some movement.

"Are you going on the sleigh ride?" Evelyn had come to stand near Holly.

Holly's shoulders slumped slightly. "Oh, I'd love to, but I should really stay behind and take care of things."

Evelyn cocked her head in Max's direction. "Even if he goes?"

Holly's chest tightened. "I don't think he's able to go, Mrs. Adler, and even if—"

But it was too late. Evelyn had gotten an idea into her head and she wasn't about to let it go. Crossing the room to where Max sat sipping his coffee, Evelyn perched herself on the edge of a footstool and removed her fur hat. She patted her silvering hair, pulled neatly into a low bun, and smiled almost…girlishly.

Holly's eyes darted to Mr. Adler, who was watching his wife from a few feet away with a bemused expression. Holly dared to near Max's chair, half dreading what she braced herself to hear.

"I don't believe we've met." Evelyn thrust a small-boned hand at Max. "Evelyn Adler. This is my husband, Nelson."

"Max Hamilton. A pleasure, Mrs. Adler." He turned to the older man and nodded. "Mr. Adler."

"Oh, call me Evelyn. *Please,*" Evelyn practically cooed.

Holly felt her brow pinch. In all the years she had known Evelyn, she had never been granted the same courtesy.

"Evelyn," Max repeated, his tone laced with amusement.

"Is this your first time at the inn?" Evelyn inquired.

"Indeed it is."

Holly's heart warmed at Max's patience with Evelyn, but she still didn't trust her most loyal guest from taking liberties. Evelyn had made herself very comfortable at The White Barn Inn over the years and, aside from a few formalities she adhered strictly to, she had taken a shining to Holly's personal life over time. Too much so.

"Mrs. Ad—" she attempted as a polite interruption but Evelyn waved her hand dismissively and refused to so much as spare a glance in Holly's direction. Frustrated, Holly began neatly stacking a pile of magazines, making sure she was just within earshot. Evelyn wasn't going to let up, and Holly couldn't resist gleaning as much insight into Max as possible.

"So you're here alone, then," Evelyn was saying now, an edge of mock disappointment in her voice. "Well, a young man as handsome as yourself must have someone special waiting back home!"

Holly cringed but held her breath, hoping to hear Max's reply above the din of the other guests in the lobby.

"Not really," Max said smoothly, and Holly felt a wave of fresh excitement wash over her. She tried to push it aside as quickly as it enveloped her. She failed miserably.

"What a pity!" Evelyn slid her blue eyes over to Holly and gave a pointed stare.

Holly clenched her teeth and wondered if Max was obtuse enough not to see through this meddling. She doubted it. Frantically searching for an excuse to pull Evelyn's attention away from Max, she bolted upright at the jungle of sleigh bells on the drive. "Sleigh's here!"

Evelyn's interest, however, did not waver. "Will you be joining us for the sleigh ride? My husband and I look forward to it every year. So...*romantic*."

Okay, this had gone far enough! Feeling out the situation was one thing. Pushing it was another. "Max," Holly said. "I think that Hank is almost finished plowing the drive. I know you were anxious to get to town."

"Oh, but he might want to go on the sleigh ride, Miss Tate!"

"Miss Tate?" Max flashed Holly a wicked grin.

Bristling, Evelyn remarked, "Of course. What do you call her?"

"Holly."

Evelyn's eyes snapped open. "Oh, I *see*," she said meaningfully, giving Holly a knowing look.

Holly bit back the urge to raise her eyes skyward. If she didn't love Evelyn so much she would throttle her!

"Unfortunately, I won't be able to join you for the sleigh ride today, Evelyn." Max set his coffee mug back on the end table. "I'm afraid I have some business in town to attend to this morning."

Evelyn deflated into her wool coat and pursed her lips. "Pity."

"Come along, Evelyn." Nelson reined in his wife by physically grabbing her at the elbow and then, more tenderly, placing her little hat back on her head. The pair scuttled toward the door to collect their thermoses and then laced fingers as they waited for the sleigh ride to board. Holly felt a sharp pang slice through her chest. She turned to see Max staring at her.

"Sorry about that," Holly said.

Max shook his head. "They're sweet."

"They are. And very loyal, too. In many ways, Evelyn reminds me of my own grandmother." Holly's mind flitted to her childhood memories in this very home. Those were happy times.

"Evelyn?" Max arched a dark eyebrow and his blue eyes gleamed. "You mean *Mrs. Adler,* right?"

Holly gave him a rueful smile. "You sure you don't want to go on the sleigh ride?"

"Nah, I should get into town."

Holly nodded, hoping she masked the disappointment she felt.

Max pushed himself from the chair and buttoned his coat. Holly winced at how inappropriately he was dressed.

"Main Street is just a few miles west, correct?"

"Correct." Noticing the silk tie peeking out from under his dress coat, Holly again pondered the reason for his visit. There was little business in the corporate sense on Main Street. With the exception of a bank, attorney's office and local doctor, only shops and a few dining options lined that stretch. Unless he was here to do something about the library... Now, that was an idea.

"Lunch is at noon?"

"Yes," Holly affirmed. She had the growing sense that he was lingering. Not that she minded, obviously. Max hadn't even left yet and already she was missing him. He was a sight she could get used to around this old house. Easily.

"I'll be back by noon, then," Max said, his eyes still locked with hers.

Breaking free from his hold on her, Holly reached for his empty mug. "Drive safe. It's slick out there."

"See you later," Max said. A devilish grin curled his lips when he added, *"Miss Tate."*

Chapter Three

The long drive to the main road was cleared, but the three-mile drive to the center of town was not. Max squinted through the snow, which was gaining momentum, the wipers doing little to keep the powder from accumulating on the windshield. Maneuvering his rented SUV through the snow banks, Max discovered he had a newfound reason for preferring city life.

It was a welcome reminder. He was becoming too relaxed in Maple Woods. He belonged in the big city; he knew it. He just needed to remember it.

Turning onto Main Street, Max clenched his jaw at the sight. Pine garlands wrapped around every lamppost, sealed with joyful crimson bows. Wreaths hung on the door of every shop. Pristine white snow covered every rooftop. Everything was almost eerily calming and peaceful.

It was like something out of a Norman Rockwell painting. But he would not allow himself to be seduced by its charm.

Pulling to a stop at the address he had jotted down, Max stepped out of the vehicle and paid the meter for the maximum time. He hoped it wouldn't take more than half an hour to convince the mayor of his plan, but if it took all day, so be it. He had no intention of leaving town without that land.

Business was in trouble and it had been for some time. People weren't shopping in malls anymore. They preferred the convenience of online shopping, the gratification of making a purchase in their pajamas at midnight, the thrill of receiving a package with their name on it in the mail five days later. Of Hamilton Properties' existing portfolio, half the centers were struggling. Development initiatives had been placed on hold for two years, but too much man power, time and energy had gone into this project. And big-name retailers were depending on him to get the job done. If he didn't, more than one department store was already threatening to pull out of under-performing centers. Without those anchors, the struggling malls would collapse.

Hamilton Properties had seen three of their competitors file bankruptcy. Only one other remained in business, and they'd already made more than one offer to buy out Hamilton's portfolio. But Max wasn't going down without a fight. He had built this company from the ground up, founding it when he was only twenty-two. It had been a roller-coaster of ups and downs over the years, and lately it had been mostly downhill, but he wasn't ready for the ride to be over. Not yet.

"Max Hamilton to see Mayor Pearson," he said confidently to the friendly woman behind the reception desk.

"Just have a seat, he'll be out shortly. Last-minute phone call and all that." The woman smiled at him as her eyes roamed over his chest, narrowing on his tie. "Not from around these parts, are you?"

Max spared a wry grin. "That obvious?"

"Most folks in Maple Woods don't wear suits and ties. Especially on days like this," she said. Her smile brightened to reveal a dimple when she admitted, "But I like a man in a suit. Always did."

Max nodded and rocked back on his heels, his eyes taking in the miniature Christmas tree on the woman's desk. She'd even hung tiny metallic ornaments on its small, plastic branches. Her sweater had a snowman knitted into it with some sort of textured yarn. Christmas carols bleated softly from the radio on the corner of her desk and at least fifty holiday cards were propped on every filing cabinet, desk, or other surface.

Seems Holly isn't the only one who loves Christmas, he mused.

Max raked his fingers through his hair and stepped away from the desk. It was definitely time to get back to New York.

A set of leather chairs was lined against the wall. Max sat down on the farthest and pulled a magazine from a pile on the coffee table. Absentmindedly flicking through it, his gaze shifted back to the woman at the desk, who was now humming along to some holiday tune, munching on a Christmas cookie and casually directing the computer mouse with her free hand.

"Oh, I'm sorry!" she exclaimed when she felt his stare. She brushed the crumbs from her mouth guiltily. "Did you want a cookie?"

Max held up a hand and gave a tight smile. "No. Thank you."

The woman frowned. "You sure? They're good. Promise. I made them myself."

Max glanced to the mayor's door. "I shouldn't, but thanks again."

He returned his focus to the magazine, feeling anxious and out of place. He shouldn't have worn the suit. It might turn the mayor off; might make him think Max was strolling into town looking to tear things down and take over. It wasn't his intention at all. But it might just look that way.

Max looked back to the receptionist, who was now plucking another cookie from her tin. "Can I ask you a question?"

The woman looked up and beamed, flattered to be asked for an opinion. "Certainly!" she exclaimed, opening her eyes wide.

"Think I should lose the tie?" Max grinned.

The woman's lips pursed in pleasure. "Definitely."

The mayor's office was decoration-free, making it easy for Max to get down to business. He sat down in the seat offered to him and accepted a cup of coffee. Mayor Pearson was an amiable sort with a warm laugh and strong handshake, and Max was immediately put at ease. So long as he didn't come across as some corporate bigwig in from the city looking to stir up trouble, he should be able to have a reasonable conversation with the mayor over what would best serve the town of Maple Woods.

And he knew in his heart that an upscale shopping center on the outskirts of town—on the land that currently housed The White Barn Inn—would be a win-win for everyone.

Everyone except for Holly, that is he thought with a frown.

"It's a stunning rendering," Mayor Pearson said, leaning over the desk to take a closer look at the blueprints. "It doesn't look like the shopping malls I'm used to frequenting."

"We try and design our centers with their location in mind," Max explained. "It's important that the mall have the architectural integrity of the town so that it just sort of…melts in with its surroundings."

The mayor gave the drawing silent consideration before releasing a long, heavy sigh. Relaxing into a high-backed swivel chair behind his desk, he said, "I'll admit that I'm intrigued. That being said, I can't be sure what the planning board will say, and they would ultimately make the decision."

Max nodded. "I understand there are lots of moving parts here, Mayor."

"Of course, there's George Miller to consider. His family has owned that land for longer than I can remember. If he's not willing to sell, my opinion doesn't even matter."

Oh, he'll sell, Max thought. To the mayor he said, "I plan to speak with him as soon as possible. I wanted to give you the courtesy first."

"I appreciate that," the older man said. "And I'd also appreciate if you kept your business here quiet unless things move forward. Maple Woods is a small town, as I'm sure you've noticed, and people around here don't like change very much."

"I'll be discreet," Max promised.

Mayor Pearson tented his fingers. "The financials you have here are very solid and I'm sure you're aware that we lack proper funding needed to re-open the town library, which unfortunately had to be closed until we can repair the structural damage that occurred in a recent fire. The library means a lot to this town—it isn't just a library. It also serves as our community center."

"I heard something about it, yes." The article mentioned that an entire wing had been nearly destroyed—Max understood firsthand the resources an undertaking like that would involve.

"People don't understand why we can't start rebuilding the portion of the building that was damaged and reopen the place. Or why we haven't already done so. It's just not as simple as that." The mayor paused. "As you can imagine, this doesn't bode well for me. Or a re-election."

Max tipped his head with renewed interest. "That's a tough position."

"Very tough. The thing I've learned about being in office is that you can't please everybody. And believe me, if we bring in engineers and construction crews to rebuild that library, someone would be in an uproar that we didn't use the money to build a new wing onto the school."

Max chuckled. "I can assure you that the taxes you would garner from the center would change things for this town."

"Oh, I know it would change things, and that's why I agreed to meet with you. If I might have a day or two to look over these papers, it would help me in making an argument to the planning committee. But I don't plan on saying a word to them unless George Miller agrees to this. I'm already on the hot seat over this library fiasco."

"I'm not sure you're aware of the urgency of the matter. It appears that George Miller plans to transfer the deed of the land to The White Barn Inn as of Christmas day," Max said.

Mayor Pearson widened his eyes. "Ah."

"I could be wrong but I have to assume that the owner of the inn—Holly Tate—might be less than inclined to sell. So you see, I would prefer to get this wrapped up before Christmas. If possible."

"You do realize that Christmas is five days away?"

Max grimaced. "I'm fully aware. I hadn't realized I

would be faced with this situation. I would have acted sooner if I had known."

The mayor lowered his brows. "Do you always do business the Friday before Christmas?"

Max decided not to give the answer to that question. He skirted it by saying, "It's not Christmas yet. It seemed as good a time as any."

"Guess that's why you make the big bucks." Mayor Pearson peered at Max, and for a split second, Max swallowed hard, nervously hooking one leg over the other. His mind drifted to Holly, to the image of her cheerfully bustling about the dining room in that soft creamy sweater and slim charcoal skirt that hugged her curves in all the right places. His stomach rolled a bit with unease.

Finally, the mayor spoke. "A retail establishment of this size will bring revenue to the town. However, it will also change the dynamic. My parting words to you are these. Tread lightly."

Max gritted his teeth and nodded in understanding. Following the mayor's lead, he stood and accepted his firm grip. The meeting was over.

"Let me know when you've talked to George Miller," the mayor said. "Then we'll have a better chat. Right now, my hands are tied. I'm of no use to you yet."

Max nodded once more and turned to the door with the sinking sensation that very little had transpired in the meeting at all. He had the mayor's approval, but it wasn't his decision to make. Max would have to convince George Miller first. And then the planning committee. And if George didn't agree…he'd have to sway Holly.

He couldn't even think about that right now.

"Oh, and one last thing," the mayor said as Max turned the door handle.

Max turned and his pulse skipped. "Yes?"

Mayor Pearson smiled. "Merry Christmas!"

The shops along Main Street had already opened by the time Max marched out of the mayor's building. Pairs of locals scurried along the shoveled sidewalks, ducking in and out of stores, stocking up on supplies before the storm and scrambling with last-minute Christmas shopping.

Max stopped and glanced at a few window displays, all of which were targeted for the holiday, of course. Santa's village in the stationery store. Elves in the children's boutique. If plans for the mall went through, independent shops along this stretch would probably struggle to survive. None of these stores would be able to compete with national retailers, or their competitive prices.

Max sighed, releasing a long ribbon of steam, and paused in front of a store window, noticing that even the bookstore boasted jolly, fuzzy snowmen in its display case.

There was no escaping it. Maple Woods was a town consumed with Christmas.

At least in New York, he could hunker down at the office or his apartment and forget about the festive activities going on around him.

Max felt his mouth slide into a smile in spite of himself. He'd dated many women in New York over the years, but he'd never encountered a girl like Holly before, and certainly none with her zest for the holidays. Although, in fairness, he'd never really dated a woman long enough to be with someone for Christmas.

Max put his blueprints in the trunk of his car and, after checking the meter and realizing that he had used very little of the time he had paid for, he strolled down the sidewalk in search of some basic necessities.

A jungle of bells chimed when he pushed through the

doors to a sporting goods store. He selected some thick wool socks, a scarf, hat and a pair of heavy-duty boots. If today's meeting was any indication of things to come, he wouldn't be leaving Maple Woods anytime soon, and he might as well make himself comfortable for the duration of his stay. He'd assumed he could come into town, meet with the mayor and spend the rest of the day getting a feel for the town before heading out the next morning. Unforeseen complications were never welcome when it came to business. Throw Holly into the mix, and Max had the unsettling sensation that personal complications were equally threatening.

From a neatly folded pile on a display table, he selected three thick sweaters and a pair of corduroy pants and, after a brief hesitation and the memory of that cold, icy wind slicing through his overcoat, he grabbed a down parka from a nearby rack.

"Do you know where I can get a cup of coffee around here?" he asked the clerk as he handed over his credit card.

The kid arched an eyebrow and studied him. "You're not from around here, are you?"

Max shrugged. "Know a good place?"

"There's not much to do in Maple Woods," the kid elaborated, and Max detected a hint of resentment in his tone. Teenagers. "You've got your bar. You've got your pizza parlor. And you've got your diner."

"Just a cup of a coffee will do," Max said patiently.

"Try Lucy's Place."

Max felt a wave of exasperation take hold. "I'm sorry, but I don't know Lucy."

"Lucy's Place. It's the name of the diner." The kid shook his head and hissed out of a breath. "You really aren't from around here."

Max inhaled sharply, but something inside him resonated with this surly kid. He was once like that. Small-town boy with big-city dreams. Desperate to break free and never look back. "Where can I find this Lucy's Place?"

The kid tilted his chin toward the window. "Just across the street."

"Thanks." Max reached for his bag and tucked his wallet back into his pocket.

"Tell Lucy that Bobby Miller sent you," the kid said, managing a tight smile. "She'll take care of you."

Max squinted as sudden realization took hold. Miller. As in George Miller? After a slight hesitation, he nodded his thanks and jogged across the street to the diner as a blast of wind slapped his face, wishing he'd had the sense to have already put on that parka.

Holly's heart flipped at the sight of Max walking into the diner and she paused mid-sentence in surprise. His broad shoulders filled that ridiculous overcoat perfectly, leaving her wishing she could see the fine details of what lay beneath. He stood in the doorway, all at once looking devilishly handsome and slightly bewildered.

Watching her reaction, Lucy Miller whispered over the Formica counter, "Who's that?"

Holly slid her eyes back to her friend. "He's a guest at the inn."

Lucy lifted her head and murmured, "Looks like you've made quite an impression on him."

Holly followed Lucy's gaze back to the front of the room, where Max caught her stare and lit up with an almost relieved smile. He held his hand up and began winding his way through the crowded tables to where Holly was perched at the counter, his athletic frame allowing him to do so with ease.

"Hey," he said, flopping companionably onto the stool beside her.

"Hi," Holly said cautiously, feeling a shiver of excitement at his proximity. "This is a surprise."

"Thought I'd get a quick cup of coffee and check out the town before I went back to the inn."

Lucy took her cue and pulled a ceramic mug off a shelf. She slid it toward Max and gave Holly a fleeting look. Holly pursed her lips and shifted her focus back to Max. "When is your, um, business meeting?"

"Already happened," Max said simply and Holly's heart turned heavy. The meeting was over. His purpose in Maple Woods was finished. He'd be leaving just as quickly as he'd arrived.

He was only booked for two nights but somehow Holly had hoped something would keep him longer. It was a silly thought, she realized now. He had a life to get back to in New York. A life that didn't include her.

She forced a bright smile. "Did it go well?"

Max pulled a noncommittal face. He shrugged. "We'll see."

Holly narrowed her eyes and looked down to her own coffee cup, not sure what to say next. Max liked his privacy, and she wasn't one to pry. If he wanted to share his reasons for being here, he would. But his evasiveness was unnerving and unfamiliar. Maple Woods wasn't a town based on secrets. If you had one, it was bound to come out sooner than later.

Max was a fresh reminder of what her life had been like back in Boston, and she suddenly realized how much she had changed since she'd moved away. And how little she missed her old life. After her parents died, the city had felt vast and empty. Cold. It wasn't until she moved permanently to Maple Woods that she remembered what it felt like to be surrounded by friends and people who genuinely cared enough to let you in, not keep you at arm's reach.

"I thought you'd be busy at the inn all day," Max observed.

"Believe it or not, I do get out," Holly said with a grin. "Abby helps hold down the fort."

"And Abby is?"

"Oh, I suppose you wouldn't have met her yet. She helps run things. Sort of a manager or housekeeper, if you will. But she's also a friend."

Max nodded, his blue gaze locked intensely with hers as if hanging onto her every word. It had been a long time since a man had paid this much attention to her, and Holly felt her nerves flutter under his gaze. Every time their eyes met, her stomach did involuntary somersaults.

The last man who had looked at her with this much interest was Brendan, her last boyfriend in Boston. And look how that had ended, she thought bitterly. But something told her Max was different.

Not that it matters, she thought sadly.

"Here are your pies, hon." Lucy placed a stack of white pie boxes in front of Holly.

Holly lifted the lid of the box on top and stole a peek at the contents. "Oh," she cried. "Apple-cranberry. My favorite."

"That's for the guests," Lucy remarked with a playful smile. She glanced at Max. "You like pie?"

Max shrugged. "I liked the pie I had last night."

"That was Lucy's creation," Holly explained. "She bakes all the pies for the inn. I drop by every morning to pick them up."

"This one keeps me in business," Lucy said.

"I find that hard to believe," Max said, an edge creeping into his once-pleasant tone. He looked around the crowded room. "This place seems to be doing pretty well on its own."

"Eh. At times. But you'd be amazed how many regulars come in, spend a buck-fifty on a cup of coffee and sip refills for two hours. Like Mr. Hawkins over there." She gave a pointed stare to the end of the counter where an older man sat sipping at his mug, the newspaper splayed in front of him. The poor man had been a fixture at the diner ever since his wife had died more than ten years ago. Holly couldn't remember a day she hadn't come in to collect her pies and had not seen him sitting in that very seat. He clearly couldn't bear the thought of being alone.

Makes two of us.

Max raised his eyebrows as he considered Lucy's logic. "Never thought about that. And on that note, I'll take a slice of pie."

A warm glow flowed through Holly at his kind effort. Why couldn't she have met a guy like Max in Maple Woods?

But then, that was the drawback to living in a small town. She couldn't find the right one in Boston. And now she couldn't find the right one here, either. Max seemed like everything she was looking for and more. But of course, he came with a hitch. He was just passing through her life. He wasn't a permanent part of it.

"What's your poison, stranger?" Lucy asked. She pointed to the blackboard on the wall. "We've got pumpkin, apple and pear."

"If apple-cranberry is Holly's favorite flavor, then I think I'll take her up on the recommendation."

Holly bit her lip to hide her smile and locked eyes with Lucy, who had approval stamped all over her face.

"Good answer," Lucy observed. She pulled a fresh pie off a baking rack and cut into it.

"Looks like we'll need a fresh one for the evening crowd," Emily Porter said, coming around the counter. Holly smiled at her friend, who was another familiar face at Lucy's Place.

"I'll get started on that after things quiet down." Emily paused, noticing Max for the first time, and then slid her eyes to Holly, barely suppressing her interest, before she disappeared into the kitchen.

"I worked in a restaurant in college," Max volunteered.

Holly perked up with interest. "So did I! I waited tables."

"You never told me about this," Lucy said, a sly smile creeping at her lips. "How long were you a waitress for?"

"Five hours," Holly admitted. It was such a short but horrifying memory that she often forgot she had ever endured it.

"Five *hours?*" Max guffawed, his bright blue eyes gleaming with amusement. He stared at her, enraptured, and Holly felt the room tilt.

He was just…perfect.

Holly shook her head and closed her eyes, just thinking of her stint as a waitress. "It was awful. I was in college and I needed a part-time job, so I applied to work at this little café. I showed up to work on the first morning and they spent ten minutes showing me how to work the espresso machine—nothing I tried helped me to succeed in foaming that milk."

Lucy nodded. "It's tricky."

"So they—wait, they fired you for not being able to foam milk?" Max's lips twitched in amusement.

"No, it went beyond the milk," Holly said. "They were short-staffed that day and my boss wanted to go golfing. He spent another ten minutes teaching me how to use the cash register—"

"Let me guess?" Max's eyes danced.

Holly gave him a playful swat, wondering for a split second if she had gone too far, but he swatted her right back. Her heart did a little jig. "So I couldn't foam the milk and I could barely use the cash register. I was the only person working aside from the cook and I had to seat people, take their orders, foam the milk, bring the food, take care of the bill, and bus the tables. It was awful. Well, *I* was awful. So awful, that one customer left me two nickels for a tip."

Max's hand was covering his ear-to-ear grin and his eyes were now wide as saucers. A heavy silence was interrupted by a sputtering of laughter and then Max tossed his head back, roaring. Lucy simply shook her head in dismay.

"Two nickels?" Max repeated, when his laughter had died down.

Holly nodded solemnly at the memory. She had never been so mortified. Never felt so ashamed. But looking back, she had to agree it was rather funny.

"I'm sorry. I'm sorry, I shouldn't laugh. But—two nickels?" Max erupted into another wave of laughter and finally composed himself, wiping at his eyes. "And here I was, just beginning to think you were perfect. Now I know you have a fatal flaw. You are a terrible waitress."

Holly's cheeks flushed deep and hot but her pulse kicked up a notch. He thought *she* was perfect. And here she thought it was the other way around.

"I bet you were a good waiter," Lucy said to Max.

Max shrugged and gave a humble grin. "I was better than Holly."

"Hey!" But she wasn't mad. How could she be? He was teasing her, and there was only one reason why boys teased.

"I'm just being honest." His eyes gleamed in merriment. "I mean, you were able to buy some penny candy with your tips and I was able to, well…pay rent."

Holly laughed but silently considered his words. Max

seemed like the type of guy who came from money. Not one who had to earn it. But then, there was a lot about Max she didn't know.

Yet.

"Restaurant work is hard work. There's a lot most folks don't think about until they're in the business," Lucy commented. She handed Max his slice of pie and placed a fork on a fresh napkin. "It's grueling at times. For everyone. Not that I'm complaining. I love this place—don't get me wrong—but it's hard work. And having a little extra cash, especially around the holidays, helps."

Max's mouth thinned. "I'm Max, by the way."

"Lucy. Lucy Miller."

Holly felt Max stiffen in his chair. She scrutinized him sidelong, questioning the reaction.

"I think I might have just met your son—Bobby, is it? Over at the sporting goods shop?"

Lucy chuckled. "So, you've had the pleasure, then? Yes, he's my son."

"Excuse me for asking, but why doesn't he work at the diner instead of the store across the street?"

"He's too cool for it." Lucy pursed her lips. "He used to help out here, but then his buddy got him that job at the sports place. It's a chance for them to hang out and earn some money at the same time. I can't complain since it keeps him out of trouble, but it would be nice to have the family help at the diner. Instead we're paying another classmate of his to help out on weekends."

Holly shook her head and heaved a sigh. Lucy often confided in her about her aggravation with her son's behavior. Bobby wasn't a bad kid. He was just a kid with dreams that extended beyond Maple Woods. "Kids these days."

Lucy tightened the apron strings at her waist. "Who

knows? Maybe he'll grow up one day and take over this place. Hope springs."

Lucy left them to tend to another customer and Holly turned to Max. She patted the pie boxes gingerly, so as to not crush the delicate contents. "I should probably get going."

A wave of possible disappointment shadowed Max's chiseled face and Holly instantly regretted her words. It wouldn't kill her to stick around for a little longer. But then, why bother getting cozier with Max when he was just going to vanish from her life tomorrow?

"You're really going to leave me sitting here all by myself? Why not stay and have another cup of coffee with me?"

She hesitated. "I should probably get back and see if Abby needs any help…"

"Fine, fine, go. But on one condition," Max insisted.

Holly's pulse skipped a beat. She carefully wrapped her scarf around her neck and gathered her stack of pie boxes. "What's that?"

"Give me a rain check?" He regarded her hopefully.

Like she'd even consider saying no.

Chapter Four

After returning to the inn, Holly continued with her normal routine, helping where needed with the lunch service and overseeing any other guest requests. She spotted Max at lunch, sitting at the same table as breakfast, under the heated gaze of Evelyn Adler from across the room. It seemed dear Evelyn's interest hadn't faded through the morning hours, but if Max was aware of her unabashed stare, he'd done a good job of feigning oblivion. Holly had hoped to be able to chat with him before he was through with his meal, but the phone hadn't stopped ringing. Guests slated to arrive in the coming days were inquiring about the weather conditions and yet another had already cancelled their weekend reservation. By the time she made it back to the dining area, Max was already gone.

Holly smiled to herself as she set down the wicker laundry basket outside the linen closet. She folded a soft ivory hand towel and placed it on its appropriate shelf, her mind firmly on Max instead of the task. She had thought her heart would nearly stop when she saw his tall, muscular frame standing in the doorway of Lucy's Place that morning—it was her usual morning stop, and his presence had shaken her routine…in a good way. She had always enjoyed her quick trip into town to pick up a stack of fresh pies and have a cup of coffee with Lucy, but something told her from now on she would always have one eye on that diner door, half expecting him to walk through, looking every bit the strapping, rugged man that had so unexpectedly appeared this morning.

It was deeply unfair that he had to be leaving town tomorrow, Holly thought with a sigh. If not sooner, considering the storm.

"Holly?" From down the hall, Abby's voice called out softly.

Holly felt her spirits perk at the sound of her friend's voice. "Back here! Folding the linens!" she cried with a smile that drooped when she saw Abby's worried expression.

"Don't get upset," Abby said, her normally pleasant tone laced with warning.

Holly stopped folding a pillow case and groaned. "Don't tell me."

"The Dempseys are checking out early."

Holly drew a sharp breath as her heart anchored into her stomach. "Of course they are."

The women exchanged a knowing look that required no other words. This was exactly what Holly had feared. The storm was scaring people away. And she would be all alone for Christmas.

The thought of the house falling dark and silent for Christmas was too unbearable to consider.

"Maybe the storm will blow over," Abby said gently, sensing Holly's distress, but Holly shook her head.

She had never been good at hiding her emotions and with the ache she felt in her chest, she didn't think she could deny her disappointment even if she tried. This was her home. Her family home. A place of so many memories, which she had promised herself she'd keep alive. This house *couldn't* fall dark and silent at Christmas. It had once, only once, and it never would again. She promised herself that.

Her voice caught in her throat when she said, "I doubt it."

She folded another towel and set it on top of the others, the task suddenly feeling useless. The thought of an empty house tonight made her feel weary with dread. She didn't want to spend Christmas alone. And, much as she loved Abby, she didn't want to spend Christmas at Abby's house. She wanted to spend Christmas here at The White Barn Inn, her own home. The one she had spent so much time and energy creating, whose doors she had opened to the public to share.

She was supposed to be spending the holiday with the cheerful buzz of her guests. Just enough company to keep her amused. Just enough work to keep her distracted, preventing her from remembering how truly alone she really was in this big house—and in the world.

And then Max had to stroll into town and remind her of what she was missing. The hope of a future and a family to replace the one she had lost.

For a fleeting second, she wished she had never met him. It was better to fill her life with guests, to keep the companionship constant, than to risk being left alone again.

"Who else?" she asked.

Abby sighed.

"Who else?" Holly repeated, realizing her suspicions were confirmed.

"The Fergusons," Abby said quietly.

"And?" Panic was starting to build and Holly's hands trembled slightly as she pulled a fluffy towel from the laundry basket.

Abby hesitated and then, as if just wanting to get it over with, she blurted, "The Browns are thinking about it."

Holly nodded gravely as she folded the towel. "Thinking about it." After a pause, she ventured, "Anyone else?"

"No," Abby said evenly. "At least not yet."

"Not yet. Exactly my sentiments," Holly said bitterly.

"It's going to be okay, Holly," Abby said firmly. "Pete and I will have you over. You can even spend the night, if you'd like. It could be fun."

Holly's mouth thinned with displeasure and she glared at Abby. "You're giving up pretty quickly."

"Oh, come on, Holly. I didn't mean it like that. I just wanted you to know you can spend the holiday with us if you need to. Or…want to."

"I know, I know. I'm sorry. I'm being silly. I'm just… It's just hard, you know?" Holly said. Tears sprung to her eyes against her will and welled into warm pools. She fanned them away with her fingers but it was no use.

"I know it's hard," Abby said quietly. And she did know, Holly thought. It was some comfort. "You've had a rough time, Holly, and it hasn't been fair. Not fair at all."

Holly nodded and brushed away another hot, thick tear. She'd have to find a way to sneak down to her quarters and clean herself up before she faced what was left of her guests.

"I know you miss them," Abby said. "And I know this time of year is especially tough."

Holly sniffed loudly and squared her shoulders. Enough crying. Wiping away the last of her tears, she blinked rapidly and let out a small laugh. "I'm being ridiculous."

Abby shook her head. "No, you're not."

But Holly couldn't help feeling indulgent. After all, her parents had died six years ago this Christmas.

Max sunk into the thick duvet and powered up his laptop. The inn had internet access, which for some reason surprised him, and he quickly scanned his email for anything new. Predictably, business was slow this week. It seemed everyone else had something—or someone—to fill their time with for the holidays. Everyone but him, anyway.

Max couldn't remember the last time he had celebrated Christmas. Never in all of his adult years, that much was certain. To him, it was nothing more than an excuse to gather with friends. Nothing more. Christmas Day, when everyone was busy with family, Max tended to work, go to a movie, or go for a long jog—anything to distract himself. Anything to make the day feel like nothing more special than any other. But it was hard not to think about what he was missing, hard not to think about that last hope-filled Christmas all those years ago, and the way his world came crashing around him so quickly. To others, Christmas was a time to build new memories. For Max, it was simply a painful reminder of what he didn't have, and he always felt a surge of relief the day after Christmas, when he wouldn't have to deal with it again for another year.

Skimming over his notes, Max then researched the library fire. The little information he found indicated that the cause of the fire had never been determined, but that it was most likely the result of a teenage prank or random accident. The library had been an historical landmark, donated by one of the founding families of the town, and was essentially irreplaceable. The age of the building lent a complication, from what Max could gather, and a structural engineer would be needed to determine the extent of the damage. Then there was the authenticity of the building itself, and the desire to restore it as close to its original form as possible. The cost of this project was monumental for a town of its size, and it appeared there was a lack of wealthy patrons standing around with their purse strings open.

Max considered the predicament for a long moment. He could understand the mayor's position. Being a real estate developer, Max knew how much a project of this size would cost to build. The mayor had a long, expensive road ahead of him and he seemed fully aware of the impossibility of his situation. Max's vision for this mall could jumpstart Maple Woods's sluggish economy and that library project. The taxes collected from the retail sales alone would fuel that development.

He had the mayor's support. That much was clear. Now he just needed George Miller's. The planning committee was something Max would think about later.

A twinge of guilt knotted his stomach when he thought of how friendly Holly was with Lucy Miller. She had mentioned George Miller in passing the night before, but Max had never stopped to consider that she would know them on a personal level. That created a serious obstacle. Holly loved this inn—why would the Millers agree to have it taken it from her? Holly would never forgive them.

Max rubbed his forehead, sensing the first hint of a headache. This project was proving to be far more difficult than he had expected. He didn't have to push it; he could just let it go. He could head back to New York and start the site selection process all over again after the first of the year. Lose most of the department stores he'd come to rely on to anchor his other centers. Throw more money away. Spend more sleepless nights trying to salvage the business he'd built from scratch.

But for what? For a woman he had met only the previous night? As beautiful as she was, even he knew this was foolish thinking. No, he hadn't come this far to back out now. And Max Hamilton was no quitter. He liked Holly. He wanted to get to know her. And he wanted to build this mall, too.

There was a way to have both, and the two were not mutually exclusive.

A knock at the door jolted him from his thoughts and he quickly shut his laptop and shoveled his papers under a pillow. He ran his fingers through his hair and stood, marching to the door with a pounding heart in anticipation of seeing Holly.

With one last deep breath, he pulled open the door, air catching in his lungs when he realized that the person who had come to see him was not Holly at all.

"Hello there, young man." Evelyn Adler stood a good half a foot shorter than Holly would have, and Max lowered his gaze to her.

A smile twitched at the corners of his lips as he peered at the older woman. Brow furrowed in confusion, he said, "Hello, Evelyn. Can I help you with something?"

A little sigh released from Evelyn's mouth and she pushed past him into his suite saying, "Nelson's taking a nap—a good, heavy meal always does it to him. I went down to the lobby to find someone to chat with and I couldn't find you anywhere, so I thought I'd come say hello."

Max watched with a stir of amusement as she made herself at home on a chair near the fireplace. She looked around the room with obvious curiosity, not bothering to hide her interest. Realizing it would be easier to humor her, Max closed the door and took the other seat near the fireplace. "How long does your husband usually nap?" he inquired.

Evelyn shrugged noncommittally. "Oh, it depends. Sometimes an hour...sometimes four."

Max raised his eyebrows but said nothing. His pulse quickened with anxiety when he thought of all the work he had planned to do that afternoon. At the top of his list was a phone call to George Miller. Evelyn was a sweet lady, but time wasn't on his side and he wasn't in Maple Woods to socialize.

Something I should keep in mind when it comes to others under the roof of this old house, he thought wryly.

"As I said," Evelyn continued, patting her hair, "a good meal does it to him every time. And they do have good food here, don't you think?"

Max pulled his thoughts away from Holly. "What? Oh, yes. Very good food."

"We live in Providence," Evelyn said. "Even with all the restaurant options we have there, nothing compares to The White Barn Inn. But then, that Miss Tate certainly has a way of making her guests comfortable."

Max swallowed a smile and dodged the question. "I take it this isn't your first time here?"

"Oh, heavens, no!" Evelyn exclaimed with a wide smile and Max noticed that she had applied a fresh coat of deep red lipstick in an almost garish fashion. "We've been coming here since it opened. This will be our fourth Christmas here."

"Really?" Now that was interesting. Evelyn must know Holly fairly well, then. Despite calling her Miss Tate, he thought with a flicker of humor.

"The first time we came here we were so charmed, we returned again in the winter. We come in the summer for the blueberry picking, you see—the orchards here are simply gorgeous. And then, of course, for Christmas."

"You don't want to be home for Christmas?" It seemed

a strange time to go away, he thought, but then, as someone who didn't celebrate the holiday himself, what did he
know? Evelyn lowered her eyes to her small, bony hands
that were tightly folded in her lap. "Little point, really. It's
just Nelson and me, you see. Everyone else has passed on
and...we were never blessed with children."

Max frowned. "I'm sorry to hear that."

Evelyn raised a hand. "It's fine. We're blessed in other
ways. Two days after Christmas, we fly down to Florida to
spend the rest of winter in Palm Beach. Probably couldn't
do that if we were busy taking care of grandkids."

Max offered her a small smile. "No, I suppose you
couldn't."

"And Miss Tate does such a wonderful job with the holiday. She has a way of pulling the Christmas spirit out of
people."

So I've noticed, Max thought ruefully.

"She's like the daughter I always wanted," Evelyn
mused, glancing at him sidelong and holding his stare. Max
fought back another smile. Evelyn's matchmaking skills
were far from subtle, but entertaining nonetheless. "Pity
that I didn't have a son to match her up with."

"Mmm," was all Max could say to that.

"Was your mother lucky enough to have a daughter?"

The questioned formed a knot in his stomach. "I was
an only child."

"I bet your mother's hoping for grandchildren soon," Evelyn observed. She stared at him expectantly, as if willing
him to just announce impending fatherhood.

"Maybe," he said. He couldn't really say what his mother
hoped for anymore. Once, he'd known what all her hopes
and dreams were, and he'd foolishly thought he could be
a part of them, too.

Max rubbed his jaw. He wondered if she had found a

way to make her dreams come true. If the sacrifices she'd made had been worth it to her.

If she ever thought about him at all.

He forced a smile, brushing aside an image of the last time he had seen his mother. Her absence was his answer. She'd followed her dreams, maybe even fulfilled them. She'd moved on with her life. A life without him in it.

"Will you be spending the holiday with your parents?" Evelyn pressed.

"Nope," Max said simply. He tried to ignore the heaviness that was forming in his chest. Sensing Evelyn's alarm, he said, "They're away."

Not the truth, per se, but not a lie, either. His parents were away. Where they were, he hadn't a clue, but away, yes. They were gone, long gone. Even before they disappeared in the physical sense, they'd always had one foot out the door, searching for escape in one form or another. His dad found it in the bottle, but his mother... Well, she had greater aspirations than caring for an unwanted kid, it seemed.

"Well, then why don't you stay and have Christmas with all of us here at the inn?" Evelyn suggested, her face lighting up at the idea. "Nelson and I would love that. And Holly, too, I'm certain... I mean, *Miss Tate*." She paused. "She's quite pretty, don't you think?"

Max bit the inside of his cheek to keep from laughing. She always found a way of squeezing Holly in, didn't she? Any thoughts he had that Holly might be spoken for romantically had been erased by Evelyn's overt matchmaking when it came to her beloved innkeeper.

"In fact," Evelyn remarked, "she's really far more than pretty. One might even say that Holly is beautiful."

Max chuckled softly but he couldn't deny Evelyn was correct. From her soft hazel eyes flecked with green to her silky chestnut hair and those perfectly full lips, Holly was truly beautiful. Both inside and out, he mused, recalling that dazzling smile that caused her eyes to twinkle.

"Mmm, quite," he said to Evelyn.

Evelyn latched onto his words. "Then you'll stay through the holiday?"

"Unfortunately, I'll need to be getting back to New York before then."

Evelyn's eyebrows knitted with indignation. "Whatever for?"

"Work?"

"No one works on Christmas!" Evelyn said, her agitation building.

"Holly does," Max pointed out.

"Well, that's *different,*" Evelyn said petulantly.

"Is it?" Max asked mildly. "How so?"

"Holly loves what she does."

Max shrugged. "So do I," he countered.

Evelyn sighed in exasperation. She was a feisty little thing, and much as she was getting irritated, he could tell she was enjoying herself, too. "It's different. This is Holly's home. And she likes having guests in her home for Christmas. It isn't work to her. It's…an invitation to share the holiday."

A hush fell over the room. Max felt a punch to the gut at the sudden revelation. Evelyn was right. This was Holly's home and she was purposefully filling it with strangers for Christmas.

Where was Holly's real family?

"And then there were five." Holly placed the key to the Orange Room in the drawer and waved sadly as the Browns rolled their luggage through the lobby and out into the cold late afternoon. The Dempseys and Fergusons were already gone, and with the departure of the Browns, that left only the Adlers, the Connellys and, of course, Max.

Abby turned to her. "Anything I can do?"

Holly glanced at the clock. "Has Stephen started dinner prep yet?"

"I could check."

"Thanks. Let him know about the new head count." Holly made a note about the change in reservations. This storm was costing her more than personal company; it was costing her money, too. And with the purchase of the estate only five days away, she wasn't in a position to be taking a financial hit.

By now, every reservation scheduled through the first of the year had called to cancel. Their money had been refunded in full. Those who checked out early were also refunded their money—Holly wouldn't have felt right keeping it from them when some, who were scheduled to leave tomorrow or the day after were simply afraid of not being able to get home in time to spend Christmas with their families. She would hardly feel justified in penalizing them for such a basic desire, even if she had been depending on their stay.

Oh, well. She had the money for the purchase of the property, and anything else would have just been a nice little cushion for getting through the slower months after the holidays. George Miller had agreed to a price that was both comfortable and fair to her. It wasn't a small sum, but it was worth it to know that the property would be hers and that her home could never be taken from her.

She'd already lost enough for one lifetime. She needed to know that some things were there to stay.

"Holly." Dana Connelly swept down the staircase. Holly knew what the woman was going to say before she even spoke. "I'm afraid we're going to have to check out early."

Holly managed a brave smile. The snow hadn't stopped

all afternoon and dusk was fast approaching. "Did you want to try and leave in the morning?" she asked.

"We think it's better to leave as soon as possible. Before the roads get worse. We can be home in two hours if we leave now." She must have sensed Holly's growing disappointment because her rich chocolate eyes softened. "I'm sorry, Holly. But if we wait until the morning, who knows what we'll be waking up to out there."

Holly forced a bright smile, knowing she had no right to feel let down. These people were her customers. They owed her nothing. She was providing them a service, not the other way around. If they wanted to leave early, she shouldn't be making them explain on her behalf.

It was just another aching reminder of how badly she wanted a family of her own. She was trying to fill the void with this playhouse she had created and, while it served its purpose, ultimately she could not depend on her guests for anything more than they were willing to give. They passed in and out of her life with pleasantries and warmth, but they were not permanent fixtures.

Her chest squeezed tight. Max was no different.

"Of course you can't wait until morning," Holly said to Dana. This was the Connellys' third visit to the inn in the last year. She would see them again. But for now, she had to let them go. "This storm is unpredictable and I'd hate for you to miss out on Christmas with your families."

"Well, I don't know about that," Dana said.

"Oh?" Holly pulled up the Connellys' records and changed their bill before sending the file to the printer.

"This year we're having Christmas with my husband's family," Dana continued in a meaningful tone. She locked eyes with Holly and Holly smiled, her first real smile since she'd left Max at the diner.

"I have a feeling you're not too excited about that."

"Oh, to put it mildly," Dana said with a sigh. "Personally, I'd rather be snowed in here for the holiday but…"

"But responsibilities beckon?" Holly flashed her a conspiratorial grin. *Guess that's one thing I don't need to worry about,* she thought, suddenly perking up a bit. In-laws.

Dana leaned in over the desk and hissed, "They never end!"

Holly laughed despite herself, feeling better than she had in hours. "Here's your bill. I didn't charge you for the weekend, of course."

"Oh, let us pay! The cancellation policy says seventy-two hours, doesn't it?"

"No, no," Holly said dismissively. "It's not like I would have filled the room anyway."

Dana lifted her eyes from the invoice. "Is everyone else checking out then, too?"

"Looks that way." Holly sighed.

Dana turned to the window. "It's really unfortunate."

"It is what it is," Holly said blandly, sadness creeping in again.

Dana suddenly smiled. "Well, one good thing has come out of all this for you. Now you won't have to worry about taking care of guests during Christmas!"

Holly managed a brittle smile as Dana ascended the stairs to fetch her husband and their luggage. *If only she knew.*

Deciding it best to tell Stephen they had lost yet another couple for the night, Holly wandered through the dining room and into the kitchen where Stephen and Abby were chopping carrots for the stew.

Holly grabbed a sugar cookie shaped like a star from the tray on the counter and took a bite, ignoring Stephen's arched eyebrow. "The Connellys are leaving."

Abby set down her knife. "What do you think we should do?"

"I honestly don't know," Holly said. "Evelyn and Nelson are still here. And Max." Her heart soared at the thought of him. Just saying his name made her feel close to him, and the image of his rugged face and dazzling blue eyes made her want to be even more close to him.

Stephen finished dicing the carrots and plucked an onion from a wooden bowl on the butcher's block. With an expert hand, he peeled and halved it, and then quickly chopped it into parallel strips. He rotated one half clockwise and ran his knife down the other side. Scraping the pieces from the cutting board to the large pot on the stove he said, "Well, there's enough here to feed twenty. So I guess we'll be having leftovers."

"How are we with supplies?" Abby asked, delicately veering the discussion back to practical matters. "If the storm hits tonight, we want to make sure we have enough to get through."

"We have enough," Stephen replied. He slung a dish towel over his shoulder and turned to Holly, meeting her square in the eye. "But before I keep going with this, you might want to check on the rest of the guests and see if they even plan on sticking around."

"Stephen!" Abby gasped.

Holly stopped her. "No, he's right. I'm being completely unprofessional, and that isn't like me. I'm going to go check on the Adlers and, um, Max. If they want to leave early, they should know they have the option. I'll go now."

Abby held her gaze. "Okay."

With more bravado than she felt, Holly pushed through the kitchen and into the dining room. Her heart plummeted when she saw Evelyn and Nelson standing in the lobby.

"Miss Tate!" Evelyn said sharply when Holly came into view.

"Yes, Mrs. Adler?" Holly asked, though she didn't need any clarification for the purpose of Evelyn's visit to the lobby. Something told her that the couple was not here for the gingerbread house decorating competition that was scheduled to start in—Holly glanced at the grandfather clock—twenty minutes.

"I'm so sorry, dear, but I think we might need to leave early."

"But—" Holly wanted to ask what better plans Evelyn could have for Christmas but managed to stop herself in time. She really was losing sight of her hospitality today, wasn't she?

But Evelyn and Holly had known each other long enough to understand the unspoken. Evelyn's watery blue eyes drooped at Holly's distress. When the older woman reached over to touch her hand, Holly had to fight to hold back the tears that were threatening to form. She swallowed a painful lump in her throat.

"You know how much it means to me to spend Christmas at The White Barn Inn," Evelyn said. "But we're supposed to be going to Florida two days after Christmas. And if we get stuck…"

Holly nodded briskly, not daring to speak for fear of choking on her own words.

"Oh, I'm torn, Miss Tate! The tree lighting is tonight, and I bought a new hat especially for the occasion. Red with black faux fur…" Evelyn glanced around the room in agony, wrestling with her own emotions. "The thought of leaving all this—" She swept her arm around the room, gesturing to the twinkling Christmas tree, the stockings hanging from the mantel, the mistletoe sprigs under every doorway and the garland framing the windows.

It was Holly's turn to comfort Evelyn. She squeezed the woman's hand tight, realizing how small and frail it seemed in her own. "It will all be here next year, Mrs. Adler."

Evelyn's worried eyes clasped with Holly's. "You're sure, dear?"

Holly smiled warmly. "Of course I'm sure."

Evelyn searched Holly's face, her gaze unrelenting until her fear had subsided. Shaking slightly, she let go of Holly's hand and turned to her husband. "Okay then," she said. "I guess we should go."

"It's the smart thing to do, Evelyn," Nelson said kindly.

"He's right," Holly mustered even though she wanted to cry out and beg them to stay through the rest of the week. "Getting home safely is most important. Do it for me, Mrs. Adler."

Evelyn pinched her lips and wiped away a tear. "Has everyone else decided to leave as well?"

Holly opened her mouth to respond when her attention was suddenly pulled to the edge of the room, where Max was sauntering down the stairs into the foyer, a pleasant expression on his handsome face. Evelyn turned to follow her gaze, her mood immediately brightening.

"Well hello again, young man!" she cooed, clasping her hands in unabashed joy.

Max stifled a smile as his cheeks grew pink. Holly herself could barely keep from laughing at Evelyn's reaction to his arrival, but a bigger part of her felt nearly sick with dread. The thought of Max leaving the inn tonight was a reality that she wasn't ready to accept. The chances of a man like him passing through her inn again were slim to none.

"Max and I had a lovely chat this afternoon," Evelyn beamed.

Holly lifted an eyebrow and smiled slyly at Max. "Oh?"

"Ah, yes. Evelyn did me the honor of stopping by my

room today," Max informed her, his blue eyes dancing with mischief.

Holly bit her lip. She didn't even want to think about what might have been said during that conversation.

"We were just telling Miss Tate that we sadly have to leave early," Evelyn explained and Holly felt a stab in the chest like she was hearing the words for the first time. "Will you be checking out early as well?"

Holly held her breath and the room went still as she waited for his response. She didn't dare look at him for fear he would see the anguish in her eyes.

"I think I'll stick around, actually," Max said easily and Holly's heart rate quickened. She hadn't seen that coming.

Evelyn could barely suppress her vicarious glee. "How lovely!" she exclaimed, fixing her large bright eyes on Holly in a less than subtle fashion.

Holly bit the inside of her cheeks to keep from laughing and Max's eyes twinkled ferociously. The fact that he was just as in tune with Evelyn's matchmaking as she was didn't bother her anymore. If anything, the private joke they now shared only made her feel more bonded to him than ever. A hidden secret was shared between them, lost on sweet Evelyn.

"I was actually coming down to see if I could extend my reservation," he said when he had collected himself.

Extend? Holly still couldn't believe her good fortune. Why on earth Max was deciding to stay longer as opposed to leaving early was beyond her understanding, but she wasn't going to question it. "Of course," she said, regaining her composure. She forced herself back into a professional role, but in the company of her favorite guests, it somehow felt unnecessary. "How long will you be needing the room for?"

"Until Christmas Day."

Holly paled. Five more nights. "Christmas Day?"

Max scrutinized her reaction. "If that's okay. I can move rooms if mine has been reserved."

Holly cleared her throat, refusing to so much as glance at Evelyn, who she could see from the corner of her eye was radiant with joy, her palm placed dramatically on her heart. "No, it's fine. Your room is free. In fact, all the rooms are free, actually."

Max spared her a quizzical look. "All the rooms?"

"We're not the only ones heading out early," Evelyn said. She rubbed her hands together as the plan was hatched. "So it looks like it will be just the two of you in this big, beautiful house!"

Holly watched as Max's eyes widened and quickly darted to hers, searching for verification. On instinct, Holly lowered her gaze, unable to look at him in that moment. Her pulse raced as her chest rose and fell with each breath. Alone in the house with Max. How would he feel about that?

"I take it that dinner has been cancelled for tonight?" Max asked, breaking the awkward silence. When Holly nodded, he suggested, "Perfect. Then you can take me up on my earlier rain check. Maybe you can show me the town tonight."

"But the roads!" Evelyn said.

Max shrugged. "The storm hasn't hit yet. By the time it does, we'll be all tucked into bed, safe and sound." He turned to Holly and grinned. "What do you say, Holly?"

Holly glanced from Max to Evelyn, whose expression was frozen in anticipation. "I'd love to," she said easily.

With that settled, Evelyn released a long sigh of content. "We should get going," she said and Nelson took his cue to take the bags out to the car.

"It was a true pleasure meeting you, Evelyn." Max

smiled down at her warmly and more awkwardly reached in for a hug.

Breaking free, Evelyn giggled like a schoolgirl and Holly noticed her cheeks were stained with pleasure. Holly shook her head, unable to suppress the contagious energy that Evelyn carried with her. "Drive safely, Mrs. Adler. And Merry Christmas," she said.

Holly pulled her in for a hug and only released her when Nelson called from the doorway that the car was ready. Evelyn slid her sharp blue eyes to Holly before joining her husband. "You have fun, dear," she purred.

Holly felt her cheeks color. She had a feeling she would do just that.

Chapter Five

Holly walked back to the kitchen as though floating on air, completely unable to banish her smile. As much as her heart ached that Evelyn and Nelson had left, she couldn't deny the glee that was building with each passing second at the thought of five whole nights with Max. Alone.

"Dinner is off!" she announced to Stephen and Abby. They both froze midaction in their tasks, their expressions transforming from concern to bewilderment.

"The Adlers are leaving?" Abby asked slowly.

"Already left." Holly shrugged. Giddily, she all but hopped over to the cookie tray and reached for a piece of fudge before stopping herself. She was about to spend a week with the most gorgeous man she had ever met. An image of the way his broad shoulders strained against the confines of his sweater filled her mind and she snatched her hand back. Now was not the time to be indulging in sweets. Now was the time to be indulging in something altogether better.

Get a grip, Holly! He was still her guest. Why was she having so much trouble remembering this?

"The Adlers already left?" Abby cried in disbelief and Holly nodded her head cheerfully. It was sad, yes, but in light of the other news… "Then why are you smiling like that?"

Holly reflexively frowned. "Am I?" she inquired. Stephen shook his head and began cleaning up while Abby stepped away from the counter, her face pale with concern and her eyes wide with something close to fear.

"I'm seriously getting worried about you now, Holly," she said gravely.

Holly smiled as Abby silently followed her back to her quarters, and only once the door was firmly closed behind her did she triumphantly proclaim, "Max invited me to dinner tonight. Even better? He extended his stay. For five more nights."

"He's staying through the *week*?" Abby's eyes flew open in shock and she threw herself down on Holly's bed and stared at the ceiling in disbelief.

"Yep." Holly leaned into the antique ivory-framed mirror above her dressing table and massaged a dollop of moisturizer under her eyes. She looked tired and stressed from the events of the day, but it was nothing a little makeup wouldn't fix. "Until Christmas Day."

"Really?"

"That's what he said." A surge of fresh glee washed over Holly's insides. Five more days with Max. Anything could happen in that time period.

Abby rolled onto her side and tucked her feet behind her. She propped herself up by an elbow and cupped her head in her hand. "But why did he decide to stay longer?"

Holly stared at Abby's reflection. She wondered the same thing herself. The mysterious nature of his visit was certainly odd. "He says he's here on business. That's all I know."

"Business?" Abby scoffed. "In Maple Woods? Over the holidays?"

Holly frowned and considered her friend's words. "It is strange. Isn't it?"

Abby was incredulous. "Strange? Uh, yes! Just a little. He didn't say what kind of business?"

Holly shrugged. "He didn't elaborate."

Abby pushed herself up to a sitting position dangled her legs over the side of the four-poster bed. "Well, it doesn't matter. Business is boring. Besides," she said, coming to join Holly in the mirror, "you can find out all the details tonight. On your date."

A flutter of nerves caught hold of Holly's stomach at the term. Date. Was that really what it was? It seemed so unlikely when she stopped to think of it—he must have an entire life in New York, so what more could he want with her than a friendly face to keep him company while he was in town? Yes, they got along, and yes, he seemed to like her. But liking someone took many forms, and with someone as gorgeous as Max Hamilton…well, chances were he wasn't often without equally beautiful female companionship. There must have been many girls who fell under Max's spell. Holly would be foolish to think she was the only one who could sense this magnetism.

Her stomach churned. A guy like Max probably had his pick when it came to pretty girls. And she was hardly exceptional. Nothing glamorous. Not rich. A plain Jane, in many ways.

She had to brace herself for disappointment. Max's intentions—on every level—were a mystery to her. Getting swept up in romantic notions would only result in heart-break and tears if the evening turned out to be nothing but platonic, albeit pleasant. She couldn't go giving her heart to a man who would rather peruse a spreadsheet than listen to what she had to say. She'd promised herself after her last failed relationship that the next man she allowed herself to develop feelings for would at least have the same priorities as she did.

Maybe Max wasn't so different from Brendan, after all. Despite his friendliness, he seemed a lot more interested in whatever business he had going on over Christmas than the spirit of the holiday itself.

"Why are you frowning?" Abby eyed her through the mirror.

"What? Oh…I wasn't frowning." Holly forced herself back to her surroundings and dabbed some gloss on her lips.

"Don't tell me you're thinking about Brendan."

Holly didn't dare admit the truth. Something told her the night ahead was going be both spontaneous and romantic, and she pushed back the wary hunch that threatened to disturb the chance of hope that was playing out in her mind. It was hard not to think about Brendan sometimes—he'd let her down when she needed someone the most, destroying any hope of a brighter future, when hope was all she'd been clinging to. She hadn't dated anyone seriously since then. And the thought of going into town with Max tonight, while thrilling, was also a little terrifying. The entire concept was so far out of Holly's normal routine that she struggled to grasp the logistics of what a real date would require.

"I'm not thinking about Brendan," she said firmly. And she wasn't. She was thinking about Max.

"Good, because all you should be thinking about right now is what you're going to wear on your date."

"It's not a date!" But even as she protested, Holly couldn't resist the warm glow that filled her.

"Then what would you call it?"

Holly considered the question. "Companionship."

Abby chortled. "Oh, please. A man like that does not need companionship."

"What does he need then?"

Abby pulled a face. "I think you already know the answer to that one. Believe me, there's only one reason that man is hanging around you so much, and it isn't because he's looking for a friend."

Holly bit her lip and considered Abby's point. And hoped to God she was right. She studied her reflection in the mirror and smiled with anticipation. She hadn't felt this nervous or alive in longer than she could remember, and her heart was hammering with possibilities. She hadn't been alone with Max in anything other than a professional setting and she suddenly felt seized with the terror of finding nothing to talk about other than the inn. She supposed they had managed just fine at the diner, but then Lucy always had a way of putting people at ease.

"You're frowning again," Abby pointed out.

Holly shifted her eyes to Abby's reflection and smiled through a sigh. "That better?"

"Nervous?"

Holly felt her shoulders slump in resignation. "Just a little."

Abby's smile widened and Holly could see her eyes begin to dance, even from this distance. "Good, that means you like him."

Of course I like him, Holly thought. "It's just been a while since—"

"Since you've had any fun?"

Holly shrugged and returned to the mirror so she could

add an extra bit of blush to her cheeks. She hadn't really thought about it but, yes, it had been a long time since she'd had any fun…unless you counted knitting circles, book clubs, and Friday movie night with her married guests as fun.

"It's just too bad that he doesn't live closer," Holly said, pursing her lips in displeasure.

"So?" Abby quipped. "A hot guy has asked you out to dinner tonight, Holly. When's the last time that happened?"

Holly pinched her lips and narrowed her gaze at her friend. Abby knew exactly how long it had been and she wasn't about to help prove her point.

"Take it for what it is, Holly! You get to dress up, go out, and have fun. And maybe if you're lucky, the date will last straight through to morning," she added with a mischievous grin.

Holly picked up a cosmetic brush and tossed it in Abby's direction. "Stop it!" She laughed, but she knew Abby wasn't joking.

"What?" Abby cried. "Come on, you can't tell me you haven't thought about it. The man is gorgeous, Holly…you may as well enjoy him!"

Holly shook her head firmly. "I'm not looking for a one-night stand. You know what I'm looking for."

Abby met her sharp gaze and tipped her head in response. "I know…but all I'm saying is…be open-minded. You've been sitting here alone night after night for as many years as you've been running this inn." Abby lay back on the bed and dramatically ran her hands over the cotton comforter. "Has this bed ever experienced anything more exciting than a pair of flannel pajamas and a romance novel?"

Nope, Holly thought, but she couldn't help but laugh.

Abby had a point—Holly *had* closed herself off to love over time. But was Max really the one to make her open to the idea of it again?

Max was already waiting in the lobby when Holly came around the corner at their designated meeting time. He was dressed casually, in dark jeans and a charcoal cashmere sweater. A heavy parka was slung over his arm along with a scarf.

Holly glanced down at her own ensemble, feeling grateful that Abby had stuck around to help her pull together her look. Gone were the uptight work skirt and heels. In her slim-fitting jeans tucked into knee-high leather boots and a black V-neck top, Holly figured she looked equally ready for a night out with a new friend…or something more. As Max's eyes roamed appreciatively over her, she couldn't help but hope it might be the latter.

She smiled shyly. She was attracted to this man like she had never been attracted to any other.

"You got some new clothes!" Holly pointed to the hat in Max's hand.

His face lit up in response to the recognition. "I picked these up in town today."

Understanding took hold. "Ah. So that's when you met Bobby Miller. Interesting kid, that one."

Max shrugged into his heavy coat and zippered it closed. "I warmed up to him by the end," he admitted. "He sort of reminded me a little of myself at that age."

"Really?" Holly hadn't seen that one coming. She couldn't think of anyone who seemed more different than Max than the Miller boy. Max was…well, every adjective Abby had cited earlier that morning. Dashing. Smooth. Warm. Bobby Miller was just…unpleasant.

She couldn't see Max ever behaving that way and she

wasn't sure she wanted to either. Allowing Max to hold the door open for her, she crossed into the cold evening. Snow fell softly on her uncovered head.

"What's this?" Max scolded, lifting a lock of her hair and then letting it drop back against her coat. "You don't have a hat? My, my, Miss Tate. And here I thought I was unprepared."

Holly hadn't wanted to look too casual on her possible date and she now realized her error. "I forgot," she lied with a smile. "It's okay."

Max questioned her with his eyes. "You sure?"

"I'm sure." Holly climbed into the passenger seat of Max's car. She hadn't even considered driving into town. Somehow, without a word, Max had taken charge of the evening.

It felt nice to be the one being taken care of for a change.

"So tell me more about your exchange with Bobby," Holly said, once Max had turned the car off the driveway. She placed her hands in front of the vents to warm them. "I have to admit that I see absolutely no resemblance between the two of you."

Max gave a small smile. "You mean you don't think I have a chip on my shoulder?"

Holly laughed. "No."

"Joking aside," Max said, flicking on the windshield wipers, "I wasn't that much different at one time. I don't know Bobby, of course, but it seemed to me like he wants more from life than Maple Woods can offer."

Holly bridled. "Gee, thanks."

"Oh—Holly, I'm sorry. I didn't mean it like that." Beside her, Max winced.

If he wasn't so damn cute… "It's okay. I know what you meant."

But something inside her twisted. Max had a point about

Bobby. Maple Woods *didn't* offer much. Certainly nowhere near the amount of opportunities that a major city could. If Max saw something of his younger self in Bobby, then it must have meant that a town like Maple Woods wouldn't work for him. That he could understand why Bobby would want to leave. That Maple Woods wasn't glamorous enough.

Already sensing the evening was headed in a disappointing direction, Holly changed the subject, feeling suddenly weary and deflated. "There's a tree lighting in the town square tonight. They always do it the Friday before Christmas."

A long pause followed as Max said nothing. Holly shifted uncomfortably in her leather bucket seat, regretting the suggestion. Max had invited her out, and if city life was something he seemed to so clearly prefer, a tree lighting was probably hardly his idea of an exciting time.

Holly chewed the inside of her lip and battled with the pang in her chest. She had been looking forward to that tree lighting, but she was hardly going to trade it in for a chance to spend the evening with Max.

Finally, Max's warm, thick voice filled the silence. "I have to say, that I'm not sure I've ever met anyone with so much holiday spirit."

The observation was pleasant but Holly detected a subtle, underlying edge. "You make it sound like that's a bad thing."

"Eh."

"You don't celebrate Christmas?"

"Not if I can avoid it," Max said simply and Holly's stomach clenched. It was one thing not to celebrate the holiday, and it was another to actively dislike it. She considered asking Max the reason behind his lack of Christmas spirit, but decided to let it go. The night was already off to a shaky start as it was.

Slumping back into her seat, Holly stared passively out the window at the snow-covered trees, but as soon as Max turned the car onto Main Street, she couldn't help but smile.

The entire street was illuminated by strands of lights wrapped around every lamp post and tree and draped over each shop awning. All along the sidewalk, a festival of lights had been assembled in every color of the rainbow. Santa and his sleigh. A slew of tiny elves. Snowmen, reindeer, and every other Christmas-themed notion. The effect was not short of magical, and cars in front of them slowed to enjoy the display.

"Quite a show," Max said tightly.

"They do it every year," she told him. Her eyes flitted from side to side, eager to take in every lighted object. "It's one of the traditions I love most about this town."

Max had turned to face her, and she distractedly met his stare. Even amidst the sparkle of the light show, she could see the blaze of mirth in his eyes at her reaction.

"I'm sorry," she chuckled, collapsing against her seatback. Her cheeks colored fiercely, and she was grateful he wouldn't notice with all the red lights pouring in from the window. Laughing at herself she said, "Maybe you're right. I really do have more Christmas spirit than most."

Max spared her a lopsided grin. "You're forgiven. Besides, it's kind of cute."

Holly's mouth snapped shut. She had forgotten what she was about to say. She merely stared. Her ability to speak, gone. Max was blissfully unaware of the effect he had on her as he pulled the car to a stop and turned off the ignition.

Cute. He thought she was cute. She replayed the exact words again, just to be sure he had really spoken them.

Butterflies fluttered through Holly's stomach and into her chest. She swallowed hard and stepped out of the car, wishing suddenly that she could climb back inside and have

Max all to herself again. She didn't want to have to share the night with anyone or anything. She wanted to focus all of her attention on him. Without distraction.

Nights like this didn't happen often in her world, and she was determined to commit this evening to memory.

Maybe it would be a story she would one day share with their children.

She banished the thought just as quickly as it formed. Ludicrous! She was getting ahead of herself, and she of all people should know better.

"Why don't we go over to the tree lighting?" Max suggested.

Holly tipped her head. "Oh…it's okay."

"Hey! I'm new in town. You're supposed to be showing me all the local attractions," he teased.

"But I thought you didn't want to go."

He peered at her suspiciously. "I never said that."

Holly flashed back to their conversation. Perhaps he hadn't spoken the exact words, but he had still managed to show a concrete lack of enthusiasm. "Okay, I guess you didn't say that. But seriously, we don't have to go. I've been to this every year. It wouldn't kill me to miss it this one time."

"So it's a tradition for you, is it?" Max began walking toward the center of the square. The decision had been made.

Running the few feet to catch up, Holly asked, "How about you? Any family traditions?"

Max sniffed and shivered in his coat. He avoided eye contact by staring in the shop windows. "Not really."

The answer was less than satisfying. Holly curbed a swell of frustration and tried again. "So, you've already established that you avoid Christmas. What do you usually do instead of celebrating?"

Max shrugged. "Work."

Something inside Holly hardened. Work. She should have known. Why else would he be in town—on business—the week before Christmas?

Holly felt her stomach curdle with disenchantment.

So there it was. A workaholic. She knew the type all too well thanks to Brendan. Men who would rather climb the corporate ladder than be tied down with a wife and kids. Men who only wanted a girlfriend when it was convenient for them. Men who didn't want to be held responsible for anything serious. Men who wanted to work hard and play hard without complications. She should have known, really. Max was gorgeous, unattached, and clearly very successful. It was a common combination. And a lethal one, in her experience.

Her heart contracted with each breath, throbbing with pressure as the reality of the situation became all too clear. It was too good to be true. She should have known. Max was who he was and she was not going to be the girl to try and change him. She'd been a fool once, and she'd be damned if she'd be one again.

He may be cute and rich and have a smile that could make her knees shake, but he'd break her heart without a bat of his curly, black lashes. If she let him.

They began to approach the town square with hands thrust in pockets, chins tucked in scarves, and quietly gathered with the other townspeople who were crowded below the base of a large evergreen. A children's choir was huddled together, waiting for their cue from the elementary school's music teacher.

"Beautiful tree this year, Holly!" someone cried out and Holly beamed.

"That's your tree?" Max whispered, his eyes wide.

"I donate one every year," she said. "With so much land, it's the least I can do."

"The owner doesn't mind?" A frown line creased Max's forehead.

Holly's breath caught. "I'm surprised you would remember that I didn't own the land," she said, feeling slightly uneasy.

But Max just threw her a devastating grin. "I learned a long time ago that when a pretty girl talks, you should listen."

Holly cheeks burned with pleasure and she skirted her eyes to her feet. When she dared to glance his way again, Max was scrutinizing her with an amused smile.

Relief finally came when the children's choir suddenly broke out in song, their small, sweet voices echoing in the night air. A chill descended over the crowd as the mesmerizing, almost haunting sound filled the silence. At the last verse, the tree immediately sprang to life, and the magnificent lights illuminated the crowd's smiling faces.

Max leaned in to her and whispered, "Cold?" The soft touch of his breath so close to her ear as he whispered such a simple question forced a rush of electricity to run the length of Holly's body. She trembled slightly and then quickly drew a sharp gust of freezing air in a vain attempt to regain some form of composure.

Mistaking her shudder for a shiver, Max draped an arm around her shoulder. His dense parka felt like a down blanket as he pulled her in closer. "That better?"

She barely managed a nod. Max's proximity began caving in on her, causing her body to respond in a primal way she had not experienced in a very long time. Even through the thick coat, she could feel the hard wall of his chest as he held her close, and the strong weight of his arm as it enveloped her shoulder, his hand gracing down to rest on her elbow. A flush of desire poured through her blood, heightening her senses. Her mind began to reel with the possibilities of what his body would feel like against hers and she had a swift and all-consuming urge to rip off that parka and press him firmly against her so she could properly feel the contours of his body, and the ripples of his muscled chest.

She knew that indulging herself with these thoughts was pointless. She could never act on them. She would only be disappointed. He was leaving in a matter of days. And he had made it clear where his priorities lay. But it wouldn't hurt to enjoy the moment…

Once the last song had been sung and the last ovation had been given, the group begin to disperse. A crowd was already working its way to Lucy's Place or the pizzeria, not quite ready for the evening to end. Max slipped his arm from her shoulder and said, "I don't know about you, but I'm famished. Shall we?"

He crooked his arm by invitation and wordlessly, Holly slipped her mittened hand through. A surge of longing choked her, drowning her in a sea of desire and conflicting emotion. Her body ached for his touch and the sensation it stirred within her.

She knew she had only just met him. He was, for all intents and purposes, a complete stranger. A stranger here for an extended stay. A workaholic. A bachelor by his own choosing. He was wrong. All wrong.

And Holly knew all at once that she was in very big trouble.

Holly slipped into the chair across from Max and unraveled her scarf from her neck. He watched as she twisted her upper body to hang her coat over the back of her chair, her tiny waist craning, and her breasts pressing against the thin cashmere of her black sweater.

Sitting so close to her, Max felt more alive than ever. The heat of her body so close to his was so intense, the sweet smell of her flowery perfume so feminine, that it took everything in him not to reach down and graze a finger along the small, creamy hand that held her menu.

"So, just so that we're clear, tonight's on me." He watched as Holly lowered her eyes and her features twisted in protest. Before she could speak, he held up a palm. "I insist."

Holly gave a shy smile as she looked up at him from under her long, graceful lashes. "Thank you."

"Now. What's good here?" Max turned the menu over and studied the specials. Lucy's Place was about comfort food, it seemed. Chicken pot pie. Mac and cheese. Fish and chips.

"I'll admit I haven't eaten dinner here very often." Holly's brows knitted as she studied the menu and Max felt himself grow curious.

"Really?" He leaned in closer to study her pretty face. Her soft, full lips were painted with a tinted red gloss that he wanted to kiss right off her mouth. His groin tightened as she met his gaze and he abruptly reached for his water glass to defuse the heat she stirred within him. Desire choked him, closing his throat and making it hard to swallow the icy liquid. He wanted this woman. Badly. But given the circumstances, she was off-limits. His mind knew it, but his body wasn't yet ready to accept it.

"I don't really get out much," she explained. Her hazel eyes darkened at the admission, and he felt a strange affection for her take hold and linger. Holly seemed like a woman surrounded by loving friends. Maybe he had misunderstood.

"Life at the inn keeps me so busy," she continued. "We serve dinner every night, so it usually makes sense for me to just eat there."

Max held her gaze with his, searching for something in

them beyond her explanation. He couldn't be certain, but he thought he detected a shadow creeping over her face.

"Well, they have wine," he noted, pulling his eyes from hers to glance back at the menu. "Want to share a bottle?"

Holly brightened. "Sure."

"White or red?"

"Red for the winter. White for summer."

Max's lips twitched. She was a funny little thing. "Red it is then."

The waitress he remembered from earlier came over to their table, grinning at Holly. "Isn't this a pleasant surprise," she said.

"Hey, Emily," Holly said. She glanced at Max, pinching her pretty little lips. "I was just telling Max that I don't get out much for dinner."

"Not enough," Emily said. "Guess it takes someone special to drag her away from the job."

From the corner of his vision, Max could see a flush appear on Holly's cheeks. He couldn't deny the twist of pleasure that stirred his belly.

"I'm Max," he said abruptly to the waitress, forcing away thoughts that shouldn't linger. "I saw you this morning, but didn't catch your name."

The young woman smiled warmly. "Emily Porter," she said. "So what can I get you?"

Max placed the order and turned his attention back to Holly, his anxiety growing in their small silences. He needed to keep pressing forward, keep talking to her. If he stopped and thought about what he was doing, he'd stand up and leave. He knew better than to be sitting here with her right now, but he was powerless to his own desire. He liked this woman, and it had been a long time since he had felt this way about anyone. Normally, the first sense of heartfelt interest made him start thinking of an excuse to end things quickly, but not so with Holly. It went beyond the way his gut tightened in response to her natural feminine curves. It was something in her voice. In her smile. Something that touched him on a level he was unfamiliar with. Something that made his heart ache.

Of all people.

"I was sorry to see Evelyn leave," he confided. "I was starting to like having her around."

Holly smiled and tucked her menu behind the napkin holder. "I was afraid she would scare you off."

"It takes a lot to scare me off."

Holly dropped her eyes once more and her lashes fluttered against her rosy cheeks. He hadn't noticed how shy she could be, and her sudden vulnerability made the man in him want to wrap his arms around her and take care of her forever.

He gritted his teeth. How ironic that the one person she needed protecting from was himself.

"Is she always like that?" he asked, pushing down the guilt as best he could. He buried it deep in the pit of his stomach and focused on their conversation.

Holly arched a brow. "Meddlesome, you mean?"

Max chuckled, recalling Evelyn sitting in his room earlier that afternoon regaling him with tales of other guests she'd had the pleasure—or displeasure moreover—of meeting over her many semiannual visits. "Yeah, I don't even know the best word to describe her. She's certainly one of a kind."

Holly slipped him a secret smile. "I think she had a crush on you."

Max felt himself blush and he broke out in laughter to cover his embarrassment. "She seems like a very special lady."

"She is." Holly cast him a challenging look, as if gauging his tolerance. "I remember one time she thought another guest was hitting on Nelson."

A peal of laughter sputtered out of Max's lips. *"What?"*

"I know." Holly rolled her eyes at the memory but the twisting of her lips betrayed her fondness for it. "It seems silly, but she was just convinced this woman was flirting with Nelson. I mean, convinced. She couldn't let it go. She went after that poor woman in the blueberry patch for asking Nelson to help her find a new bucket. Chased her all the way back to the barn."

"What about Nelson?"

Holly waved a hand through the air dismissively. "He just stood there and watched. Completely bewildered."

Max shook his head, wishing he could have been there. "She's a firecracker."

Holly tipped her head to the side. Her eyes roamed over his face lazily. "That's a *very* good description."

"Well, thank you," Max said, grinning.

Emily brought the wine to the table and he sipped at his glass, enjoying the anecdotes about the inn. The more Holly talked, the more captivated he became. She was a compelling woman with a knack for putting people at ease. No wonder she was so at home at the inn; why she made so many others feel at home there, too. She was sweet in a quiet, nurturing sort of way. Her world seemed calm. Peaceful. For a moment, he dared himself to imagine what it would be like to live in that world.

He had an uneasy feeling that he would like it there.

He knew he could ask her, right then and there, when she was reminiscing about experiences at the inn, if she would ever think of giving it up, moving back to the city. But for some reason, he couldn't. Now wasn't the time. If she said no, he would be left with no alternative but to admit the truth. This dinner—and any hope of others to come—would grind to a halt. Any chance of getting to know her better would be gone. She was a trusting sort, and he couldn't take complete advantage of her. So for now, he'd rather not know her stance.

Besides, there was always a chance that he'd sway her view, especially if she was as charmed with him as he was by her.

After all, he still had five days until Christmas.

The diner looked different this evening than it had earlier in the day. The lights were dimmed and the room was lit predominantly by dozens of strands of multicolored lights. Around the perimeter of the walls, an electronic train worked its way around the room. Max smiled as he watched it go around, the sight of it filling his chest with an ache he couldn't fight.

"I remember asking Santa for a train like that one year," he said.

At the mention of Christmas, presumably, Holly perked up. "Did you get it?"

"No."

Holly's forehead creased into a frown. She clearly hadn't been expecting that response. "Oh. That's sad."

Max shrugged and watched silently as the train passed by them once more. "North Pole Express," he mused, reading the label. "That's a good one."

Holly watched it passively, her attention fixed on his story. "Did you get the train the next year?" she asked hopefully.

"Oh, it was too late by then," Max said evenly. He inhaled deeply, wishing he had never mentioned the train. Or Christmas.

"Why's that?"

"Because by then, I no longer believed in Santa." He

managed a smile and quickly shifted the conversation. "I hope it's okay that I'm sticking around through Christmas."

Holly drifted her eyes from the train to his. "I'm really happy you're staying, actually."

His stomach tightened. He didn't know whether to feel guilty or excited or both. "I'm not intruding on any plans?"

Holly tucked a strand of chestnut hair behind her ear and toyed with the stem of her wine glass. She cast her eyes downward. "I tend to rely on my guests for company." She dragged her attention away from her glass and watched him with a guarded edge. "You really spend your Christmas working most years?"

"Don't you?"

Holly stiffened, but the corner of her lip curled into a smile. "Touché."

Max drew a sharp breath. "I don't mind working. And Christmas is…highly overrated."

She watched him with a critical squint, her eyes darkening. After a pause she gave a noncommittal "Maybe."

Max suspected she didn't hold the same view. Her outward joy at anything related to the holiday was proof. She couldn't cover up her feelings even if she tried. And he was glad she wasn't trying. He liked a woman who could hold her own. Holly was true to herself.

And true to those around her. A ripple of shame passed through him.

"Do you celebrate at all? Even just to get together for a party with friends?" She watched him carefully, searching his face for an explanation.

"It's not my thing."

Holly's eyes narrowed slightly, but her attention was quickly pulled to a man approaching the table.

"George!" she said, smiling once more.

"Nice to see you in here this time of evening, Holly. I hope I'm not, uh, interrupting you."

Holly's cheeks turned a fleeting shade of pink. "I don't think you've been introduced," she said. "This is Max Hamilton, a guest at the inn. Max, this is George Miller. He and Lucy own the diner."

Max stiffened. He held out a hand. "Pleased to meet you," he said, giving George a firm handshake. "I met your wife and son this morning."

"Max is already a fan of Lucy's pies," Holly chimed in.

"My second time here today," Max said. "And I only just arrived last night."

George grinned. "Already a regular, then!"

Max managed a thin smile, feeling sly and underhanded. This wasn't like him, but he didn't know what else to do. "Guess so."

"How long are you in town?" George continued. Across from Max, Holly stared at him expectantly.

"Through the holiday," he replied.

"Family here?"

"Just me."

George's eyes narrowed in surprise but he recovered quickly. Refilling Holly's wine glass, he said, "Let us know if you need anything. We like to keep our customers happy."

Max gave a watery smile. "Just like Holly."

"Must be something in the air." George inched back as the door jingled and a new pair of customers shuffled in from the cold. He lifted his chin and raised a hand in greeting. "Better go seat them. But good to meet you, Max. Hopefully I'll be seeing you again before you head out."

"I'm sure of it," Max said.

More sure than you know. He turned to Holly. "Shall we?" he asked, tipping his head toward the door. "I wouldn't mind walking around town before the storm hits."

She nodded. "Another glass of this wine and you'd be carrying me back to the inn."

"Would that be so bad?" Max asked, and Holly's cheeks flared.

"If I didn't know better, I might think you were trying to flirt with me," she said as she shrugged into her coat and buttoned it closed.

Max watched her thoughtfully, noticing the way her eyes blazed a brighter shade, the way the high color in her cheeks set off the tint of ruby in her lips.

"Maybe I am," he murmured.

Holly pressed her lips together, but he could tell she was pleased. Maybe none of this was as complicated as he worried it would be. Holly was young, single and trapped in Maple Woods. Sure, she loved her inn, but that didn't mean she wouldn't embrace change. She had lived in Boston before this, after all.

"Do you ever get back to Boston?" he asked, holding the door for her.

Holly wound her scarf tighter around her neck and began leading them down the snow-covered sidewalk. "Not really," she said, stopping to glance at a window display in the stationery store. "The inn keeps me so busy, I can't exactly get away without closing down business."

"That must be difficult," Max ventured.

Holly sighed, releasing a plume of steam into the brittle night air. "Oh, life is full of sacrifices, I suppose."

Max frowned at her choice of words, wondering if he should dare to read more meaning into them than she'd intended. She loved the inn, that much was clear in the way she lit up around her guests or when she spoke of the place, but she'd chosen to give something up to keep it going. Max knew well enough what happened when people sacrificed too much for one thing. Eventually they came to resent it, and soon after, they left it. Just as his mother had.

Falling into easy silence, they walked a lap around the town square, their feet crunching over the frozen snow, pausing here and there so Holly could enjoy the decorations, until the wind picked up and the snowflakes grew thick and wet.

"We should probably head back to the inn," Holly said, looking up to the sky.

Disappointment settled heavy in his chest as they approached the car. As the lights from the town faded behind them and The White Barn Inn came into view, Max had a momentary vision of the bulldozers coming and knocking it to the ground, leveling it to a field and later paving it with cement. Only a matter of weeks ago, he had gazed at the plot of land and imagined his sleek shopping center standing proudly at the edge, but now the thought of this big, beautiful house being gone felt sad and unfair.

He turned to Holly as he pulled the car to a stop and popped his seat belt. Letting go of the past was hard—he'd learned that at an early age. But letting go of the past was the only thing that kept you moving forward. Surely, Holly would be the better for it? Maybe this was the opportunity she needed to start living for herself instead of always taking care of others.

"I had a lot of fun tonight," Holly said as they slipped through the front door. Just off the foyer, the lobby area was dimly lit and the fireplace was dark. Not a sound could be heard through the giant house, forcing all of Max's attention on the beautiful girl in front of him.

"See, it's fun to get out and go to dinner once in a while."

She gave a slow smile as she looked up at him. "You're right," she admitted. "I think I do need to get out a bit more."

He hesitated, lured in by the slight parting of her lips, the lingering hold in her gaze, by the awareness that there was no one else in this house but the two of them.

"I should go check some emails," he said, his voice husky and low. Firm. He was convincing himself, not her, and he was doing a damn poor job of it.

Her cheerful expression faded ever so softly, and without thinking, knowing only that he didn't want to see that look cross her face or know that he had caused it, he reached out and set a hand on her arm and leaned down. She blinked up at him, her eyes flashing in awareness of their sudden proximity, and then he turned his head ever so slightly and brushed her cheek with his mouth. Her skin was smooth and light against his lips, and his groin tightened at her sweet smell. Everything in him was telling him to graze his mouth to hers, to taste her lips.

Max stepped back. Not tonight. Not with the conversation with George Miller on the table.

He was still in town for four more days. And in that time period, anything was possible.

Chapter Six

"Good morning," Max said from the kitchen entrance, his voice deliciously thick and scratchy from slumber. Holly's heart lurched and she felt the color drain from her face as she turned to sweep her eyes over his chiseled, unshaven face. Her pulse quickened as his mouth tipped into a knowing grin, and his blue eyes twinkled. She knew he would most likely come into the kitchen—it was breakfast time after all—but the sudden sight of him standing there was still enough to send a shock through her and she found herself completely flustered and unprepared.

Max leaned against the doorjamb, tall and strong, folding two thick arms across his broad chest. His hair, she noticed, was slick and wet, and a vivid image of him in a shower with water streaming down his hard body flashed through her mind before she could stop herself. Instinctively, she brought her hand to her mouth and bit down on the side of her thumb, staring at the object of her desire under the hood of her long lashes.

It had been a long, sleepless night.

"Hey!" she replied, gathering her wits. She had to pull it together today; she'd promised herself that much. She was going to behave today. She had to.

He was all wrong for her. A workaholic who didn't even live in town. And—though she was quick to forget— he was her guest.

Amazing how quickly both facts could mean so little when he strolled into her kitchen looking like that.

Max ventured farther into the sun-filled warmth of the kitchen. He crossed behind her to the coffeepot on the counter and his hip brushed casually against hers. Something flipped inside her at the involuntary connection.

This was going to be more difficult than she thought.

She pressed her lips together, fighting her weakening resolve. She had tossed and turned all night thinking of the way Max's sharp blue eyes had pierced hers last night, the way his lips had tenderly brushed her cheek when he said goodnight. The way his strong, heavy hand had lingered on her arm. The way her heart had missed him from the second he turned and ascended the stairs to his room. The way her bed had never felt so vast. Or so empty.

She still didn't know if their evening had constituted a real date, but it was real all right. Too real. So real that she feared it would take her a long time to forget it and come back to reality. Because the reality was that in four days Max would be gone and she would be all alone.

And the reality she knew before his arrival had somehow come unraveled in the two days since she'd first set eyes on him.

How strange that only a couple of days ago she was so content with her life, so seemingly fulfilled, and now all she could think about was how much she was missing. She'd always known how much she wanted a family of her own, but she'd managed to fill that hole in her heart—and this house—with a makeshift family. The variety of personalities shuffling in and out of The White Barn Inn made this old mansion a home. But Max's arrival served the opposite purpose of the coming of her other guests. Instead of warming her heart, it just made it ache.

She liked him more than she wanted to. And the harder part was that she thought he might like her, too.

She chewed her lip in thought. New York *was* only two hours away…

No. She banished the notion immediately. Maple Woods was her home. It had given her a sense of community that she had never known. A feeling of belonging. Of comfort. Of safety and security. She had a place here. A purpose. She could never leave it all behind.

Recalling his words last night, it was to Holly's chagrin that she knew Max preferred a much different way of life. It was just one of the many strikes she held against him.

But then…what were the others? Her mind was clouded by his all-consuming presence; she was so rattled she couldn't even remember if she'd salted the eggs yet. Or if she'd set the timer for the toast. She was a mess, and the more desperate she became to find composure, the more fuzzy her thoughts grew.

With a mental flip of a coin, she grabbed the saltshaker and doused the eggs. It was a gamble, but it would have to do. Besides, keeping her hands busy with her task was the only way to keep them from innocently wandering over to Max and doing things they really shouldn't.

Max leaned against the counter and took a gulp from his mug. "I have to ask. What exactly do you put in this coffee? Or…is it a secret?"

"Cinnamon."

"Ah," Max said, taking another sip. His lips turned into an easy smile. "Nice touch."

"Thanks," she said. She sprinkled some rosemary over the diced potatoes that were sizzling in the frying pan, grateful for an excuse to look away from that irresistible face. Her knees felt weak just sensing his rugged body so close to hers.

For not the first time since he'd entered the room, she wished he'd just grab her and press her close to that hard, ripped chest.

You stop it, she chastised herself. Honestly, this was getting out of control. She was powerless to her own desire for him. It wasn't like her.

Leave it to Max to unleash a whole side of her she didn't even know existed.

"Looks like the snow has stopped," Max observed.

Holly looked up from the stove and followed his gaze out the window over the sink. Only a mere two feet of snow had gathered over night—hardly the snowstorm of the year that the forecast had warned. Not that she was complaining. The threat of more had left her alone with Max; she couldn't have orchestrated the outcome better if she had tried. She almost had to laugh over the irony of her concern only twenty-four hours ago, when the thought of everyone checking out early had seemed so devastating. Amazing how sometimes things just worked out the way they were meant to. If she were more of a romantic sort, she might have called it fate. "Maple Woods is used to handling snow like this. I'm sure the roads will be plowed in two hours."

"Look like a lot to me," Max said, eyes fixed out the window. "But I guess the road conditions are the biggest factor."

"Does that mean you'll be leaving early?" Her heart

flipped as she spoke. She didn't know what was keeping him in town. The weather. Business. Or her.

"That eager to get rid of me?" His eyes danced at the banter.

She took his response as a no, her chest rising and falling with relief. "I hope you like omelets."

"You don't need to cook."

"Of course I do. You're still my guest."

"Holly." His tone was deep in sound, gentle in protest. He dropped his head to the side, his eyes locking with hers. A heavy silence took over the room.

Holly drew a shaky breath. "I told Stephen to take the rest of the week off, so hopefully my cooking will do."

"If it's anything like yesterday morning, I'll be a happy man."

"Good. Why don't you pick a spot and I'll bring everything in," she said, feeling nervous under his watchful eye.

"You're not going to make me eat alone, are you?" He lifted an eyebrow and pulled himself from the counter.

"Of course not. I'll be out in ten minutes." She kept her eyes on the frying pan until he finally left the kitchen and only then did she release an enormous pent-up breath. She clutched the counter and bent over it, feeling all at once dizzy and lightheaded. She stood to fan her face as her body temperature continued to rise.

The effect that man had over her was unparalleled. And ridiculous. She filled a glass with cold water from the tap and took a long sip, tipping her head back to consume every last drop, and set it back on the counter. After wiping the back of her hand over her mouth, she fanned her face once more, taking deep breaths to calm her pounding heart.

Honestly. Was this what she had come to, spending year after year holed up in this house? By the way she was responding to his slightest flirtation, you would have thought she'd been living in a convent!

She grinned wryly to herself. Considering she hadn't dated anyone since leaving Boston, the analogy had more truth in it than she cared to admit.

Gathering her wits once more, Holly finished preparing breakfast and carried the food into the dining room. Surprised to find it empty, she set the heavy tray down on the nearest table and ducked her head into the lobby. Max was sitting on a leather club chair, an ankle propped on the opposite knee, a cell phone clutched to his ear. He promptly ended the call when he spotted her.

"You didn't need to hang up on account of me," she said as she neared him. "I would have waited."

Max waved away her concerns. "Nah. Just business. Boring stuff."

There was that word again. Business.

"Well, breakfast is ready when you are."

Max rose to his feet and Holly reflexively raked her eyes over the length of his body. "Smells good," he said.

"Thanks," she said, crossing back into the dining room. She arranged the plates on the table and pulled out a chair to join him. "Do you have any plans for the day?"

As soon as she said the words, she immediately regretted them, fearing her phrasing might be misconstrued as an invitation. Not that she wouldn't mind spending the day with Max, but she didn't want to seem…needy.

"I have some work to do this morning in town," he said and Holly felt a twinge of dismay.

"I'll be in town today, too, actually," she said, remembering her own plans with relief. "Every weekend in December the town hosts a Christmas Market in the town square. I help out each year."

"See?" He waved a fork playfully in her direction. "You work through the holidays, too. It's not just me."

"It's different." Holly bristled. "I'm still participating in the holiday."

Max met her stare from the corner of his eye. He didn't buy it.

"Don't you ever feel like you're missing out on Christmas?" she asked.

Max cut into his omelet. "Christmas doesn't hold any meaning to me. No good feelings, at least."

Holly frowned, and something deep inside her seared open. She swallowed hard, pushing away the thought before it could surface. "I'm sorry to hear that."

Max shrugged and reached for his coffee mug. "No sympathy needed. I have work to keep me busy through the holiday. It's not like I feel I'm missing anything." He smiled tightly, holding her eyes for a fleeting second, before lowering his gaze to his plate.

"Hmm," Holly said, watching him carefully. His jaw seemed hardened as he focused on his food.

"Besides," Max continued, "Christmas is for children, for families. I have neither."

That makes two of us, she thought grimly. "Do you ever wish you could leave the office behind for a few days, maybe…make time for a child or family?" she ventured.

Max chewed a wedge of toast thoughtfully. "I try not to wish for things that can't happen."

Can't or won't?

She supposed it didn't matter. The heaviness in Holly's heart was replaced with emptiness at his words. His work was his life. By his choosing. And it didn't seem as though he was open to sacrificing his time. Or making an effort. It didn't seem as if anything more held any meaning to him.

Sadness coated her stomach. He was confirming her

worst suspicions. He wanted to focus on a career, not everything else that mattered so much to her.

An old wound opened. She'd still never forgotten the way she felt returning home after that last dinner with Brendan. Thinking it was the night he was going to propose, she'd bought a dress just for the occasion and even splurged on a manicure at a little spa around the corner from her apartment. All through dinner she could barely eat, so sick was she with anticipation, wondering how he would do it, what the ring would look like, what she would say. Would he get down on one knee?

But Brendan had no intention of proposing that night. Or any night. The romantic occasion had been his way of telling her that he was being transferred to Los Angeles. He had no intention of returning to Boston and at no point in the conversation did he broach the idea of her moving with him, not that she would have wanted to go. Her grandmother was all she had by then, and her parents' sudden death six months prior was still unbearably fresh. Staying in close proximity to Maple Woods and her grandmother was too important.

Watching Brendan's beaming face nearly burst with pride over his promotion, without any regard for the heartache she was feeling at his expense, without any consideration for the two years of her life she had given him, she couldn't help wonder what she had done wrong. Knowing that there was nothing she could have said or done to make him want to stay, she had reached the obvious conclusion. The only thing she was at fault for was giving her heart to the wrong man. When she looked back and thought of the time she had spent with him, spending so many weekends in Boston when she could have spent more time in Maple Woods with the last of her family, she felt a pang of regret so deep, she thought it would break her.

And that was a mistake she was determined to never repeat again.

With a hardened heart she went on a few dates over the years, but the pickings were slim in Maple Woods and eventually she just stopped altogether. But still, she dared to hope that someday she'd find a family of her own again. That her home would be filled with love and laughter and memories.

As an only child of two deceased parents, all she wanted was someone to share her life with. It was a simple thing to wish for, wasn't it?

George Miller lived in a small house behind the diner. He'd agreed to meet Max there, rather than in the open setting of Lucy's Place, where they would be sure to garner suspicion from the other locals. Max had been brief in their phone conversation, not even stating the nature of the visit and only hinting that he was a real estate developer when he asked George if they might talk at his convenience. If George was curious about the reason for the meeting, he didn't reveal it.

George was shoveling the front sidewalk when Max rolled to a stop. "Come on in," he said, propping the shovel against the front porch. "Lucy's at the diner and Bobby's out with friends, so the house is quiet. I'm afraid I don't have much time. I need to get back to the diner in about half an hour."

Max pounded the snow off his boots on the mat and followed George into the cramped living room. "Is Bobby still in school?" he asked.

"Winter break," George replied.

"Ah," Max said.

"Those were the days, weren't they?" George said ruefully, and Max felt his lips thin.

He had loved the academic side of school—the distraction and hope that reading and learning provided. When he was very young, he looked forward to the school year, seeing it as an escape from his unhappy home life. By the time he was in middle school, his classmates had grown mean, and Max dreaded the shame he felt from the judgment in the eyes of his classmates, the pity in the faces of his teachers. They knew all about his father—about the brawls down at the bar, about the black eyes and drunken tirades. Those who lived close enough heard the doors slamming, the glass breaking as it hit the walls. They saw the flashing lights from the police cruisers late at night. It was a common sight, but the dread Max felt the next day never faded.

And they all knew about his mother, of course.… His teachers had been particularly kind to him as a result, he knew. But he didn't want their sympathy. He didn't want anyone's sympathy.

Holly's words that morning at breakfast had made him pause. He'd almost opened up to her then and there. What had he been thinking? He didn't open up to anyone. Those who knew his story taunted and teased or felt sorry for him. He didn't want anyone to think that way of him again.

"I loved school, actually," Max managed. And despite it all, he had. He'd considered dropping out more than once by the time he was in high school, but he knew that a good education was his only chance at a better life, so he stuck with it. *And look at me now,* he thought. He should feel proud, he should feel successful, but being here in the Miller house, a house not much bigger than the one he'd grown up in, just depressed the hell out of him.

It was this damn town, he told himself. It was making him soft. Making him wish for things he could never have.

"Is Bobby a senior?" Max inquired, shifting his thoughts back to the conversation.

"A junior," George replied.

"I imagine he's busy applying to colleges, then. Isn't this the year for it?"

George dodged the question by taking Max's coat and hanging it in a hall closet. Eventually he said, "We'll see about college. He's hoping for a scholarship. He's quite good at football."

Max nodded, thinking of how quickly circumstances could change.

"So you're staying at The White Barn Inn?" George asked, sinking down into a well-worn armchair.

Max took a seat on a sofa, noticing the threadbare quality of the fabric. "I am," he said. "It's a beautiful establishment."

"Holly does a good job with it," George mused. "She's a sweetheart, that one."

Max allowed himself an internal grimace. It seemed Holly had succeeded in charming the whole town, not just him. "I take it you know her well?"

"She's friendly with my wife. Lucy supplies the inn with those pies you like so much."

Max gave an easy smile. "Your wife is very talented."

George did a poor job at masking his pride. "What can I say? I'm a lucky man."

Looking around the cramped, simple room, Max had a moment of clarity. George *was* happy with his life. It didn't suit Max's needs any more than it seemed to suit Miller's son, but to George it was enough.

And that wasn't good. Max had thought it impossible for the Millers to turn down the sum he was ready to offer, but now he wasn't so sure. They didn't seem to yearn for much more than they had. They were uncomfortably friendly with Holly. What reason would they have to sell the land to him?

If it wasn't for cold hard cash, than what other motivation could he give them?

"Has Lucy thought about branching out with her pies?" Max asked.

"Oh, she's got dreams of opening a little bakery," George said, "but she's too busy running the diner to pursue that right now. He smiled fondly. "She wants to call it Sweetie Pie. She's been saving for years, but it hasn't added up to much."

"You could bring in extra help at the diner to free up her time for another business," Max offered.

"Help doesn't come free, and neither does another rent payment," George replied and Max felt a flicker of hope spark. "We'd hoped Bobby would help out more at the diner, but he's too busy running around with his friends to roll up his sleeves on our account."

Max rearranged himself on the couch and gave a benign smile. It wasn't his place to comment on a situation he had only just come into.

"Lucy thinks getting him out of Maple Woods for a while will be good for him, but I'm not so sure. The kid needs to grow up and once he does, I think he'll decide to follow in his old man's footsteps. We'd love for him to take over the diner one day, maybe grow it into something bigger even."

Max said nothing, using the time instead to consider his best approach. George Miller was a man of deep roots. He was tied to Maple Woods. The situation—from Max's view—was bleak.

"Enough about me," George finally said. "You wanted to meet with me and I have to say, I'm curious. What can I help you with?"

Max inhaled deeply. This was it. If George Miller shot him down, his efforts in Maple Woods would be finished.

His purpose for staying gone. He'd have to head back to New York immediately to start salvaging the project and he would most likely never see Holly again. If George turned him down, news of Max's attempts to swipe her home out from under her would travel back shortly, possibly before he'd even have time to pack his bags and peel out of town.

"My company, Hamilton Properties, is a major retail developer. We have centers throughout the country. Twenty-six in total."

George nodded his head gravely. "Impressive."

"I'll get right to the point, George. For some time now my company has been strategizing to build a shopping center approximately halfway between Boston and New York City. We've done extensive research and planning, including securing several major retailers in order to get the bank to approve the loan. All of these efforts are hinging on one thing, location. We've pulled the demographics and we've driven around several sites. We feel very strongly that your parcel would be the ideal location for our center."

George's jaw slacked. "My parcel? You mean…The White Barn Inn?"

Max was brisk. "Yes."

Gobsmacked, George sat back in his chair, saying nothing as he digested the information. "Wow. I don't even know what to say."

"I understand this must feel random. I wasn't informed that you owned the land until two days ago."

"Are you aware that I have a verbal agreement with Holly Tate to sell her that land?"

Max swallowed the bitter taste in his mouth. "Yes, I'm aware. Is this why you never put the land up for sale before? A parcel of this size is worth a lot of money."

George's brow creased with trouble. "Holly's our friend.

Her family has leased the land for generations... It just didn't feel like it was ours to sell."

"Well, I can assure you it is your land to sell."

George's expression fell and after a beat, he tossed up his hands. "I've had this arrangement in place with her for... years. I'm supposed to transfer the deed to her on Christmas Day. It's already been decided. I'm...I'm sorry, but I'm afraid you're too late."

Max blew out a breath. Slipping his hand into the leather briefcase at his feet, he pulled out the offer he had drawn up before coming to Maple Woods. He extended his arm across the coffee table to George. "If you wouldn't mind taking a look at this before you make your decision, I'd appreciate it. I'm under the impression that there is nothing legally binding the sale to Holly at this point, correct?"

"That's correct. However, there was a stipulation in the original lease that said the lessee—Holly's family—would have first rights to the purchase of the property on the expiration of their lease. That thing is ninety-nine years old. And here we are, less than a week before it expires." George sighed and reached for the paper Max was extending. The color drained from his face as his eyes scanned the page.

"It's a fair price for the land, I can assure you," Max said evenly. He could only imagine what George Miller must be thinking right now. Though he didn't know how much Holly and the Millers had agreed on for the purchase of the land, he thought it safe to assume it was less than five percent of the offer he was making.

"What about Holly?" George asked when he managed to find his voice.

"So long as we come to an agreement before Christmas Day when the lease expires, I don't think there should be a problem." Max cleared his throat. He had four days before that land essentially transferred to Holly for a fraction of its value, and he couldn't risk trying to sway her to sell. His best bet was dealing directly with George Miller.

"And the inn?"

Max's stomach tightened.

"I'm afraid it will have to be razed." He paused. *May as well say it.* "The barns would have to be torn down, as well. I understand there are some orchards. Those would be leveled. Basically, everything would have to be cleared to leave room for the foundation and the parking lot. A center of this size requires a lot of land."

"But why our land, specifically? Surely there must be other—"

Max shook his head. "No. Believe me. A lot of time has gone into finding the perfect location for this development. We have to look at the size of the parcel, the proximity to competing centers, the distance to major highways, the general age range and income of the population within radiuses of various mileages. Consumer behavior... I could continue, if you'd like."

"And all that led you to our land?"

"Yes." Max steepled his fingers and looked down at the scuffed floorboards. swallowed hard and gritted his teeth. Everything he was stating was a fact. A cold, hard fact. There was no other option. The only way for this development to flourish was if it was built on the land that housed Holly's inn.

So why was he having so much trouble accepting that himself?

George let out a long whistle and looked around the crowded room, processing some inner thought. "Understand the position I'm in, Max. Holly is a dear friend of my wife's and I'm fond of her as well. The town loves her. And that inn—everyone loves that inn."

"I wish I could say we could save the inn, but we can't.

It sits too far back from the road, and it cuts into too much of the acreage. Believe me when I say that I wish it could be different. But…it can't." Now that his plans were being spoken aloud and set into motion, Max felt dizzy with guilt. The metallic taste in his mouth was a physical reminder of how corrupt his behavior was, even to himself. He meant what he said, that he wished this could be different. But he was a realist, and he knew that some things just were what they were. And he was going to tear down The White Barn Inn the first chance he had.

"Will the town even approve this?" George asked.

"That's a good question," Max said. "I spoke to the mayor yesterday. He said it was your decision. If you agreed to the sale, the plans for the mall would go to a vote with the planning committee."

"Does anyone else know?"

"No, and I think it's best if we keep it that way," Max said as his thoughts again drifted to Holly. "The mayor would rather not make this public knowledge as he anticipates a polarizing reaction from the community. If you decide to sell the land to me, I'll call him and let him know and he will take it from there."

George opened his eyes wide as the enormity of the decision he was faced with became a reality.

"If the planning committee doesn't approve the mall, I have a clause in the contract that permits Hamilton Properties to rescind the offer," Max explained.

George lowered his eyes to read over the papers once more. "I'd like to take some time to talk this over with Lucy."

"Of course," Max said. "But please bear in mind that time is running out. If you agree to sell to me, I will need some time to put the project before the planning committee, and Christmas is only four days away."

"I'll have an answer to you one way or the other as soon as I can," George assured him. He rose from the armchair and Max held out a hand.

"Thank you for your time," Max said. "And if we can keep this from Holly, I'd appreciate it. I know Lucy and she are friends, but I'd rather not have to upset her if there isn't reason to."

"I couldn't agree more," George said. He handed Max his parka and shoved his hands into his jeans. "You're sure there would be no way to save the inn? Put the mall behind it maybe?"

Max shook his head. "Impossible. The blueprints are all drawn up and there simply isn't room. The inn is located in the middle of the planned parking structure. There's no other way to allow for enough spaces. I can show you the drawings if you'd like. They're in my car."

George waved his hand dismissively. "No, no. I just thought I'd ask. If you say it won't work then I trust you."

Trust me. Max clenched a fist, feeling suddenly suffocated and claustrophobic. The parka was too heavy to wear inside. The ceilings were too low. The room too stuffy. He needed air. He needed to breathe and clear his head and stop, stop, stop thinking about Holly.

Holly trusted him, too. And look what he was doing to her right under her nose. He wished he could just tell her, admit the truth, convince her to leave Maple Woods and start building a life for herself, but he didn't think he could. Yet.

"I'll be in touch," George said as Max trotted down the porch stairs to the driveway, gasping for the cold fresh air.

Max climbed into his rental car and turned the ignition, desperate to get out of George's driveway before anyone spotted his New York plates. He realized as he gripped the steering wheel that he was shaking. The magnitude of what he had just done was taking effect. He felt confused, lost and out of control. He hadn't felt this way in years—he had made it a point to avoid ever having to feel this way again. He lived his life in a self-preserving way. And then…then he had met Holly.

The offer was made. It was in George Miller's hands now. And only one thing was certain. There was no going back now.

Chapter Seven

By midmorning, the Christmas Market was vibrant and crowded as familiar faces strolled through the town square clutching steaming paper cups of hot chocolate and snacking on roasted chestnuts. It seemed the entire town had made it out that morning, despite the couple feet of snow that had gathered overnight. Holly had snagged the cart just next to Lucy, who had been up all night making fresh pies in preparation for the festivities. The Saturday before Christmas was always the busiest, and Holly expected to sell what was left of her homemade preserves before the market closed for the day, as she did every year. No matter how much time she spent preserving and jarring the blueberries she had harvested, it seemed there was never enough to keep up with the demand. She'd worked long into the night for weeks in preparation for the annual tradition, but she didn't mind. Keeping busy, she had learned, was a good way to keep from giving in to the loneliness that sometimes crept in late at night, when the guests had turned in and the house grew quiet.

"Where's George?" Holly asked, as she pulled some more jars from a box at her feet.

"He had some bookkeeping to do at the house this morning," Lucy said. "But I doubt he'll make it to the market today. Someone has to cover the diner. We can't leave the staff unsupervised all day."

"Guess not." Holly shivered and turned on her heat lamp. "At least the sun's out today."

"Some big storm," Lucy said ruefully. "Did all your guests head out early just in case it hit hard?"

Holly hesitated. "All but one."

Lucy slid her a glance from her neighboring stall. "Don't tell me. That man who came into the diner yesterday. The one who likes my pies."

Holly's face flushed with heat despite the frost in the air. "None other."

Lucy let out a long whistle. "Well, looks like Christmas came early for you this year!"

Holly lowered her eyes but she couldn't resist a smile. "It's not like that."

"No?" Lucy didn't look convinced. "Because it sure looked like something to me. Do you like him?"

What's not to like? Holly wanted to say. But something in her sinking heart told her there was plenty not to like. She paused to consider the question, knowing it required no thought at all. She did like him. Of course she did. But Max was sadly all wrong for her.

"He lives in New York," Holly explained.

"So?"

"So, that's two hours away." Holly gave her friend a measured stare but Lucy looked unimpressed with her excuse.

"People move all the time," Lucy said casually. She

pulled an apple crumble pie from a box and placed it on a cake platter.

"I think he prefers city life," Holly continued.

"You grew up in Boston," Lucy pointed out. "Would you ever consider going back to that kind of life?"

Holly grimaced. She didn't even want to think about leaving Maple Woods and she felt agitated by how ahead of herself she was getting. "He doesn't seem to want the same things I do."

Lucy pulled a face. "That's too bad. He seemed really interested in you to me."

Holly's heart spasmed. "Really?" Her mind raced as she flashed through the sequence of their conversation at the diner yesterday morning. She was itching to ask Lucy for more specifics on her observation.

Taking notice of Holly's inner struggle, Lucy's lips twisted in satisfaction. "Aha! I *knew* you liked him."

"Of course she likes him!" Abby sauntered up to Holly's cart and handed her a cup of cocoa. Eyes gleaming, she asked, "So how was last night?"

"What was last night?" Lucy inquired, perking up in interest.

"Our little Holly had a date," Abby announced proudly.

"What?" Lucy squealed. "And you didn't blurt it out as soon as you saw me? Holly, we have been here for over an hour. When were you going to mention it?"

Holly blew out a sigh and held Abby's stare. She hadn't planned on telling Lucy about her evening, partly because she didn't want to think about it herself. Recounting the details would only conjure up images of Max's handsome face so close to hers, his strong, broad arm around her shoulder, that irresistible grin, and those were thoughts she couldn't afford to have.

"I didn't want to make a big deal out of it," she told Lucy with a shrug.

"Well, I am making a big deal out of it," said Abby.

"I noticed." Holly picked up her hot chocolate and took a tentative sip to test the temperature.

"Am I missing something here?" Lucy asked, eyes darting from one woman to the next and back again. "I met that man—Max, right? You should be shouting from the rooftops, my girl! Why aren't you more excited?"

Holly's shoulders slumped and she toyed with the lid of her cup. "I just don't want to fall for him. He's leaving in a matter of days, and I don't think he wants anything more than a fling."

Abby peered at her. "What makes you say that?"

Holly tried to remember Max's exact words but her thoughts were muddled with a devastating image of his smooth grin and dazzling blue eyes. "He said that he doesn't have time for much in his life besides work, essentially. It just…it just felt like Brendan all over again."

"Holly." Abby's voice was stern. "Max is not Brendan. Just because Brendan disappointed you in the end doesn't mean that Max will, too. They are completely different people and the circumstances are, too. Max deserves a fair shot. It isn't right to judge him based on your past experiences."

Holly's heart sank as she listened to her friend's lecture. "No, you're right. But at the same time, tell me exactly how this would even work? He is a self-diagnosed workaholic. He lives two hours away. He has an aversion to small-town life. And oh, he hates Christmas."

Abby and Lucy gasped simultaneously. "He hates Christmas?" Abby hissed.

Holly nodded her head victoriously, satisfied in a twisted sort of way that she had managed to prove her point to them. Max was all wrong for her. She would be a fool to fall for him.

Ever the pragmatic one, Lucy clarified, "Does he just not celebrate Christmas, or does he actually hate it?"

"He hates it!" Holly's voice was shrill with defense, hoping for any reason to validate why Max was all wrong for her and why she should be allowed to just forget him. She met Lucy's suspicious gaze and added, "He said it isn't his thing."

"But who hates Christmas?" Abby asked again.

Holly threw up her hands. "Exactly!" But even as she said it, she couldn't shake the rest of his words from her thoughts. Christmas brought back bad memories, he'd said. A feeling she knew all too well.

She would never forget the first Christmas after her parents had died. First the dread leading up to it, then the incessant ache in her heart and finally the relief she had felt the next day, when it was all over. She'd feared ever having to spend another holiday that way—raw with hurt and an overwhelming sense of loss.

She set her jaw. Well, she never had again. Christmas was a busy and happy time. That's the way it was meant to be. It was better that way.

She let out a shaky sigh and began frantically arranging her jam jars in a pyramid, realizing the other two women were watching her carefully. She glanced up at one of the accusers. "What?"

"Who cares if he hates Christmas," Lucy said. "A man that looks like that is allowed to hate anything he wants."

Abby laughed heartily and took a sip of her cocoa. "Seriously, Holly. You're just talking yourself out of this with one flimsy excuse after another. It's okay to like him, you know."

"I know," Holly said halfheartedly, feeling lightheaded

over it all. The thought of allowing herself to indulge in these feelings was so far outside her comfort zone she almost couldn't bear it. She had spent years creating this cozy, safe environment for herself, and now everything felt uncertain again. She didn't know why, but she had an uneasy sensation that everything was about to fall out from under her. That Max's arrival had permanently shattered her comfortable, complacent life.

"You sure you know?" Lucy asked. "Because that face looks like it needs some persuading."

Believe me, Holly thought, *I don't need any persuading at all.*

And that was half the problem.

"What if he goes back to New York next week and I never see him again?" Holly voiced. Saying it out loud felt good, like a weight had been lifted. She was so tired of loving people only to have them leave her one way or another in the end. There was nothing more painful than being left behind. She'd much prefer to be the one leaving first for a change.

"I've got a few years on you, so let me give you a piece of advice, Holly. Anyone who disappears from your life isn't worth having in it." Lucy gave her a hard stare from under the hood of her lids.

The corner of Holly's mouth turned in a small smile. "You're a good friend, Lucy."

"Don't you forget it." Lucy winked.

"Well, speak of the devil," Abby murmured and Holly's heart skipped a beat.

Across the town square, Max was weaving his way through the stalls, stopping every few feet to pause at a cart. At the mere sight of him, Holly's stomach dropped and a wave of nausea engulfed her.

Lovesick, she thought bitterly.

There was really no point in fighting the inevitable. She was smitten. And who could blame her?

She watched him through the crowd until he disappeared behind the massive Christmas tree in the middle of the market. Before he could appear again, she turned herself away, planting a smile on her face when a little girl in a bright pink coat and matching hat asked for a jar of preserves.

"Five dollars," Holly said absentmindedly. She scanned the crowd quickly once more, but she couldn't spot Max or his navy blue parka anymore.

"I only have four," the little girl said.

Heart pounding, Holly's eyes swept over the Christmas Market once more, wondering if he had come to find her, and if so, what he wanted to say. Perhaps he had already left.

"Take it. That's fine," she said, handing the little girl a jar with barely another glance.

"If you keep running your business like that, you'll go broke." At the sound of his voice, Holly jumped. "Sorry to startle you." His deep, smooth voice sent a warm rush through Holly's blood. Her heart reeled.

Turning to face him, she swallowed hard before saying, "What a nice surprise."

"Thought I'd come see what all the fuss was about," he said. He was holding a small brown paper bag full of roasted chestnuts and he popped a few in his mouth as he looked around the town square.

Holly could feel the heat of Lucy's stare boring into her from the next cart. She mentally dismissed it as she studied Max's profile. Every inch of it was perfect, from the loose lock of dark hair that spilled over his forehead to the strong nose to the square jaw. "I didn't think this would be your kind of thing."

Max lifted a mischievous brow. "I'm a man full of surprises," he bantered and Holly gave a weak smile.

Beside her, Abby cleared her throat and Holly jolted. Squaring her shoulders she said, "Max, I don't think you've officially met Abby yet."

Max took off his glove and held out his hand. "I've seen you around the inn. And Holly's mentioned you a few times, as well."

"Nice to meet you, *Max*," Abby said, with more meaning than Holly cared for. "I've seen you around the inn, but you were always being snatched away by Evelyn Adler before I could introduce myself."

Max chuckled. "Will you be back at the inn today?'

Holly stiffened as Abby said, "No, Holly here was nice enough to give me the week off since everyone's gone home. Guess she figures she can handle you on her own."

Max slid his blazing blue eyes to Holly and held them there. The corner of his lips lifted in a lazy smile. "I might be more trouble than she expected."

Holly felt her cheeks color a shade of pink she didn't even want to envision. Under the cart, where Max couldn't see, she gave Abby a less than gentle kick with the toe of her boot. Abby turned to her with a frozen smile, but her eyes were warm and dancing. She was enjoying herself. Of course. Easy for her, being married already. Not having to put herself out there. Risk her heart.

But she couldn't stay mad at Abby. Not really. Abby was her closest friend and she wanted what was best for her. And it seemed everyone around Holly thought what was best for her was Max Hamilton.

"So how do you like Maple Woods?" Abby inquired, because Holly was sure, she simply couldn't resist.

"It's quaint!" Max said heartily, his smile open and genuine. He slipped a glove back on his hand; his nose and cheeks were turning pink with cold.

"Well, hopefully you'll stick around," Abby said. "At least long enough to cover my spot." She stepped away from the cart. Would you mind? I have to go find my husband."

If Max was opposed to the suggestion, he didn't show it, and he swiftly stepped behind the cart once Abby had shuffled out. Before any excuse could be made from anyone, she darted into the crowd, her hand-knitted scarf flying behind her until she disappeared into the swarm of people.

Holly bit her lip to hide its smile.

"So what are you selling here?" Max held up a jar and studied the label. She'd printed them up herself with The White Barn Inn logo, as well as tied a twine bow around the bottom of each parchment-paper covered lid. "Wild Blueberry Preserves," he read.

"From the bushes out back," she said quietly.

"The bushes that witnessed Evelyn Adler's breakdown one afternoon?" He cocked a brow and looked at her sidelong.

Holly laughed. "The very same ones."

Max studied the jar once more before setting it back on the display table. "Let me guess. You made them."

"Is it that obvious?" she sighed.

"More like that impressive," he corrected and her heart flipped at the compliment. "You've got everyone here fooled into thinking you're perfect. But luckily I happen to know your dirty little secret."

Holly gasped. "What's that?"

"That you are the world's worst waitress. Hostess. Barista. Cashier."

At the stall next to them, Lucy snorted with mirth.

"You're never going to let that one go, are you?" Holly asked, searching his handsome face.

"Nope." He grinned ear-to-ear and took another handful of chestnuts out of the bag.

"I should have known better than to tell you that story," Holly said ruefully, but she couldn't help but laugh at herself.

"Hi, Lucy," Max said, holding up his hand to the neighboring stall.

Lucy smiled, "Pleasure to see you again. What do you think of our little Christmas Market?"

"Never seen anything like it," he said. "Usually I'm too busy to notice these types of things."

Holly flashed Lucy a pointed look and then swiftly returned to her task. She scanned the crowd for Abby, who was standing near the tree talking to Pete and gesturing back toward the stand.

"You mean too busy to notice the holidays?" Lucy was asking Max.

"Guess you could say that. It's pretty hard to avoid it here, though."

His smile didn't waver but Holly bristled at his word choice. Why would he want to avoid the holidays? What bad memories did it conjure up for him?

"Well, I'm excited for Christmas this year," Holly announced, lifting her chin.

"Holly, you're excited for Christmas every year." Lucy chuckled.

Not every year, Holly thought darkly.

She steeled herself, forcing herself back to the present. "Well, this year is different."

"And why is that?" Max popped another chestnut in his mouth and chewed, his eyes clasped on hers as he waited for her answer.

"Because this is the Christmas I finally get my inn," she said, glancing to Lucy, who smiled.

"Aw, honey. I'm so happy for you," she said. "It's been a long time coming. I know this holiday is a special one for you."

Despite the chill in the air, Holly felt a warm flood wash over her. Every time she stopped to remember that in only a matter of days the inn would be hers, she felt the same flicker of excitement mixed with relief.

She knew the inn had always been hers in spirit. The Millers had never put any demands or restrictions on the land or its uses. They had inherited the land in the same fashion she had inherited the lease, and with it being leased to the Tate family for coming up on ninety-nine years, most people in town didn't even know Holly didn't own it outright. For as long as anyone could remember, some generation of the Tates had lived in the old mansion her great-grandfather had built on rented land. It was her home, and George and Lucy treated it as such.

But that didn't keep Holly from wanting to make it official.

She'd had too many close calls in life. Too many times where she thought something was a sure bet, only to discover that everything she had poured her heart and soul into could be taken at a moment's notice. And without warning.

Beside her Max was surprisingly quiet.

"Everything okay?" she asked and he shrugged his response. She shifted uncomfortably from one foot to the other, racking her mind for what could have caused this transition in his mood. "If you need to get back, the inn is open. You can come and go as you please," she offered.

"You just left the door *open?*" Max was immediately pulled from his brooding mood. His eyes flinched as they bore into hers and his brows met in the middle.

Holly stopped to register the question and laughed softly when she realized how trusting this must seem. When she had first moved here from Boston, she never would have dreamed of doing such a thing; if anything, she had been scared living alone in that giant house. Everywhere she turned was a shadow of something past, a memory of something that was long gone. She had certainly changed a lot in five years, she mused, but some things did remain the same.

She hated being alone in that house. It was much better when it was filled with people. It would be even better if it was filled with her own family, too.

"We're all friends in Maple Woods," she said easily.

"So," he said, leaning in closer to her once more. Her pulse quickened as she waited for his next words. "If you told Stephen and Abby to take the week off, did you do the same with the rest of the staff?"

"Yes."

"So it's just you and me, alone in that house?"

Her heart plummeted. "Yes," she said slowly, not daring to say much more, and a slight smile formed at the corners of her lips. She glanced at him sidelong, catching the flash of the electric blue of his eyes piercing hers.

"So that means no cook again tonight?"

Holly furrowed her brow. "No, but I can make something."

Max grinned. "Not if I can help it."

Holly looked up at him quizzically. "Excuse me?"

"I'm making dinner tonight. For both of us. Unless you have other plans, that is?"

Holly chuckled, unsure of how to handle the flirtatious look in his sparkling blue eyes. She had never before encountered a man so confident in his approach. His gorgeous face was only enhanced by the powerful way he commanded their situation. He wasn't going to take no for an answer, she realized.

Not that she was arguing.

* * *

Max wasn't sure what he was doing, but frankly, he didn't care. He knew what he *should* do: walk away. Today. Now. He should get in his car and drive back to New York. He should be gone by the time Holly got back to the inn that night.

What he wanted to do, however, was vastly different.

He was fairly sure that the inn's kitchen was stocked with more food than he would need, but just in case, he decided to stop in the local grocery for the ingredients he would need for the dinner he had decided to make. The thought of going back to that inn by himself bothered him. He had become fond of being surrounded by the cheerful din of guests, and he had to admit it saddened him to think that Evelyn wouldn't be knocking on his door at some point today.

A sharp stab halted his breath when he realized the domino effect of the events he had set into action. Evelyn Adler depended on The White Barn Inn to give her a special Christmas each year. And he was single-handedly taking that from her.

She was an older woman, with only her husband to keep her company. What would she do next year? And what would Holly do?

Not for the first time since his meeting with George Miller, Max had to physically restrain himself from marching straight back to the Miller cottage and rescinding his offer. But he knew that as much as he wished he could do this, it wasn't exactly an option, unless he was willing to sacrifice everything else in his life.

And he had worked too hard and come too far to do that. If he took back his offer on the land, there would be no new development, and from there it would be only a matter of time before they'd have to merge or sell to a competitor, as so many rivals had already done. This development was his road to recovery—it would offset the revenue loss and keep his options open.

If he didn't build on this land, he didn't build at all, it was that simple. None of the anchors would take a gamble on weak demographics any more than Hamilton Properties would, and the research for this project was rock solid. Sales projections were strong. He couldn't risk letting the major retailers down now. He was depending on them as much as they were him. If he didn't deliver this project and they started pulling out of other centers…it wouldn't be long before everything unraveled.

His life's work. Gone. He couldn't bear to think about it.

"Mr. Hamilton."

Max darted his gaze to the left, where Bobby Miller was seated on a bench outside the grocery store. "I don't remember telling you my name," he said, walking closer.

Bobby shrugged. "You're the first new face we've seen here in ages. Everyone knows your name."

Max did a quick mental calculation of how many hours had passed since he'd left the Miller cottage. Long enough for George to have said something to his son, or for Bobby to have overheard something he shouldn't have.

"What have you been up to today?" he inquired, studying Bobby's face for any insight into what the kid might know.

Bobby shoved his hands in his pockets. "Just hanging out with my friends," he said. "There's not much to do around this town."

Unsatisfied with his answer, Max probed further. "I met your dad last night at the diner. He's a nice guy."

Bobby gazed at him warily. "If you say so," he said at last.

"What's he up to today?" Max asked.

"Beats me. Probably working. I haven't seen him."

Max let out a long sigh of relief. "Well, I should be going. It was good seeing you again, Bobby."

Bobby waved his hand unenthusiastically as Max pressed on. As he rounded the corner to the automatic doors of the store, a pungent whiff of cigarette smoke cut through the fresh country air and caught Max's attention. He turned his head reflexively, but there was no offender in sight. Out of curiosity, he poked his head back around the corner of the building, but Bobby was already gone and the smell of smoke had already started to fade.

Still shaky from the exchange, he forced himself to concentrate on the dinner ahead with Holly as he pulled one item after another off the shelves of the quaint store and tucked them into his basket. Rounding to the produce section, he looked up and locked eyes with Mayor Pearson.

The older man shifted his eyes from the left to the right before walking slowly over to Max. "Good to see you again, Mayor," Max said.

The quizzical expression on his face must have been apparent for the mayor explained, "The office is closed on weekends and I've got a new assignment for this afternoon." He tilted his basket to reveal several boxes of candy canes. "I've been cast in the starring role in Santa's Village. Right down to the fat suit." He offered a dry smile. "If you haven't noticed, Christmas is a big deal in our little town."

Max widened his eyes at the obvious. "I've just come from the Christmas Market, actually."

The mayor spared a wry smile. "It's a cheerful time for everyone, which is why I hate the thought of disrupting the spirit. Do you mind me asking where things stand on the matter we discussed yesterday? Has any progress been made?"

Max nodded his head slowly. Lowering his voice, he said, "I met with George Miller this morning."

"And?"

"He's asked for some time to consider the offer, but seemed receptive."

Mayor Pearson raised his brows. "Did he say when he would give you his answer?"

Max shook his head. "He needs to discuss it with his wife first, but he knows that time is of the essence. He promised he would have an answer to me with ample time to put the project before the planning committee."

The mayor leaned in and asked, "Does anyone else know?"

"No," Max's tone was firm. Of this much, he was certain. His moment of paranoia had been a fleeting lapse. When he stopped to think about the overwhelming ramifications of the proposal, he knew that George Miller wouldn't say a word to anyone but his wife. This was a tight-knit community. Word of something of this magnitude getting out would have a disastrous ripple effect on everyone.

His stomach tightened. Was George Miller really ready to put himself in the middle of a firing squad? Max hadn't stopped to think about the impact the local outcry might have on the diner. But then, with the amount of money the Millers would reap, they wouldn't need to rely on their customers anymore.

"What about Holly?" the mayor pressed.

"What about her?" Max was quick to reply. The mere mention of her name prompted him to rush to defense. But who was he protecting? Himself...or her?

"Does she know that you have made an offer to George?"

"No," Max said, feeling disgusted with himself. "I

thought about talking with her about it, but I get the impression she wouldn't be happy about this."

"That's an understatement," the mayor said. He shook his head. "I've been up all night thinking about this, but ultimately one person can't hold the rest of the town back from progress. Holly is sitting on something that can be put to better use, and that's the way I have to approach this." He sighed. "Who knows, maybe if that library hadn't caught fire I would be saying something different."

Max paused to think about this last statement. If the idea of building on the Miller site had never been possible, would that have been better? Then he could have just enjoyed his time with Holly for what it was. Because where he stood now, one thing was inevitable: in a matter of days—if not hours—Holly would learn his real reason for being in Maple Woods.

And then she would hate him.

The thought of her feeling betrayed by him was almost too much to bear. Especially when he himself wished it didn't have to be this way. Tonight he would try and tell her the truth. Cooking dinner was the least he could do for her, in light of everything else.

"I suppose I should get going," the mayor said, starting to walk away. "But I have a feeling we'll be in touch soon."

"It was good seeing you again, Mayor."

"Talk to you soon, Mr. Hamilton." The mayor made his departure, and Max quietly watched him disappear down an aisle until the man was out of sight.

A domino effect, he thought to himself once more. That's exactly what it was. He had knocked the first chip yesterday morning, and now there was no chance of him halting the breaks without it all crashing down on him anyway. If he at least let the plan stay in motion, it had a chance of falling neatly into a pile.

And why was he even questioning his actions anyway?

This was what he had wanted. This was what he had worked for. This was what he had come to town to do. And then he had met Holly.

And now...now he didn't know what he wanted anymore. All he knew was that he had the sickening feeling he was going to come out of all of this with nothing.

Max turned to pull some pears from a bushel against a wall and his heart pitched at what he saw.

Standing only a few feet from him was Abby, staring at him intensely, her gaze steady and lethal. The friendly smile was gone from her small face, her eyes clouded with confusion. How much she had overheard, he didn't know. She looked away hastily and was gone before he could say anything to stop her.

Chapter Eight

A loud clanging of pots and pans greeted Holly as she made her way into the warm, heavenly scented kitchen a few hours later. For a fleeting second she wondered if she should have allowed Max into her kitchen. If he damaged one of Stephen's prized sauté pans, the wrath she would face from the chef would be fierce.

Oh, well. A small price to pay for such an attractive invitation.

Holly nervously ran her hands through her long, thick hair. After returning from the Christmas Market, she'd managed to duck inside through her personal entrance at the back of the house to shower and dress. She wanted to arrive in the kitchen as she would for any other intimate evening. Even if it wasn't a date. Technically.

She had no idea what Max had planned for the night or what his intentions even were. She had a feeling that tonight would be a turning point, but maybe that was just wishful thinking.

Max stood at the stove, stirring a creamy sauce with one hand and adding handfuls of dried pasta to a boiling pot of water with the other. He set his culinary skills to the side when he saw her, greeting her with a hundred-watt smile.

"Hello there," he said and Holly felt her heart pool into something warm and thick that spread through her body like melted chocolate.

"Hi," she managed, unable to pull her eyes from him. She stood awkwardly in the doorway, never having felt so out of place in her own kitchen and resisting the urge to push up her sleeves and tie on an apron.

"Wine?" he asked rhetorically, as he filled two glasses from a decanter. Holly accepted hers with a smile and clinked his glass before taking a sip. It was smooth and rich. Perfect. He flashed her a lazy grin and Holly's pulse quickened with longing.

"So, what's for dinner?" she asked in a forced casual tone, settling herself onto a counter stool that lent an excellent vantage point to Max's activities.

"Penne with vodka sauce," he said as he picked up a dish towel and bent down to pluck a loaf of steaming, crusty bread from the oven. His back was wide and strong. Holly indulged herself in a long stare at Max's broad shoulders straining against the confines of his shirt, imagining what it would be like to stroke his bare skin with the tips of her fingers, and explore every inch of his raw, masculine physique...

She immediately gave herself a silent scolding. If she kept up this type of thinking, there was no telling where the night would end.

She'd left the Christmas Market with a new sense of hope. Talking with Lucy and Abby always made her feel better, and confiding her fears in them this morning had put her mind at ease. They were right; she was coming up with one excuse after another to keep herself from falling for Max and she was dangerously close to letting a chance for real love pass her by as a result. Practicalities aside, she had a connection with Max that she couldn't deny any longer. She had come to a point where she had to risk her heart again; if she didn't, how would she ever find that true love she so desperately wanted?

She hadn't been this attracted to a man in as long as she could remember, if ever. There was something about Max— his quiet strength mixed with a touch of vulnerability made her want to squeeze him close and never let him go. It was as if he had been brought here just for her. The realization that she could have gone through life never feeling this way, never knowing him, was fast becoming inconceivable.

"Where'd you learn to cook?" she asked, taking another sip of her wine.

"Oh, you learn a lot of things when you've been single as long as I have." Max grinned. "Like how to make your bed. Do laundry. Do the dishes."

"Very funny," Holly chided, but she smiled. "In all seriousness, you really seem to know your way around a kitchen."

"I have a weakness for cooking shows," he said. "Makes for good background noise."

Holly squinted with interest. "I take it you live alone then?"

"Always have," Max said mildly.

Deciding to go for it, Holly took a deep breath. "Do you prefer it that way?" she ventured.

Max threw her a noncommittal shrug. "Never really thought about it," he said, but something in his tone was unconvincing.

Unsatisfied, Holly toyed with the stem of her glass. Not willing to relinquish the topic just yet, she blurted, "I hate living alone," and then lowered her eyes, instantly realizing how reckless her declaration had been.

If Max was put off, he didn't show it. "I figured that was the case," he said as he stirred the sauce.

"Why?"

"You run an inn," he said. "It would be a bit inconvenient for you to have all these people in your house everyday if you preferred them not to be there."

Holly laughed at his logic. "Good point."

"So you like what you do then? Running the inn? Taking care of people day after day?"

"I love it!" she exclaimed.

"It never gets tiring?" He was watching her carefully, leaning back against the counter and clutching his wineglass.

Holly shook her head slowly. "No...I guess some days can be long, but I'm sure that's the case with any job."

Max's hooded stare held hers until she squirmed under the scrutiny. "Guess so," he said, finally releasing his hold on her to return to the pots on the stove.

What was that all about? Holly wondered. But while the topic remained on work, she decided to use it to her advantage.

"How about you?" she asked. "Do you like your job?"

"I do," he said.

She waited, but he didn't elaborate. "What do you do exactly?"

His strong, wide shoulders heaved slightly. He stopped stirring the sauce for a fraction of a second before resuming. "Real estate," he said.

Holly wasn't sure what she had been expecting to hear, but she felt inexplicable relief. He had been so cryptic about the business that was keeping him in town that her mind had started to needlessly reel with sinister possibilities.

Real estate. It probably was something to do with the library. Or maybe—a sudden thought caused Holly's hopes to soar—maybe he was planning to purchase something in Maple Woods? Her heart began to thump with the implications. Any kind of real estate investment that he was making would surely bring him back to Maple Woods often. If not permanently. She didn't know much about real estate, but she had reason to hope, at least.

Barely managing to hide her bursting smile, Holly took another sip of wine and watched as Max continued his cooking efforts. "It smells delicious," she observed.

Max turned and flashed her a grin over his shoulder. "Thanks. Hopefully it tastes good, too." He plated the pasta and turned to face her. "Dinner is served."

The fire was roaring in the lobby and the tree twinkled invitingly as she followed Max into the dimly lit room. He set the tray down on the coffee table and without a word, sunk into the sofa next to her. A stir of excitement ran down her spine.

This was cozy.

Max held up his wine glass. "To…chance meetings."

Holly stomach tightened as she clinked his glass with hers and took a long, delicious sip. She knew by sitting here like this, it would be harder than ever to back out of… whatever this was.

Her mind began to race with possibilities.

Watching him over the rim of her glass, Holly wasn't sure how much longer she could hold back. In the few days she had been with him, her heart had felt something foreign and wonderful. Something seemed to click and tell her this was right despite how much she had desperately tried to convince herself otherwise. It was only a doubtful corner of her mind that told her to fight what her heart so desperately wanted.

Didn't any real love involve a risk or sacrifice?

"This is delicious," Holly commented, taking a bite of the warm, creamy pasta.

"I'm a man of many talents, believe it or not," Max joked and that adorable grin came over his mouth.

"Oh, yeah? What other tricks do you have under your belt? I'd like to see what you're keeping down there." As soon as the words were out, Holly felt the color drain from her face. Max's eyes burst open in surprise, and his expression froze until his lips began to twitch.

Holly tittered nervously but Max's sudden roar of laughter muffled her own feeble sounds. She slid her pasta around her plate, unable to eat from humiliation and wondering what exactly Max would say when he had finally settled down. She furiously scrambled for a delicate way to change the subject.

"Sorry," she settled on. "That didn't come out right."

Max's eyes were sharp in their hold on hers. "Darn, I was hoping it came out exactly right."

Holly's cheeks burned with heat and she knew this time the flush didn't go unnoticed. She forced a bit of food into her mouth and chewed slowly, barely able to swallow due to the knot that had formed in her throat.

Needing physical distance, she set her plate on the table and crossed the room without a word. With the press of a button, soft music poured through the speakers and broke up the silence.

From afar, Holly could see Max's brow furrow. She immediately knew why.

"Christmas carols," she said. "What can I say? 'Tis the season."

Taking in the large lobby—from the stockings over the

crackling fire to the enormous tree, to the garland wrapped around the banister in the adjacent foyer—Holly thought back on her conversation with Max the day before. "I hope all this doesn't offend you," she said, hoping she wasn't being insensitive.

"It doesn't offend me. It's just—"

"Not your thing," Holly finished, managing a wry smile. Max matched her expression. "Does that bother you?"

Holly fell back onto her cushion next to Max and studied his face. "No," she said honestly. "It just makes me curious. And a little sad," she added softly.

Perhaps it was the wine, perhaps it was the warmth from the flames flickering in hearth, perhaps it was the damn music…or perhaps it was just Holly. Sweet, beautiful Holly. Max didn't know the reason, but for the first time in years, he felt at peace.

"I think I told you the first night we met that I grew up in a small town like this." His voice was low and husky, his eyes firmly on the fire.

"I remember," Holly said softly. She waited, patient for him to continue.

Max took another forkful of pasta and chewed, his mind in two places at once. Here in the safety of this homey room, and back in his childhood home. Which was hardly a home at all.

"It was awful," he blurted.

Holly raised a questioning brow. "Small-town life?"

"All of it." He grimaced at the memories. A series of images he had pushed aside. A life he had put behind him.

Holly's brow furrowed in concern. "What was so terrible?"

"My mom got pregnant with me out of wedlock when she was…very young. It was a scandal, especially back in those days, and the small-town lifestyle didn't help matters."

Holly frowned. "That would be hard."

Max nodded and watched the flames grow in the fireplace. "She had so many things she wanted to do with her life," he mused. Turning to Holly he said, "She was a musician. A singer, actually. And a very good one. She had a music scholarship to college."

"Impressive," Holly said but Max shook his head to show she had misunderstood.

"She couldn't go."

He met Holly's gaze. Her eyes flickered in realization. Her lids drooped slightly until she lowered her eyes, her long black lashes skimming her cheeks.

"Because—"

"Because of me." Max nodded.

"That must have been hard," Holly said quietly.

"More than you know," Max said as a swell of resentment built inside him and turned his heart heavy. "It was as if, all my life, I could sense this unhappiness in her. This longing to be somewhere else. Doing something else. And there was nothing I could do to make her happy."

"But couldn't she pursue her music in another way?" Holly asked. "Could she teach at school or give private lessons?"

Max shook his head. It wasn't just about the music, which represented everything she wanted and didn't have— couldn't have. His gut twisted when he thought how different his mother's life might have been if he had never been born. But when he grew older—and, after everything happened—he knew that she had made her choice. She had done the best she could. She had thought she could make it work. She just…couldn't.

"For a long time, when I was very little, she would walk

around the house singing." A faint smile tugged at the corner of his mouth at the memory of his mother, so young then, in a housedress and apron, standing over a sink of dirty dishes crooning Sinatra and old show tunes like there was an audience in the living room just waiting to throw roses at her bare feet. "I remember sitting on that old linoleum in our kitchen playing with my toy cars and just listening to that voice…no sweeter sound."

Holly smiled and locked her eyes with him, encouraging him to continue.

"Sometimes, when I was about two or three, she'd turn on the record player and just dance around the house, singing, holding my hands, twirling me around…and the next thing I knew, she'd stop and just burst into tears. And I never understood it."

"That's so sad," Holly murmured, her voice cracking.

Max forced a smile. The last thing he needed was Holly thinking he was feeling sorry for himself. Once he might have, but not anymore. Time had a way of fading the rawness of pain, even if it didn't always heal the wounds.

"And your father? Was he around?" Holly said the words hesitantly, as if not sure she should be asking.

Max emitted a deep sigh. "They got married when my mother was pregnant," he said and before Holly's expression could shift any further in the direction of hope he added, "It was the worst decision my mother could have made."

Holly's hazel eyes shot open in surprise and then crinkled as her brows met in the center. "How so?"

"He was the town drunk," Max said simply. He clenched his jaw, all sadness evaporating at the thought of his father. There was no place in his heart for that man. Any time he happened to think of him, ice filled his chest. "I just remember that night after night, he would come home late, sometimes when I was already in bed, reeking of booze, stumbling around, crashing into lamps, and he and my mother would just *scream* at each other. For hours." Max chuckled. "I tried putting cotton in my ears, and one time it got stuck. My mother had to take me to the doctor to fish it out."

He slid a glance at Holly. She gave a watery smile. "You didn't have any brothers and sisters?"

"No."

"Me, neither."

He wasn't sure why, but something about this shared bond made him feel closer to her. Even if—judging from this place—her circumstances had been quite different than his own.

"Money was always tight," he continued. "Especially around the holidays. My dad spent all the money he made at the mill on booze at the town bar after work. More than a few times a week my mom would get a phone call from the owner of the tavern, telling her to come collect him, that he was too drunk to drive home. She'd have to ask the lady next door to come sit with me. I'll never forget the shame in her face. Or the fear in her eyes."

"She was afraid of him?" Holly asked gently.

"My father was a mean drunk," Max said. "A mean, mean drunk. When he got like that…my mother didn't know what she was about to step into. She walked on glass. As did I.

"Did he ever hurt her? Or—" Holly paused as the horrifying thought took hold, but Max waved away her concern with his hand.

"He never hurt either of us. Nah, he preferred to punish my mother in other ways."

"But why?"

Max shrugged. "For trapping him. For getting pregnant with me. He was miserable."

"But she didn't do it on purpose!" Holly protested.

"Oh, I know. But he didn't care." Max swallowed when he thought about the truth in Holly's statement. She hadn't meant to be hurtful, but the words cut him to the bone. She was right. His mother hadn't gotten pregnant on purpose. He hadn't been planned. *Or wanted.*

"But what did he do then? To punish her?"

Max felt almost grateful that Holly was asking so many questions. It made opening up to her so much easier. She sensed his need to tell her this—to finally talk about it. That was what made Holly so easy to approach, he realized. She didn't just feign an interest in people's lives. She genuinely cared.

"Oh…he would break things that were special to her. He always apologized once he'd sobered up, but some things couldn't be replaced."

"Like her record player?" Holly ventured.

Man, she was good. "Yep," Max said with a bitter smile. "And since money was tight, she never got another."

Holly frowned, her eyes holding his almost pleadingly. "Is that when she stopped singing?"

Max sighed deeply. "No, she stopped long before that. Around the house, at least. You asked about her giving music lessons? She did that once."

"Just once? What happened?"

Max swallowed hard. "Remember how I told you about that train I wanted for Christmas one year?" Holly nodded and Max continued, "I never connected it until much later, but she took a job giving singing lessons to a girl in town. A daughter of one of her friends from high school."

"That was the only time?" Holly was squinting at him, trying to piece the nuggets of information together.

"She isolated herself over time," he explained. "You know how it is living here in this small town. Everyone knows you. Everyone knows your business. It's fine when you have nothing to hide, but when you do, it can be really tough. People would whisper when she'd take me to the store—some just loving the gossip, some feeling pity—and her face...I just remember the look on her face. The way she would hang her head. The way she wouldn't make eye contact. The way the light in her eyes was just gone. It just became too much for her."

And for me too, he thought.

Holly shifted her eyes to the fire. "That would be very hard," she reflected. "Small-town life isn't always easy."

"No, and in this case, it was impossible. Everyone knew my father. And everyone heard the screaming."

Holly grimaced. "That must have been difficult to listen to every day."

"You get used to it. What other choice do you have?"

"Did your mother every think about leaving?"

Max leaned forward and stoked the fire. "That year when I asked for the train, she gave music lessons twice a week to save for that train. Two days before Christmas, my father found the money. They had a terrible fight. I was too young to understand at the time. Heck." He chuckled. "I still believed in Santa."

Holly eyes searched his. "What happened?"

"He spent all the money my mom had earned on a round of beers for his buddies down at the tavern," he said simply.

"The money for the train," Holly summarized quietly.

Max shrugged. "The next day, she was gone. No train. No mother. Nothing under the tree. And that," he said, "is when I stopped believing."

Holly wiped away a tear with the back of her hand and let her gaze drift to the fire. They lapsed into silence, watching the flames crackle and dance. Eventually she asked, "Did you ever see her again?"

Max inhaled deeply. "She said she'd be back for me once she found a job and had a place for us."

Holly gave him a measured look, already knowing the ending to the story. "But she never came back."

"No."

"Did you ever try to find her?"

"I went looking for her when I moved to New York. I thought she might have gotten into some off-Broadway show, that type of thing. But there was no trace of her." He paused. "She probably changed her name."

She wanted to start fresh. Just like I eventually did, he thought.

"And your father?"

"I left that town when I was eighteen and never looked back," he said firmly. "No reason to."

Silence fell over the room until Holly finally spoke. "I am so sorry, Max."

He turned to her, shrugging dismissively to curtail the enormity of what he had just told her. "I survived."

Beside him, Holly remained solemn. "It isn't fair."

"Who said life has to be fair?" he asked. He reached for his plate, pleased to find the food was still warm from the heat of the fire.

"It would be nice if it could be," Holly said, giving him a thin smile.

His stare held hers as he took a the last bite of pasta and set the empty plate back on the table. It was a comforting feeling, to be under her protective gaze, and when her hand slid over to tentatively graze his, he grasped for it, squeezing it in his large palm and feeling more connected to her in that moment than he ever had with anyone before her.

"Should we have our dessert now?" Holly forced a cheerful smile as she eyed Max cautiously, gauging his mood.

Her own heart still ached when she thought of the story he had shared. She could only imagine how he must feel. Unless it was something that was so much a part of him it didn't touch him in the same way anymore.

Max smiled in relief. "What's on the menu?"

Holly hesitated. "Oh. You didn't—" She'd assumed he had made the final course, but the expectant look on his face told her otherwise. She smiled to herself. The innkeeper in her wanted to scold him, but his oversight only endeared him to her.

"How about pie?" she suggested. He was still her guest, after all.

"Sounds great," Max said, standing to help her load the tray.

Holly watched him carefully as he went about the menial task. Max didn't open up easily from what she'd gotten to know of him so far, but for some reason, he had chosen to share his innermost thoughts with her tonight. The look of loss and pain in his eyes when he spoke of his childhood tore at Holly's heartstrings. She felt a stab in the gut as she looked around at the festive decorations, wondering what kind of painful reminder they might be causing him.

Once they would have hurt her, too.

"Do you want me to take down the tree?" she blurted.

Max's bright blue eyes flung open. "What? Why?"

Holly shifted uncomfortably from one foot to the next, looking desperately from the tree back to Max. "I understand now why Christmas is a difficult time for you. I don't want to do anything to make it worse."

Max's eyes softened as he threw her a lopsided, boyish smile and Holly felt her stomach flutter. God help her. She wasn't sure how much longer she could resist him. As it was he consumed her every thought when she wasn't with him. And when she was…

"The truth is that I normally don't spend this much time with women who listen to Christmas carols or bake gingerbread houses," he said, motioning to the candy house perched on an end table.

Holly's frowned in. So there it was. She wasn't his type. Just as she had suspected. "Oh."

She glanced up to see Max's mouth curl into a smile. He took a step toward her, and she felt her body stiffen at his nearness. Their eyes were locked, each looking to the other to make sense of the situation.

"And you probably aren't used to spending so much time with someone who would rather ignore Christmas."

"Well, no—" Holly shook her head in protestation, but her words were lost as Max dipped his chin, lowering his mouth to hers.

"I'm willing to make an exception if you are," he murmured. His fingers traced the curve of her waist, lingering just above her hip. She shifted with desire and twisted her body closer to his.

His face was so close to hers, she could feel the heat of his breath, catch the scent of musk on his skin. His eyes flamed with hunger and Holly shuddered in anticipation. His lips met hers once again, grazing them gently at first and then opening to explore her further. Her stiff, shocked body slowly relaxed in his arms, and she felt herself giving in to him as his strong, determined hands pulled her body against his own.

Max's tongue danced slowly with hers, and then adjusted its rhythm as he sensed her arousal, probing her in a way that caused her knees to go weak.

Dropping the napkin she'd been holding on to for dear life, she pressed herself closer to him. His chest was firm and tight and she could feel the hard planes of his muscles through the thin material of his shirt. She slid her hand farther up his strong, wide back, taking in the contours of his broad torso, the heat emanating from his skin. She molded herself into him, pressing the swell of her breasts against his body, breathing in his masculine scent. A mixture of soap or aftershave, it was distinct and intoxicating.

She sensed him smile before he released her lips. His breath was hot in her ear, sending a tingle down her spine.

"You know, I've been wanting to do that for days," he said, his voice low and husky.

"Why'd you wait so long?" she asked through a grin, glancing up at him.

His arms slid to her waist, his blue eyes piercing. "I could get used to that."

So could I, Holly thought.

Chapter Nine

Max tossed and turned into the early-morning hours. By four, he admitted defeat, and turned on the bedside lamp. Sleep would be impossible as long as his mind searched for a solution to ease the knot in his gut that tightened every time he imagined Holly's face when she discovered his true purpose here. He couldn't get his mind off Holly—the way her lips had felt against his, the way the soft, feminine curves of her body had made his groin tighten with arousal. There was no denying that he wanted her. He wanted to touch her, kiss her...but he couldn't think about these things now. He had to keep a level head.

Pulling out his laptop, he reviewed the materials for the umpteenth time. Everything for an impending pitch to the city planning board was in place. The financial and demographic reports were solid. The architectural renderings were polished and attractive. The retail tenants that had already committed to the project were appealing and upscale, indicating others would follow. It was all there for the taking.

But for Max, the project had lost its luster.

He tried in vain to create a secondary plan, seeing if it was even feasible for the company to restore their existing projects rather than pursue new developments. But as he examined—and reexamined—the spreadsheets detailing how much money had already been poured into the planning of this new development, he knew he had to see it through. There was no denying it. If Hamilton Properties was going to stay in business, the project had to be built. It was the only thing that would save the existing centers and generate new revenue for the company.

Financially, he would be fine if Hamilton Properties went bust. But was he really thinking of sabotaging years of hard work over a woman he barely knew? A woman he knew he couldn't even have a future with...

His work—the business he had worked so hard to build from nothing, when he'd started with nothing—was his life. It represented who he was now. The obstacles he had overcome.

He would have to be a fool to just throw it all away. But would he be a bigger fool to throw Holly away?

The kiss last night had been more promising than he'd expected. Sure, Holly was pretty and sweet, but the electric bolt he'd felt as their lips explored each other was more than he could have anticipated. His mind was clouded, reeling with memories of her touch, flooded with anxiety over the fallout of this project. Time was ticking fast. And he had a bad feeling everything was about to explode.

And that he'd be the one getting burned.

Max stood up from the desk in his room and stared out the window onto the snow-covered fields that surrounded the inn. He rubbed at the stubble on his chin and thought long and hard, but his mind was blank. The White Barn Inn was sitting on a gold mine. It could be put to much better use.

Or so I keep telling myself, he thought.

Max drew a deep breath and glanced at his watch, surprised to realize that it was already almost nine. Heaving a sigh, he ran his fingers through his bedraggled hair. He'd deal with the business matters later. Surely by now Holly would be busy in the kitchen, whipping up something fragrant and delicious as she did every morning, and that was all the distraction he needed at the moment.

Besides, maybe George Miller wouldn't even accept the offer.

Max pushed the thought away as quickly as it formed. *Ludicrous.* He liked Holly…a lot. But he couldn't go throwing away a project this big based on attraction…no matter how deep.

His mind flashed to an image of Holly standing in the sun-filled kitchen in that red Christmas apron, humming carols to herself and sprinkling cinnamon into her coffee. Something inside him swelled as he recalled the sensation of her full breasts against his chest. Had that only been last night? It felt surreal now. To think he had held her in his arms. In that moment she had been all his. When he allowed his mind to wander there, he knew he couldn't let her go.

But he wasn't sure he had a choice.

Showering and shaving quickly, he dressed in one of the new sweaters he had bought in town and crossed to the door, mentally talking himself through the next part of the day. As difficult as it was going to be, he had to talk to Holly today. It was only three days until Christmas, and for all he knew, Abby had overheard too much of his conversation with the mayor. Or Bobby Miller had overheard his parents talking and told his friends. It was a small town and Max knew all too well how quickly gossip could spread.

Holly was going to learn the truth sooner rather than later anyway. It would be better if it came from him.

Now was the time to go after everything he wanted. Full force. The business and Holly.

There was no other way.

As he pulled the door to his room closed behind him and made his way down the sweeping staircase to the lobby, something told him that her attachment to the inn extended beyond it being her business or even her grandmother's home. There was something deeper keeping her here, something that might be pivotal to the situation, and he intended to figure out exactly what that was. Today.

Holly pulled a few logs of kindling from the pile stacked neatly against the back of the house and sniffed. The biting cold was already making the tip of her nose burn and her eyes tear. Clutching the firewood to her chest, she threw her head back and allowed the morning sun to wash down over her face. A fresh wave of excitement tickled her spine when she thought of seeing Max again today. It had been a long time since she had felt this powerful flush of desire, and the heat he had awakened in her kept her warm all through the night.

A tapping at the glass from the kitchen window caused her to jump. Her eyes flew open to see Max smiling at her and waving. Her heart dropped to her stomach and stayed there as she turned the handle to the mudroom and, after hanging her coat on the rack and setting her boots on the rug to dry, emerged into the warm, fragrant kitchen.

Max was leaning against the counter, already clutching a steaming mug of coffee. "Morning." He grinned sheepishly, and she smiled in return.

"Sleep well?" she asked. Unable to look him in the eye, she grabbed a mug and filled it with coffee and a splash of cream.

"I've slept better," he admitted.

Holly darted her eyes to his and he threw her a lopsided smile that had the distinct hint of...guilt.

Disappointment flooded Holly's chest and sunk her heart into the pit of her stomach. So he was regretting the kiss, then. She balled her fists at her sides to keep them from shaking. She should have known it was all too good to be true. That she had given her heart away too quickly. That she'd been fooled yet again. That she was silly for getting caught up in the romance of their circumstances, and the hope that Christmas still ironically brought her year after year.

"I'm sorry to hear that," she managed, her tone cool.

"You should be," he said. "Because it's your fault."

Holly frowned at the accusation and wrapped her hand around the coffee cup still on the counter. "How's that?" she asked.

Max shrugged and the corner of his lip tugged in amusement. "I could have slept better if I wasn't thinking about that kiss."

Holly's pressed her lips together so he couldn't see how much this pleased her. She searched his face in bewilderment. "I...I see," she stammered.

"Is it too much for a guy to hope that you might have been thinking about me, too?"

He met her gaze from under the hood of his lashes, his rugged face suddenly taken over by a vulnerable expression. Holly's nerves immediately dissolved and her insides flooded with warmth. "I didn't sleep much, either," she admitted.

"Guess we'll both be in need of a nap today, then," Max

said. His blue eyes twinkled mischievously in the sunlight that poured through the window.

Holly offered a noncommittal shrug as she watched him. "That might be nice."

The corner of his lip curled into a suggestive smile. He stepped toward her, reaching out a hand to skim her waist, and Holly shuddered back a surge of fresh heat at the pleasure the small gesture ignited.

"How about a little something to tide us over?" he asked, his voice husky with desire as he leaned into her.

Holly lifted her chin as her lips met his. His mouth was familiar now, his lips sweet to the taste. She ran her hands down his chest, feeling the soft wool of his sweater. As Max's strong hands cupped her hips she slid her hands higher up against the back of his neck, massaging the silky locks of his hair as she pressed her body close into his, her body throbbing with arousal and need.

Sensing her response, Max groaned into her mouth as his tongue continued its dance. Grazing his hands lower to clutch the back of her thighs, he lifted her effortlessly onto the counter, and she parted her knees to allow him to press closer against her. Their mouths were frantic now, insatiable in the pleasure the union of their lips could bring. Max slid his hands from her hips and pulled at the bottom of her shirt until his fingers were free to wander up her bare stomach. Holly shuddered at the sensation—a long, deep quiver that pulsed the insides of her thighs. She wrapped her legs tighter around Max's chiseled frame as his fingers splayed to caress her breast over the lace of her bra. He found the center and began to tease the bud with the tips of his fingers until Holly groaned and tore her lips from his mouth. She buried her face in the nape of his neck as he stroked her tender flesh and then slowly pulled back the flimsy fabric until his warm hand was smooth and soft against her skin.

Tilting her head, she accepted the spine-tingling graze of his mouth against the nape of her neck, clutching the broad strength of his shoulders against her as his fingers performed their magic.

Max sighed into her ear as her body shuddered against his. He slid his hand slowly down her stomach and glanced up from beneath his hooded brow. His cheeks were flushed and his eyes glazed as he met her heated stare. Holly's chest rose and fell with lingering desire and with a grin, she reached over and smoothed his hair.

Sliding off the counter, Holly ran a shaking hand through her own chestnut locks, her skin still quivering from Max's touch. "I suppose we should eat…" She glanced halfheartedly toward the stove.

"You certainly have a way of stirring up my appetite." Max grinned, lifting an eyebrow and Holly felt her insides melt. Turning to the stove, he lifted a lid off a saucepan and asked, "What's for breakfast? Mmm… French toast." He turned to her. "Why don't you let me serve you for a change?"

Holly smiled. "With pleasure, sir."

Max plated the food, then pulled a stool away from the counter and sat down, patting the chair next to him for her to join him. She couldn't remember the last time she had sat in her kitchen and enjoyed a meal. It was usually taken over by staff. Not that she minded, but she had to admit there was something deliciously casual about eating breakfast in this setting.

"Are you going back to the Christmas Market today?" Max asked as he cut into his food.

Holly took a gulp of coffee, trying to pull her mind away from the intensity of their embrace. "No, I sold out yesterday, actually. Five hundred dollars richer."

"Really?" Max raised a brow.

"Why do you sound so surprised?"

"Last I saw you were handing the jars away for free," he said with a shrug.

Holly stifled a smile and sipped at her coffee, unable to fully tear her mind from the experience of his touch. The sensation of his hands on her skin had only served to make her want more. She no longer had an appetite. Not for food, anyway. There was only one thing she had a taste for and it was Max's mouth pressed firmly on her own. Listlessly, she dragged her fork over the plate. Even the waft of cinnamon and vanilla couldn't entice her.

"Do you have more business in town today?"

Max paused. "Maybe. Depends how the day goes."

Holly nodded slowly, trying to comprehend. "You're almost finished with it, then?"

Max set down his fork and turned to her. "I'll actually be disappointed to leave," he said, his voice husky.

Then don't, Holly wanted to shout. Instead, she asked, "Will you still stay through Christmas?"

Max shifted his eyes. "That's the plan."

"And then back to New York," she stated sadly.

Max stirred in his seat and reached for his coffee mug. "Do you ever miss city life?"

Holly had considered the question herself many times over the years, and dozens more times in the past week. There were elements of city life that were inevitably attractive: the shopping, the excitement, the din of the crowds, the buzz of the traffic. There were times when life in this small town felt almost too quiet, but those times were fleeting and rare. She made sure of that.

"Occasionally," she answered honestly.

Beside her, Max's posture seemed to shift. "Do you get back to Boston often?"

"No," she said. "I haven't been back since I moved to Maple Woods."

Max appeared baffled, a line creasing his forehead. "Not even to visit your family?"

"Oh," Holly said. She hesitated, lowering her eyes and forcing a shy smile to cover the awkwardness she felt. "I don't have a family, actually. Not…anymore."

She lifted her gaze to Max. He was watching her with an unsurpassed intensity, his eyes flashing with shock. "I'm sorry. I didn't know."

"How could you?" she asked mildly, setting down her fork. She realized that all this time she had been suspicious of Max, sensing that he was being evasive and overly mysterious, when she herself had hardly been forthcoming.

He slid a large, heavy hand onto her knee. A tingle rushed the length of her spine and pulsed at her tailbone as he grazed his thumb over her thigh. "Can I ask what happened?"

Holly took a deep breath and held it there. "It's not—not something I've talked about in a long time, really."

Tears sprung to her eyes, hot and thick and precariously close to spilling over and turning her into a blubbering idiot. She forced them back. She couldn't fall apart again. Not now. There had to come a time when she could talk about this without getting choked up. Maybe this was the time.

"My parents died in a car accident six years ago," she said quickly.

"Oh, my God," Max whispered. His hand moved from her knee to grab her hand.

Even in the heat of her despair, she welcomed the warmth of his touch on her cold fingers. "It was…awful," she said shakily. "We were driving back to Boston, from Maple Woods, actually, and the car hit a patch of black ice."

Max leaned forward. "You were in the car?"

A knot had locked in Holly's throat. She nodded her response, unable to speak. If she permitted herself, she could still hear the squeal of the brakes, her mother's piercing scream, the devastating crunch of the metal. And then, almost worse, the silence. "I was in the backseat," she managed. "It was a frontal-impact collision. The car—it crashed into a guardrail. I got out with some bad bruises, but basically walked away without a scratch. Physically, at least."

Max rubbed his forehead, digesting this information. "And you've been on your own since then?"

Holly tipped her head to the side. "Well, I had my grandmother until she passed shortly after and left me this house."

"That's a lot of people to lose in such a short period of time."

Holly's mouth thinned. It definitely was.

"But you stayed in Boston after…"

"After my parents died?" Holly finished, sensing his unease. "I did. And I wish I hadn't."

"Why?"

"My priorities were in the wrong place. I should have moved here to be with my grandmother. I…I didn't realize she would be gone soon, too. I thought I had time, that life couldn't be so cruel…. I had this boyfriend, and I thought we had a future together. I thought I was moving on with my life, moving past the hurt, looking toward the next phase instead of holding on to the past. But…it turns out I was spending my time with the wrong person. I should have been here, with my grandmother." She gritted her teeth, thinking once again about how much she had sacrificed by pinning all her hopes on Brendan. If she had known he didn't see a future with her, she would have come back to Maple Woods and spent the last months of her grandmother's life at her side.

"Everyone has regrets, Holly," Max said.

Oh, she knew all about regrets. And that was why she was so determined not to make the same mistake twice. She had learned the hard way what it meant to give your heart to the wrong person. Life was too precious to waste on people who didn't truly care about you.

Maybe that was why she was so attached to Maple Woods and The White Barn Inn. Even if these people weren't her family, they cared about her. She knew they did.

"I know that you think it's a bit strange of me to get so enthusiastic about Christmas—"

"Oh, now. I wouldn't say that," Max objected.

She shot him a good-natured accusatory look and his cheeks colored with guilt. "Well, maybe I *have* hinted at that impression," he admitted. "But that wasn't entirely fair. Besides, it's quirky. And it...it made me want to get to know you."

Holly's heart leaped at his confession. Maybe he wasn't the Scrooge she had come to believe him to be.

"But what does all this have to do with your unbridled passion for Christmas?" he asked, and she appreciated his attempt to lighten the mood.

Despite herself, Holly grinned. Only Max could succeed in making her smile in times of sadness.

"That Christmas six years ago was the last day I can remember being really truly happy," she said. "We were here, in this house, and it was just so perfect. My mom and I made cookies, and my dad cut down the tree." She grew quiet, thinking back on that day, not knowing in that moment that everything was about to change forever. "The car accident happened the day after, on our way back to Boston. I guess that every year since I opened the inn I go a little overboard with the holiday, just to keep the memory of that day alive a little longer. This house is meant to come alive at Christmas."

Max squeezed her hand tighter and sat in companionable silence with her for a long time. When he spoke, his voice was hoarse with emotion. "I guess I'm not the only one with a family tragedy," he said.

He reached up and tucked a strand of loose hair behind her ear, his eyes closing softly as he bent toward her. Holly's pulse quickened as she leaned in to meet his lips with hers. She had longed for this moment since the second his lips had last left hers, and just as her mouth brushed his, a sharp clearing of a throat was heard from the doorway, jarring their lips apart.

Abruptly, Holly turned and with surprise said, "Abby."

"I've been trying to call you," Abby whispered urgently, clutching Holly's upper arm and dragging her through the dining room and into the lobby. "Haven't you been checking your phone?"

Holly craned her neck back to the dining room, eager to get back to Max who was still sitting in the kitchen eating. She felt trapped with sudden impatience. The heat of the moment they had just started to share was gone; breakfast wasn't the only thing getting cold since Abby's arrival.

"I'm sorry," Holly said, not feeling the least bit guilty. "But I've sort of been busy."

"With *him?*" Abby hissed, referring to Max.

Holly's eyes flew open at the insinuation. "Yes, with him. Who else?"

Abby tightened her arms across her chest. Her eyes blazed through Holly's. "Do you even know what you're getting yourself into here, Holly?"

Holly faltered. "Abby, where is this coming from? I thought you liked Max. You were practically pushing me onto him yesterday!"

"Well, that was before," she huffed.

"Before what?"

"Before I started thinking that something doesn't add up here."

Holly groaned. "Abby."

"I'm just saying, what do you even know about this guy?"

A lot, Holly wanted to say. *Enough*.

"He's a good guy," she settled on.

Abby's face creased with worry. "Are you sure?"

"Abby," Holly said sharply. "Where is this coming from?"

"I'm just worried about you."

Holly sighed. "I appreciate that, I do. But just yesterday you and Lucy were basically telling me I was being ridiculous for being so apprehensive. And now you're telling me the exact opposite."

"Okay," Abby said, taking a deep breath. She held Holly's gaze with hers and lowered her voice. "After I left the Christmas Market, I went to the grocery store to pick up a few things for dinner. And I ran into Max. He was talking to Mayor Pearson," she added meaningfully.

Holly searched her friend's face in confusion. "And?"

"They were in some really heated conversation. Speaking in low voices. It was really suspicious," Abby finished.

Holly stared deep into her friend's warm brown eyes. "And...did you hear anything?"

Abby crossed her arms and looked shiftily around the room. "Well, no."

"Abby!" Holly cried. She knew her friend's heart was in the right place, but already her resolve to give Max a chance was breaking down, wariness seeping in through the cracks.

"I'm sorry," Abby said. "Maybe I'm overreacting."

Holly's anger wavered. "No, I know you're just concerned." She paused. "Are you sure you didn't overhear anything?"

Abby's lips twisted. She stared at the ground, pensive. "I guess not. It just…it just seemed odd that they knew each other. I don't know…"

Holly shrugged dismissively. "It's a small town. And you know how friendly Mayor Pearson is. I'm sure he was just trying to be friendly."

But even as Holly spoke the words, she felt her stomach begin to twist.

Abby looked equally unconvinced. "It just seemed like more than that. Like they knew each other."

"Maybe they do," Holly said, throwing up her hands. "Max is here on business, after all. I guess it would make sense that he could have met the mayor." Holly's mind flitted to the library. The more she thought about it, the more convinced she was that Max's involvement here was tied to it.

Abby nodded. "I feel like an idiot."

"Don't." Holly pulled her friend in for a hug.

"So tell me," Abby whispered, a glint reappearing in her eyes. "Did I just interrupt something?"

"You did," Holly said ruefully.

"Then I should probably let you get back to it!" Abby gave her a sly smile and said, "I want every detail. Promise?"

Holly nodded and waved her friend away with false cheer. Standing halfway between the dining room and lobby, she had the deflating sensation that she wasn't going to be able to just get back to it. The moment was lost and Holly's old fears had returned stronger than ever.

"Everything okay with Abby?" Max asked in what he hoped was a breezy tone as Holly strolled back into the kitchen. His heart was still pounding, despite the smile in Holly's eyes. This was all happening faster than he had prepared himself for, even if he had set it into motion.

"Oh, yeah. She just forgot something the other day and I needed to help her find it," Holly said, refusing to meet his eye. She pulled the sticky French toast pan from the stovetop and placed it in the sink, filling it with water to soak. Max watched her silently, his gaze shifting down her spine, lingering on the curve of her waist before she abruptly turned to face him, her expression unreadable. He eyed her as she smoothed her sweater over her hips. A rush of heat filled him as he imagined his own hands following her slim curves.

Max's gut clenched as her eyes bored into his from beneath the shadow of her long lashes. He studied her carefully, trying to gauge what she knew. What Abby had told her. This was what he feared the most—that news would spread to Holly before he could come clean himself.

He couldn't wait any longer. He had to talk to her. Now.

"I have to ask... Do you really plan to run this inn for the rest of your life?" he asked.

Holly refilled both of their mugs with coffee and turned to face him. "I do," she said simply. "I don't think I would ever leave Maple Woods. My life is here now, in this house. It's where I'm supposed to be."

Max clenched his teeth. So there it was. So final. So official. He knew it. She wasn't going to leave on her own. And that meant he'd have to force her out. Out of her business. Out of her home.

And inevitably, out of his life.

"Even with all the sacrifices you mentioned?" he pressed. "Even though you never get time away, and you're always busy with your guests?"

Holly considered his question. "I like dealing with my

guests, meeting new people. I know what I want out of life and I guess I feel like right now, the closest I am to having it is by staying here, in my inn."

"And what is it you want, Holly?" he asked softly.

She tucked a loose strand of chestnut hair behind her ear, seeming to debate whether she should tell him. Finally she looked him square in the eye and said, "A family. A family of my own."

Max groaned inwardly. He should have known. A woman like Holly was looking for marriage. Kids. A house. Probably this house. He could never give her any of those things. All he could ever do was break her heart.

"Are those things that *you* want?" she asked, her eyes searching his.

Max looked at her and knew right then and there what he had to say. "No."

Holly visibly paled. The light disappeared from her eyes. "Because of work?"

Max shook his head. "I love my work. My work has filled my life with purpose. But that's not the reason."

"Then what is?"

"I don't believe in family," he said, realizing as he spoke the words that he had never articulated his feelings so concisely. *I don't believe in family.* Was it even true? For years he clung to this belief, but something about being here with Holly these past few days, confiding in her, listening to her, laughing with her, made him start to wonder.

Holly's jaw set. She folded her hands across her chest. "Well, that's really sad."

Max gave a casual shrug, feeling like a callous bastard. He could see the contempt in Holly's eyes, the hurt and pain he was causing her. It was better this way, he told himself. Better for him to end it like this, to let her go. It would make it easier when the truth came out. She wouldn't be so blindsided.

He wasn't the man she thought he was. Maybe he wasn't the man he'd led her to believe he was.

His chest tightened with realization. He wasn't the man he wanted to be, either.

"Holly—" His voice was firm, his heart was pounding. He was going to tell her. Now.

"I should probably go tend to some things," she interrupted coolly. "Let me know if you need anything." She refused to meet his eye as she pushed through the kitchen door, leaving it swinging in her wake.

For a long time after she left, Max sat stone-faced at the counter, staring out the window onto the serene landscape that, in a few months' time, would be paved with cement.

There was no alternative other than to give up all his plans and live happily ever after with Holly. And that was never going to happen.

The ringing of his cell phone pulled him from his rambling thoughts. With a skip of his pulse he retrieved it from his pocket. He recognized the number from the call display as George Miller's. And he knew before he even answered what the verdict would be.

Chapter Ten

Holly pressed her palms against her eyes as hot tears spilled down her face and soaked the white eyelet shams of her feather pillows.

She knew she had no right to cry. The warning signs were all there. She had seen them all along; it was everyone else who was telling her otherwise. But she wanted to give Max a chance. She wanted to have some hope. She wanted to believe.

What a fool she had been.

Finally dragging herself into a sitting position, Holly glanced at her watch. She had work to do to prepare for the New Year's guests, and she couldn't spend half the day crying over this man who she wouldn't ever see again after Christmas. Oh, if only he would leave sooner, she suddenly wished.

Holly crossed to her bathroom, splashed water on her face and ran a brush through her hair, trying to perk up, even though his words still haunted her. How callous could he be? To just shut down any chance of something they could have had only minutes after she had poured her heart out to him.

She never talked about her parents' death. To anyone! Sure, Abby knew. And Lucy and George. A handful of others, of course. But other than that, it was something she had locked in a box and tucked away somewhere deep inside her. It was easier that way, somehow. Not thinking about her painful past was her only way of plodding through each day and looking forward, not back. But then Max had gone and spilled his own story to her, and she felt so instantly bonded to him, so close in the trust he had put in her, that she had just reflexively done the same.

And the strange part was that it had felt *good* to talk to him about it. To let him see a side of her she didn't reveal very often, not merely the woman who smiled and charmed her guests every day as she worked at the inn. The real Holly.

The Holly he clearly had no desire to get to know any better.

She just didn't understand it. Why had he bothered being so open with her last night if he didn't feel something for her? She had known all along, of course, that he was only in town for a few days, that he wasn't here to change his entire life around, but the rest…

I don't believe in family. His words echoed again and again. It was worse than she had even thought. It was one thing to be married to your work like Brendan had been. But to keep the world at arm's reach—to be so cold and alienating—was entirely a different matter.

Holly lifted her chin and studied her reflection. If Max Hamilton thought he could waltz into town, have a little fun with her, and then waltz back out, he was sadly mistaken.

He had picked the wrong woman for that. Holly didn't do flings.

She believed in family.

Well, forget him, she decided.

Holly plucked a tube of lip gloss from a drawer and swiped it over her mouth, but it did little to help. Her eyes were swollen and glistening. Her cheeks blotchy and red. She realized that she hadn't seen herself like this in longer than she could remember. Not since…

Something in her stomach twisted. Maybe she wasn't the only one keeping people at arm's reach. It was the only way to keep from getting hurt. From going through this. She had protected herself for years from moments just like this, steeling herself from the possibility of more pain. In many ways, Max wasn't much different. Was it worth it?

Holly felt her anger subside. A strange calm came over her, leaving her with nothing but a heavy lump of sadness in her already aching heart.

With everything he had been through, could she really blame him for feeling the way he did?

She shook her head and flicked off the bathroom light. Regardless of his reasons, he was who he was. And Max was not a family man.

And that meant that he was not the man for her.

Keeping busy, Holly had learned, got her through the tough times, and today was no exception. She spent the morning organizing the activity list for New Year's Eve, and going over her receipts for the month. Max's car was gone, and before he had a chance to return, Holly decided to use the opportunity to visit Abby. The roads were manageable and she could use a friendly face right now.

Abby was already waiting on her front porch by the time Holly's snow tires ground to a halt on the shoveled driveway. She stood hugging her thick wool cardigan against her frame, her expression a mix of surprise, concern, and curiosity.

"This is a pleasant surprise," Abby said.

Holly forced a smile. "I'm sorry I didn't call first," she said.

"Oh, please. You know you don't need to bother with that." Abby folded an arm around Holly's shoulders and led her up the stairs to the porch and into the warm comfort of her cottage.

"I was just sitting by the window working on my knitting when I saw your car pull up," Abby said. She pulled the door closed behind them and guided Holly over to the couch. "Pete's at work so you don't need to worry about anyone interrupting. It's just us girls."

Holly sighed. "I'm sorry. You must be wondering what's going on."

"Let me guess," Abby said. "Is it Max?"

Holly looked around the room, wondering just why she had allowed herself to get this upset about someone she barely knew. But see, that was the thing. He had let her get close. After last night, she felt like she *did* know him.

Guess I was wrong, she thought bitterly.

"I was right about him after all," she said to Abby with a watery smile. "Or, maybe you were."

Abby's eyes narrowed. "What do you mean, I was right?"

"When you came and warned me this morning," Holly said.

"Did he say something to you about that? About his talk with the mayor, I mean?"

Holly shook her head. "No. I still don't know what that was all about."

Abby's face softened. She picked up a pair of bamboo

knitting needles and wrapped a strand of thick, hunter green wool around one tip. "Sorry," she said, lowering her eyes. "But I planned to make this sweater for Pete before Christmas and time is running out. I can't exactly work on it when he's home."

"Got any spare yarn?" Holly asked.

Abby handed her a ball of pink wool from her basket under the coffee table. She fished around for a spare pair of needles. "This will make you feel better," she said.

"Thanks," Holly said, managing a small smile. She randomly casted on a few stitches, the softness of the wool on her fingertips instantly soothing her frayed nerves.

"So what exactly happened?" Abby asked, glancing up from her project.

Holly shrugged. "It's just what I said. I was right about him all along. He doesn't want a relationship. He isn't that kind of guy."

Abby studied her. "But you only just met him. Maybe in time…"

Holly stopped her. She knew better than to reach for hope that wasn't there. "He was pretty clear about it. He has no intention of getting married."

Abby frowned. "He said that?"

Holly paused, recalling the exact hurtful, horrible words. "He didn't have to. He said he doesn't believe in family."

"What?" Abby gasped.

"That's what he said," Holly repeated. "I don't believe in family."

Abby's brown eyes widened, her knitting paused. "Wow," she said, lowering her gaze. She wrapped the yarn over the bamboo stick and pulled it through a few more times, shaking her head. "That's…"

"Horrible?" Holly finished. She gave a feeble smile when she met Abby's stare.

"Yes. Horrible." Abby furrowed her brow as she worked on the sweater. When she finished another row, she quietly set her knitting on her lap and looked at Holly. "But why would he say such a thing? There has to be a reason."

Holly gave a reluctant sigh. "Well, I suppose there is."

"Hold that thought," Abby announced, standing up. "I have a feeling we're in for a long chat and I don't know about you, but I need some hot chocolate. With a splash of something to take the edge off."

Holly managed her first real smile since Max's announcement and settled back against the chenille throw pillows while Abby disappeared into the kitchen. The couch was positioned against a large picture window looking out over the front stretch of lawn where Abby had stuck a plastic Santa and his reindeer.

"Tacky, aren't they? But I couldn't resist," Abby said as she came back into the room. She smiled out the window before handing Holly a steaming mug of cocoa generously heaped with whipped cream.

"Yum," Holly said, perking up.

"We were out of marshmallows. Sorry." Abby blew on her cocoa and then, deciding to let it sit and cool, returned it to the table. She curled her feet under her on the couch and said, "Okay, so tell me everything."

Holly hesitated. She sensed that Max's childhood was something he had harbored close and shared with few people. She frowned when she considered that he had felt comfortable opening up to her.

She gave Abby a brief recount of the past few days, leaving out the details of Max's past that he had trusted her with, and ending with Max's hardened proclamation.

"I just don't think he wants the same things that I do," Holly finished.

Abby pursed her lips. "But you like him, Holly, I know you do. Maybe there's still a chance."

Holly thought about this. "I don't think so," she said, shaking her head. Even that flicker of hope she had just felt was enough to remind her of how much she stood to lose. Max had stood his ground. Now it was time to move on.

Abby reached for her mug and took a slow sip. "Maybe he just needs time."

"No, I don't think that's it, either. He's been alone for a long time, you figure. I think he prefers it that way."

Abby shook her head. "What a shame. A man that looks like that…" She blew out a breath. "Seriously, though, all joking aside, I know that I was a little wary of him this morning, but he seems like a really nice guy from everything you've told me, Holly."

"I know!" Holly cried, desperation filling her chest. "That's what's so frustrating!"

"I still don't understand what led to this big statement on his part. What happened after I left? Did he just blurt out that he didn't want a family?"

Holly chuckled. "No. Of course not."

"Then what?" Abby asked, getting impatient.

Holly slumped against the pillows and skimmed her eyes over the room. "He was asking me what I wanted out of life, and so I asked him the same."

Was that how the conversation had begun? Holly chewed the corner of her lip. Somehow this didn't seem so dire when she said it aloud. "He asked if I intended to run the inn for the rest of my life."

Abby was looking at her with round eyes and a telling smile. "Let me guess? You said you did."

"Of course. Maple Woods is my home. You know how much that inn means to me"

"Would you be open to leaving Maple Woods if you

could have that family you want so much somewhere else?" Abby asked shrewdly.

Holly already knew the answer and it terrified her more than she wished it did. She loved Maple Woods. But if leaving meant she could have those things… "I want to get married. I want to have children. But I want to live in Maple Woods. In my house. My family's house. It's all I have left."

Abby sighed. "I just don't want to see you throwing away a good thing because you aren't ready to give up some of your creature comforts."

"What do you mean?"

"I mean that you have been holed up in that inn for so long that you don't even know how to get out there and live a little. You are far too young to live like that, Holly," Abby said. "You've built this cozy little nest for yourself and filled it with lots of strangers. But you haven't stopped to open yourself up to something real. And lasting. So how are you ever going to even find the one thing you really want the most?"

The words stung, jolting her to reality. She knew it was true. She knew what she had done. But she liked the safety and comfort of the life she had created for herself. Perhaps too much… "I should talk to him. We have had a few nice days together."

Abby nodded. "I think you should."

But something still remained true. "But he doesn't want the things I do. He doesn't want a family, Abby. Not in Maple Woods. Not in New York. Not anywhere."

"Maybe he felt rejected!" Abby said. She adjusted her expression and muttered, "The male ego is a fragile thing, Holly."

Holly wasn't persuaded. "No, it isn't his ego. I think it has something to do with his own family." Her heart feeling heavy as realization formed. "His own family hasn't been around in a long time. Maybe—"

"Maybe he's afraid of people leaving him? Of getting close?" Abby asked, raising an eyebrow. "My, my. Doesn't that sound familiar."

Holly gave her a dirty look.

"Where is he now?" Abby inquired.

Holly lifted her hands. "I have no idea. He's probably still working out his business dealings."

"He still hasn't told you any more about that?"

"No. Should he?"

Abby pinched her brows. "Huh."

"Abby!"

Abby burst out laughing and clapped a hand over her mouth. Her eyes widened in apology. "I'm sorry, Holly. I'm awful. I just can't help but think it's strange that he has all this urgent business in town three days before Christmas. In Maple Woods of all places."

Holly chuckled. "It is bizarre. I know. But it's harmless, I'm sure. He said he's in real estate."

"Real estate?" Abby repeated. "Well, that's boring."

"I know," Holly said wryly.

"And here I was hoping he was a federal agent or a fugitive or something. Well, I'm sure that I was overreacting about his conversation with Mayor Pearson, then." Abby sighed "Besides, whatever he does for business really doesn't have anything to do with you. It's two separate matters."

Holly realized she was right.

"Sit and stay a little longer. Calm down. Think about what you want to say. And then go back to that inn and talk to him before he's gone and it's too late."

Holly considered this tactic, and realized this is exactly

what she needed to hear. "I guess it can't hurt to talk to him once more."

"If he's anything like the guy I talked to yesterday, he probably feels terrible. He likes you, Holly. I know he does. And that's why I'm telling you that this one is worth fighting for. If he still walks away after you talk, then let him go. But not yet."

Holly nodded and picked back up her knitting needles. Not yet.

Max sat in his rental car outside Maple Woods's biggest pub, The Corner Tap, for over an hour after he had left the Millers' cottage. He left the car running to keep the heat blasting. The radio station crackled over the speakers. The reception was poor, but it was the only channel not playing Christmas carols, so he was willing to put up with a little static.

The signed contract sat beside him on the passenger seat, a quiet reminder of what he had done and what he was about to do. The Millers had agreed. George had signed. Lucy had been too tearful to do anything but hide in the bedroom. Bobby, at least, had been gone. At another friend's house, presumably.

Even though Max had once hoped they would sign, somehow now that they had, he was left with the burning wish that he had never approached them at all. That he had taken one look at Holly's sweet face and just let the whole matter of the property drop.

But he hadn't done that. And now it was only a matter of hours before Holly would learn the truth. The horrible, awful truth about why he had come to Maple Woods. And why he had stayed.

The Corner Tap. The lights flashed invitingly on the sign in the window. Inside he could see a heavy crowd, all merrily cheering and toasting, some wearing Santa hats, their faces illuminated by the multicolored strands of Christmas lights that framed the frosted windows.

His mind flashed once again to his father, who was probably sitting in a similar bar right this moment, buying rounds for people who didn't care about him with money he didn't have, and stumbling home at the end of the night to a dark, empty house. His wife, gone. His son, gone. Did he even miss them? Did he even care?

Max had done everything in his power to make sure that he paved his own way, creating a different path for himself that would take him as far from his childhood as possible. The misery of his youth had fueled him for years, giving him a sense of purpose and determination. But he was so busy running away he hadn't stopped to ask himself where he was going. Or where he wanted to end up. Or if he was happy.

He had thought he was happy. He had thought escape was enough. But these past few days with Holly had made him realize how much he was missing out on. How much more there was to life.

Shifting the car into gear, Max pressed his foot on the accelerator and swerved back onto Main Street, driving to The White Barn Inn as quickly as the icy roads would allow. He didn't know what she knew. He didn't know what she would say. All he knew was that he had to talk to Holly. Tonight.

It was dark by the time Holly stepped out of the car and glanced up at the top corner of the inn that housed the Green Room. While she was calmer now than she had been this morning, her mind was still at war with her heart.

She heaved a sigh, her breath escaping in a plume of steam against the cold night air, and trudged through the snow to the front door. She hadn't a clue if Max would be there or not, and her pulse quickened with the possibility that he had packed his bags and left for New York. After their exchange this morning, she wouldn't be surprised.

Almost gingerly, she turned the handle of the door. Holding her breath, she stepped into the foyer. The lobby was lit by the lamps and Christmas lights on automatic timers, but the inn was hushed. She craned for a sound of life somewhere, anywhere, and found it lacking.

With a heavy heart, she crossed to the front desk and hung her scarf and hat on the rack. She paused once more, listening for any sound of Max, but all she heard was the pounding of her own heart.

"You're back."

His deep voice cut through the silence. Holly jumped, and turned to face him. He stood in the door to the dining room, holding a few logs against his broad, sculpted chest. If he was uncomfortable with how things ended this morning, he gave no sign of it. The only reminder of their last words was the sad smile he offered as he walked to the fireplace and began tenting the logs.

"I thought maybe you had gone," Holly said softly, moving hesitantly away from the front desk. She couldn't peel her eyes from him as he went about starting the fire.

"Where would I go?" he asked. His back was still to her but she could hear the smile in his voice. He wasn't angry.

But then, maybe she was the one who should be angry.

"Back to New York," she suggested.

"Didn't you notice my car parked out front?" he turned and arched an eyebrow. Holly glanced out the window and saw his car in the lot to the side of the house. She'd been so distracted planning what she would say when she saw him she hadn't even bothered to register her surroundings as she drove up to the house. Realizing her folly, she managed a small smile. "Oh."

Max rolled back on his heels, having stoked the fire enough to get the flames roaring. He stood and turned to face her. "I had a meeting in town. Besides, I never would have just left without saying goodbye."

Relief washed over Holly as she let out a pent-up breath.

"It's good to see you," she said. The words gushed out and she realized how much she meant them.

Max gave her an apologetic smile. "It's good to see you, too."

He stepped toward her and she didn't pull back. Any earlier trepidation vanished as her body took over her mind's reasoning. He bent his head down to touch her lips, softly, almost hesitantly. But the emotion of the day had awakened something in her, and she pulled him against her aching body, willing him to claim her and finish things they had started that morning. As her lips became more demanding, she felt him return the favor, his kiss becoming aggressive and bold. She entwined her tongue with his and began running her fingers along the back of his neck, feeling the heat from his skin as he pressed her to his body until she could barely breathe.

Finally, he gently pushed himself back, looking into her searching eyes. She wanted to believe his kiss was full of unspoken words, that the things he had said this morning were untrue or said in hurt. His blue gaze was clouded, but the spark of desire was undeniable.

"I'm sorry if I upset you this morning," Max said heavily, as if relinquishing his own burden with the words. "It wasn't my intention."

"I'm sure it wasn't," Holly said. Hesitantly, she added, "But is that really how you feel?"

Max sighed and sat beside her. He raked his fingers

through his hair and studied the fire, avoiding eye contact. "The thing is, Holly, that there's still a lot you don't know about me."

"I know," Holly said simply. "There's still a lot you don't know about me, either. We've only just met."

Max turned and met her gaze. "Yeah, we only just have, haven't we? It's strange because somehow it feels like I'm closer to you than anyone else."

Holly smiled at the compliment and fought off the warm spark of hope that took hold of her bloodstream.

"I'm not used to letting people in," Max admitted. "Maybe I'm not very good at it."

Holly offered him a smile. "It takes time."

Max nodded, his brow furrowed. He hesitated long enough for her to sense that this might not turn into the happily-ever-after she had hoped it would be. That maybe he still meant what he had said this morning.

Max locked eyes with her and the intensity she saw in his gaze caused her breath to catch in her lungs. "I like you, Holly. A lot. And I don't want to hurt you."

Holly searched his face, unsure of what he was telling her, looking for an answer that wasn't there. She licked her lips, still tasting him. "I don't understand."

Max drew a breath. "Holly, there's something you need to know. Something that I think will change the way you feel. I…I don't even know how it got to this point."

Holly felt a flood of concern at his sudden loss for words. Her mind raced with possibilities as she watched his eyes darken and shift back to the fire.

Her heart was pounding. "Max? What is it?"

Max shook his head and swallowed hard. When she reached for his hand, he moved it away.

"Max. Please." She reached out to grab hold of his arm,

eliciting a quiver down her spine as her skin touched his. "Just tell me. What is it?"

The ring of her cell phone cut the tension. Holly felt a wave of irritation so strong it almost exceeded the relief she felt at its timing. On shaking legs she stood and walked to the front desk where she had set her phone, immediately recognizing the number on the screen.

"George, hi." Her voice was raspy and breathless from emotion.

"Holly, I hope I'm not catching you at a bad time." George Miller's voice was weary and she immediately recognized that something was wrong.

"Is everything okay, George?" she asked worriedly, her anguish over Max instantly replaced with fear. The roads were slick, it was already dusk. She gripped the phone tighter. When he didn't reply right away, she pressed, "Has something happened to Lucy or Bobby?"

"We're all fine," George explained. "But…"

Holly's stomach knotted. She barely managed to form her words. "What is it, George?"

"I don't know how to say this, Holly, but someone has made an offer on the land."

For a moment the room went still and all she could hear was the blood rushing in her head. She tried to make sense of what he was telling her and failed. "I—I don't understand," she finally said, grasping the corner of the desk for support.

"I'm sorry, Holly," George's voice was strained, tight with emotion.

Holly's mind fumbled through the fog. "I don't understand. What do you mean? What are you saying?"

"I'm sorry, Holly," George said again. "But I accepted the offer. I sold the land. It's…it's done, Holly. I'm sorry."

Chapter Eleven

Holly set the phone down and silently stared at the back of her hands as she pressed her palms flat against the rich surface of the front desk. They were her mother's hands. The same long fingers, the same small knuckles. The same curve of the thumb. The same hands that had held hers when she was little. And stroked her hair. And wiped her tears. They were so familiar. So constant and reassuring in their sameness.

The cool grain of the wood warmed under Holly's palms and she pulled back, dropping her hands at her side. She had thought it impossible to feel this way again, to feel so lost and alone and hopeless. This house was the only thing she had left of her family and her memories of them. And it was gone. Just like that. No longer hers. As sudden as that car crash that took her parents' lives. It was all just snatched out from under her, without any warning.

How could life be so cruel?

She had thought she was too old to feel this way. That nothing could replicate the loss of her parents. But standing there, staring at that phone that had so instantly shattered her world, Holly felt an emptiness that nothing could fill.

She let her gaze drift over the room, her mind bleary as she tried to comprehend the implications of George's words. Was none of this really hers anymore? But it was her *home*. The only home she had. Where would she go?

Max was standing now, across the room, staring at her. His face was lined with concern. She had forgotten about him.

"Oh, Max." She shook her head, trying to clear the fog. Her voice came out like a hoarse whisper. "I'm sorry…I've had some bad news."

Her eyes lowered once more to the desk. She didn't trust herself to walk. She didn't even know where she would go.

"Holly." Max's voice was soft, but firm.

She looked at him again, noting the ashen pallor of his cheeks. "I'm sorry, Max. I just… That was George Miller. My inn…" She trailed off, her mind reeling with the fresh hurt of George's words. He had sold the land. Sold her home, without even consulting her. In less than seventy-two hours it was supposed to be hers. For years she had been waiting for this Christmas. And now, suddenly, it was just gone.

How long had he been planning this?

A burst of anger erupted in her. Lucy. Lucy must have known all along and she had never even said a word! Not even hinted. Instead she had so callously told Holly how happy she was for her, knowing how important this was to her. Knowing what it meant to her. It wasn't just about keeping her business going. Forget the business. It was about preserving what was left of her family.

Holly's eyes blazed with hot tears as she looked wildly

around the room, seething with anger for people she had thought were her friends. Her mind spiraled as she wondered who else knew about this. Abby? Stephen? It was a small town and people talked. What a fool she had been to think anyone in this town cared about her. She had put too much faith in them.

"Holly." Max's tone was pained, the expression in his eyes pleading.

She looked at him expectantly then stopped. Her heart suddenly froze with awareness. "Holly. I am so, so sorry."

Holly's eyes widened as the reality of the situation took hold. He was in town for business. Real estate, he'd said. His anguished stare met hers, unblinking. It couldn't be, she told herself. Not Max. "No," she whispered, not ready to hear the words just yet.

"Holly."

"No." She shook her head, her gaze never leaving his, silently begging him to make this go away, willing his expression to change. For none of this to be true. "No. *No*."

Max's lips pinched. His brow knitted as he shook her gaze from his. And she knew.

"No," she pleaded, her face crumbling in grief. The tears that had been forming spilled over, relentless in their fall, soaking her cheeks and dripping onto her sweater. She didn't even bother to brush them away or try and fight them.

"Please understand," Max said, his eyes holding hers. "I didn't know you owned the inn when I started this. If I had known…"

"What? What?" Holly insisted. "If you had known, you wouldn't have done it? You wouldn't have taken my home from me?"

Max shook his head, dropping his gaze, and Holly felt a fresh wave of frustration mount. She looked wildly around the room, desperate for someone to take this pain away.

But the only one there was the person who had brought it upon her.

"You wouldn't have done it!" she insisted.

Max looked up at her with a helpless shrug. "Maybe..."

Holly's heart sprang with hope. "Then take it back, Max. Take it back!"

Max shook his head, his eyes drooping with honesty before listlessly raising to meet hers. "I can't, Holly. It's too late."

"It's not too late!" Holly cried, her pitch becoming shrill in her frantic need to reverse the actions that had been set into motion. "The Millers will give you your money back. They know what this place means to me!" She lowered her voice to an urgent whisper. "Just take it back."

"Believe me when I say that I wished this could be different. But...it's business, Holly. It's not personal."

Holly's eyes flashed with fresh fury. "It's not personal?" she spat. "It's personal to *me,* Max!" she cried, her anger turning to despair as sobs racked her body. "It's personal to me."

She covered her eyes with her hands and cried deeply into her palms, feeling her shoulders shake violently. She felt nauseous. Dizzy and sick. Max reached out and placed a hand on her shoulder and she shook it off, glaring at him. "Don't touch me."

Max sighed and took a step back. He looked exhausted. Defeated. But it didn't bring her any solace.

"What are you going to do with it?" she asked quietly. "You're going to live in my house?"

Max's face whitened further. "George didn't tell you what the land will be used for?"

"No," she said cautiously.

Max heaved a sigh. "I'm a real estate developer, Holly. This land has been targeted for a shopping mall."

Holly gasped. Her tears momentarily ceased before silently welling again. "A mall?" she repeated, her voice so small it was barely audible even to her. "You mean, you're going to...tear it down? My *home*? For...a *mall*?"

Max's jaw twitched. He swallowed hard. "They might not even approve it, Holly," he said feebly, but his words were lost on her.

"A *mall*? That's why you were in town? That's why you were staying here? Meeting with the mayor?" She shook her head as the pieces of the puzzle fell into place. "Abby saw you. She warned me. I should have known..."

"I know how much this house means to you, Holly."

"No, you don't! You couldn't." Holly choked on a sob. "You don't *believe* in family. You said so yourself. You can't even *begin* to understand. This is all I have left!"

A silence filled the room and for one, heart-aching second Holly thought that maybe, just maybe he might change his mind.

"Please," Max said so softly she could barely him.

Holly swallowed hard, and looked him dead in the eye. Shaking with emotion, she narrowed her eyes at the man who had only a short while ago seemed so tender and kind. And perfect. "I *hate* you, Max Hamilton," she hissed, glaring at him through hot, blinding tears. "And I will *never* forgive you."

Max nodded slowly. "I'll leave."

"I think that's best," she said, and then turned on her heel and left him standing there alone.

December 23. She had been counting down the days all year, waiting for that sense of security, the comfort in knowing that her home was hers, that even though her family was gone, their memories could live on.

A soft tapping broke the silence of the room. Holly rolled

over in the strange bed to see Abby standing at the open door wrapped in a chenille robe. Soft light from the outside world was already peeking in through the blinds.

One day closer, she thought. The deed on the land expired on Christmas Eve.

"Thought I'd bring you some tea," Abby said quietly, coming inside to sit at the foot of the bed.

Holly pulled herself up to a sitting position and propped some pillows against the wrought-iron headboard. She sank back into them wearily, feeling drained and despondent.

"Thanks," she said, reaching for the hot mug.

Abby frowned, and patted her knee under the patchwork quilt. "How are you doing?"

Holly shook her head as tears threatened to form again, but never managed to surface. Her eyes were swollen and irritated, too dry for any further damage. "Not good," she mumbled, feeling every bit as miserable as she had since she first arrived at Abby's the night before. As much as a part of her wanted to stay in that house as long as she could, a greater part needed to be around someone that still cared about her.

"I figured as much, but I thought I'd ask just in case." Abby looked around the room, frowning. "I just still can't believe it."

"Tell me about it," Holly muttered bitterly, blowing on the steam rising from her mug.

"I just feel so guilty," Abby said, tightening her lips. She stared at a framed print on the wall, but her mind was clearly elsewhere.

"Don't feel bad," Holly said mildly. "It's not your fault."

"But I feel like it is in a way," Abby said, turning to face her. Dark circles had formed beneath her eyes. Holly realized with a sinking heart that Abby hadn't slept either. "First I pushed you on him, despite your apprehensions, and then I didn't listen to the little voice in my head that told me something was amiss."

"You did come and warn me," Holly reminded her.

"The way Max was talking to the mayor…something wasn't right. And instead of following through, I let it drop."

"Because I wanted you to," Holly said. "I wanted you to let it drop."

Abby held her gaze, unwilling to relinquish responsibility. "I should have known better," she chastised herself.

"Stop," Holly ordered gently. "You're a good friend. The best I could ask for. There is nothing you could have done differently. You did what you thought was best. Honestly."

Abby wasn't persuaded. "If you say so."

"I do," Holly said. "Besides, we both know who the real culprits are here."

Abby narrowed her eyes and fixed her gaze on the framed print once more. "When I think of the way that guy had us all fooled, it makes me sick."

Holly sipped her tea, which was sweetened with an almost overly generous amount of honey. She set it carefully down on the nightstand so as to not spill. "It isn't like Max acted alone, Abby. Lucy and George are just as responsible."

"I don't know who to be more upset with," Abby confessed. "Lucy has been such a dear friend to both of us. Why would she do this?"

"I've been asking myself the same thing," Holly said, suddenly feeling weary. No amount of scouring for answers was going to change the outcome or explain away the decision.

"Money," Abby commented bitterly.

"Probably."

Abby shifted on the bed, tucking a slippered foot up under her. "See, but that's what makes no sense!" she said, leaning in toward Holly. "You know the Millers don't care about getting rich. It doesn't add up."

Holly gave a listless shrug. "Does it matter why they did it?"

Abby's lips thinned. "I guess not."

They lapsed into silence, each consumed with confusion and misery, hurt and unanswered questions. It was Holly who finally broke the silence.

Thinking aloud, she said, "Max did say something interesting last night."

Abby peered at her sharply. "What was that?"

"He said the project still had to go before the planning committee."

"Huh."

For a fleeting moment, Holly felt her heart swell with a twinge of hope, only to feel it deflate just as quickly when reality came rushing in. "I guess it doesn't make a difference, though. Max bought the land. The Millers accepted the offer. Whether the mall gets built or not doesn't change anything. It is what it is."

"When is this planning committee meeting?" Abby asked.

Holly shrugged. "Who knows. But again, it doesn't matter."

Abby exhaled a breath. Her shoulders slumped. "Guess not."

"Do you mind if I stay here a little while longer?" Holly reached for her tea and choked down a sweet sip. It was the day before Christmas Eve, and that meant that tomorrow was her last real day in her home. It just didn't seem possible. "The thought of going back there right now...I can't bear it. It's too painful. If I went back it would just be harder to leave. Why prolong the inevitable?"

"Is he still there?" Abby voiced the same question Holly herself wondered.

"I told him to leave," Holly replied.

"Good." Abby's face was red with fury. "I can't even believe he had the nerve to stay at your inn, knowing what he had in store for it!" She clenched her jaw and grunted in disgust. "He has no heart."

Holly said nothing. A stir of unease rolled through her stomach. She reached once more for the tea, hoping the sweet honey would help, but it was no use. As much as she wanted to believe that Max had no heart, something deep within her knew it wasn't so. She had seen the pain in his eyes last night. She had seen the anguish and the guilt.

But then why did he do it?

She had thought their connection was real. He had felt it, too; she was sure of it. He wouldn't have opened up to her like that otherwise. He wouldn't have looked so helpless when she discovered the truth.

"He wanted to tell me," Holly thought aloud.

Abby turned to her, her expression impassive. "What do you mean?"

"He wanted to tell me. Last night, when I went back to the inn, he was trying to tell me something. And then George called."

Abby looked pained. "But why did he do it, Holly? Why string you along if he was planning this the entire time? Why be nice to you?"

"Why kiss me?" Holly added.

Abby shook her head. "Maybe he was really torn."

"Maybe," Holly said quietly. "But I guess it doesn't matter. In the end, he still decided to make the offer on the property. Knowing what it meant to me."

"In a way, that's worse."

Holly nodded slowly. "Yes. It really was."

But then, what else could she expect from someone who didn't believe in family?

Abby huffed out a breath. "I suppose I should go get showered. Are you going to rest a little longer?"

Holly nodded and pulled the quilt up tighter around her shoulders. She couldn't think about facing the day just yet. That required doing things and going places. She had nowhere to go. And nothing to do.

The inn. She hadn't even thought about it in the haze of her grief. The inn would have to be closed down. She would have to refund dozens of reservations.

"You stay here as long as you want," Abby said with a reassuring smile. "You'll get back on your feet again. Until then, our home is your home."

"Thanks," Holly said, managing a weak smile. She knew Abby was trying to be kind, but she couldn't ward off the ache in her chest. She loved Abby, and she was grateful to have a place to stay. But it wasn't the same.

She just wanted to be home for Christmas.

Max rubbed his eyes and looked at his watch. Somewhere during the night he had managed to fall asleep. He hadn't thought it possible with the way his mind was racing.

He knew he shouldn't be here. He should have left, as he said he would, but he couldn't. Not until Holly returned. Not until he had his final say with her.

Pulling himself off the couch where he had spent the night, he stumbled over to the massive fir tree and crouched down to inspect the gifts. His pulse quickened when he saw one labeled with his name.

Holly.

After a beat, he picked it up. The box was heavier than he had expected it to be somehow. There was a sturdy weight to it. On instinct, he shook it, feeling the hidden object shift slightly. He set the box back under the tree, smiling at himself for this childish indulgence before a sweet sadness crept in once more.

He couldn't remember the last time someone had given him a Christmas present. It was such a small, simple gesture. So very much like Holly to do.

Rolling back on his heels, Max stood and looked around the empty lobby. Only a few days ago the room had been buzzing and alive, filled with Christmas music and a pleasant buzz from the guests' cheerful conversation. Now the house was still and vacant. Everyone was gone, except for him. And he had no right being here.

Wasn't this exactly how the rest of his life had unfolded? He had built himself an empire, and he was living in it alone. The White Barn Inn was no different.

He had hoped that Holly would have come back during the night, and he had waited in the lobby for her. What he would say when he saw her, he didn't know. But he needed to see her. It was an all-consuming need. He couldn't let her go.

He pulled his phone from his pocket to call her and realized with a strange pang that he didn't even know her phone number. She was probably at Abby's house, but he didn't know where that was. He could ask someone in town, he supposed, but what would he even say when got there? There was nothing he could say that could take back what he did.

The memory of her parting words rang out, echoing in the empty corridors of this old mansion. She would never forgive him.

And why should she? He had taken the one thing that meant the most from her. He'd taken everything from her.

Max's stomach churned with self-loathing. Was this really who he was? The person he had become? He had tried so hard to better his life. To redeem his childhood. But this wasn't the man he had set out to be.

It took Max only fifteen minutes to get to the Millers' cottage. He took the icy porch stairs two at a time and tapped his knuckles firmly on the door. A tearful Lucy Miller pulled it open. Her brow creased when she saw him standing on her porch.

"I'm sorry to bother you, Lucy. Is George here?"

"He's at the diner," Lucy said, holding the door open wider so that he could enter.

Max stepped into the cramped living room. It was only his third time here, but already it felt familiar. The Millers were kind people, and it sickened him that he had dragged them into this.

"I need to speak with George, if possible."

Sensing the urgency in his tone, Lucy nodded solemnly. "I'll just call him," she said, ducking into the kitchen. From behind the thin wall, Max could hear her frantic whisper. "He's coming right over," she announced, reemerging. "Can I get you some coffee?"

Max managed a grateful smile. "Coffee would be great."

"I think I'll join you," she said. She disappeared once more before quickly returning with two mugs. "I didn't sleep a wink last night," she confessed, coming to sit across from him.

"That makes two of us then," he said, taking a hearty gulp. Adrenaline was pumping through his veins and the caffeine made him shaky.

A pounding of footsteps was heard quickly clambering up the porch stairs and the door swung open to reveal George Miller, his face creased with confused. "What's going on?" he demanded.

"Come sit down, George," Lucy quietly commanded.

She turned her attention back to Max. "My nerves can't take much more, Max. If you wouldn't mind telling us why you're here, I'd appreciate it. Has the planning committee already decided? Was all this for nothing?"

"No, it's not that." Max set the empty mug on the end table and leaned forward on his knees, feeling more clear-headed than he had in years, despite the lack of sleep. He stole a glance at the Millers, who were sitting side by side, clutching hands. Lucy's knuckles were white and her face colorless. Realizing they were waiting for him to explain, he cleared his throat. "I need to let you both know that I no longer plan to present the project to the planning committee."

The Millers turned to face each other. Max could see the mixture of panic and relief in their eyes. Before they could protest, he held up a hand. "I am a man of my word, believe it or not. I offered you a price for the land and I chose to back out. The money is still yours to keep."

The Millers exchanged another glance. Lucy nodded her head, silently communicating with her husband and George turned to meet Max's stare. "This wasn't an easy decision for my wife and me to make, Max. Lucy here has been crying for days over this. We agonized about selling this land to you, when we had already given our word to Holly Tate. She's our friend, and a member of this community."

"I understand that," Max said, his voice low.

"But the thing is…" George's voice failed him. He swallowed hard, collecting himself. "The thing is that Lucy and I have another responsibility that extends beyond Holly. And that's our son. And our town."

Max squinted, trying to follow their logic. He nodded for George to continue.

"I'm sure you've heard about the library fire," George said. "But what you probably don't know is that our son is responsible."

"It was an accident! He was smoking behind the library," Lucy interjected desperately.

A wave of shock slapped him, leaving him momentarily speechless as he struggled to comprehend the multiple layers of the Millers' situation. His expression, he knew, revealed his astonishment. "Does anyone else know?" he asked, trying to piece the facts together.

Lucy shook her head, lowering her gaze. "No. But it wouldn't have felt right to let it go. We…we needed to do something to set things right. But not at the expense of our son. He has an entire future ahead of him. I had dreams of him going to college in a couple of years! He's a smart boy…and we hoped he would get a football scholarship."

Max nodded. "You won't have any trouble sending him to college now," he said.

"We didn't know what we were going to do, but we knew we didn't want to keep this a secret forever. We kept thinking that if we could just pull the money together we could set it right… My father runs a construction business here, but he's not well and I'm afraid to burden him with this. We want to pay for it ourselves, to do the right thing, but the diner doesn't bring in enough. And when your offer came to us…" Lucy trailed off, swallowing back tears. "It was both a blessing and a curse."

"The money is still yours," Max reiterated. "You can send Bobby to college now. You don't have to worry about anyone finding out what happened."

"No," George said. "We're fair people. Honest. It might not seem like it, but we are. We'll go through with the sale of the land, Max. But we have a new condition."

Max sat and listened, first in awe, then in wonder, as the Millers detailed their wishes. When they had agreed to everything, Max stood to leave, feeling a hundred pounds lighter. It was time to go back to the inn, and time to let the Millers get back to their life.

"But, what will you do with the land?" Lucy asked as Max shrugged into his parka.

"I don't think I will do anything with it after all," he said.

Lucy followed him to the door, her brow pinched in thought. "Can I ask why?" she asked softly. She raised her eyes to meet his, searching his face in confusion.

Max gave her a small smile. "Holly has come to mean a great deal to me in the short time I've been here," he said. The words were true, but it felt foreign to be speaking them aloud.

Lucy beamed and reached out to touch his arm. "She has a way of doing that to people."

Max nodded and turned, walking down the stairs and back to his car, chuckling at the irony of the situation. He had spent his entire adult life pushing people away. How on earth did he end up falling in love with someone he had known for only a matter of days?

Chapter Twelve

As a child, Christmas Eve had always been Holly's favorite day of the year, even more so than Christmas Day.
By noon on Christmas Day, the presents had been opened
and excitement had peaked. But Christmas Eve was the
epitome of anticipation and hope, of dreams yet to come
true, of magic yet to be made.

But this year was different. There was nothing to look
forward to now. No preparations to be made. This year it
just felt like the beginning of the end.

Holly pulled onto the long drive and parked. Even though
she'd been away for only two nights, it was the longest she
had been away from the inn since she'd moved to Maple
Woods. She stared at the property, already missing it, wondering if she would ever get used to being away from it.

It had been a long time since she had stopped to look at
the old house from this distance. Sitting in the car at the
edge of the estate, she felt almost in awe of its grandness of

scale, its richness of history. She'd spent the first few days
of December wrapping the posts in garland, carefully hanging a wreath on each of the windows and the front door.
It didn't seem possible that somewhere in the near future,
the house would be demolished and in its place would be
a shopping mall of all things.

She shifted the gears and slowly crept up the drive, allowing her eyes to roam over the acreage. From the snow-
covered blueberry bushes to the white barn far to the side,
barely visible against the snow from this vantage point.
She loved that barn—from its cheerful red doors to the
weathervane standing proudly on the roof. Behind it was
the pond, now frozen over for the winter. On a normal day,
she would be down there skating, tracing figure eights into
the ice. When she was a child, she and Abby would swim
in the cool, murky water while her grandmother sat under
an umbrella on an old plastic chair, flipping through fashion magazines and sipping sun tea.

Holly's heart tightened. She wondered what would happen to the pond. They'd probably fill it, pave it over.

As she finally neared the top of the drive, she couldn't
help noticing Max's car was gone, and she felt strangely
sad about it. The feeling was fleeting, but confusing in its
effect on her. She was just disoriented and exhausted, she
knew. She had gotten used to looking forward to seeing
him and missing him when he wasn't there.

She pulled her car around to the back of the house and
climbed out into the crisp air. A biting wind slapped at her
cheeks and stung her eyes. Crunching through the snow to
the front of the house for what would probably be the last
time, she felt her heart sink further as her mind flitted back
to Max. He had seemed so sincere! She'd thought she had
softened his hardened heart. But maybe some hearts were
just permanently damaged.

It would take her a while to remember that he wasn't the man she thought he was. That his advances had been nothing more than flirtatious banter, meant to cover his betrayal. That she had been duped, used.

Holly's pulse skipped as it did every time she came around to this sad, hard fact. No matter how much evidence was pointing to the contrary, something deep inside her still told her that her time with Max had been real and true. She'd seen it in his eyes, heard it in his laugh. Maybe he was this way with every woman he met, but her gut told her otherwise. Or maybe she was the one with an ulterior motive. Maybe she just wanted to see him so achingly badly because she knew in her heart that he was the one person who had the power to make this all go away. And she couldn't stop wishing he would.

The front door was locked to Holly's surprise—Max must have locked it when he left—so, after a bit of fumbling, she slid the key into the lock and turned the bolt. Already she felt like a stranger as she closed the door behind her. The house was empty, eerily still. Unlike it had ever been since she first converted it into an inn. Even during her slowest months, there was always the cheerful rumble of conversation from a handful of guests or members of staff.

The staff. Holly groaned as she realized the ripple effect of this horrible situation. She couldn't imagine a worse time than Christmas to let everyone know that they no longer had a job to return to, but she had been left with no other choice. She winced when she thought of Abby, who was so busy comforting her that she hadn't even bothered to indulge in the setback this had caused her personally.

A wave of shame took over when she thought of her oversight. When she got back to Abby's house, she would figure something out for her. A severance of some sort. It was the least she could do.

Holly moved quickly through the lobby, not bothering to linger. The longer she stayed in this house, the harder it would be to leave again. She didn't need to sit here and reminisce. There would be plenty of time for memories later. That was all she would have left soon. Memories and nothing more. At least those would be hers to cherish and keep forever—something Max or anyone else could never take from her.

Abby had been kind enough to offer to help her pack, but Holly knew it was better for her to do this on her own, despite how much of a toll the effort was taking on her broken spirit. She needed to do this at her own pace, with her own thoughts to keep her company, to have the closure she needed to be able to walk out of her house and shut that door behind her for the very last time.

Max gripped the steering wheel as he drove through town, recalling the dozens of terse emails he'd received from his senior staff, the confusion and anger he'd sensed in their voices during a conference call earlier that morning. People were upset, and understandably so. He'd told them a half-truth—that the site had slipped through, that it wouldn't work out. They didn't need details beyond that. It was his company, and he'd deal with the fallout. The anchors would be let down. It was possible several would act on their threats to pull out of underperforming centers. Hamilton Properties would take a major financial hit.

But it would be worth it.

He took a left and began to climb the long driveway to the inn. He held his breath, looking for any sign of Holly. He had spent another night sitting in the lobby, waiting for a sign of headlights, bracing himself for her return. He ached with a need to see her, speak to her. He needed to make things right, and he didn't want to wait any longer.

His tires chomped up the drive and he pulled to a stop. No car.

Max fought back the bitter taste that filled his mouth. There was still a chance to set things right; Holly would have to return to the inn eventually. It was her home, after all. She couldn't stay away forever.

By now he had resigned himself to letting her go, if that was what she wanted. He was used to people walking away from him; it was all he had ever known. If Holly was determined to never forgive him or see him again, that was her choice. He couldn't stop her.

But it wouldn't stop him from doing what he had to do.

Max turned off the ignition and stepped out into the chilly air. It was going to be a white Christmas this year— even the sun's rays couldn't cut through the cold. He pulled his collar up to shield his neck from the wind and darted to the front door of the lobby, fumbling in his pocket for the key. He hesitated, his brow furrowing in confusion when he realized the door was unlocked, even though he had made sure to lock it before going into town.

Holly.

He held his breath, his heart pounding as he quietly pushed open the door and stepped inside. With eerie calm he stood perfectly still, his eyes skimming the lobby, looking for any sign of her.

But all he was met with was silence.

Max inhaled deeply, and nodded to himself. He had set this into motion and now he was paying the price. It was time to leave The White Barn Inn once and for all.

But first, there was one last thing he needed to do.

It didn't take Holly long to pack up her clothes and toiletries. Her personal photos and mementos all fit neatly in a few brown packing boxes. She had fit her entire world into the bedroom, sitting room, and bathroom that constituted her living quarters. The rest of her home was open to the public; the door was always open for any passing stranger who wanted to enter her world, even for just one night.

She did want to keep some of the furniture, though. When she landed on her feet, she would need it to make her feel like she was home again. Abby had suggested she have an estate sale for the rest; she could use the money to start a new life for herself. Although, what that life would be, she didn't even know anymore.

Maple Woods no longer seemed the place for her. She couldn't bear the thought of driving through town and seeing a shopping mall on this very spot she now stood. It would kill her.

And even her friends... Abby and Pete and Stephen were dear, but some pain cut too deep and some towns were too small. She understood now why Max had left his childhood town behind and never looked back. It was time to do this with Maple Woods. She couldn't imagine ever facing the Millers again after this. Their smiles, their diner, all of it would just be a constant reminder of their betrayal and of her loss.

Holly had a sudden urge to hide. To run from her life and leave her memories packed up in the boxes at her feet. Maybe she *would* go back to Boston, where she could get a new job and get lost in the crowd. Or maybe she could get a job at a hotel in another city, someplace where no one would know her or her sad story or would have even heard of Maple Woods.

She sealed another box. It was almost time to leave. Dragging this out would only make things worse. Holly took one last look around the bedroom, feeling strangely detached and peaceful. It was too surreal to accept yet. Someday it would hit her, but not today. Not while this house still stood intact, at least. Not while she was still a part of it.

As much as she wanted to load up her car and drive away right then, before the inevitable flood of tears took hold, there was still business to be done. Holly smiled weakly to herself—she had taken such pride in making over this building as an inn and providing for her guests. She had run a tight ship, and she would still do so now, to the bitter end.

She wandered back through the corridors, growing dim in the fading sunlight, mentally forming a list of everything she would have to grab from the front desk, but stopped dead in her tracks when she saw the golden flames crackling in the fireplace at the far end of the room. Her heart wrenched, her chest heaving with each breath.

Max. He was still here.

"Max." Her voice caught the knot in her throat, barely coming out as a stifled whisper, its tone laced with hope she didn't even know was there.

She slowly put one foot in front of the other as she tiptoed further into the vast space, her eyes scanning for any sign of him. Gingerly, she crossed the room to the hearth, her eyes focusing on something else that hadn't been there just a short while ago.

She reached out to the mantel and touched the stocking that hung beside Abby's and the other members of the staff. The ones Abby had knitted and that Holly had hung so carefully. The stockings had been empty all this time, meant for nothing more than a decoration and eventually a small gift from the Secret Santa exchange they did every year and she knew at once that the gift tucked into her stocking was not from Abby or Stephen or any other member of the small group that ran The White Barn Inn.

It was from Max.

Holly sucked in a sharp breath and let her fingers graze

the creamy paper that was tucked inside the stocking, poking out from the top just enough to make it visible. She pulled it out slowly and held it in her hands, pondering the possibilities. The paper had been rolled into a scroll, tied with a scrap of twine that she now set on the mantel.

Unfolding the crisp paper, she was surprised by the length of the letter. Her trembling hands caused the paper to shake and she scanned the words quickly, barely absorbing them and then reading them over and over until her tears blurred her vision and dripped onto the ink, smearing his last words to her.

Max halted at the bottom of the stairs, his hand gripping the banister. Holly stood with her back to him, her dark hair pulled into a loose ponytail that flowed down her back, glistening in the light of the fire. She looked so small, standing there alone in the huge room. So innocent in a way that touched him deeply and seized his heart. She hadn't done anything to deserve this. All she had wanted was something that was rightfully hers all along. He'd had no business coming in and trying to steal that from her.

Sensing his presence, Holly suddenly turned. Her eyes locked with his, and even from this distance he could see her tears, and it made his heart ache to know that he had caused them.

"I thought you'd left," she said, staring at him as if he were a ghost.

"I should have, but I needed to see you one last time first. I needed to try to make things right." He watched her, his breath caught in his chest, not ready for this moment to be over. In this moment there was a still a chance, still hope, and he clung to it.

"I read your letter," she said with a watery smile. She

lifted it in the air, the fire illuminating it from behind. "Is it official? The deed to the property is mine?"

Max nodded. "It was never mine to take in the first place."

Holly looked down at the letter that accompanied the deed and back to him. "I just don't understand. Why did you change your mind?"

"It's like I said in the letter. I know what this place means to you. I understand how it could never be replaced."

"No," Holly said. "It can't."

"I shouldn't have gone through with it in the first place, Holly," he apologized, coming closer to where she stood near the large hearth. "I had no business being here or involving you in this mess."

"You didn't know at first," Holly said, but her tone had a hard edge. She was still bruised. He wouldn't have expected otherwise.

"No, I didn't," he said. "I honestly thought I was coming here to make an offer to the owner of the inn. That it would be a clear-cut business arrangement and that everyone would walk away with what they wanted. When I learned of the situation, I didn't walk away. And I should have."

"It was business. You said so yourself."

Max shrugged. "I guess I just didn't realize that the project wasn't worth it until it was too late."

Holly lowered her gaze and stared at the letter in her hands. She ran her fingers over the formal deed to the land. Her eyes shot up to his. "Was it really important to you? The project?"

It was now or never, Max knew. He had fought so hard to build a safe world for himself—his business and nothing else. Now it was time to fight for something else. Something that meant a great deal more to him than anything else ever had.

"None of it matters, Holly," he said, fighting to form the words, "if it costs me the one thing that has come to mean so much to me."

Holly's eyes held his, unblinking. "What's that?"

"You."

Holly looked down at the deed to the property that lay flat against the smeared ink of Max's letter. She clung to the paper, thinking it odd that something that could mean so much could be both so simple yet official in form.

The tenderness of his confession tore at her heartstrings.

She looked deep into his blue eyes, noticing the way they crinkled at the corners, the way a faint line had formed between his brows. He had opened his heart to her, and now it was up to her to step inside.

A memory of how deeply he had hurt her cut fresh. He had broken her trust, blindsided her when she had finally dared to let her guard down. And now he was standing here, telling her everything she wished to hear but didn't know if she could believe.

"Max—" she started and then stopped as her mind waged war on her heart.

"What is it? What more do I need to say? Just tell me what more I need to say to convince you that I will never hurt you again. I'll say anything, Holly."

Holly searched his eyes. "Tell me what you want, Max. Tell me what this is all for."

His eyes didn't waver from hers, and when he spoke, his voice was strong and clear. Certain. "I want this, Holly. I want your world. I want *you*." He gestured to the room, to the tree. "Being here this past week has made me realize how much I've chosen to miss out on. I thought it was better to keep to myself, but I was wrong." He paused, giving her a lazy smile. "I want the tree and the stockings and the small town where everyone knows your business. I want to live my life feeling the way I've felt every day that I've been here. I don't want to go back to the way it was before."

Holly beamed. "You don't have to," she said.

Max's smile widened. "You really mean it?"

"I've never been more sure of anything," she said as she took a step toward him. He leaned down toward her, his eyes never breaking their hold with her own, until the moment his lips finally touched hers. His kiss was light and tender at first, sending a tingle down her spine.

He wrapped his arms around her waist, pulling her to his hard chest. His fingers traced lower down her curves, drawing her in as his mouth claimed hers with more passion. Holly ran her hands over the nape of his neck, through his hair, feeling the urgent heat radiating from his body.

Barely breaking their kiss, he whispered in her ear, "I'll never betray you again, Holly." The delicate rush of his breath in her ear and the featherlight touch of his lips on her skin made her shiver with need and she wrapped her arms tighter across his wide chest, pulling him close.

They continued to kiss, their hands tracing the other's chest, hips, back, until step by step they were moving together in the direction of Holly's bedroom.

"I didn't think guests were allowed back here," Max teased.

Holly laughed, letting her lips linger softly on his. "There are exceptions to every rule."

They fell back onto her bed, and Holly let her head drop back as Max traced his mouth along the length of her neck. She sighed, barely believing life could transform so quickly.

His tongue traced her bottom lip, teasing her for more, and higher still, sending a warm current rushing through her. She opened herself to his embrace as he pulled her sweater free, and she quickly released him from his shirt. His chest was taut and firm, and the warmth of his skin on hers made her ache for him to touch her more intimately.

Her nipples strained against the lace of her bra, and Max slowly pulled the straps off her shoulders, one by one, before unhooking the clasp and lowering his mouth to her breasts. His tongue circled each nipple softly as his fingers traced over her stomach, her hips and the rim of her panties, teasing her with his touch.

Her hips lifted with anticipation. She raked her hands through the silkiness of his hair and craned her neck to recapture his lips when his mouth met hers once more.

"I want you, Holly," he said, looking her in the eye.

She nodded, unable to speak as she looked deep into his blue eyes, noticing for the first time the slight dusting of freckles that covered the bridge of his nose, the flecks of brown that surrounded his pupils.

She lay back against the pillow as Max's lips trailed down her stomach, over her hips, his touch so light, yet her body so achingly aware.

He pulled her jeans off, then slid her panties down her legs. Kneeling before her, he released his belt, and he was soon hovering above her in only his plaid boxers, and then nothing at all.

She opened her mouth to his deep kiss as he sheathed himself in a condom and then entered her in one long, slow thrust. Easing back slowly, he pushed forward again until their bodies found their rhythm, his mouth never leaving hers until the end, when he groaned into her ear and collapsed against her chest.

They lay against the soft flannel sheets, which, as Abby had observed earlier that week, had up until this moment never seen anything more exciting than a romance novel. Their bodies entwined, each lazily stroked the heat off the other's bare skin, sighing with happiness or possibly relief.

"You know," Max said eventually, "I think your Christmas spirit might be contagious. All this mistletoe has clouded my judgment."

Holly smiled to herself. "So you're looking forward to another day of festive activities, then?"

"Do you know what's even crazier than that?" he asked in a husky whisper, his lips curling into an irresistible grin as his blue eyes danced. "I love you, Holly Tate."

Holly smiled. "I love you, too."

Bright sunlight poured through open curtains, filling the bedroom with a golden warmth and stirring Holly from her slumber. She smiled as the memory of the night before came back to her, and she rolled over on the mattress to run her hands over Max's smooth skin.

It seemed like an eternity since she had first met Max, when really it had been only a week. A mere matter of days, and her whole world had been turned upside down. She almost had to chuckle, thinking of the events that had brought them to this perfect moment. She could still picture the look on Evelyn Adler's face when Max had appeared in the dining room for breakfast that first morning.

"What are you laughing about?" Max mumbled. His voice was muffled with sleep and his eyes remained closed, as if clinging to the remains of a fading dream.

"Nothing, really," Holly whispered. She traced her finger down the contours of his bare chest and again let her arm fall lazily around his waist as she sank down deep into the burrows of his warm body. "Just happy."

Holly felt the shift in Max's torso, the twist of his limbs. Rolling over to face her, he wrapped a strong, heavy arm over her waist. "Mmm," he murmured into her hair. "This is nice."

"It is," Holly managed to whisper as desire overwhelmed her senses and caused her insides to quiver.

A smile began to play at Max's lips as he slid his hand down the length of her thigh. Holly sighed ever so slightly as a surge of warmth filled her. "It's Christmas," he said, leaning down to skim her lips with his.

And it was. Christmas Day. The Christmas she had been anticipating for years was finally here. She had imagined it so many times over—what it would feel like to know her home was really and truly her own—but never could she have imagined she'd be sharing it with the man who had swept into town and nearly taken it from her.

"It's your first official Christmas in your home," Max said, roaming his blue eyes over her face. He pulled his hand from her hip and brushed a loose tendril of hair off her cheek. "Was there anything special you had in mind?"

"I think this will do just fine," Holly whispered, nestling into the smooth curve of his neck.

"Mmm," Max murmured as he wrapped both arms tightly around her waist. She could hear the smile in his voice, and her curiosity was piqued. "There's just one little surprise I hadn't mentioned.…"

"What's that?" Holly lifted her gaze to his, her eyes wide in alarm when she saw the mirth dancing through his.

The sudden chime of the doorbell tore through the house, interrupting their moment and jolting Holly away from the warmth of the bed. She sat up, wrapping the sheet around herself as confusion mounted. The bell rang again and again, the sound echoing off the walls of the large house.

Holly's brow furrowed in confusion and her heart began to race as she turned warily to Max, who was laughing so hard he was clutching his stomach. "What in the world?" Holly demanded.

Max wiped at his eyes as another round of chimes began, and finally groaned as the remains of his laughter faded away, until a fresh round of ringing caused him to sputter once more.

Holly was on her feet, frantically pulling on a sweater and socks, her mind reeling with the possibilities of what could be going on, of who could be all but tearing down her front door. Had she forgotten about a guest? Surely they had all canceled. No one was scheduled to arrive until New Year's Eve…unless… "Max?"

She slid her eyes to him knowingly as her heart lurched with hope. Max sat up in bed, propped on an elbow, his hair tousled, his eyes warm. He nodded to her just once, and that was all it took.

"The Adlers," she said, releasing a sigh.

He grinned. "It wouldn't be Christmas for you without a house full of everyone you love the most."

Holly beamed. "Present company included."

Epilogue

The White Barn Inn really did come alive for Christmas. Max smiled as he walked into the warm kitchen, drinking in the fragrant air.

"Smells delicious," he said, stomping the snow off his boots. He'd never in a million years have thought he would hear himself say it, but it smelled like Christmas. And he liked that it did.

"Turkey will be ready in an hour," Stephen announced from his familiar post in front of the stove. His girlfriend stood behind the island, placing appetizers on a sterling silver platter, and Evelyn Adler was perched on a counter stool, arranging cookies on a tray. When she noticed Max, she plucked the biggest cookie from the tray and handed it to him, smiling.

"Don't tell me Stephen's put you to work!" Holly said to Evelyn as she swept into the room with a half-empty punch bowl. Max's pulse skipped at the sight of her. She seemed to have grown more beautiful overnight. Her eyes twinkled and her rosy lips were perpetually spread in a warm smile.

"It's not work, it's dinner!" Stephen countered. "And you're in charge of the wine."

Holly added more eggnog to the bowl and garnished it with a sprinkle of nutmeg, smiling brightly. Her expression changed when she saw the freshly chopped logs Max was holding to his chest. "What are those?" she asked, her voice an octave higher than usual.

"Wood for the fire. I thought I'd pitch in."

Holly's eyes blazed with mirth as she took in the jagged and splintered cuts of wood in his arms. She wagged a teasing finger. "I never want to hear you make fun of my stint as a waitress ever again."

Max grinned. "Deal."

As everyone trickled into the dining room and lobby, Holly finished up a few quick tasks in the kitchen, smiling as she listened to the laughter and conversation flowing through the rooms. She had lived in this house for five years, had spent plenty of holidays here as a child, yet this was her first *real* Christmas here. Oh, her guests were lovely, of course, but she had never realized how wonderful it was to be surrounded by the real people in her life for the holiday. In her real home.

Picking up the bowl of eggnog and balancing the cookie platter in her other hand, Holly walked into the lobby and set both items on the coffee table. A shiver of excitement zipped down her spine at the mere sight of Max who was now sitting in a club chair, chatting easily with Abby's husband Pete, looking very much at home. It was almost impossible to believe that this was the same man, who, only days before, had looked more uncomfortable and out of place in this house than any guest of hers ever had before.

"I had a feeling it would all work out," Abby said, coming to stand next to her.

Holly turned to her, unable to suppress the smile she had worn all day. "Sure, you did."

"I'm just so glad that it did," Abby mused. "But there's just one thing that still doesn't make any sense."

"What's that?" Holly pulled her stare from Max and turned to meet Abby's furrowed gaze.

"The Millers. Why'd they do it?"

Holly shifted in her shoes. Max had explained everything to her—including the fact that the Millers had refused to accept any money for the sale of the land. The money would serve as a donation only. After Holly's fury had faded, she had been left with an overwhelming sadness that Lucy had harbored this secret for so long, and that she hadn't trusted Holly enough to share it. To think that Bobby had been responsible for the destruction of the library, and that Lucy had kept the knowledge bottled inside this entire time…it broke Holly's heart to imagine the burden her friend had carried.

"They had their reasons," she said to Abby. "I understand now. And I've actually invited them here today before they visit Lucy's parents."

Abby peered at Holly for a long moment and eventually said, "Well, if you're at peace with it, then so am I."

"I am," Holly affirmed, nodding her head.

"Miss Tate," Evelyn said, squeezing her way in between the two friends. "I read the most interesting thing in this morning's paper."

"What's that, Mrs. Adler?" Holly looked down at her dearest guest, finding it still almost impossible to believe that she was even here. Just when she had thought her Christmas wish list was complete, she had opened the door this morning to find Evelyn and Nelson standing on her doorstep, demanding to know why on earth the door was locked.

Max was full of good surprises, Holly thought, feeling all warm and fuzzy again. Though she couldn't have wanted more than for her house to be filled with her own makeshift family for Christmas dinner, a part of her couldn't wait for everyone to leave so that she could be alone with Max again…

"They're going to begin rebuilding the library in the spring!" Evelyn recanted.

"Really?" Abby asked, disbelieving. "But how? I thought there wasn't enough funding."

"Apparently an anonymous donor has come forward," Evelyn remarked.

Abby's wide eyes darted to Holly's, but Holly refused to feed into the knowing stare. "I think I heard about that," was all she would comment and she left the two women to go and greet George and Lucy, who had just arrived.

"Holly." Lucy's eyes were bright and tearful, and Holly could see the toll the past few days had taken on her. With shaking hands, she thrust a white pie box into Holly's hands, saying, "Peppermint chocolate cream. I thought it seemed…festive."

Holly smiled and reached out a hand to grab Lucy's wrist. "It sounds perfect," she said.

Lucy exhaled in relief and blurted, "Please forgive me, Holly. Some things have happened, you see, and we…we didn't know what to do."

"Lucy, it's okay. Max told me everything."

Lucy sighed and her shoulders slumped with release. With pained eyes, she held Holly's gaze. "I'm so sorry."

"I just wish you had told me what was going on," Holly said quietly. "You could have confided in me. We're friends."

Lucy squeezed her eyes shut. "I don't think you know how much it means to me to hear you say that."

"You and George have been like family to me since I moved to Maple Woods. There's no need to discuss this anymore. It's over. We're just going to keep moving along." She nodded her head into the room and flashed Lucy a smile. "Now come on in and get some eggnog. Dinner's almost ready and I think Max wants to talk to you about some other business venture he has."

Lucy paled. "What now, Holly?"

Holly laughed. "What would you think about branching out with these?" she asked, holding up the pie box. "Now that Max is planning to stay in Maple Woods, he's looking for some new investment opportunities."

"Oh, is he, now?" From behind them Evelyn's voice chirped. Holly turned to her, trying to suppress her smile at the obvious glee in the woman's eyes. "Should I presume I'll be seeing Max again during future stays at the inn?"

Holly laughed softly. "I think that's a safe assumption, Mrs. Adler."

Evelyn's blue eyes gleamed. "This place just gets better and better."

Holly watched as Evelyn scurried off to find Nelson. Although they usually didn't exchange presents until after dinner, she couldn't wait any longer to give Max his gift.

"Come here," she said as she brushed past his chair.

"What is it?" he asked, sensing her need for privacy.

"You haven't opened your present yet," she said. She pointed to the tree and Max's eyes sparkled as he leaned down and picked up the small box with his name on it.

"Should I just open it here?" he asked.

Holly nodded as Max quickly shed the box of its wrapping paper and lifted the lid. His expression folded, first in confusion and then in recognition, and a warm glow filled her heart as his eyes met hers in a tender, knowing gaze. The red-and-black toy train looked small in his hands, but not in the least out of place.

"It's just the engine, but I couldn't let you go through life without that train," she said. "Even if it is about thirty years after you asked for it."

Max grinned. "Some things are worth waiting for," he said, leaning in to kiss her.

Holly wrapped her arms around his waist and snuggled into his chest, enjoying the weight of his arms around her shoulders, and the security they provided. She looked around the room at all the wonderful people that filled it and she smiled to herself. A week ago this house was an inn. Yesterday it was empty. And today, it was officially home.

* * * * *

LET'S TALK
Romance

For exclusive extracts, competitions
and special offers, find us online:

Get in touch on 01413 063232

For all the latest titles coming soon, visit
millsandboon.co.uk/nextmonth